THE BATMAN STRIKES!
DUTY CALLS

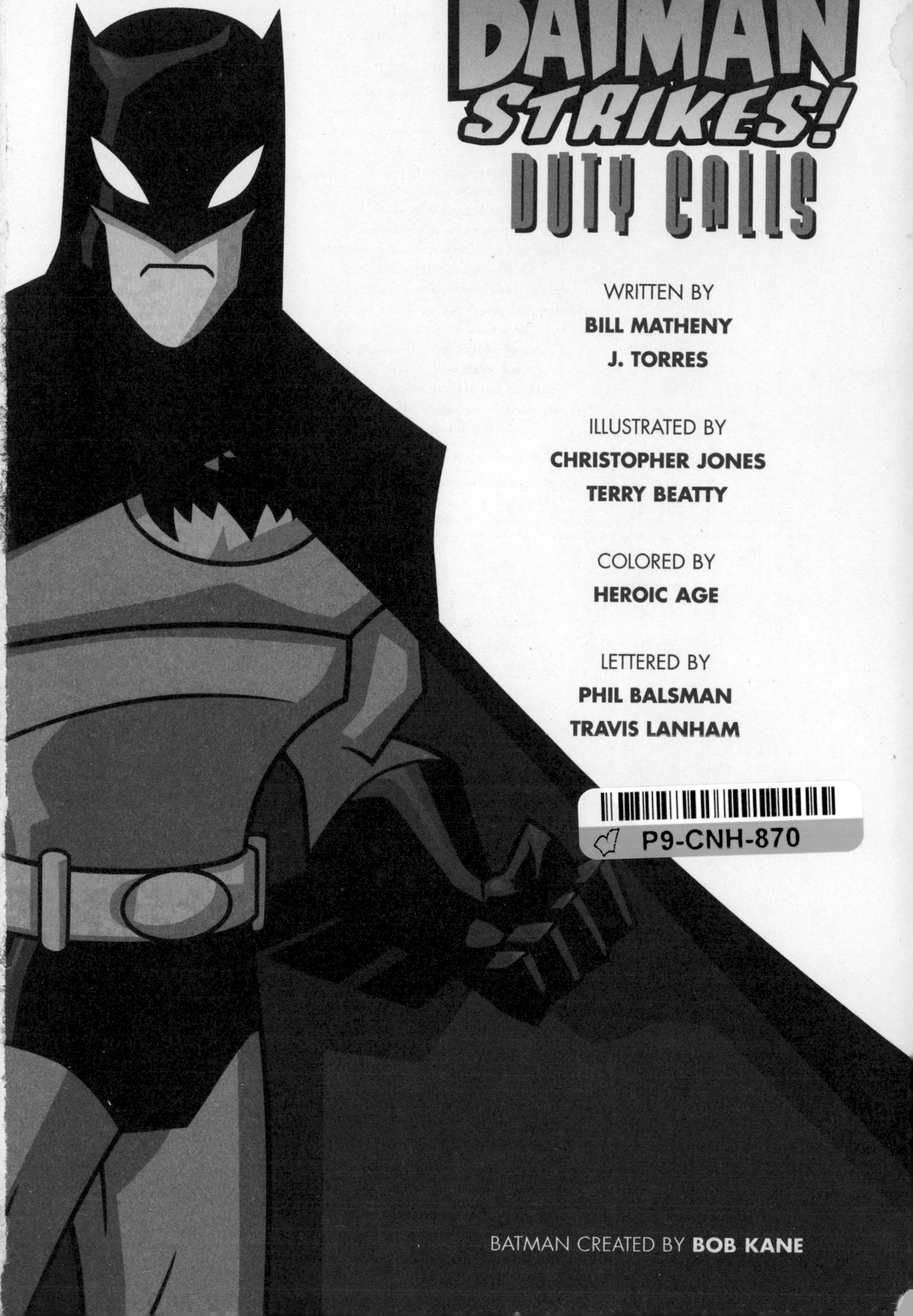

WRITTEN BY
BILL MATHENY
J. TORRES

ILLUSTRATED BY
CHRISTOPHER JONES
TERRY BEATTY

COLORED BY
HEROIC AGE

LETTERED BY
PHIL BALSMAN
TRAVIS LANHAM

BATMAN CREATED BY **BOB KANE**

Cover illustration by Jeff Matsuda Cover color by Dave McCaig Publication design by Robbie Biederman

THE BATMAN STRIKES!: DUTY CALLS

DC Comics
1700 Broadway, New York, NY 10019
A Warner Bros. Entertainment Company.
Printed in Canada. Second Printing.

ISBN: 978-1-4012-1548-4

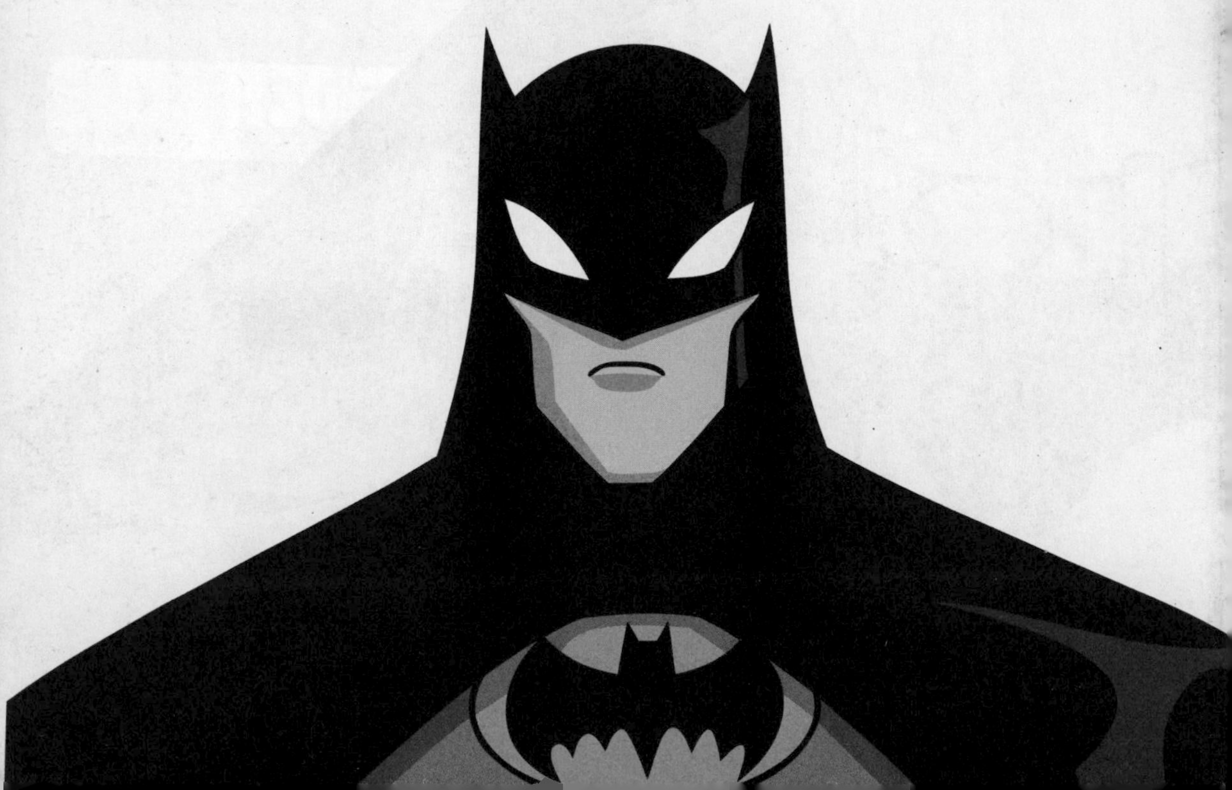

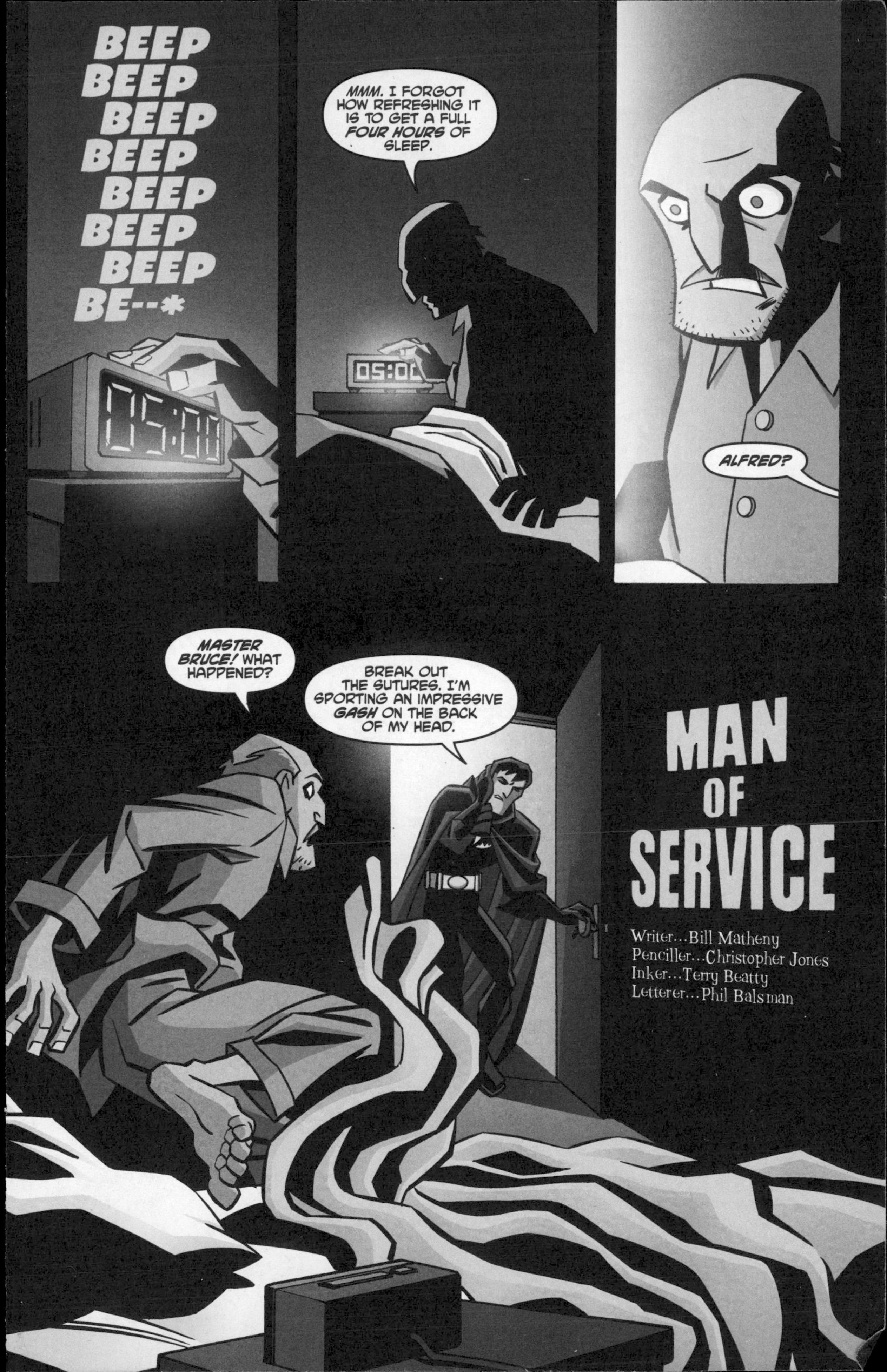
BEEP BEEP BEEP BEEP BEEP BEEP BEEP BE--*
05:00
MMM. I FORGOT HOW REFRESHING IT IS TO GET A FULL FOUR HOURS OF SLEEP.
ALFRED?
MASTER BRUCE! WHAT HAPPENED?
BREAK OUT THE SUTURES. I'M SPORTING AN IMPRESSIVE GASH ON THE BACK OF MY HEAD.
MAN OF SERVICE
Writer...Bill Matheny
Penciller...Christopher Jones
Inker...Terry Beatty
Letterer...Phil Balsman

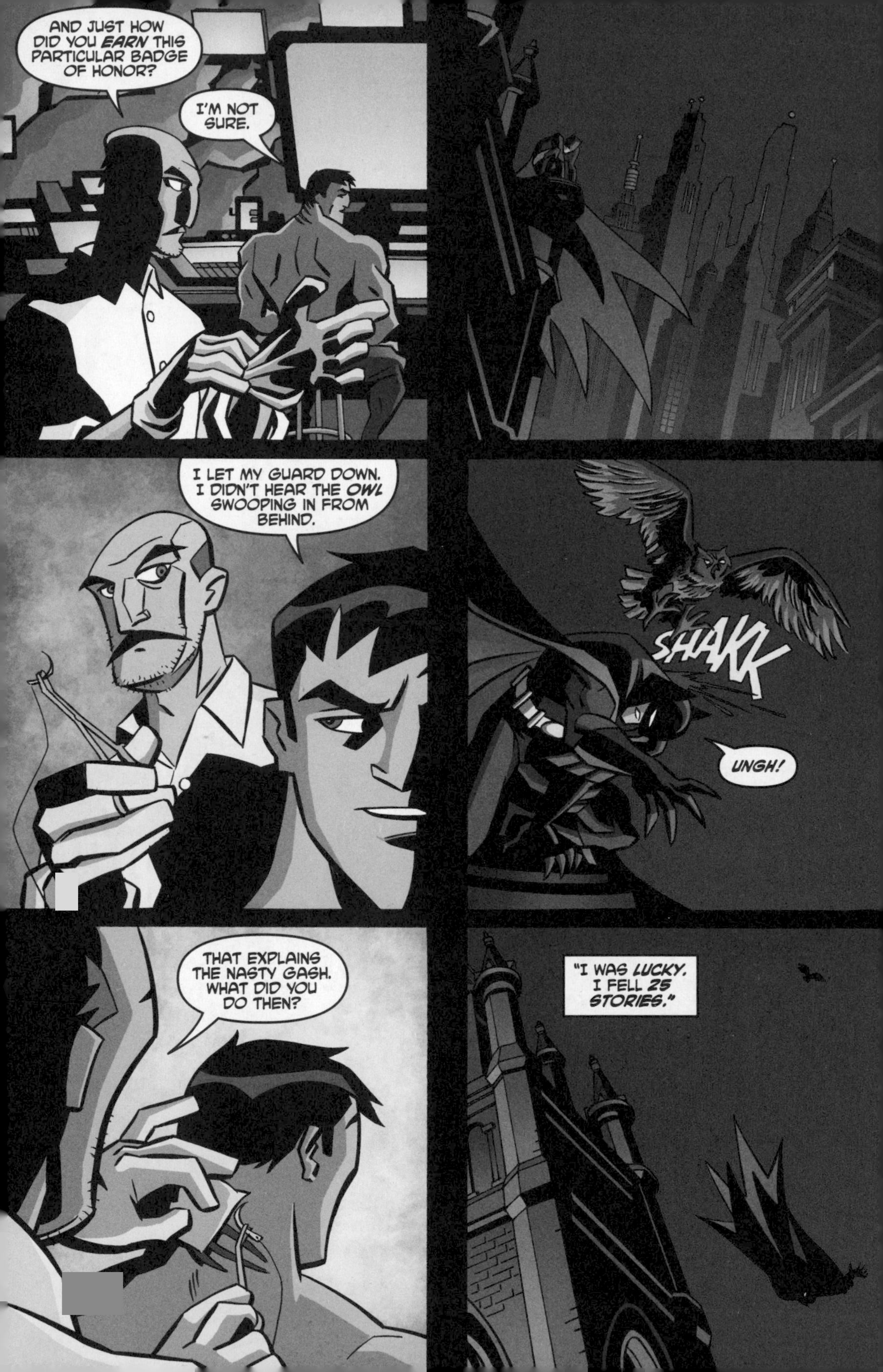
AND JUST HOW DID YOU EARN THIS PARTICULAR BADGE OF HONOR?
I'M NOT SURE.
I LET MY GUARD DOWN. I DIDN'T HEAR THE OWL SWOOPING IN FROM BEHIND.
SHAKK
UNGH!
THAT EXPLAINS THE NASTY GASH. WHAT DID YOU DO THEN?
"I WAS LUCKY. I FELL 25 STORIES."

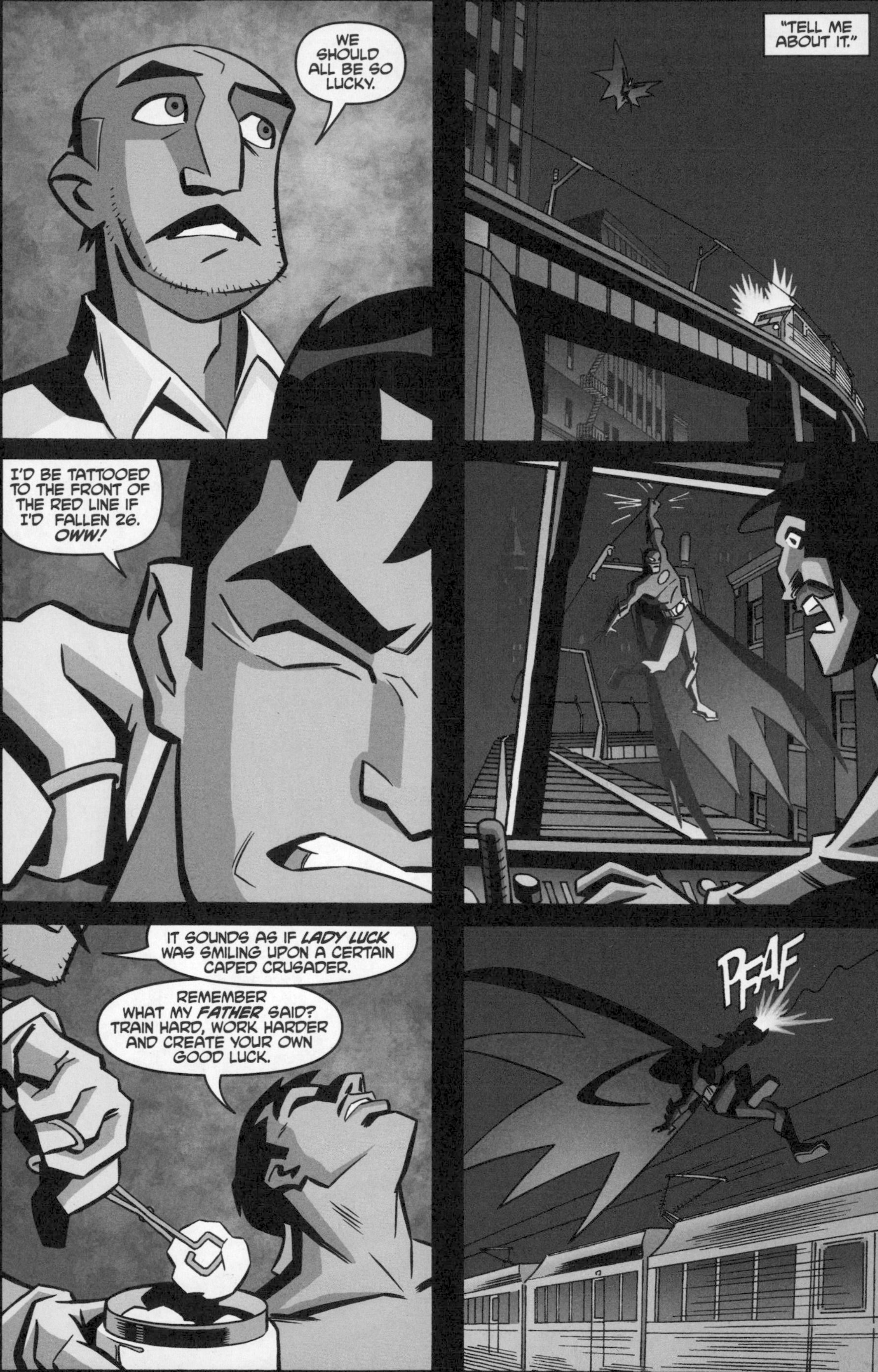
WE SHOULD ALL BE SO LUCKY.
"TELL ME ABOUT IT."
I'D BE TATTOOED TO THE FRONT OF THE RED LINE IF I'D FALLEN 26. OWW!
IT SOUNDS AS IF LADY LUCK WAS SMILING UPON A CERTAIN CAPED CRUSADER.
REMEMBER WHAT MY FATHER SAID? TRAIN HARD, WORK HARDER AND CREATE YOUR OWN GOOD LUCK.
PFAF

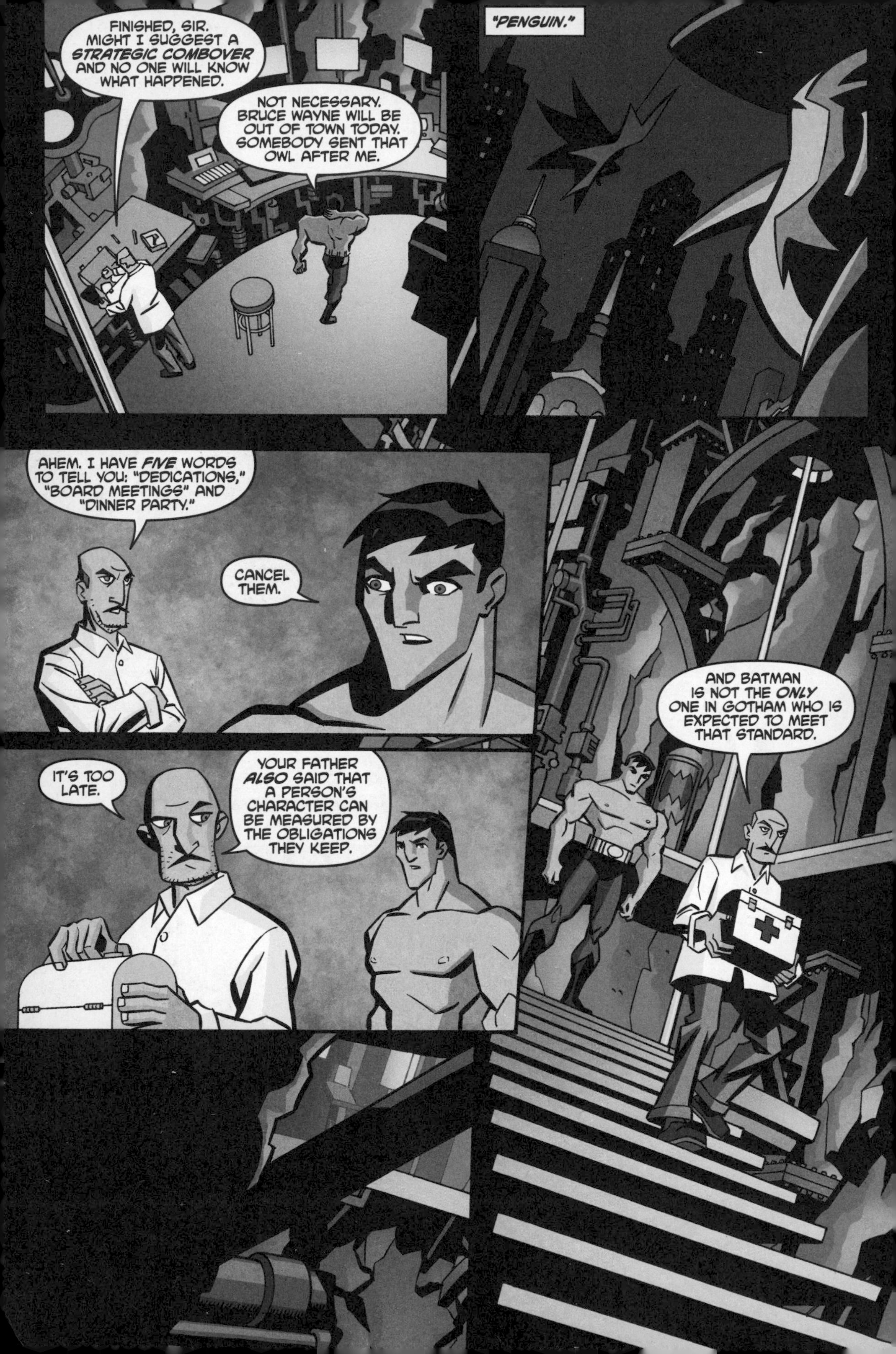
FINISHED, SIR. MIGHT I SUGGEST A STRATEGIC COMBOVER AND NO ONE WILL KNOW WHAT HAPPENED.
NOT NECESSARY. BRUCE WAYNE WILL BE OUT OF TOWN TODAY. SOMEBODY SENT THAT OWL AFTER ME.
"PENGUIN."
AHEM. I HAVE FIVE WORDS TO TELL YOU: "DEDICATIONS," "BOARD MEETINGS" AND "DINNER PARTY."
CANCEL THEM.
IT'S TOO LATE.
YOUR FATHER ALSO SAID THAT A PERSON'S CHARACTER CAN BE MEASURED BY THE OBLIGATIONS THEY KEEP.
AND BATMAN IS NOT THE ONLY ONE IN GOTHAM WHO IS EXPECTED TO MEET THAT STANDARD.

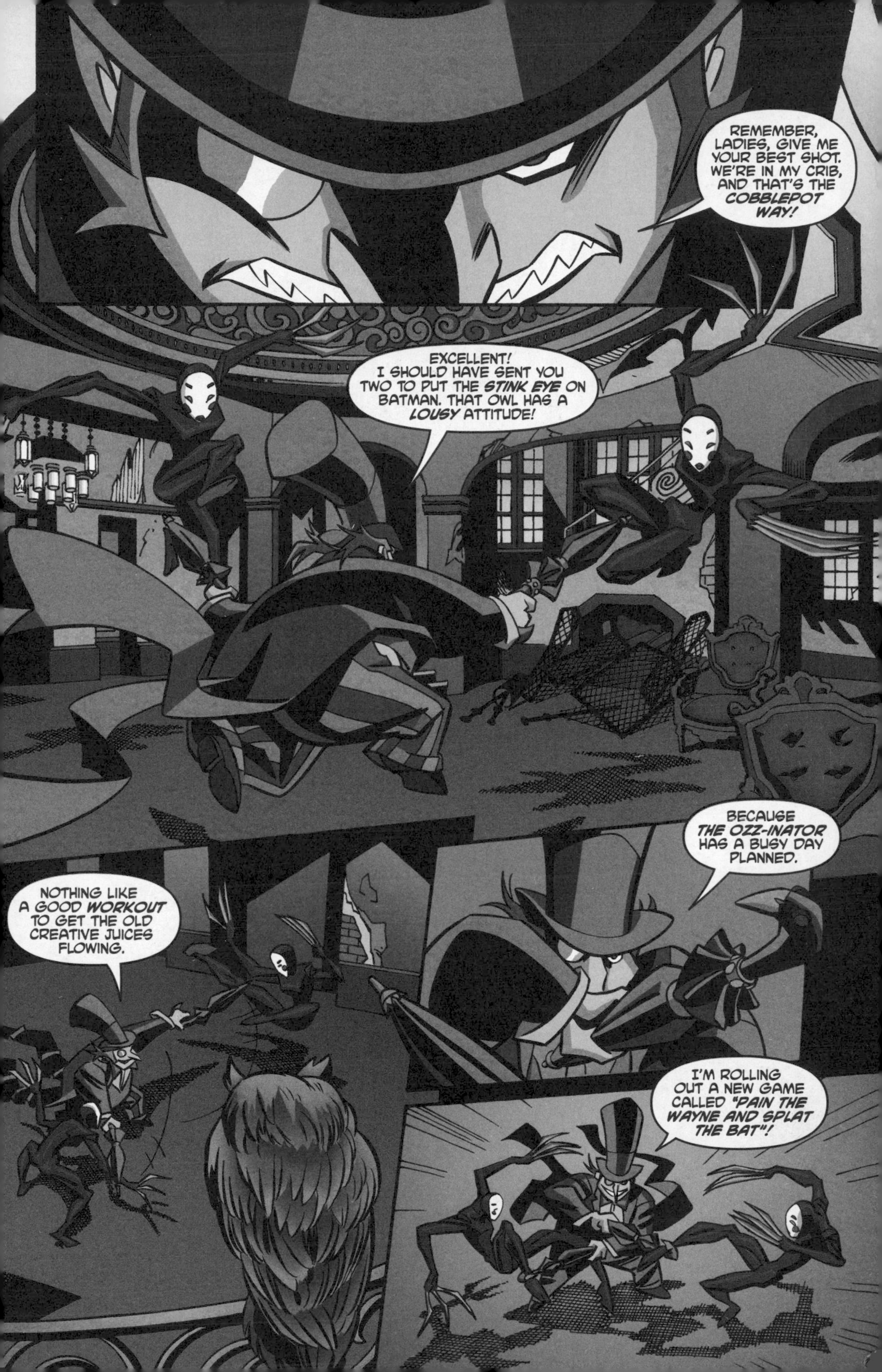
REMEMBER, LADIES, GIVE ME YOUR BEST SHOT. WE'RE IN MY CRIB, AND THAT'S THE *COBBLEPOT WAY!*
EXCELLENT! I SHOULD HAVE SENT YOU TWO TO PUT THE *STINK EYE* ON BATMAN. THAT OWL HAS A *LOUSY* ATTITUDE!
NOTHING LIKE A *GOOD* ***WORKOUT*** TO GET THE OLD CREATIVE JUICES FLOWING.
BECAUSE *THE OZZ-INATOR* HAS A BUSY DAY PLANNED.
I'M ROLLING OUT A NEW GAME CALLED *"PAIN THE WAYNE AND SPLAT THE BAT"!*

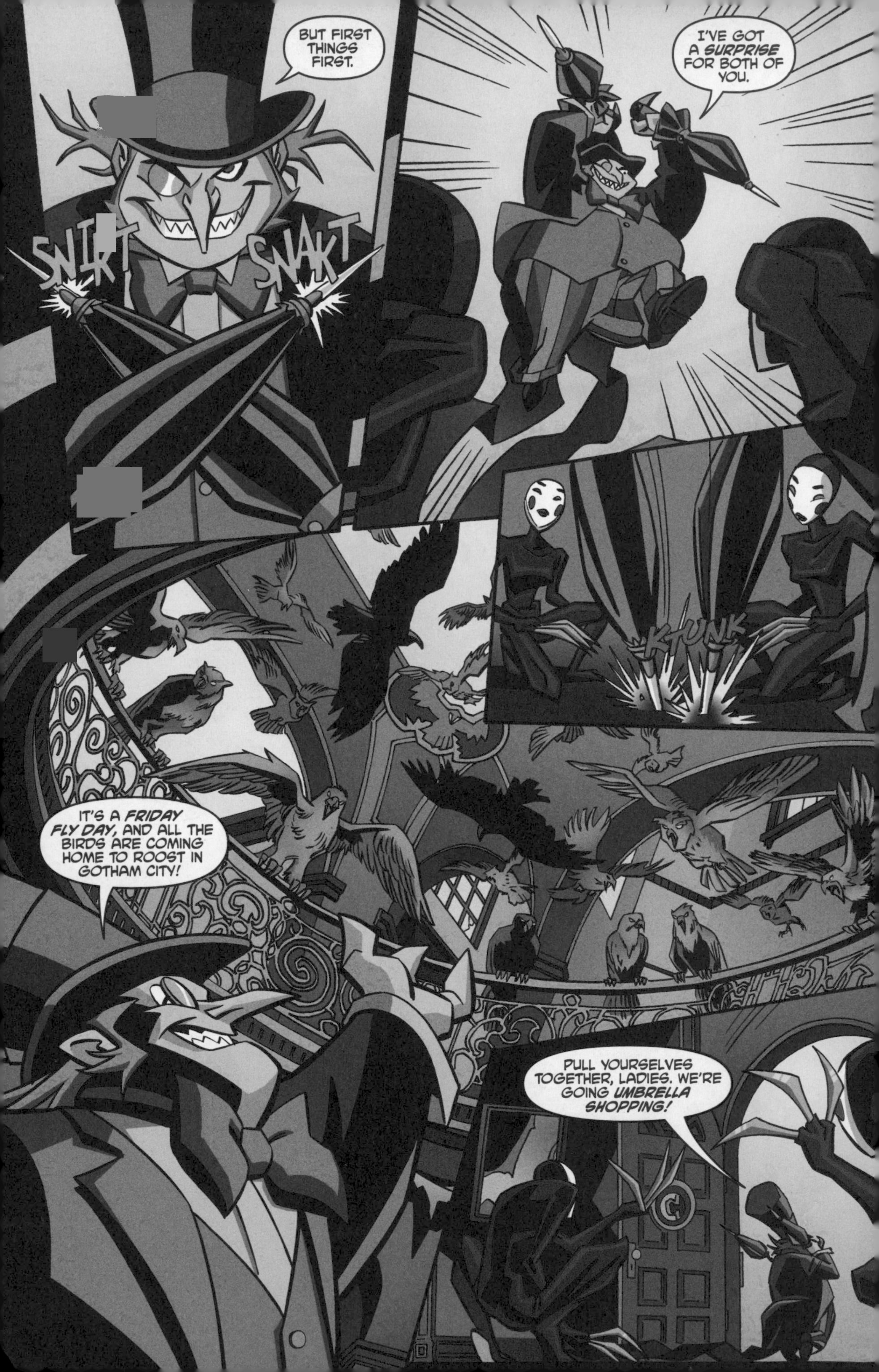
BUT FIRST THINGS FIRST.
SNIKT
SNAKT
I'VE GOT A SURPRISE FOR BOTH OF YOU.
KTUNK
IT'S A FRIDAY FLY DAY, AND ALL THE BIRDS ARE COMING HOME TO ROOST IN GOTHAM CITY!
PULL YOURSELVES TOGETHER, LADIES. WE'RE GOING UMBRELLA SHOPPING!

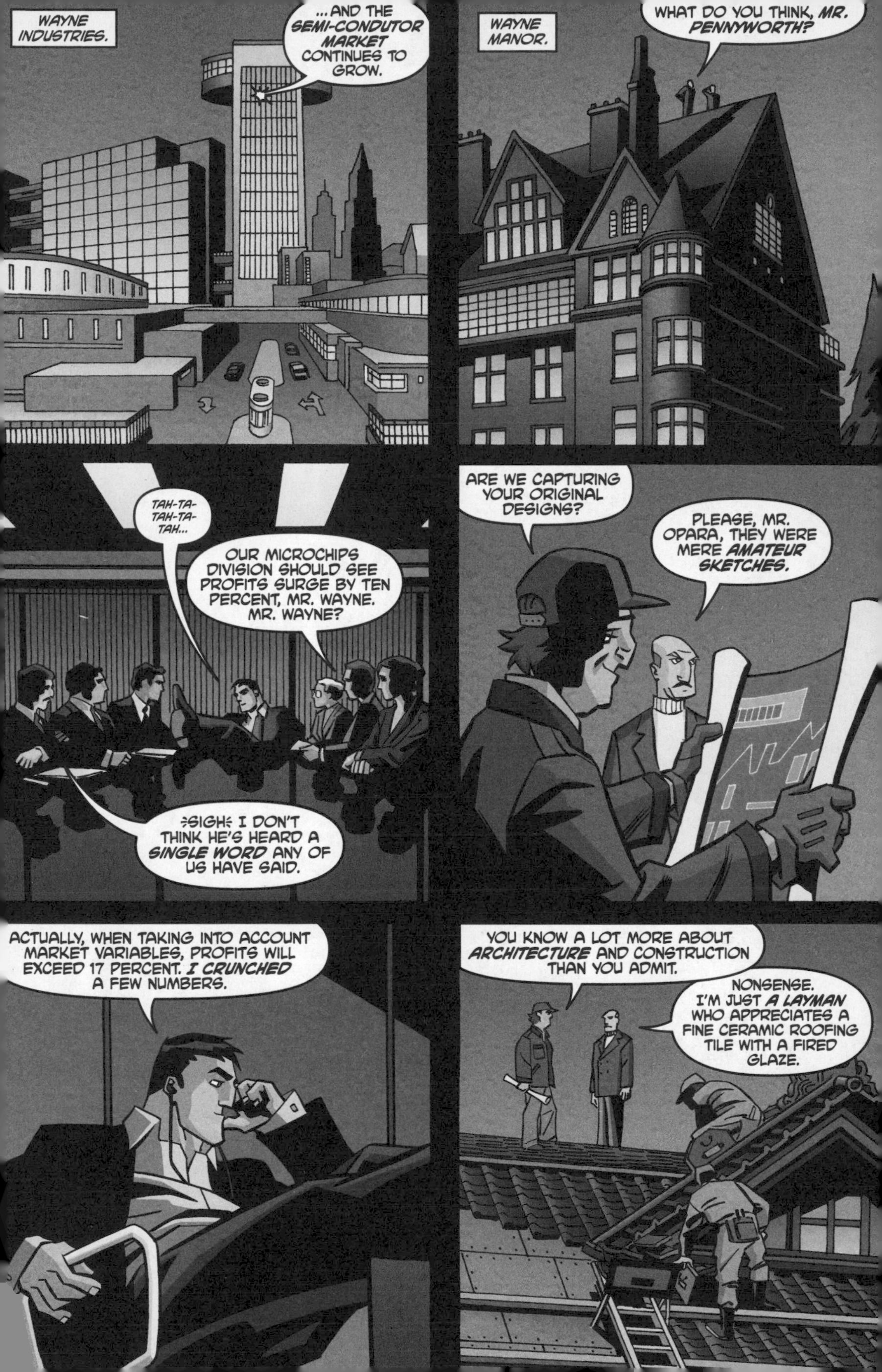
WAYNE INDUSTRIES.
...AND THE SEMI-CONDUTOR MARKET CONTINUES TO GROW.
WAYNE MANOR.
WHAT DO YOU THINK, MR. PENNYWORTH?
TAH-TA-TAH-TA-TAH...
OUR MICROCHIPS DIVISION SHOULD SEE PROFITS SURGE BY TEN PERCENT, MR. WAYNE. MR. WAYNE?
⫶SIGH⫶ I DON'T THINK HE'S HEARD A SINGLE WORD ANY OF US HAVE SAID.
ARE WE CAPTURING YOUR ORIGINAL DESIGNS?
PLEASE, MR. OPARA, THEY WERE MERE AMATEUR SKETCHES.
ACTUALLY, WHEN TAKING INTO ACCOUNT MARKET VARIABLES, PROFITS WILL EXCEED 17 PERCENT. I CRUNCHED A FEW NUMBERS.
YOU KNOW A LOT MORE ABOUT ARCHITECTURE AND CONSTRUCTION THAN YOU ADMIT.
NONSENSE. I'M JUST A LAYMAN WHO APPRECIATES A FINE CERAMIC ROOFING TILE WITH A FIRED GLAZE.

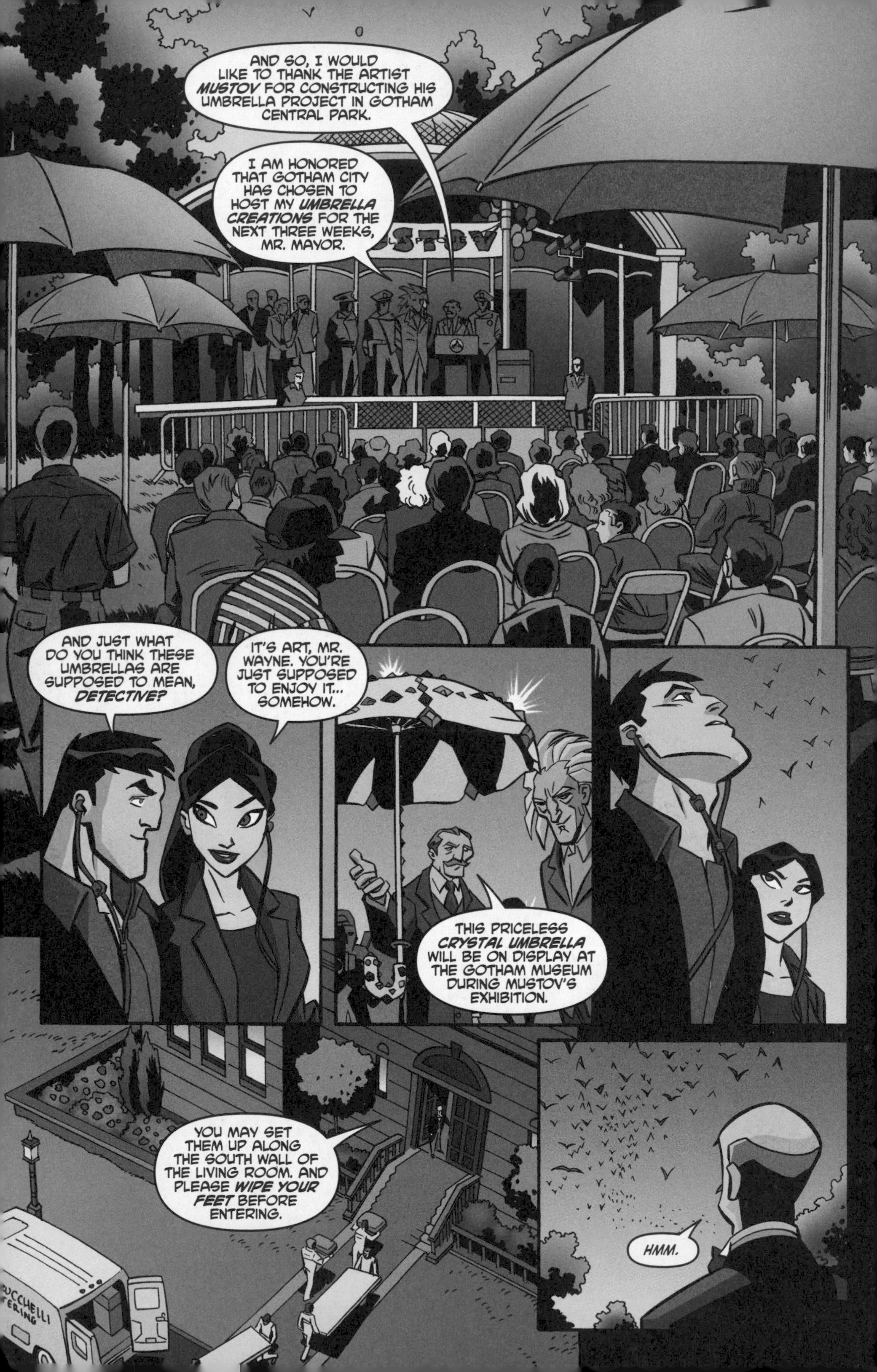
AND SO, I WOULD LIKE TO THANK THE ARTIST MUSTOV FOR CONSTRUCTING HIS UMBRELLA PROJECT IN GOTHAM CENTRAL PARK.
I AM HONORED THAT GOTHAM CITY HAS CHOSEN TO HOST MY UMBRELLA CREATIONS FOR THE NEXT THREE WEEKS, MR. MAYOR.
AND JUST WHAT DO YOU THINK THESE UMBRELLAS ARE SUPPOSED TO MEAN, DETECTIVE?
IT'S ART, MR. WAYNE. YOU'RE JUST SUPPOSED TO ENJOY IT... SOMEHOW.
THIS PRICELESS CRYSTAL UMBRELLA WILL BE ON DISPLAY AT THE GOTHAM MUSEUM DURING MUSTOV'S EXHIBITION.
YOU MAY SET THEM UP ALONG THE SOUTH WALL OF THE LIVING ROOM. AND PLEASE WIPE YOUR FEET BEFORE ENTERING.
HMM.

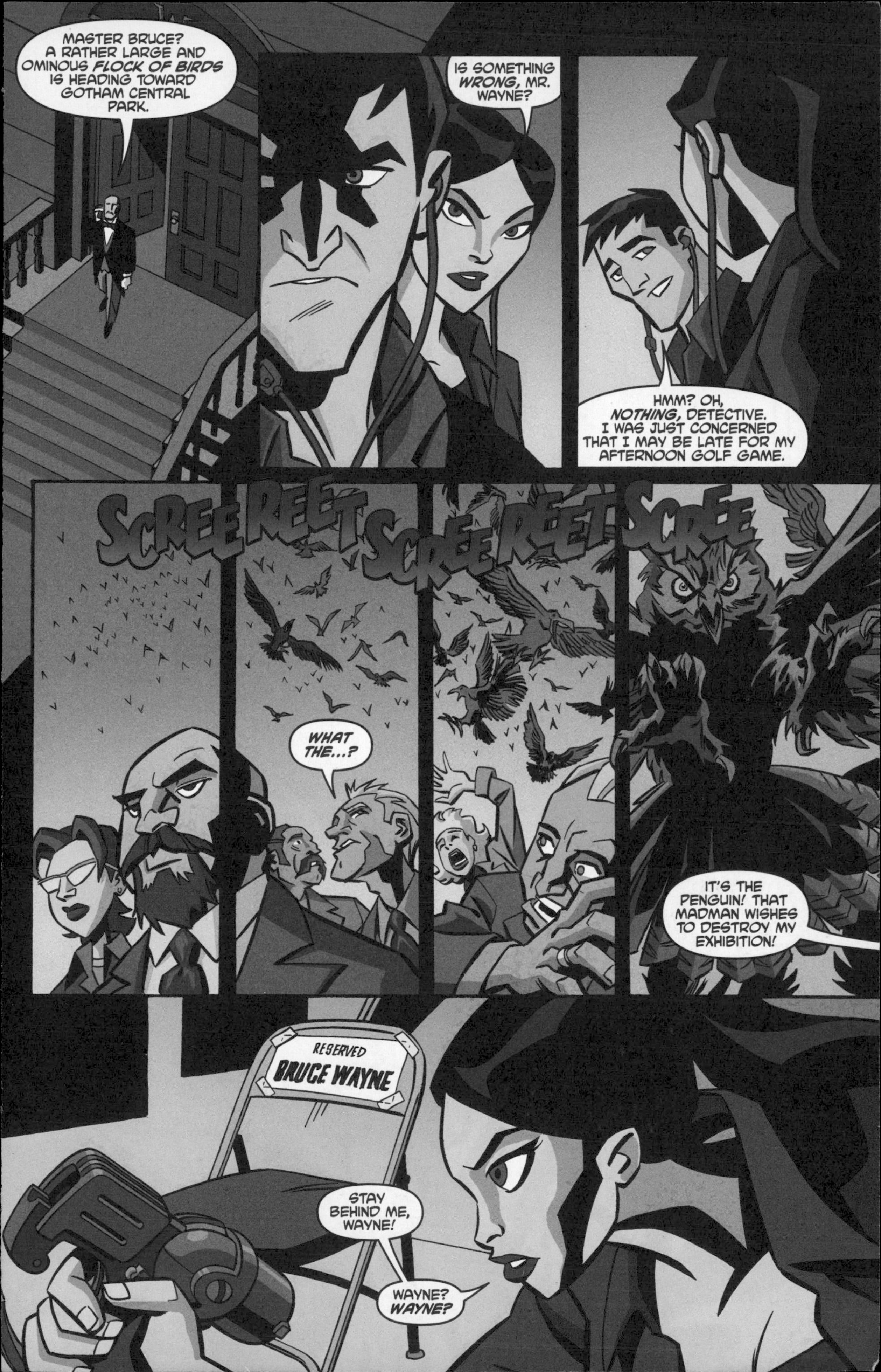
MASTER BRUCE? A RATHER LARGE AND OMINOUS FLOCK OF BIRDS IS HEADING TOWARD GOTHAM CENTRAL PARK.
IS SOMETHING WRONG, MR. WAYNE?
HMM? OH, NOTHING, DETECTIVE. I WAS JUST CONCERNED THAT I MAY BE LATE FOR MY AFTERNOON GOLF GAME.
SCREE REET SCREE REET SCREE
WHAT THE...?
IT'S THE PENGUIN! THAT MADMAN WISHES TO DESTROY MY EXHIBITION!
RESERVED
BRUCE WAYNE
STAY BEHIND ME, WAYNE!
WAYNE? WAYNE?

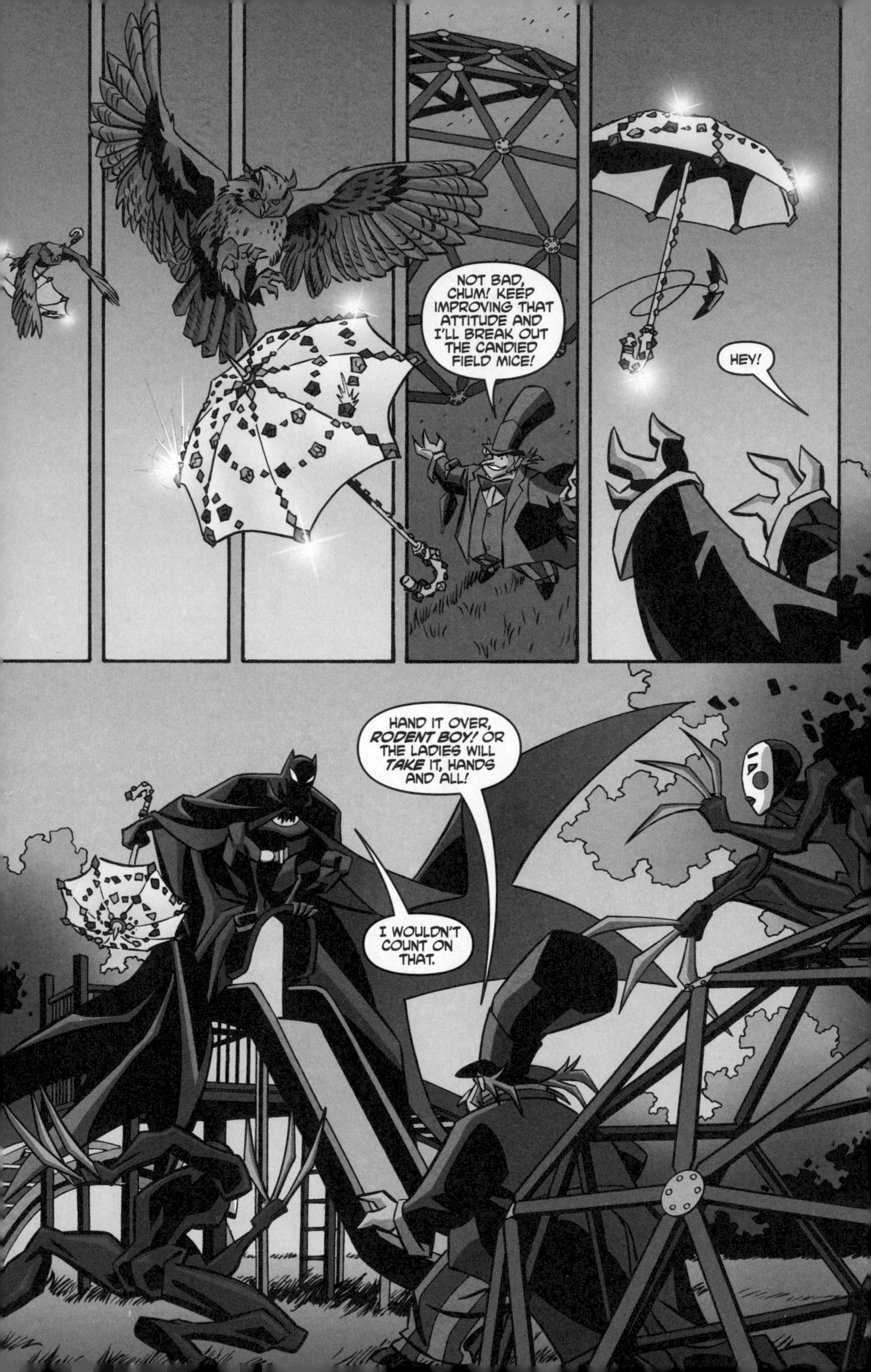
NOT BAD, CHUM! KEEP IMPROVING THAT ATTITUDE AND I'LL BREAK OUT THE CANDIED FIELD MICE!
HEY!
HAND IT OVER, *RODENT BOY!* OR THE LADIES WILL *TAKE* IT, HANDS AND ALL!
I WOULDN'T COUNT ON THAT.

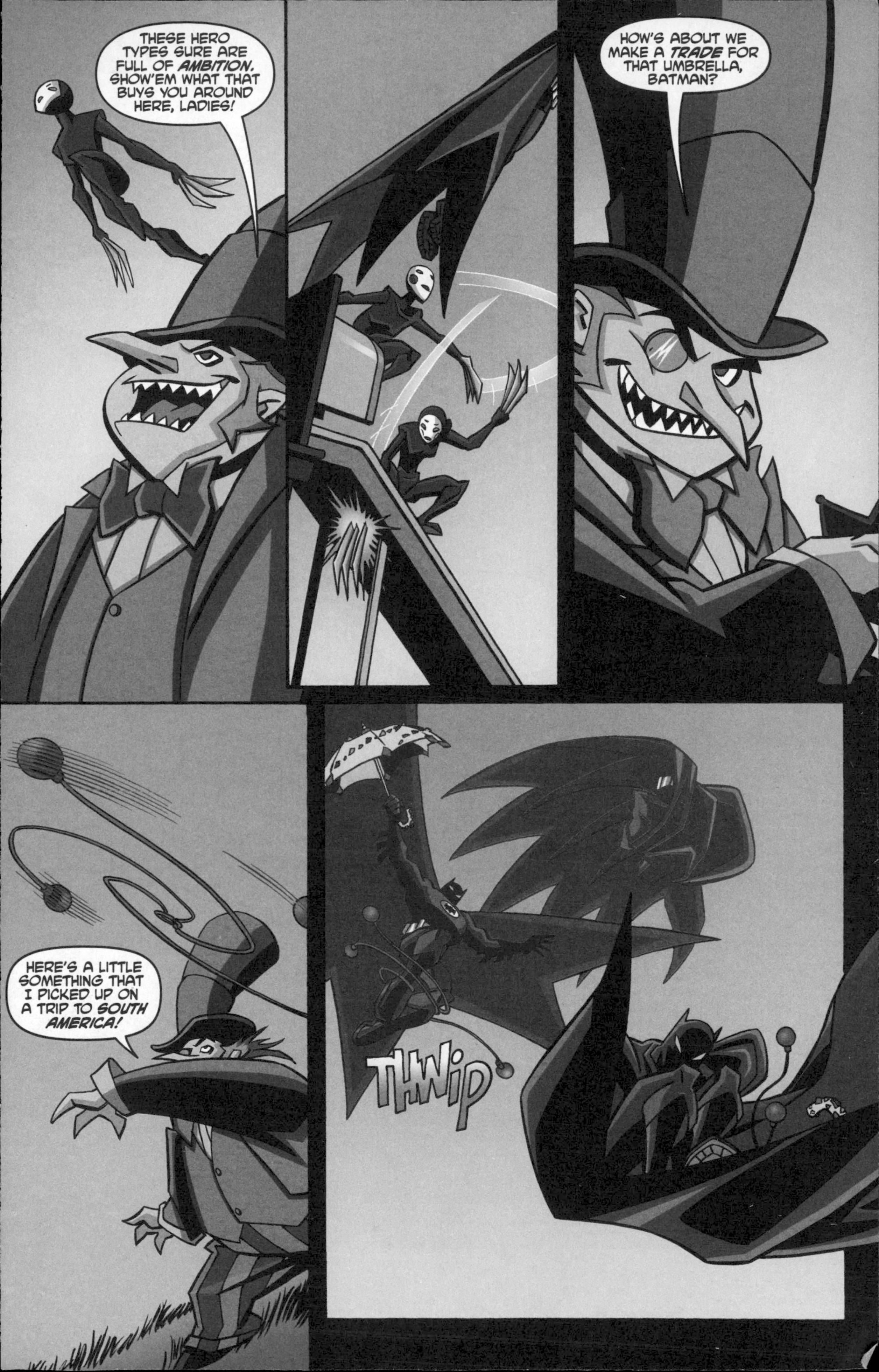
THESE HERO TYPES SURE ARE FULL OF AMBITION. SHOW'EM WHAT THAT BUYS YOU AROUND HERE, LADIES!
HOW'S ABOUT WE MAKE A TRADE FOR THAT UMBRELLA, BATMAN?
HERE'S A LITTLE SOMETHING THAT I PICKED UP ON A TRIP TO SOUTH AMERICA!
THWIP

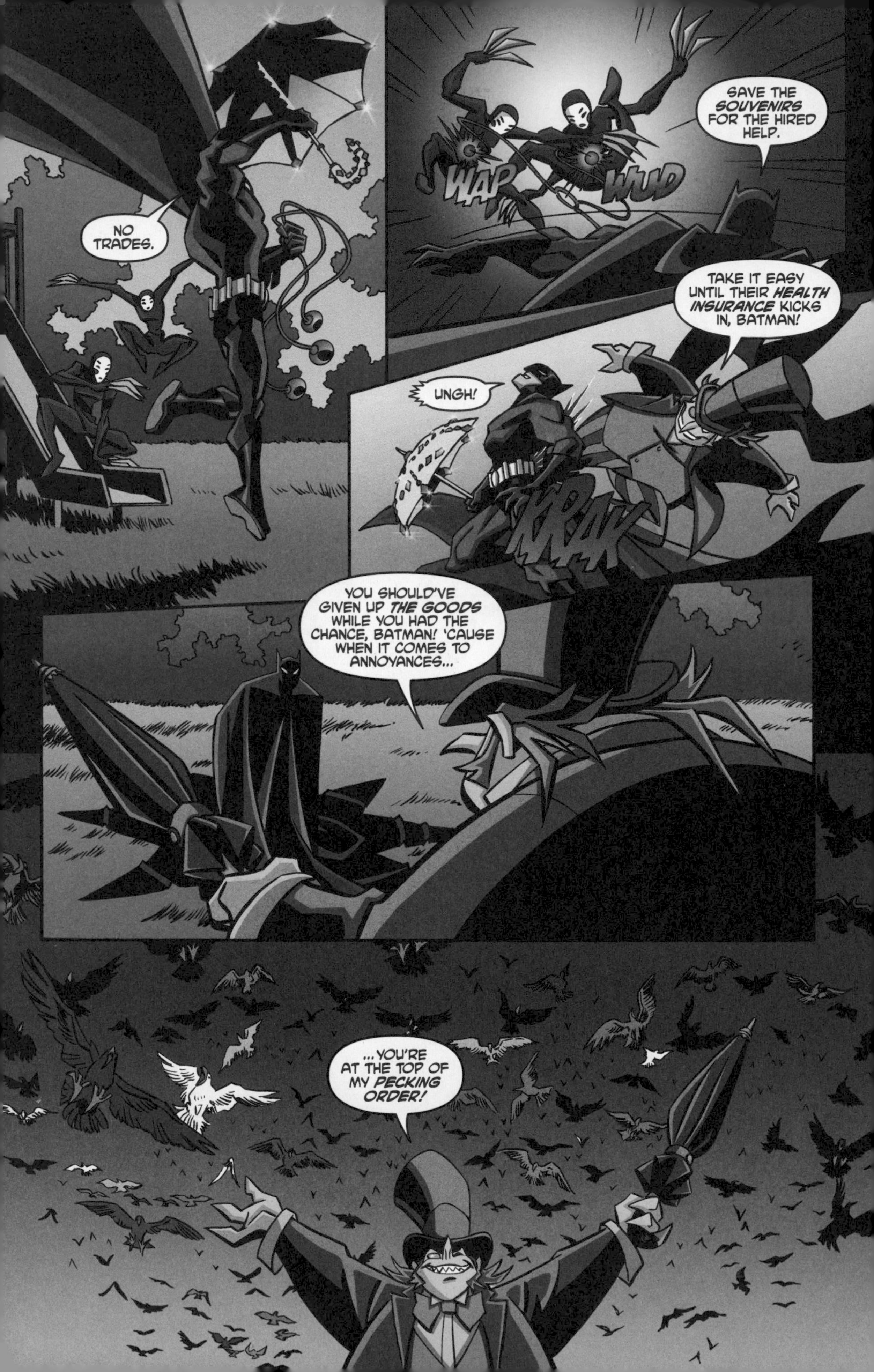

NO TRADES.
WAP
WUD
SAVE THE SOUVENIRS FOR THE HIRED HELP.
TAKE IT EASY UNTIL THEIR HEALTH INSURANCE KICKS IN, BATMAN!
UNGH!
KRAK
YOU SHOULD'VE GIVEN UP THE GOODS WHILE YOU HAD THE CHANCE, BATMAN! 'CAUSE WHEN IT COMES TO ANNOYANCES...
...YOU'RE AT THE TOP OF MY PECKING ORDER!

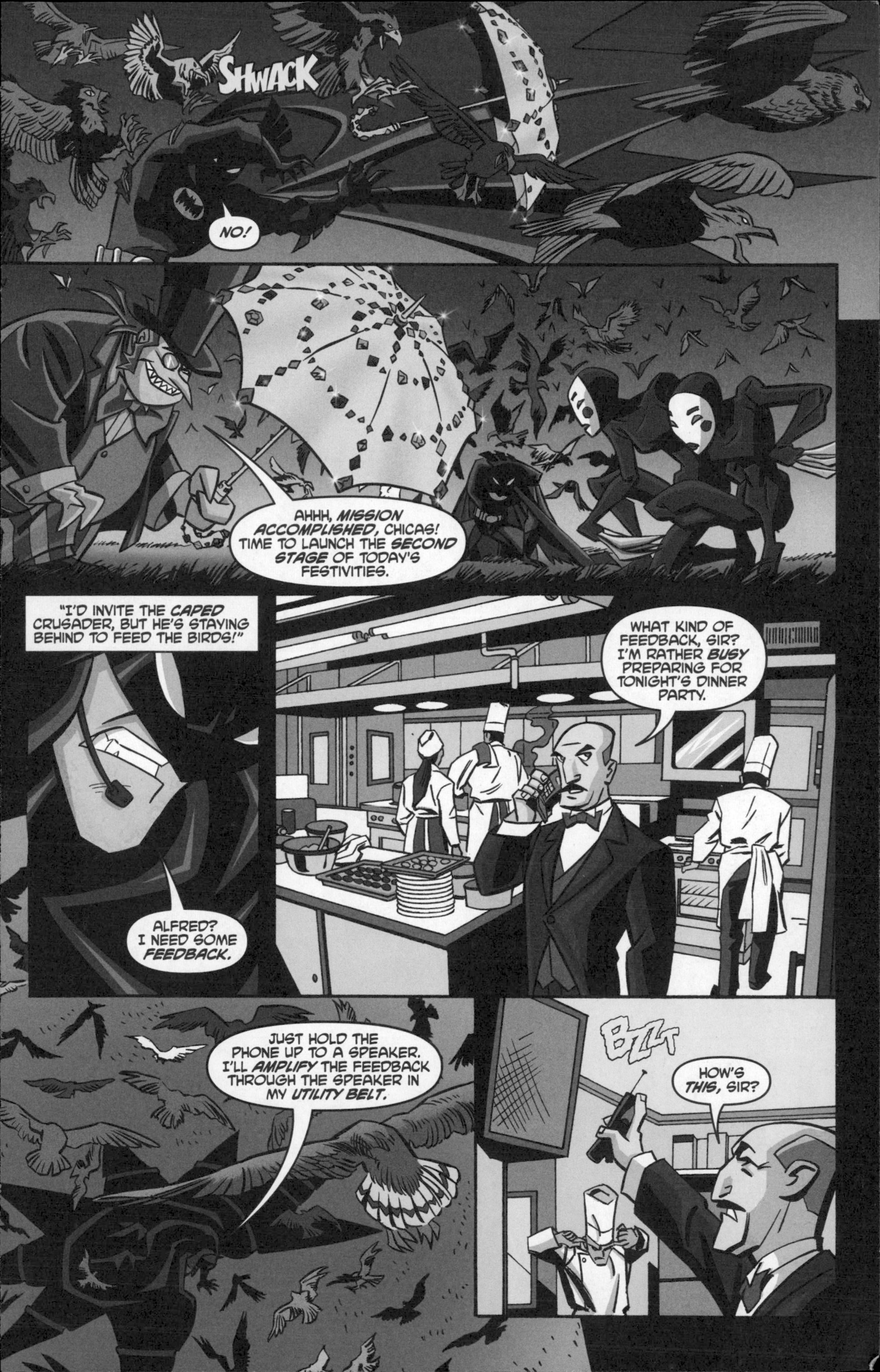
SHWACK
NO!
AHHH, MISSION ACCOMPLISHED, CHICAS! TIME TO LAUNCH THE SECOND STAGE OF TODAY'S FESTIVITIES.
"I'D INVITE THE CAPED CRUSADER, BUT HE'S STAYING BEHIND TO FEED THE BIRDS!"
ALFRED? I NEED SOME FEEDBACK.
WHAT KIND OF FEEDBACK, SIR? I'M RATHER BUSY PREPARING FOR TONIGHT'S DINNER PARTY.
JUST HOLD THE PHONE UP TO A SPEAKER. I'LL AMPLIFY THE FEEDBACK THROUGH THE SPEAKER IN MY UTILITY BELT.
BZZT
HOW'S THIS, SIR?

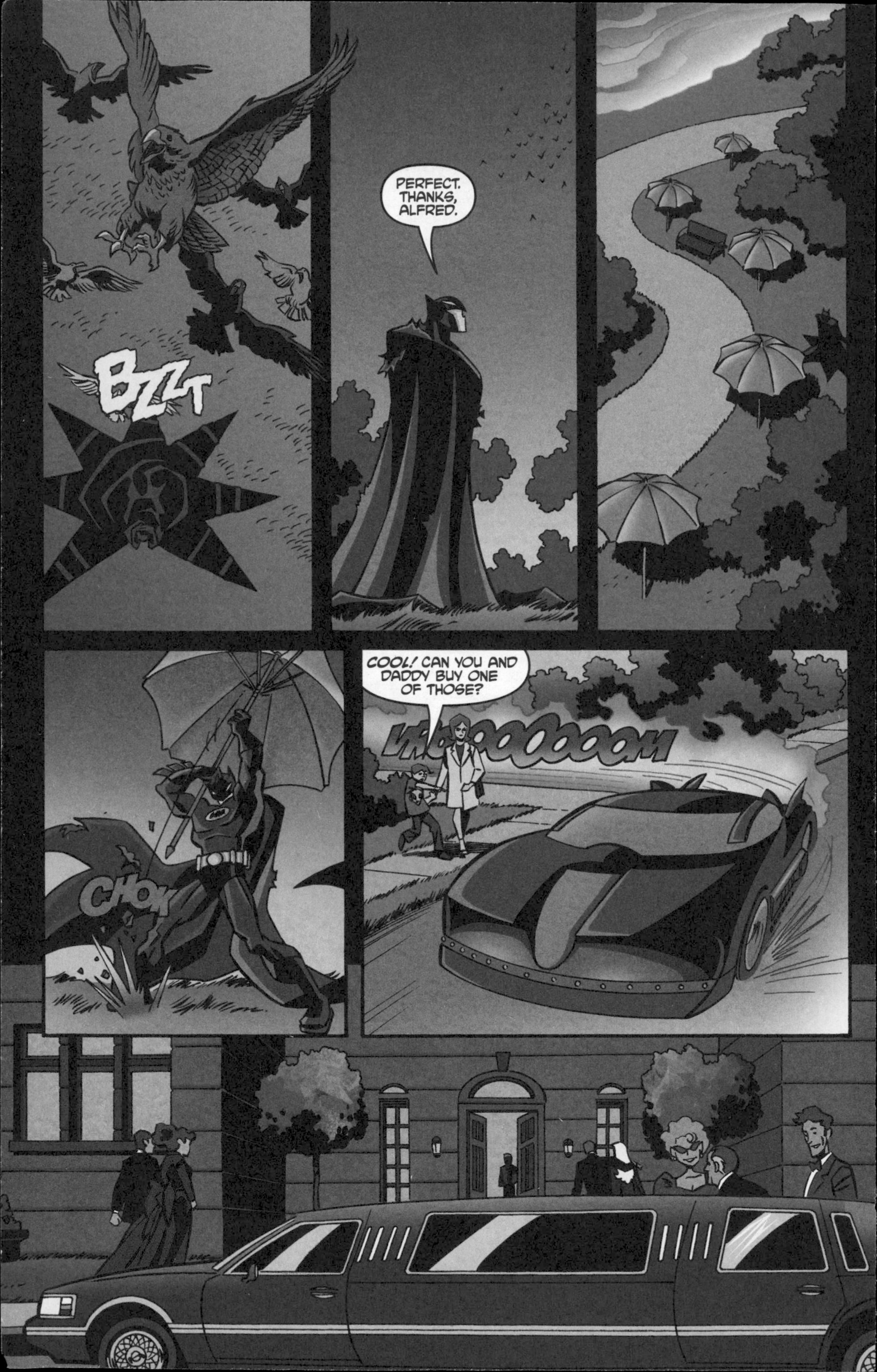
BZZT
PERFECT. THANKS, ALFRED.
CHOK
COOL! CAN YOU AND DADDY BUY ONE OF THOSE?
VROOOOOOOOM

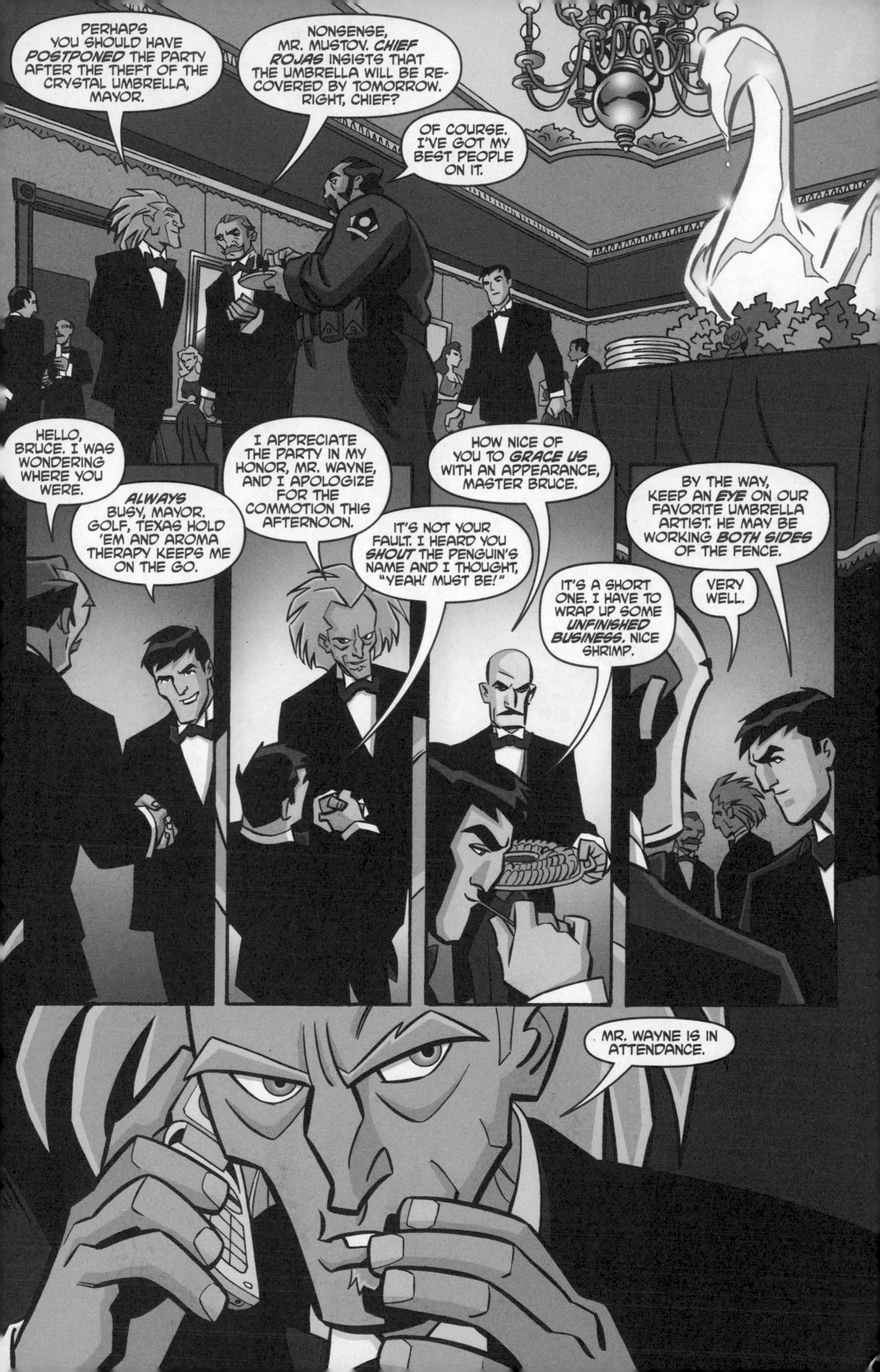
PERHAPS YOU SHOULD HAVE POSTPONED THE PARTY AFTER THE THEFT OF THE CRYSTAL UMBRELLA, MAYOR.
NONSENSE, MR. MUSTOV. CHIEF ROJAS INSISTS THAT THE UMBRELLA WILL BE RE-COVERED BY TOMORROW. RIGHT, CHIEF?
OF COURSE. I'VE GOT MY BEST PEOPLE ON IT.
HELLO, BRUCE. I WAS WONDERING WHERE YOU WERE.
ALWAYS BUSY, MAYOR. GOLF, TEXAS HOLD 'EM AND AROMA THERAPY KEEPS ME ON THE GO.
I APPRECIATE THE PARTY IN MY HONOR, MR. WAYNE, AND I APOLOGIZE FOR THE COMMOTION THIS AFTERNOON.
IT'S NOT YOUR FAULT. I HEARD YOU SHOUT THE PENGUIN'S NAME AND I THOUGHT, "YEAH! MUST BE!"
HOW NICE OF YOU TO GRACE US WITH AN APPEARANCE, MASTER BRUCE.
IT'S A SHORT ONE. I HAVE TO WRAP UP SOME UNFINISHED BUSINESS. NICE SHRIMP.
BY THE WAY, KEEP AN EYE ON OUR FAVORITE UMBRELLA ARTIST. HE MAY BE WORKING BOTH SIDES OF THE FENCE.
VERY WELL.
MR. WAYNE IS IN ATTENDANCE.

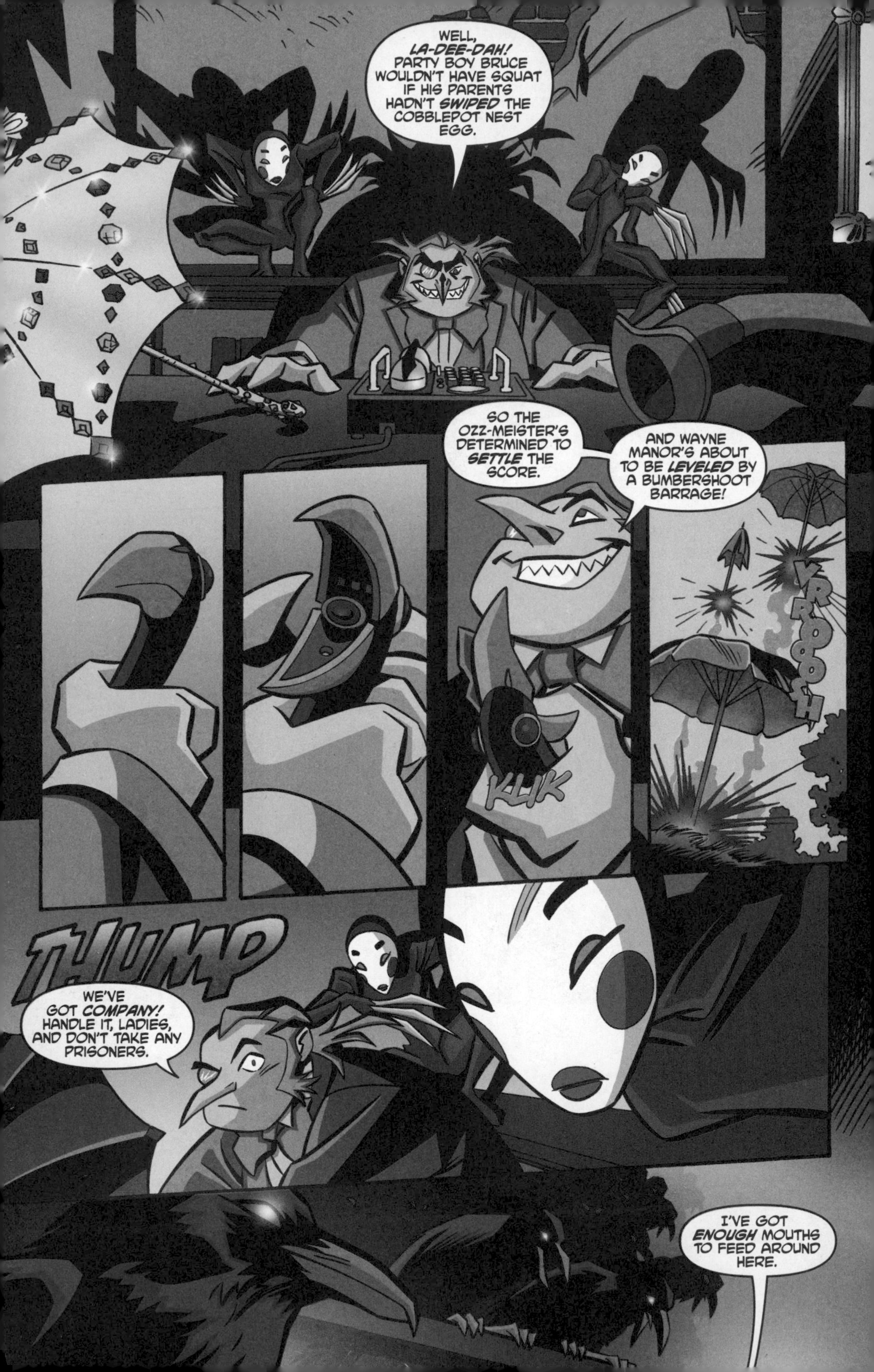
WELL, LA-DEE-DAH! PARTY BOY BRUCE WOULDN'T HAVE SQUAT IF HIS PARENTS HADN'T SWIPED THE COBBLEPOT NEST EGG.
SO THE OZZ-MEISTER'S DETERMINED TO SETTLE THE SCORE.
KLIK
AND WAYNE MANOR'S ABOUT TO BE LEVELED BY A BUMBERSHOOT BARRAGE!
VRROOSH
THUMP
WE'VE GOT COMPANY! HANDLE IT, LADIES, AND DON'T TAKE ANY PRISONERS.
I'VE GOT ENOUGH MOUTHS TO FEED AROUND HERE.

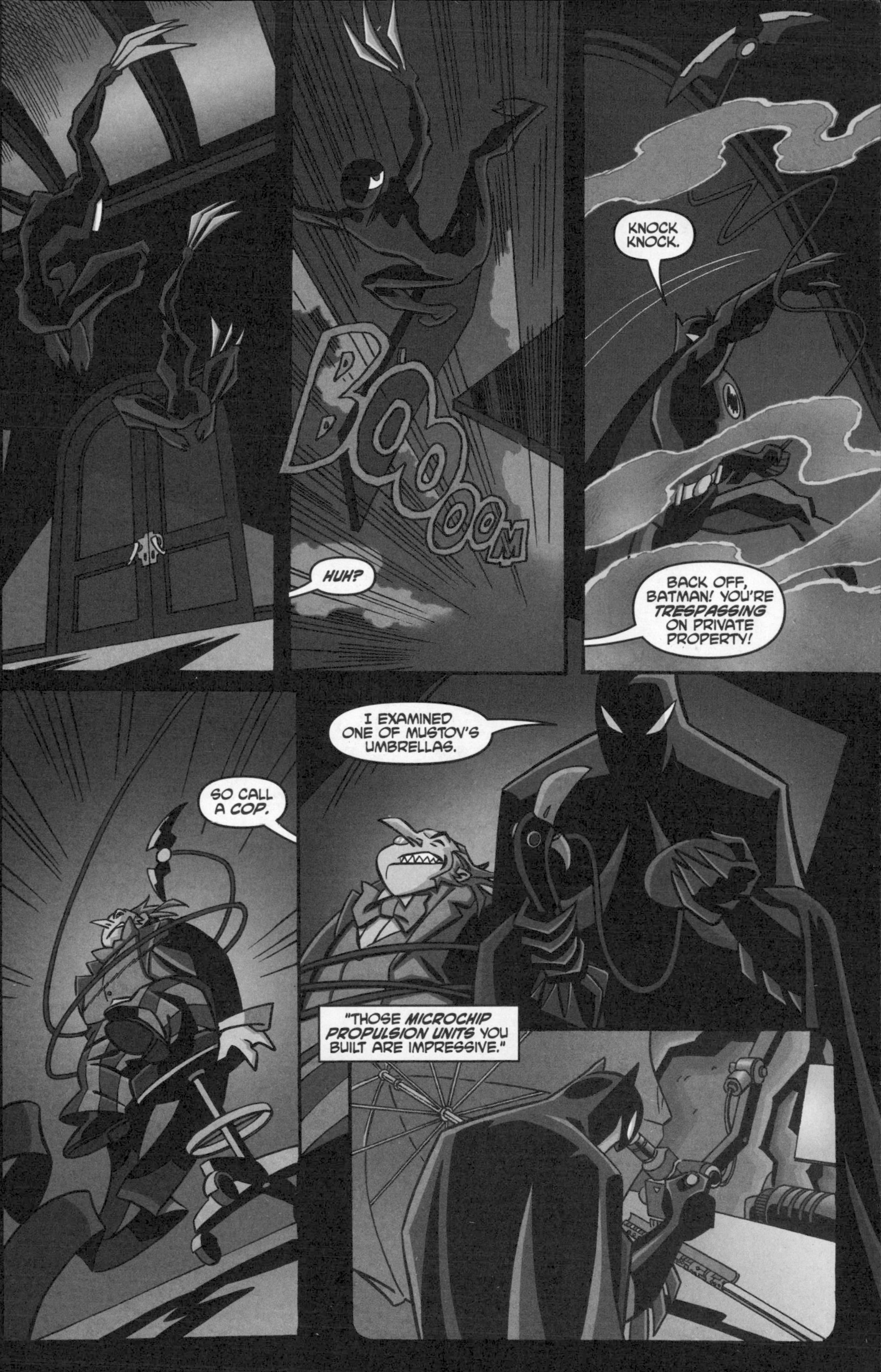

BOOOOOM
HUH?
KNOCK KNOCK.
BACK OFF, BATMAN! YOU'RE *TRESPASSING* ON PRIVATE PROPERTY!
SO CALL A COP.
I EXAMINED ONE OF MUSTOV'S UMBRELLAS.
"THOSE *MICROCHIP PROPULSION UNITS* YOU BUILT ARE IMPRESSIVE."

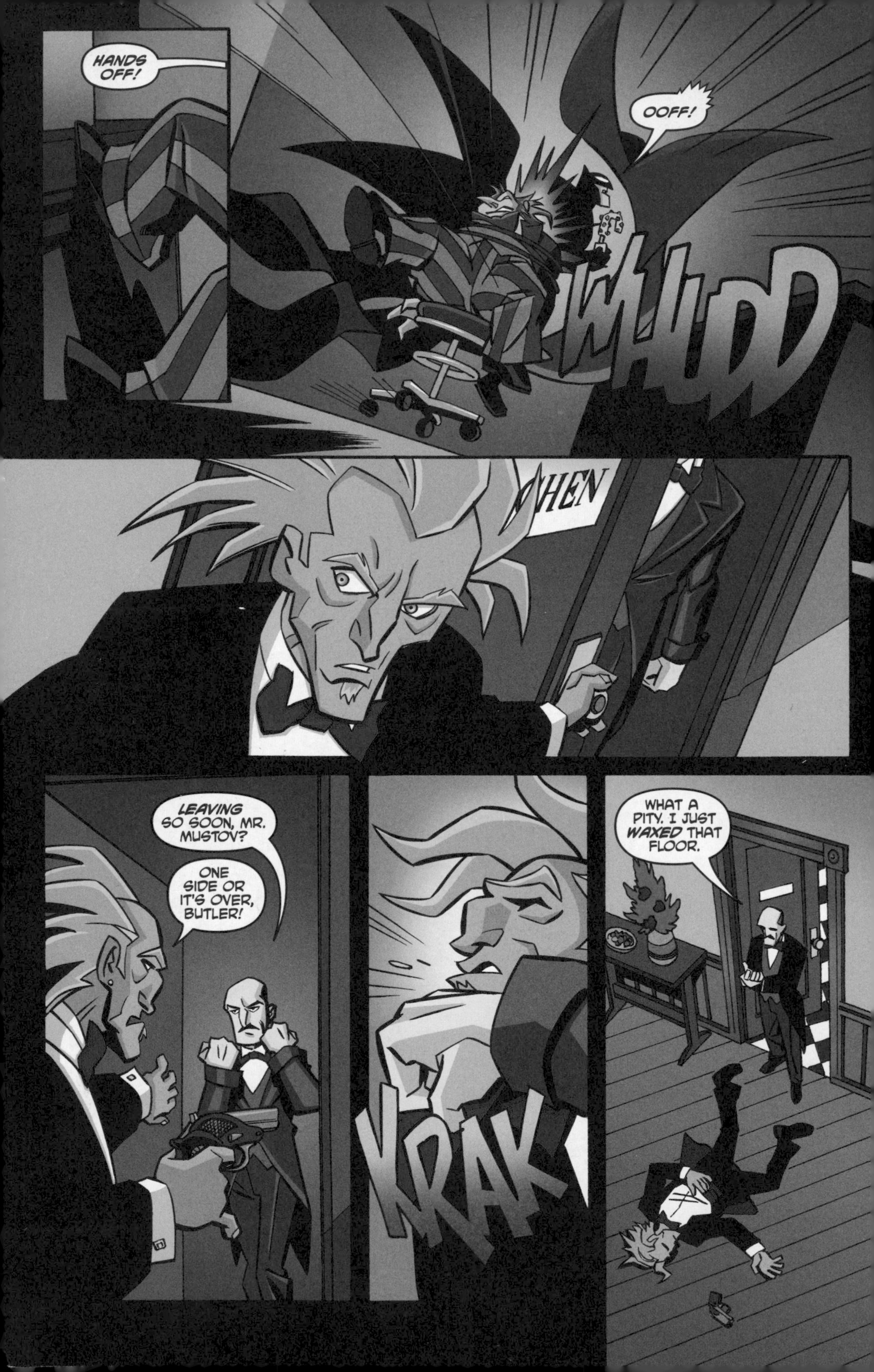
HANDS OFF!
OOFF!
WHUDD
HEN
LEAVING SO SOON, MR. MUSTOV?
ONE SIDE OR IT'S OVER, BUTLER!
KRAK
WHAT A PITY. I JUST WAXED THAT FLOOR.

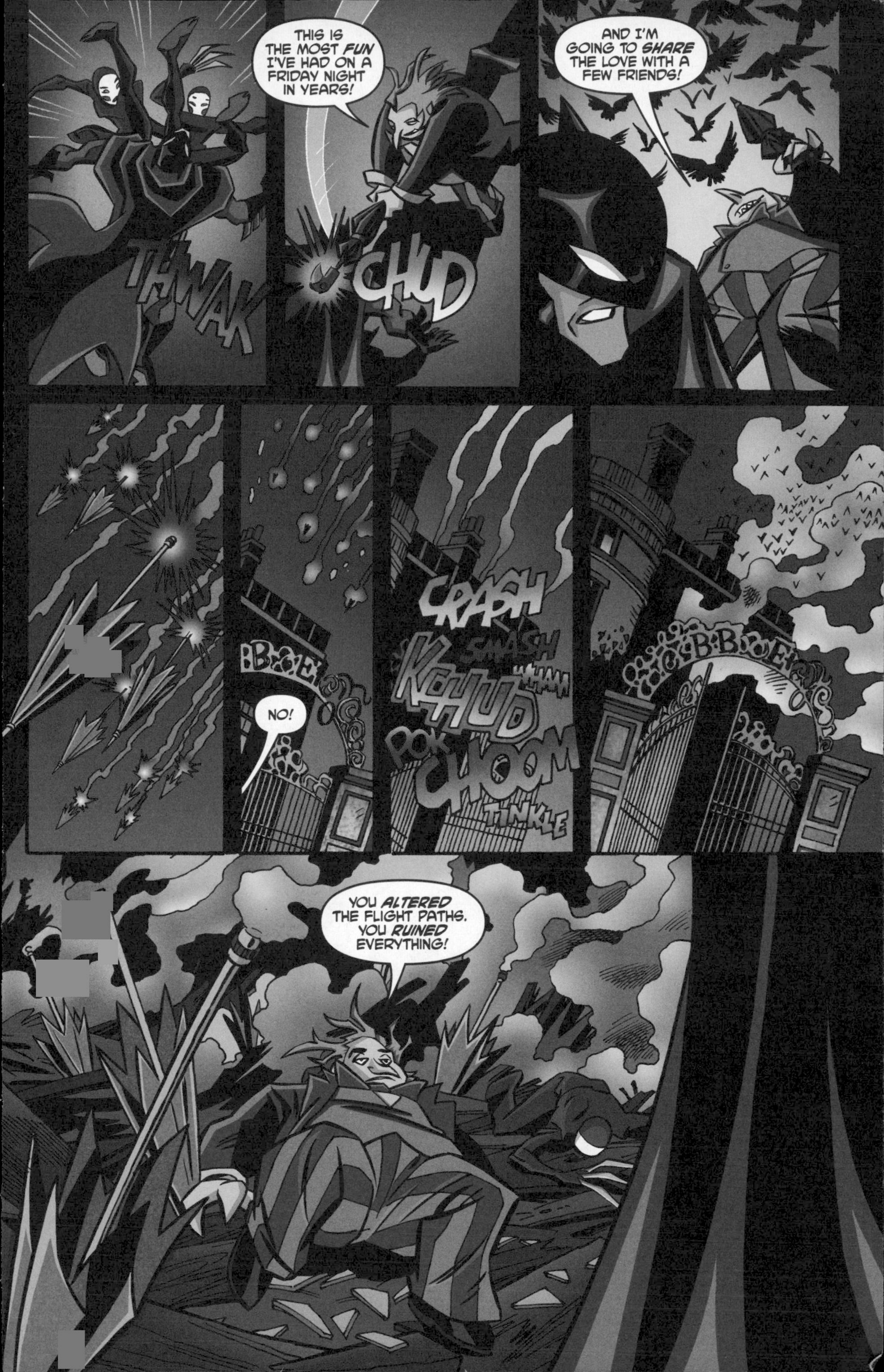
THWAK
THIS IS THE MOST FUN I'VE HAD ON A FRIDAY NIGHT IN YEARS!
CHUD
AND I'M GOING TO SHARE THE LOVE WITH A FEW FRIENDS!
NO!
CRASH
SMASH
WHAM
KCHUD
POK
CHOOM
TINKLE
YOU ALTERED THE FLIGHT PATHS. YOU RUINED EVERYTHING!

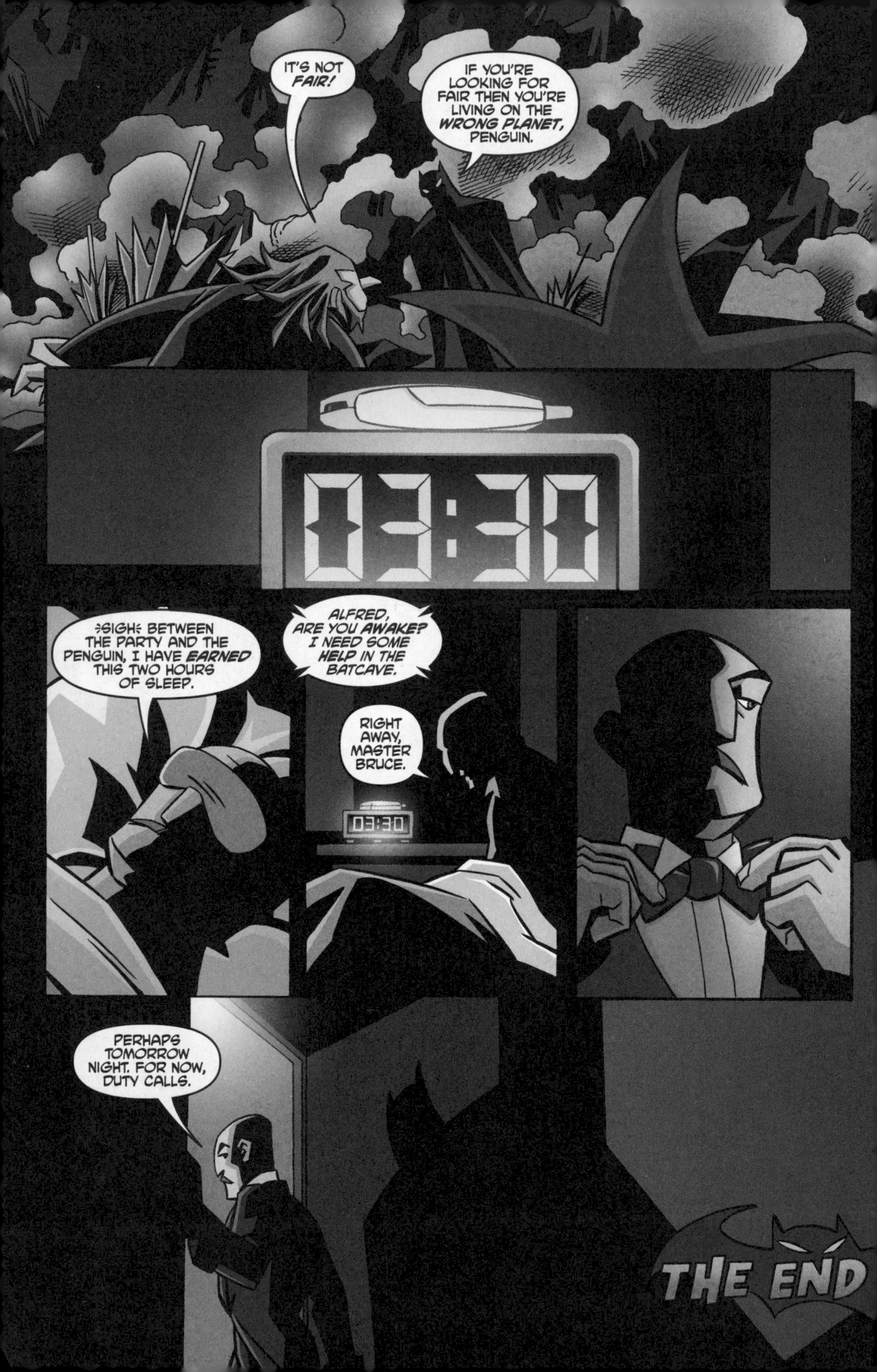
IT'S NOT *FAIR!*
IF YOU'RE LOOKING FOR FAIR THEN YOU'RE LIVING ON THE *WRONG PLANET*, PENGUIN.
03:30
SIGH BETWEEN THE PARTY AND THE PENGUIN, I HAVE *EARNED* THIS TWO HOURS OF SLEEP.
ALFRED, ARE YOU AWAKE? I NEED SOME HELP IN THE BATCAVE.
03:30
RIGHT AWAY, MASTER BRUCE.
PERHAPS TOMORROW NIGHT. FOR NOW, DUTY CALLS.
THE END

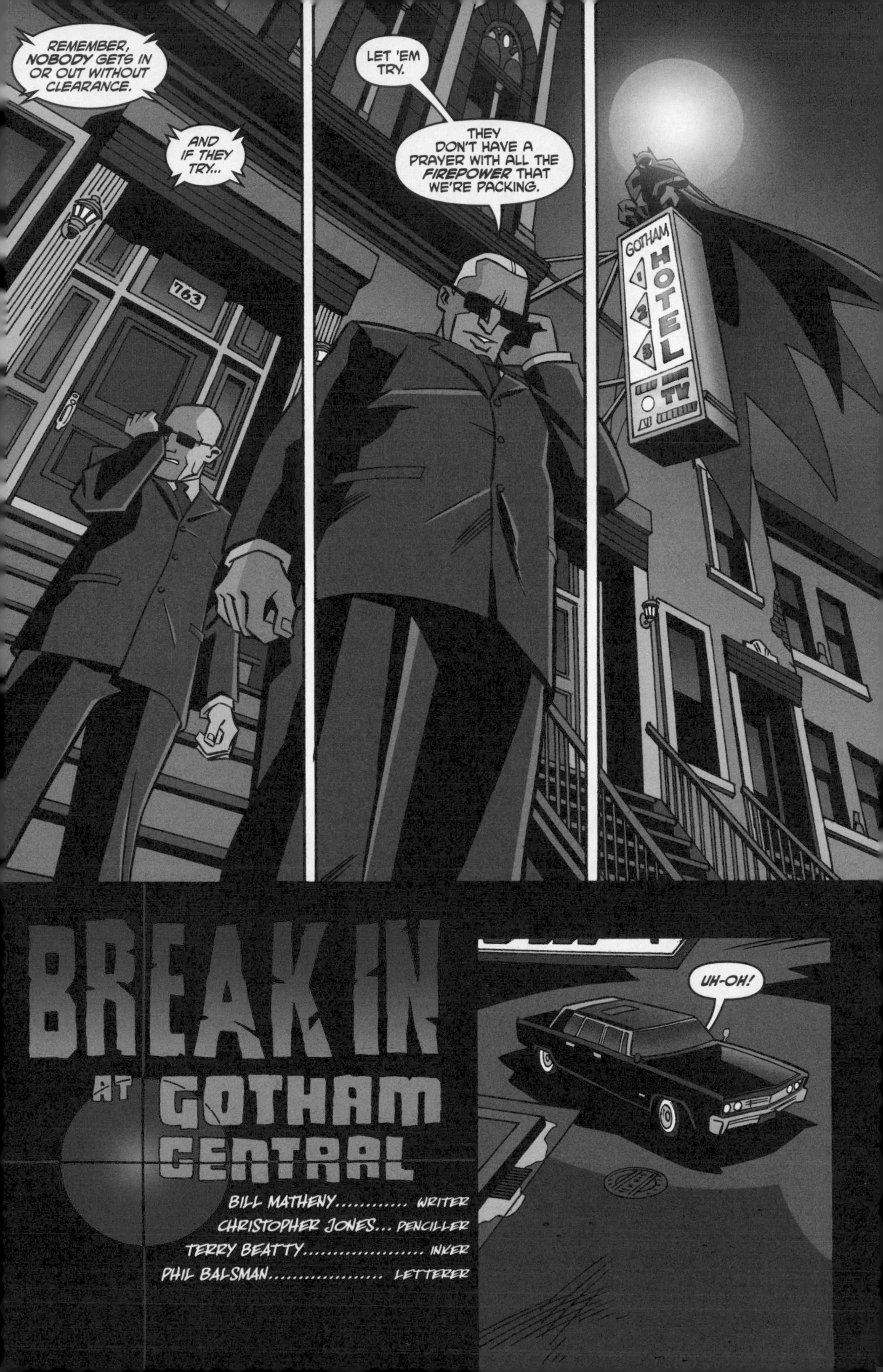
REMEMBER, NOBODY GETS IN OR OUT WITHOUT CLEARANCE.
AND IF THEY TRY...
LET 'EM TRY.
THEY DON'T HAVE A PRAYER WITH ALL THE FIREPOWER THAT WE'RE PACKING.
763
GOTHAM HOTEL
TV
BREAK IN AT GOTHAM CENTRAL
BILL MATHENY............ WRITER
CHRISTOPHER JONES... PENCILLER
TERRY BEATTY..................... INKER
PHIL BALSMAN................... LETTERER
UH-OH!

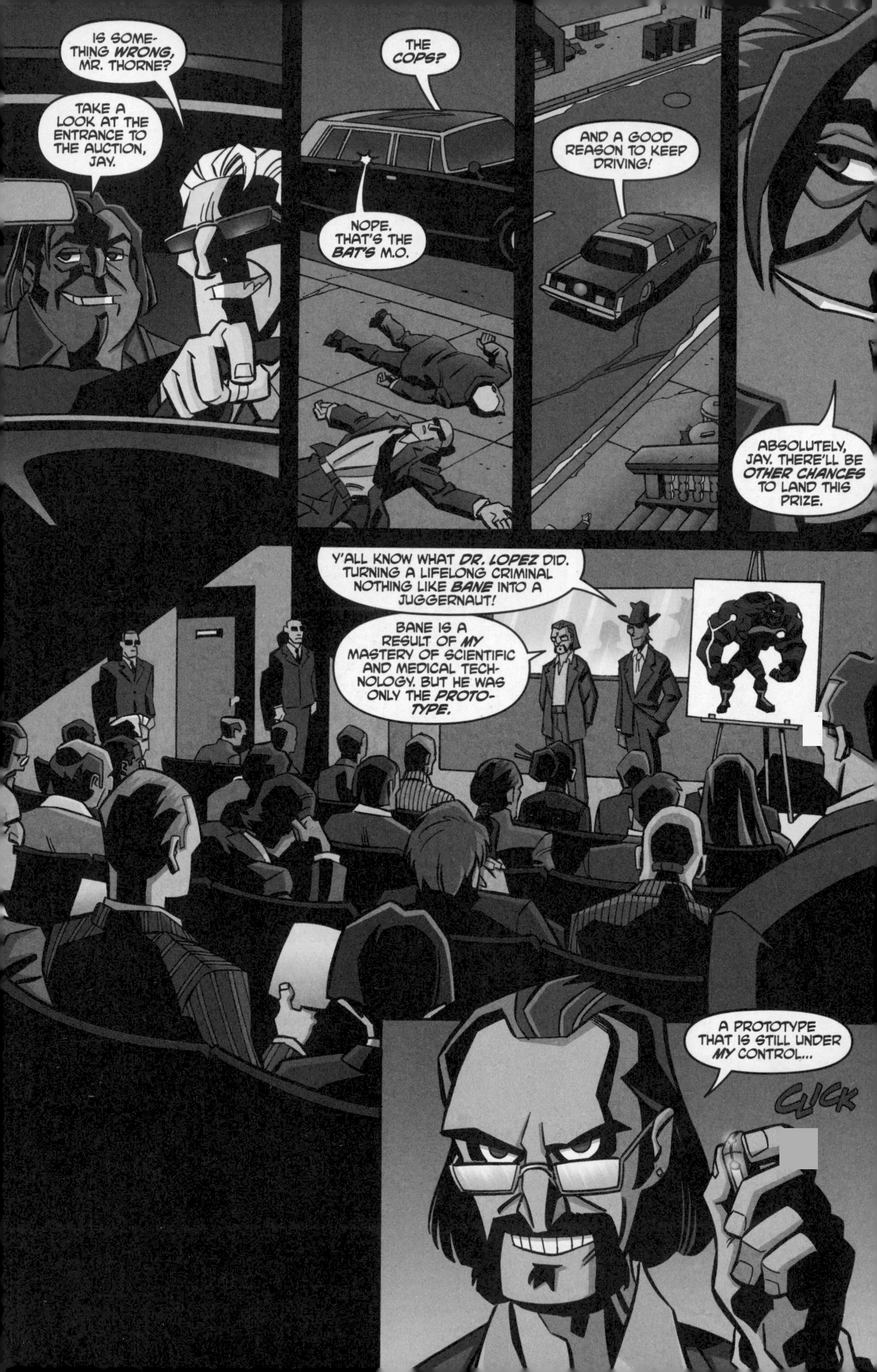
IS SOMETHING WRONG, MR. THORNE?
TAKE A LOOK AT THE ENTRANCE TO THE AUCTION, JAY.
THE COPS?
NOPE. THAT'S THE BAT'S M.O.
AND A GOOD REASON TO KEEP DRIVING!
ABSOLUTELY, JAY. THERE'LL BE OTHER CHANCES TO LAND THIS PRIZE.
Y'ALL KNOW WHAT DR. LOPEZ DID. TURNING A LIFELONG CRIMINAL NOTHING LIKE BANE INTO A JUGGERNAUT!
BANE IS A RESULT OF MY MASTERY OF SCIENTIFIC AND MEDICAL TECHNOLOGY. BUT HE WAS ONLY THE PROTOTYPE.
A PROTOTYPE THAT IS STILL UNDER MY CONTROL...
CLICK

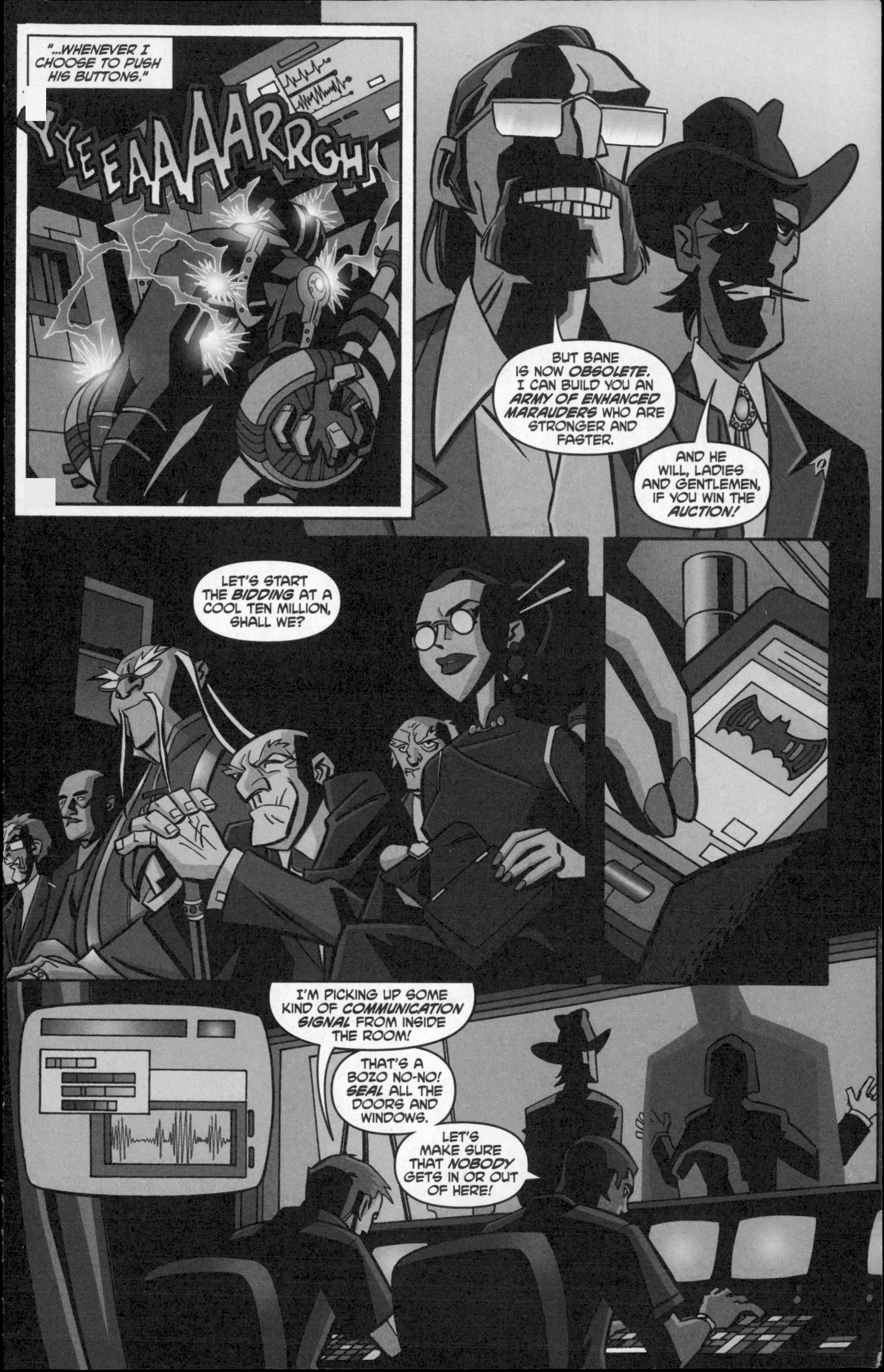
"...WHENEVER I CHOOSE TO PUSH HIS BUTTONS."
YYEEAAAARRRGH
BUT BANE IS NOW OBSOLETE. I CAN BUILD YOU AN ARMY OF ENHANCED MARAUDERS WHO ARE STRONGER AND FASTER.
AND HE WILL, LADIES AND GENTLEMEN, IF YOU WIN THE AUCTION!
LET'S START THE BIDDING AT A COOL TEN MILLION, SHALL WE?
I'M PICKING UP SOME KIND OF COMMUNICATION SIGNAL FROM INSIDE THE ROOM!
THAT'S A BOZO NO-NO! SEAL ALL THE DOORS AND WINDOWS.
LET'S MAKE SURE THAT NOBODY GETS IN OR OUT OF HERE!

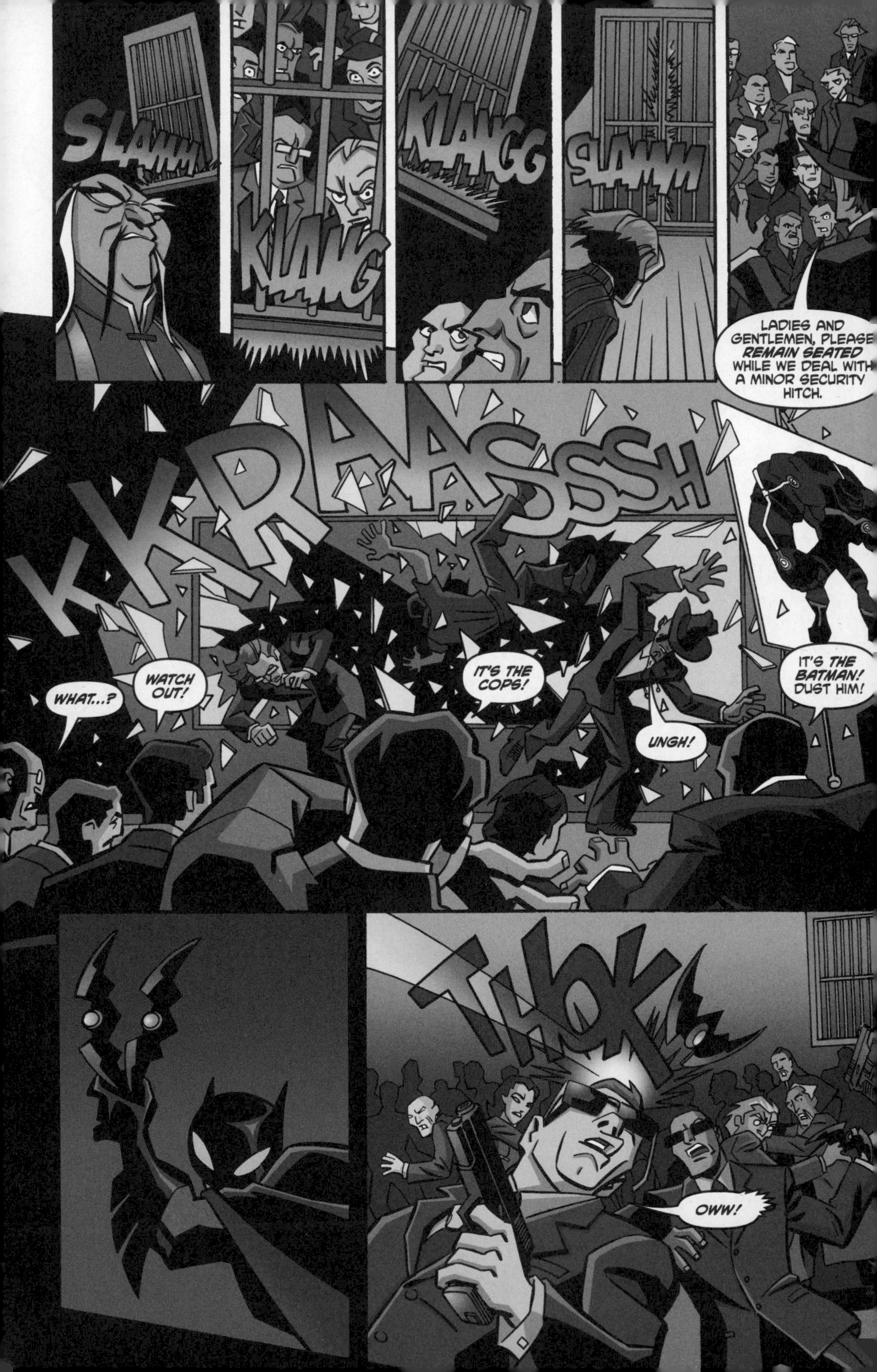
SLAMM
KLANG
KLANGG
SLAMM
LADIES AND GENTLEMEN, PLEASE REMAIN SEATED WHILE WE DEAL WITH A MINOR SECURITY HITCH.
KKRAASSSH
WHAT...?
WATCH OUT!
IT'S THE COPS!
UNGH!
IT'S THE BATMAN! DUST HIM!
THOK
OWW!

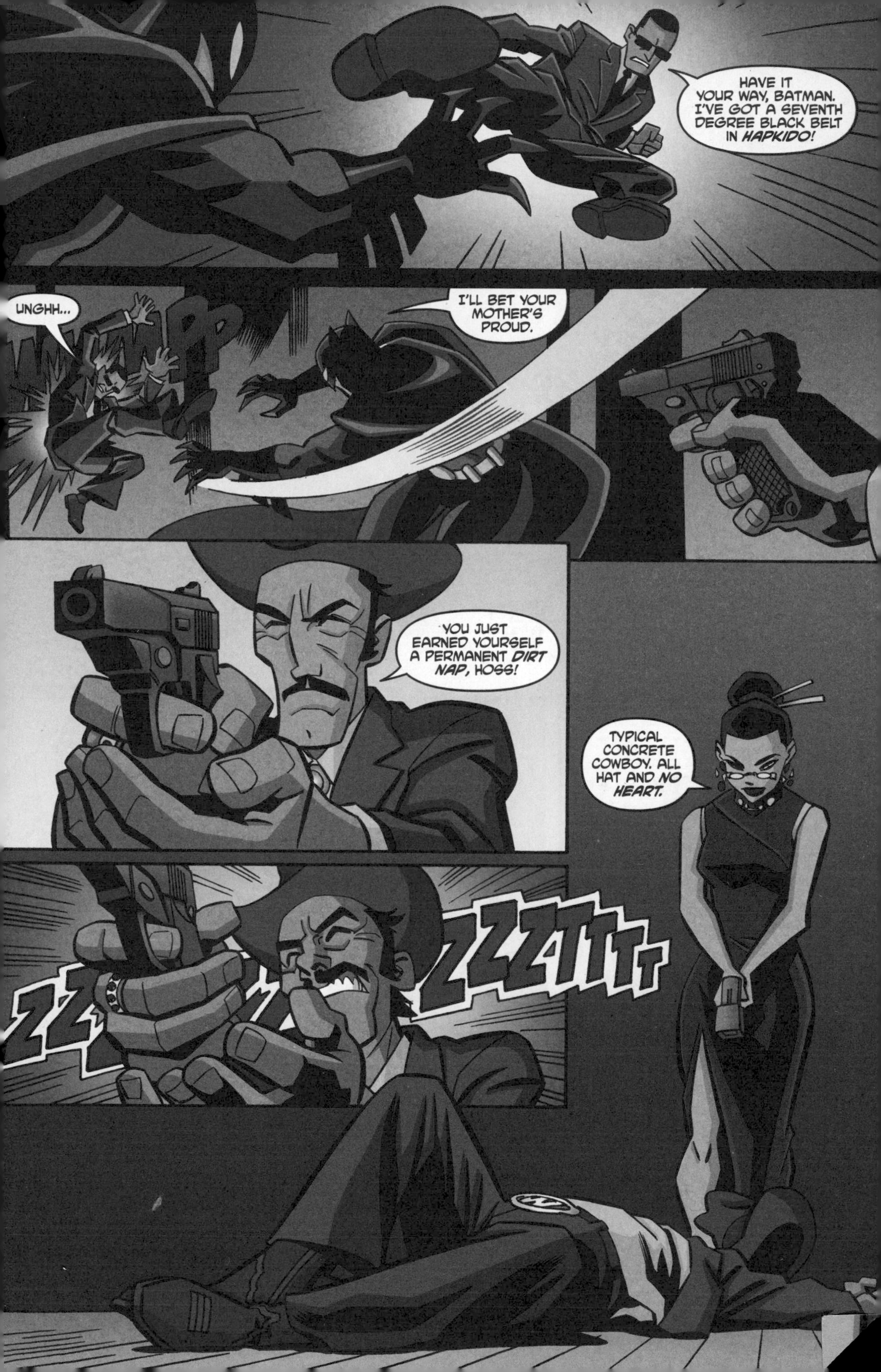
HAVE IT YOUR WAY, BATMAN. I'VE GOT A SEVENTH DEGREE BLACK BELT IN *HAPKIDO!*
UNGHH...
I'LL BET YOUR MOTHER'S PROUD.
YOU JUST EARNED YOURSELF A PERMANENT *DIRT NAP,* HOSS!
TYPICAL CONCRETE COWBOY. ALL HAT AND *NO HEART.*
ZZZZZTTTTt

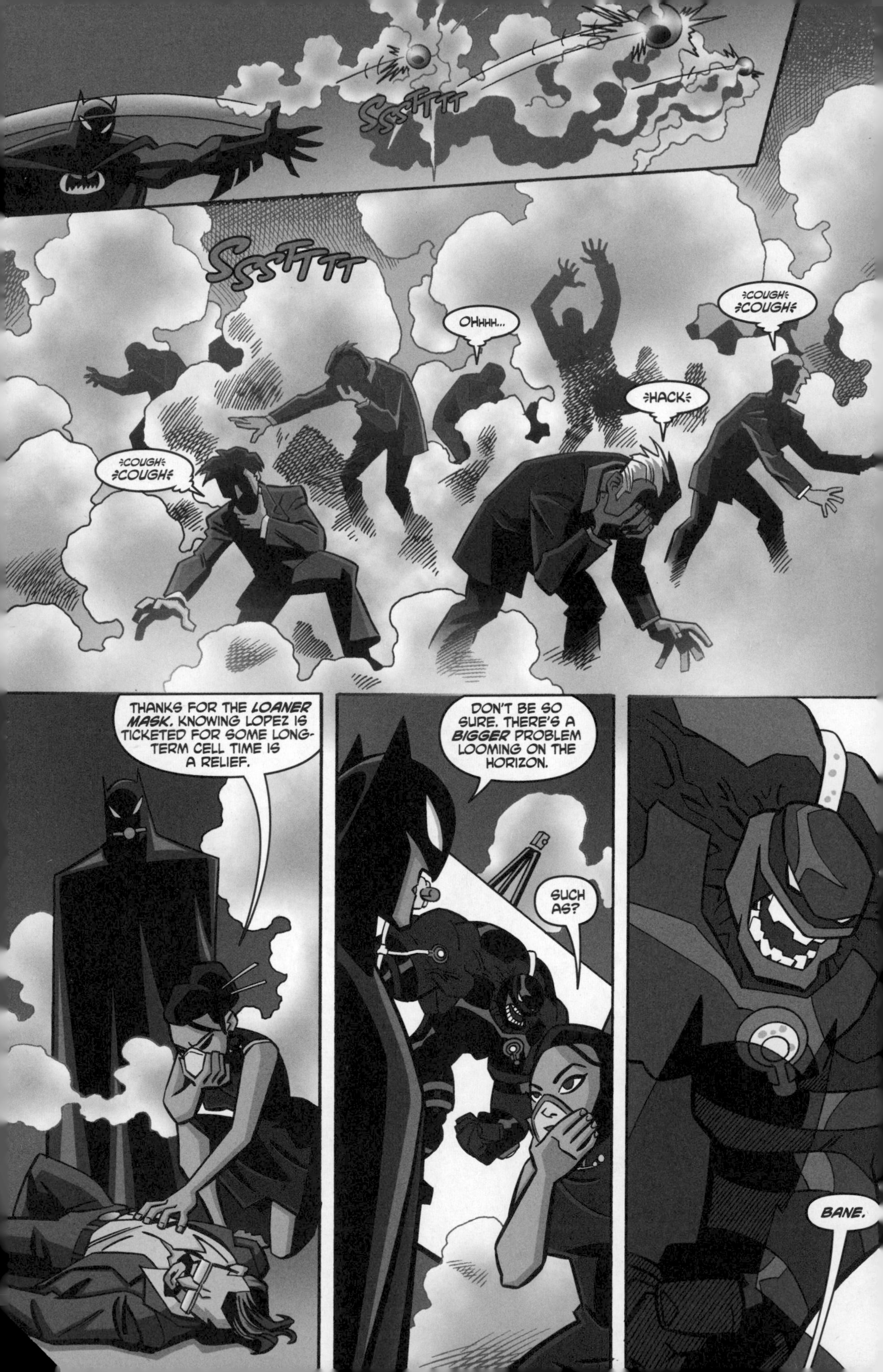
SSSFTTT
SSSFTTT
OHHHH...
COUGH *COUGH*
HACK
COUGH *COUGH*
THANKS FOR THE LOANER MASK. KNOWING LOPEZ IS TICKETED FOR SOME LONG-TERM CELL TIME IS A RELIEF.
DON'T BE SO SURE. THERE'S A BIGGER PROBLEM LOOMING ON THE HORIZON.
SUCH AS?
BANE.

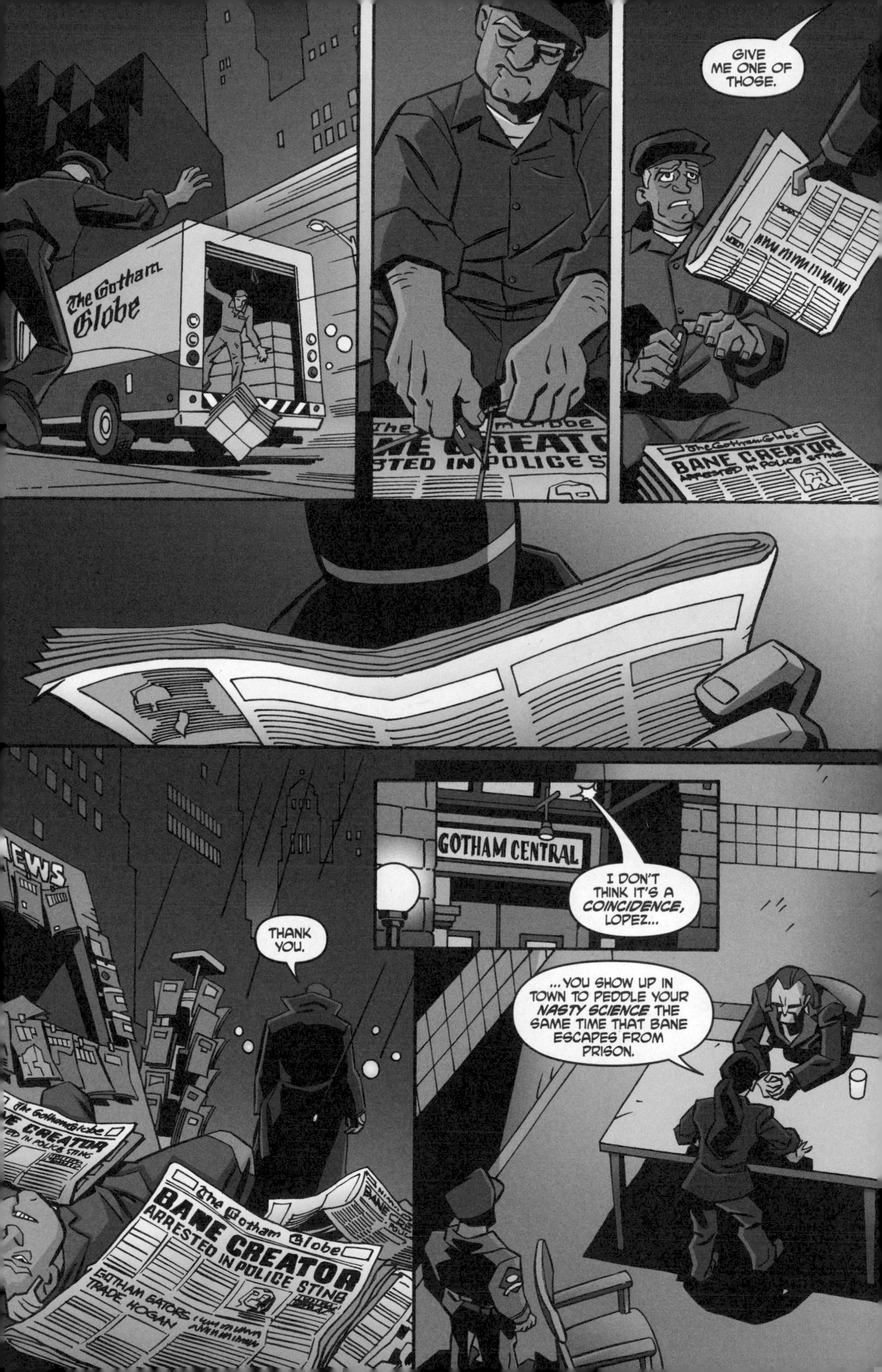

The Gotham Globe
GIVE ME ONE OF THOSE.
BANE CREATOR
ARRESTED IN POLICE STING
THANK YOU.
BANE CREATOR
ARRESTED IN POLICE STING
GOTHAM GATORS TRADE HOGAN
GOTHAM CENTRAL
I DON'T THINK IT'S A *COINCIDENCE,* LOPEZ...
...YOU SHOW UP IN TOWN TO PEDDLE YOUR *NASTY SCIENCE* THE SAME TIME THAT BANE ESCAPES FROM PRISON.

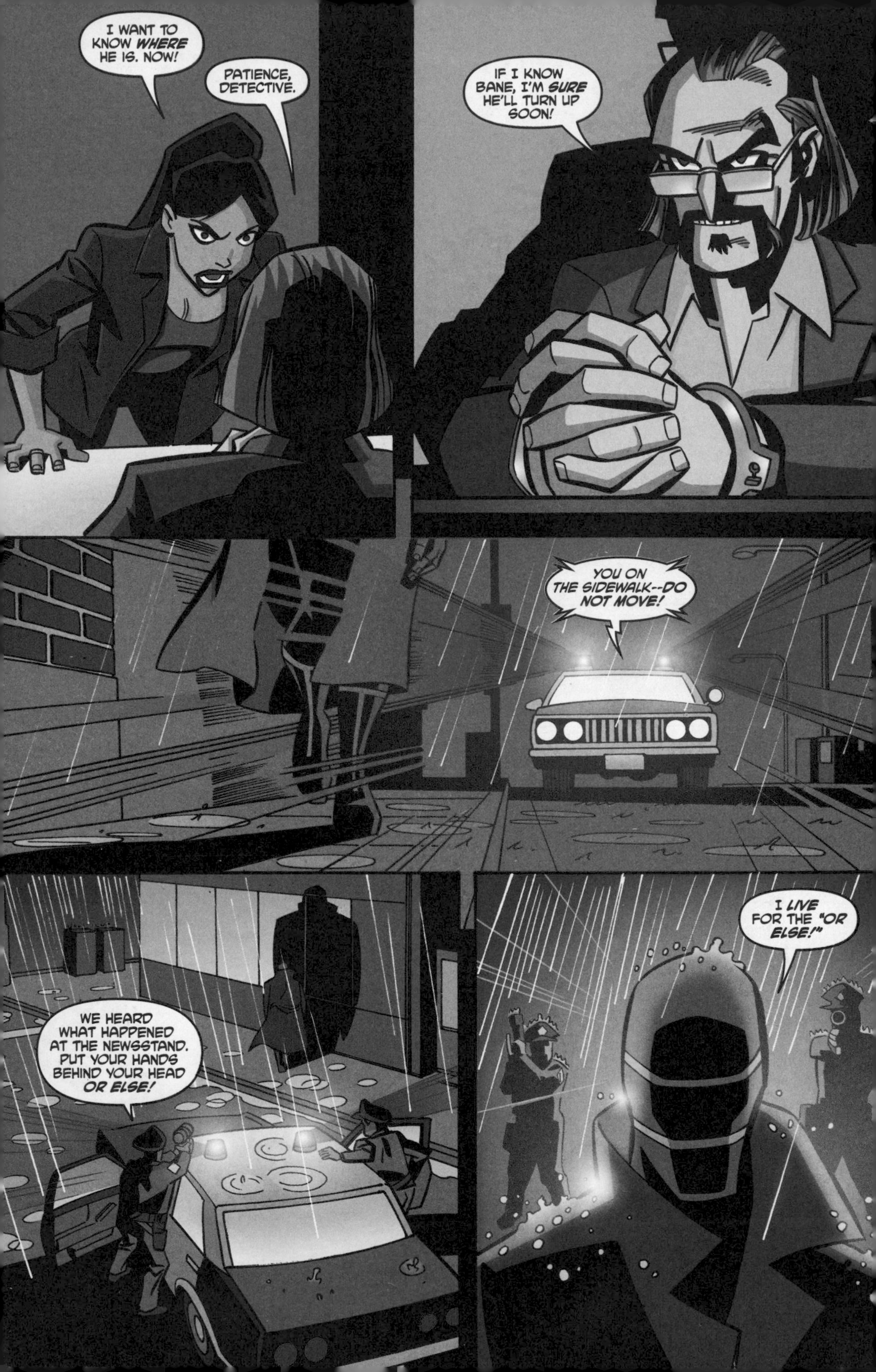
I WANT TO KNOW *WHERE* HE IS. NOW!
PATIENCE, DETECTIVE.
IF I KNOW BANE, I'M *SURE* HE'LL TURN UP SOON!
YOU ON THE SIDEWALK--DO NOT MOVE!
WE HEARD WHAT HAPPENED AT THE NEWSSTAND. PUT YOUR HANDS BEHIND YOUR HEAD *OR ELSE!*
I *LIVE* FOR THE "OR *ELSE!*"

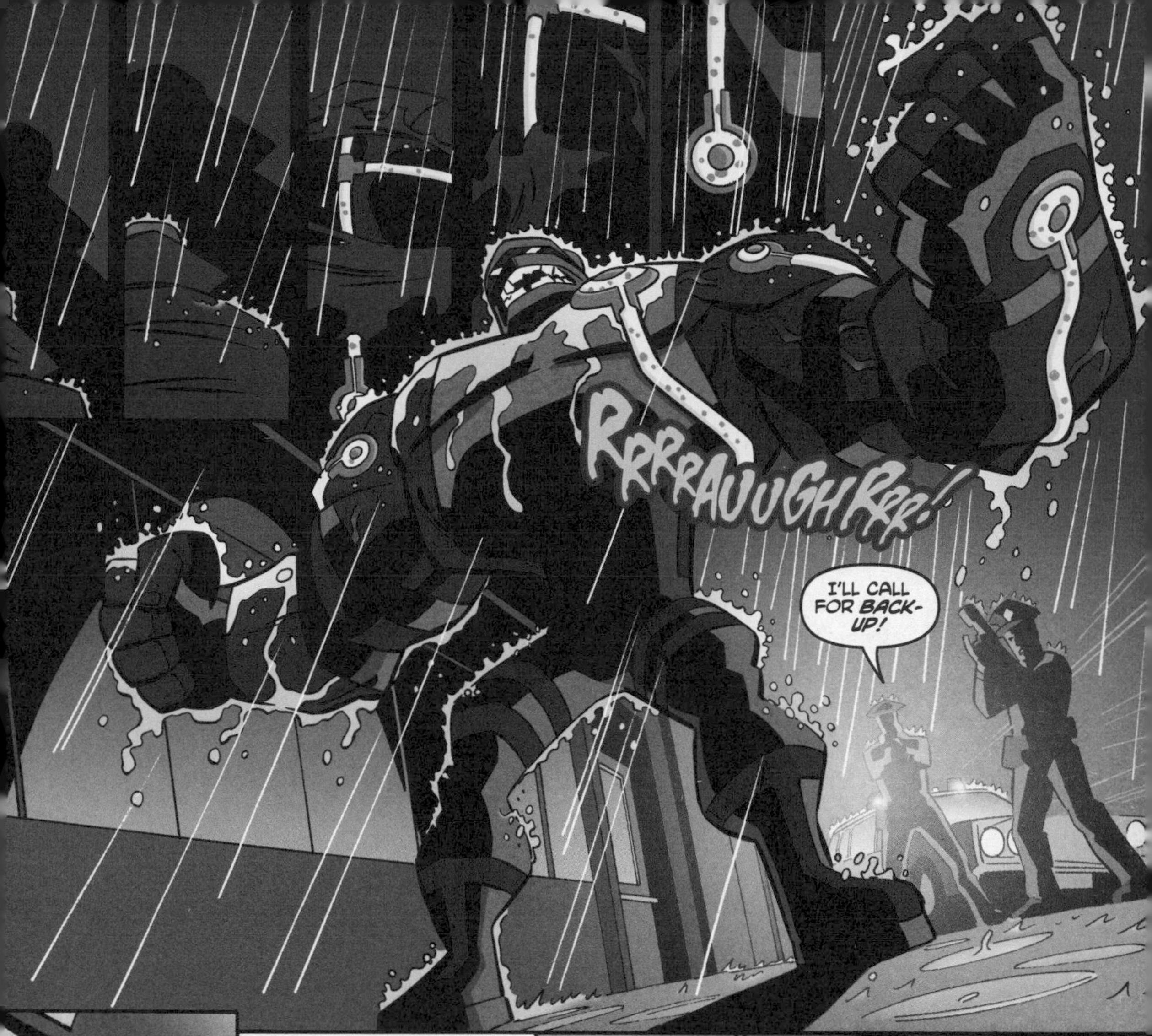
RRRRAUUGHRRR!
I'LL CALL FOR *BACK-UP!*

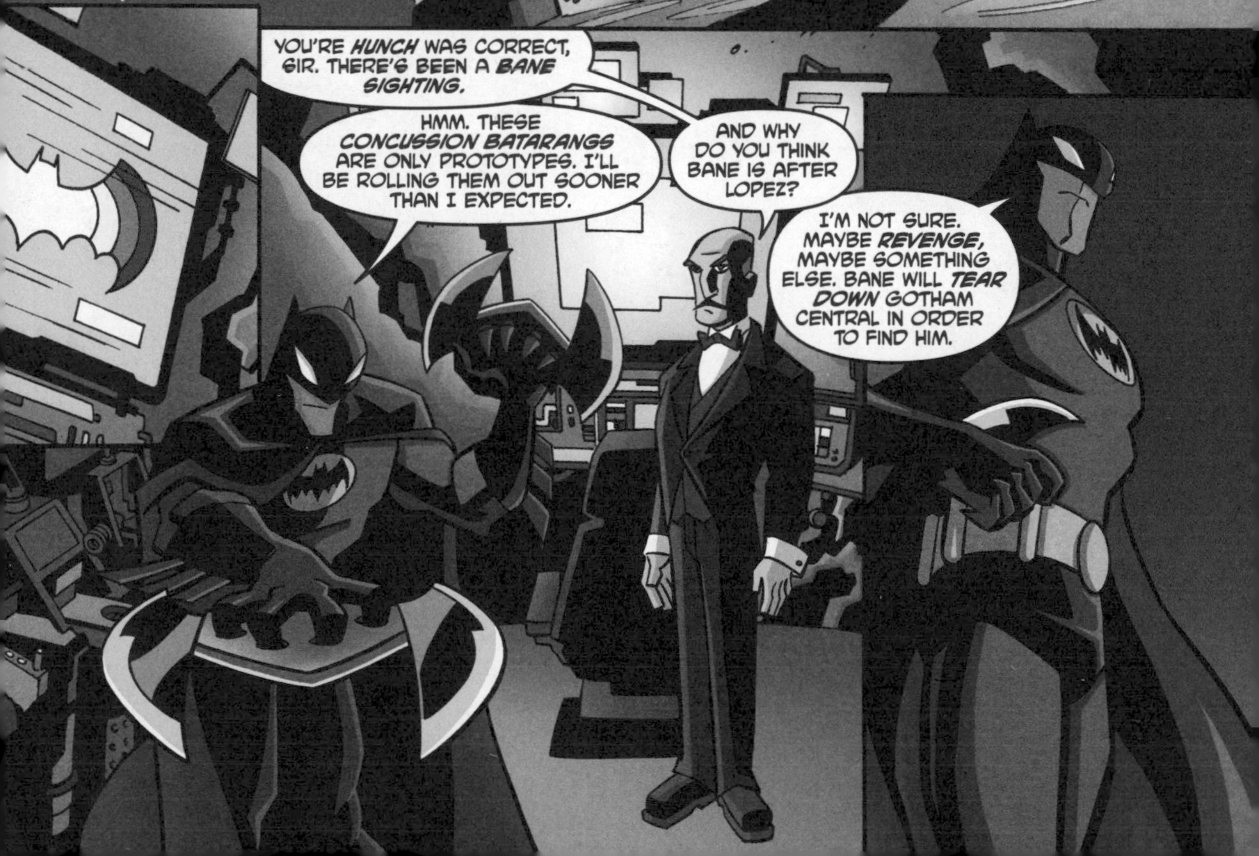
YOU'RE *HUNCH* WAS CORRECT, SIR. THERE'S BEEN A *BANE SIGHTING.*
HMM. THESE *CONCUSSION BATARANGS* ARE ONLY PROTOTYPES. I'LL BE ROLLING THEM OUT SOONER THAN I EXPECTED.
AND WHY DO YOU THINK BANE IS AFTER LOPEZ?
I'M NOT SURE. MAYBE *REVENGE,* MAYBE SOMETHING ELSE. BANE WILL *TEAR DOWN* GOTHAM CENTRAL IN ORDER TO FIND HIM.

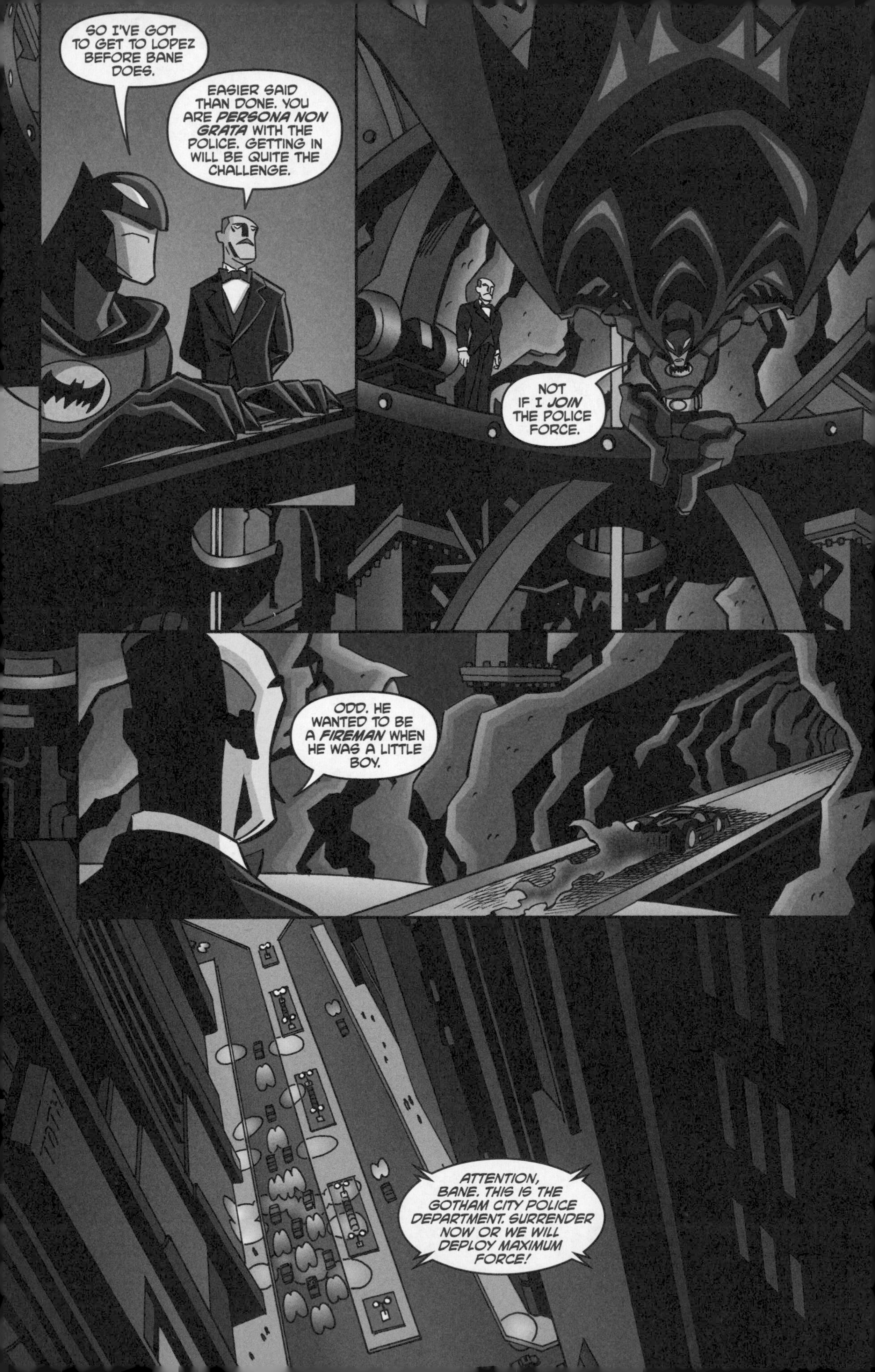
SO I'VE GOT TO GET TO LOPEZ BEFORE BANE DOES.
EASIER SAID THAN DONE. YOU ARE *PERSONA NON GRATA* WITH THE POLICE. GETTING IN WILL BE QUITE THE CHALLENGE.
NOT IF I *JOIN* THE POLICE FORCE.
ODD. HE WANTED TO BE A *FIREMAN* WHEN HE WAS A LITTLE BOY.
ATTENTION, BANE. THIS IS THE GOTHAM CITY POLICE DEPARTMENT. SURRENDER NOW OR WE WILL DEPLOY MAXIMUM FORCE!

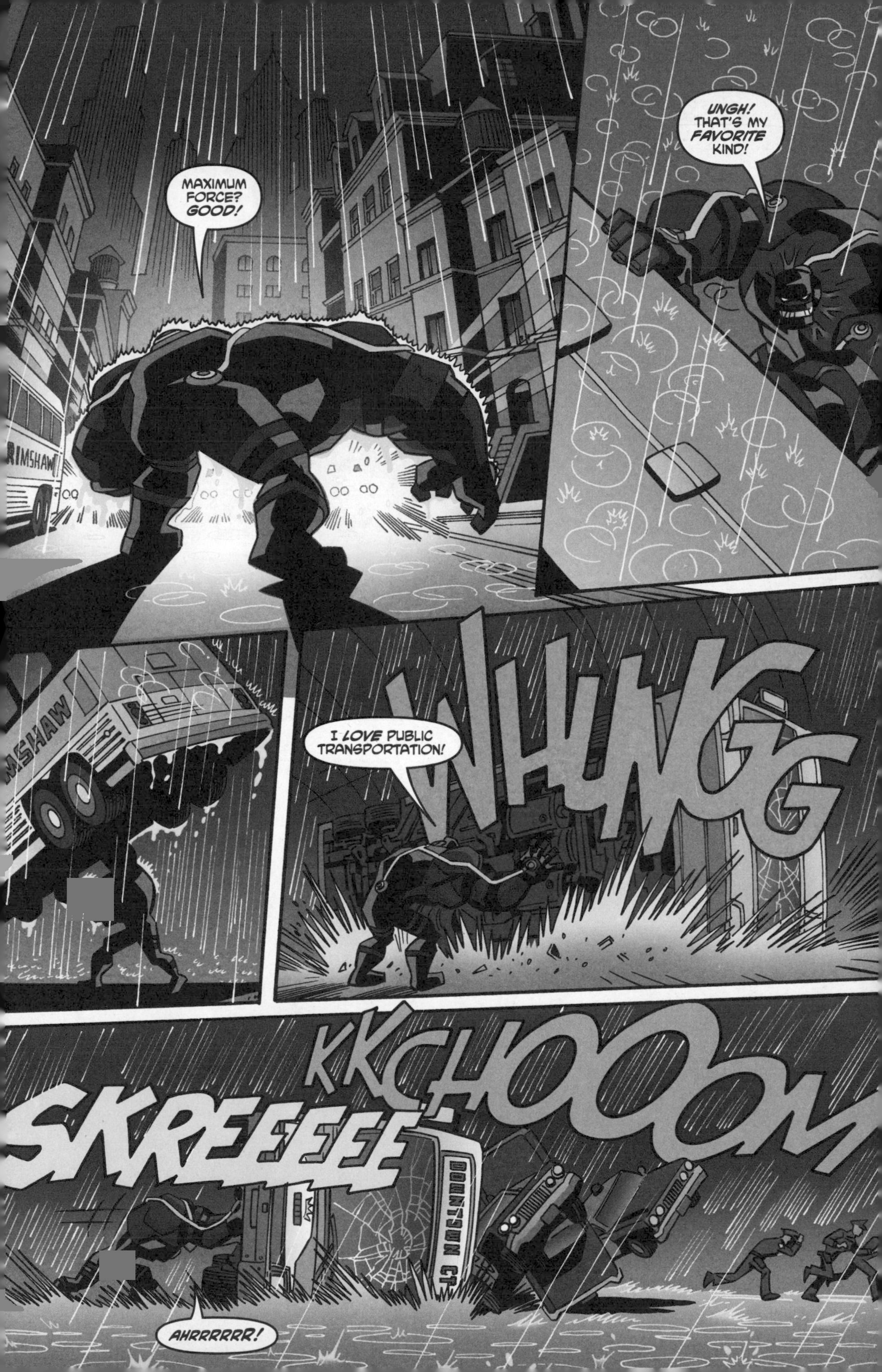
MAXIMUM FORCE? GOOD!
UNGH! THAT'S MY FAVORITE KIND!
I LOVE PUBLIC TRANSPORTATION!
WHUNGG
KKCHOOOOM
SKREEEEEE
AHRRRRRR!

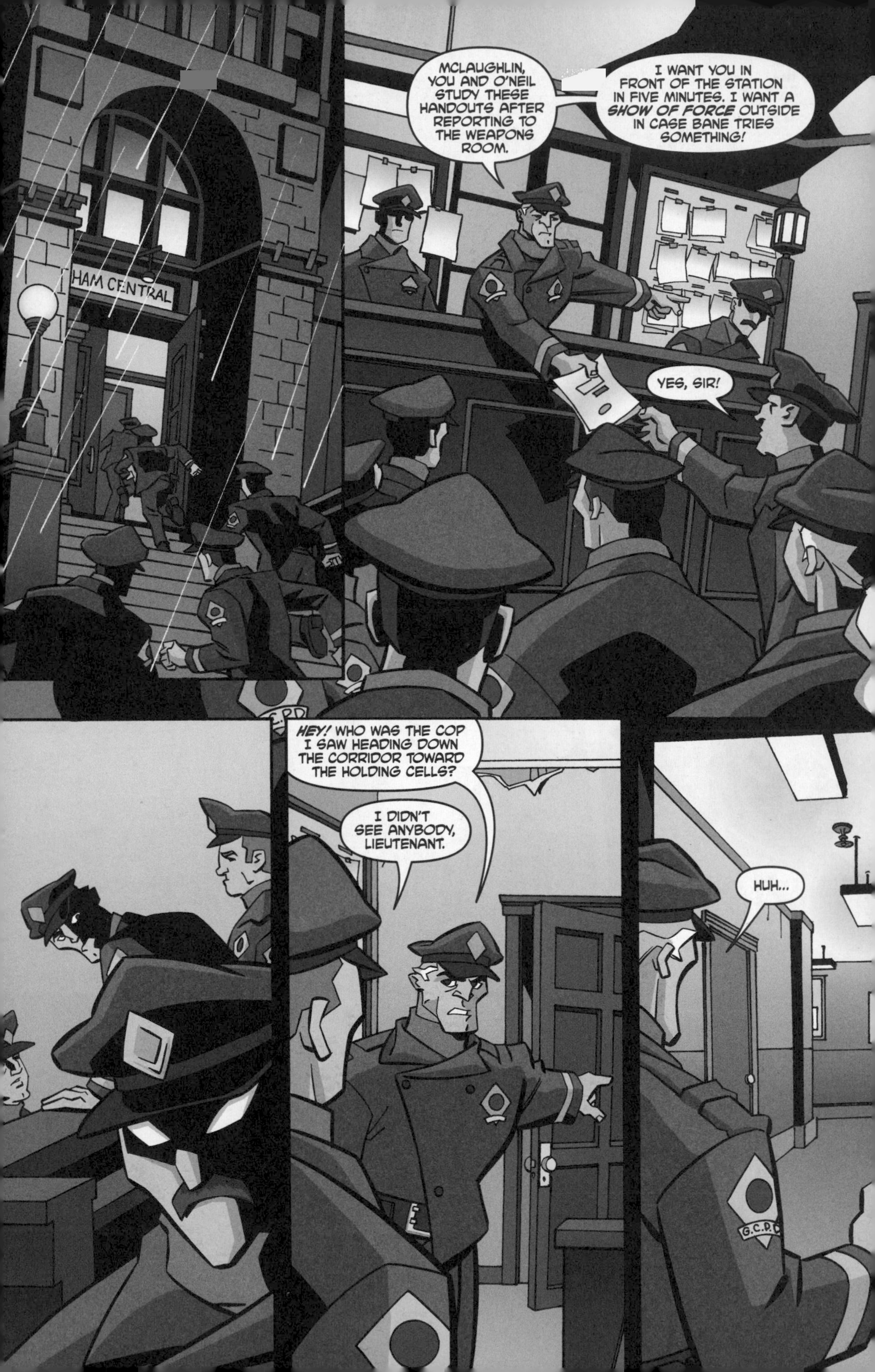
HAM CENTRAL
MCLAUGHLIN, YOU AND O'NEIL STUDY THESE HANDOUTS AFTER REPORTING TO THE WEAPONS ROOM.
I WANT YOU IN FRONT OF THE STATION IN FIVE MINUTES. I WANT A *SHOW OF FORCE* OUTSIDE IN CASE BANE TRIES SOMETHING!
YES, SIR!
HEY! WHO WAS THE COP I SAW HEADING DOWN THE CORRIDOR TOWARD THE HOLDING CELLS?
I DIDN'T SEE ANYBODY, LIEUTENANT.
HUH...

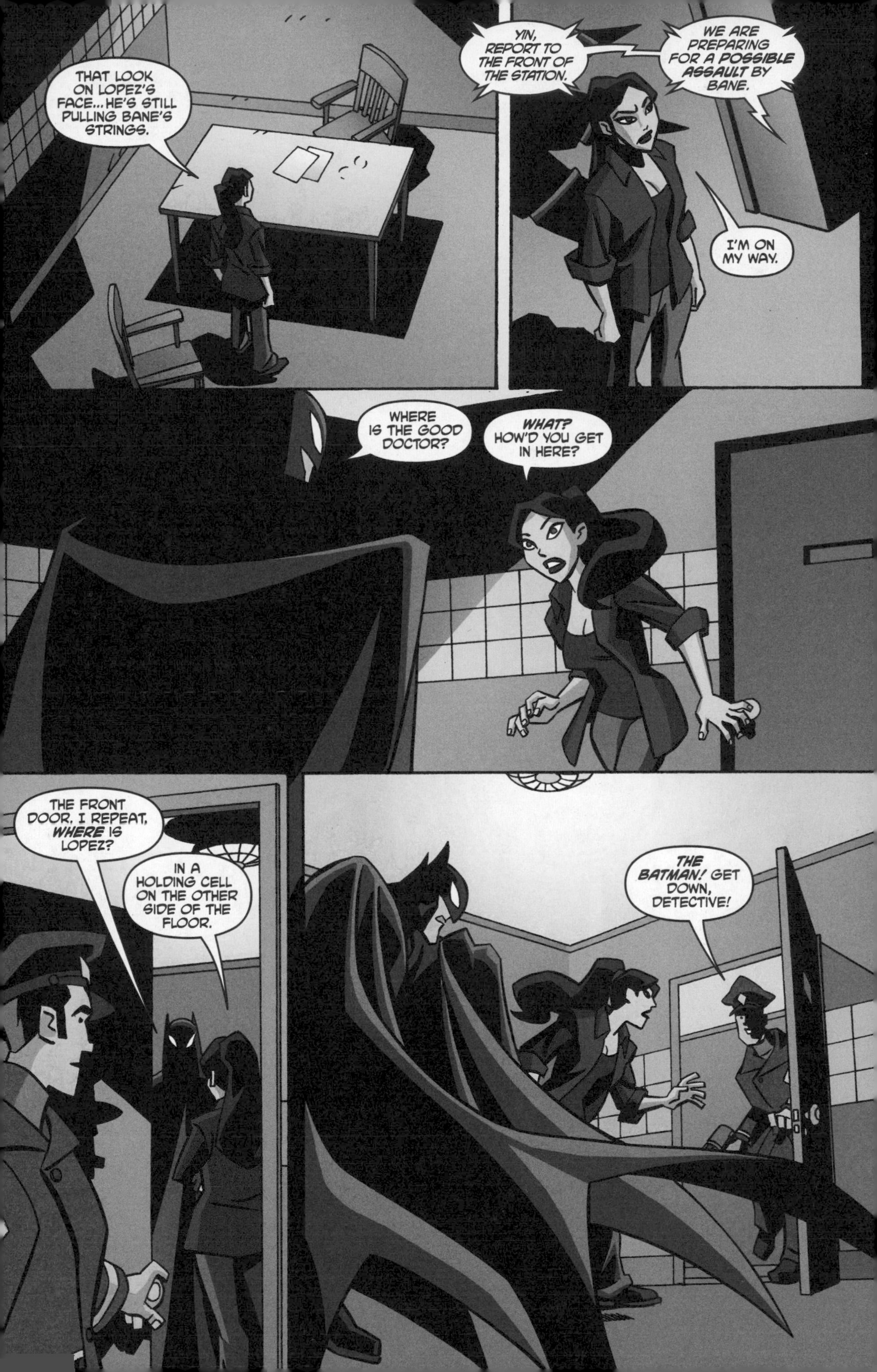
THAT LOOK ON LOPEZ'S FACE... HE'S STILL PULLING BANE'S STRINGS.
YIN, REPORT TO THE FRONT OF THE STATION.
WE ARE PREPARING FOR A POSSIBLE ASSAULT BY BANE.
I'M ON MY WAY.
WHERE IS THE GOOD DOCTOR?
WHAT? HOW'D YOU GET IN HERE?
THE FRONT DOOR. I REPEAT, WHERE IS LOPEZ?
IN A HOLDING CELL ON THE OTHER SIDE OF THE FLOOR.
THE BATMAN! GET DOWN, DETECTIVE!

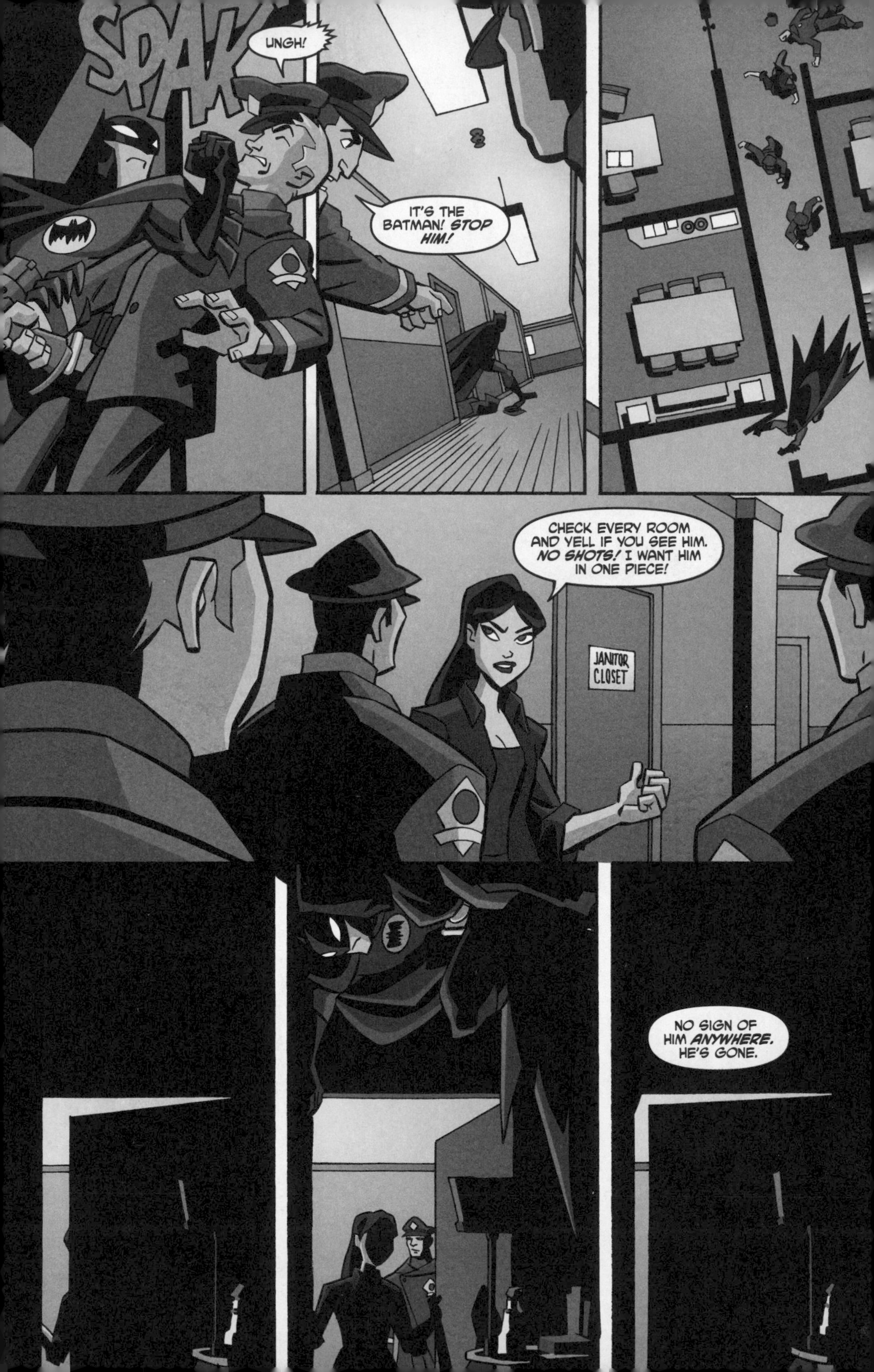
SPAK
UNGH!
IT'S THE BATMAN! STOP HIM!
CHECK EVERY ROOM AND YELL IF YOU SEE HIM. NO SHOTS! I WANT HIM IN ONE PIECE!
JANITOR CLOSET
NO SIGN OF HIM ANYWHERE. HE'S GONE.

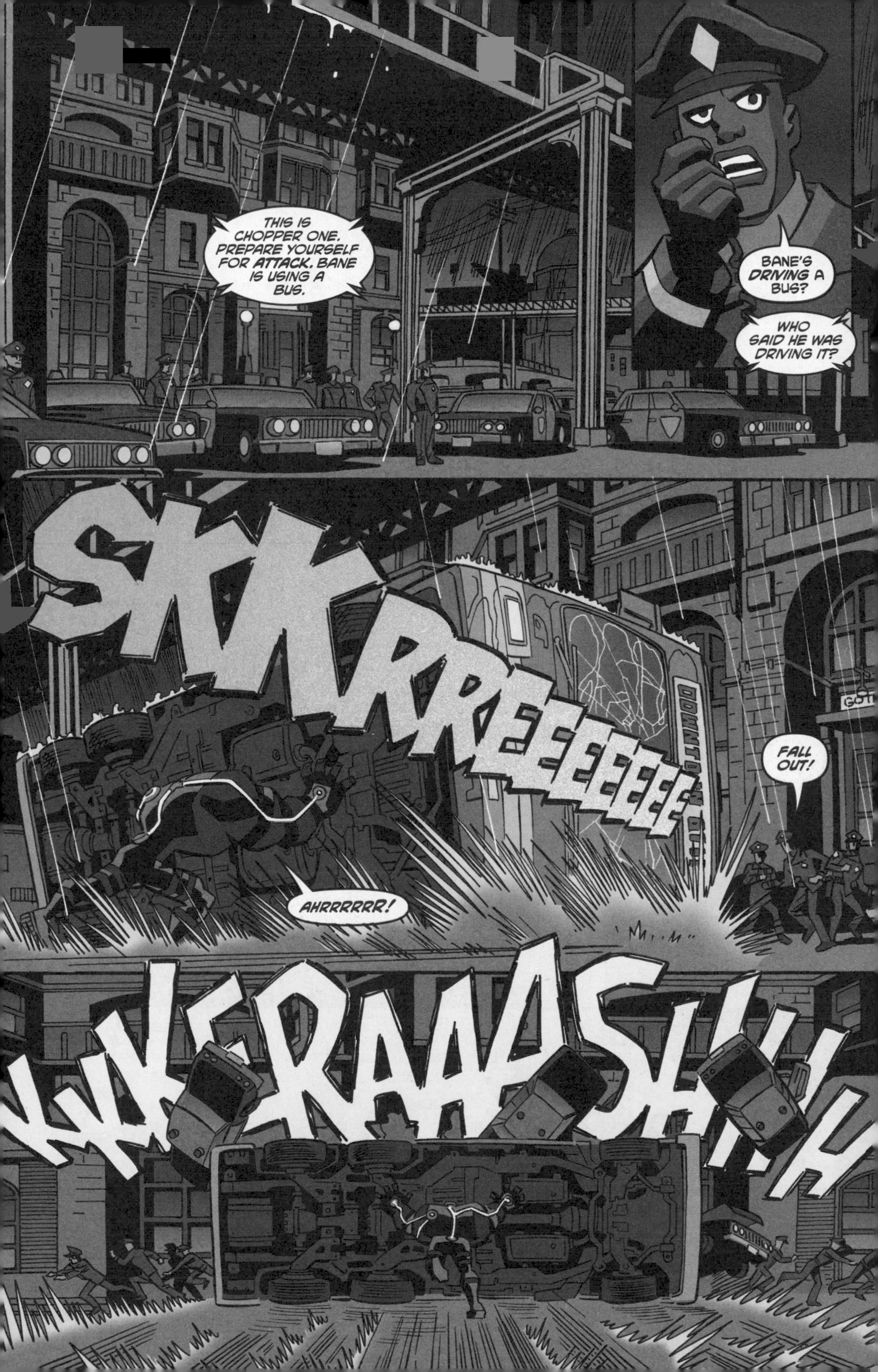
THIS IS CHOPPER ONE. PREPARE YOURSELF FOR ATTACK. BANE IS USING A BUS.
BANE'S DRIVING A BUS?
WHO SAID HE WAS DRIVING IT?
SKKRREEEEEEEEEE
AHRRRRRR!
FALL OUT!
KKKRAAASHHH

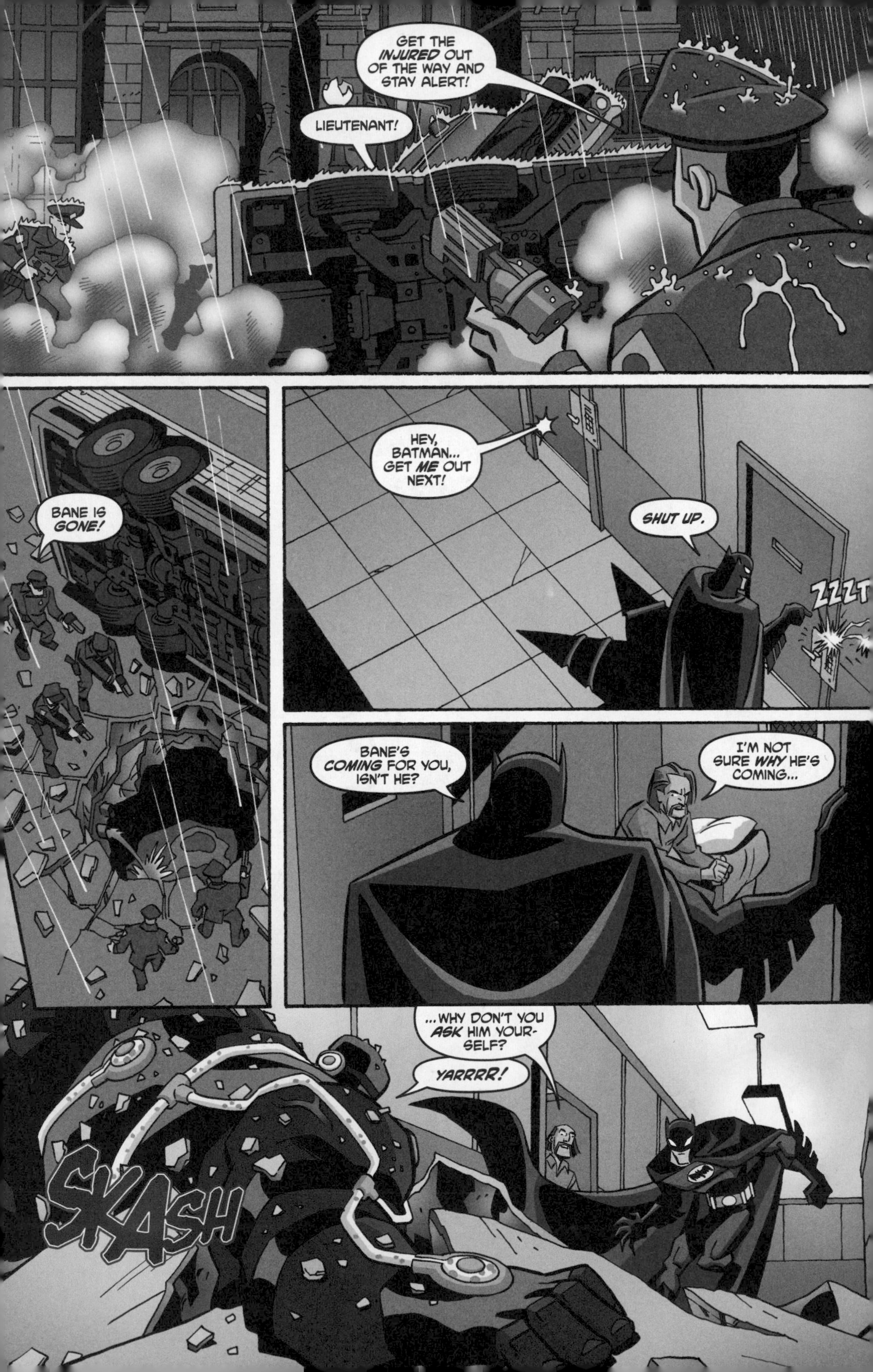
GET THE INJURED OUT OF THE WAY AND STAY ALERT!
LIEUTENANT!
BANE IS GONE!
HEY, BATMAN... GET ME OUT NEXT!
SHUT UP.
ZZZT
BANE'S COMING FOR YOU, ISN'T HE?
I'M NOT SURE WHY HE'S COMING...
...WHY DON'T YOU ASK HIM YOUR-SELF?
YARRRR!
SKASH

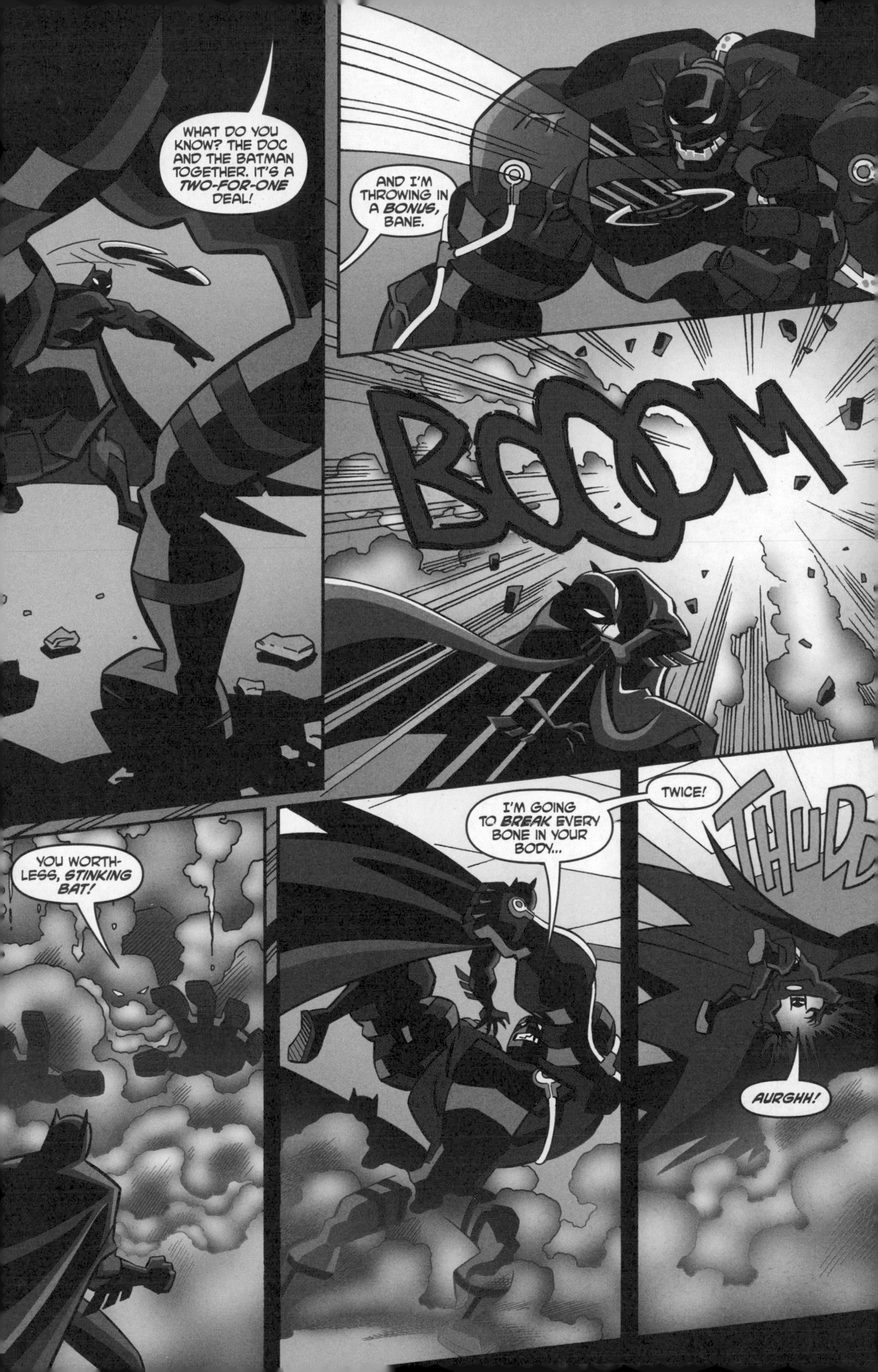
WHAT DO YOU KNOW? THE DOC AND THE BATMAN TOGETHER. IT'S A *TWO-FOR-ONE* DEAL!
AND I'M THROWING IN A *BONUS,* BANE.
BOOOM
YOU WORTH-LESS, *STINKING BAT!*
I'M GOING TO *BREAK* EVERY BONE IN YOUR BODY...
TWICE!
AURGHH!

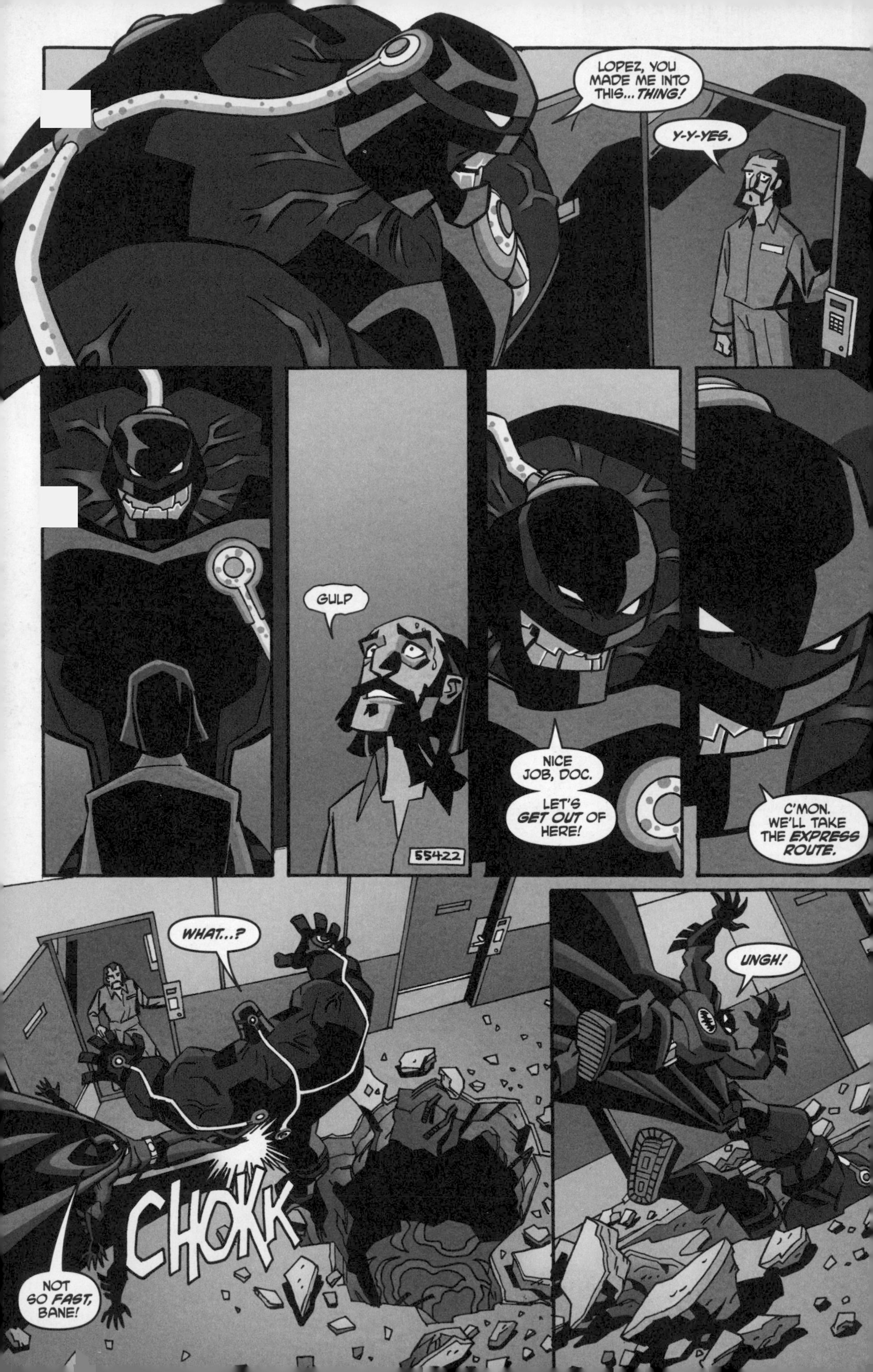

LOPEZ, YOU MADE ME INTO THIS... *THING!*
Y-Y-YES.
GULP
55422
NICE JOB, DOC.
LET'S *GET OUT* OF HERE!
C'MON. WE'LL TAKE THE *EXPRESS* ROUTE.
WHAT...?
CHOKK
NOT SO *FAST,* BANE!
UNGH!

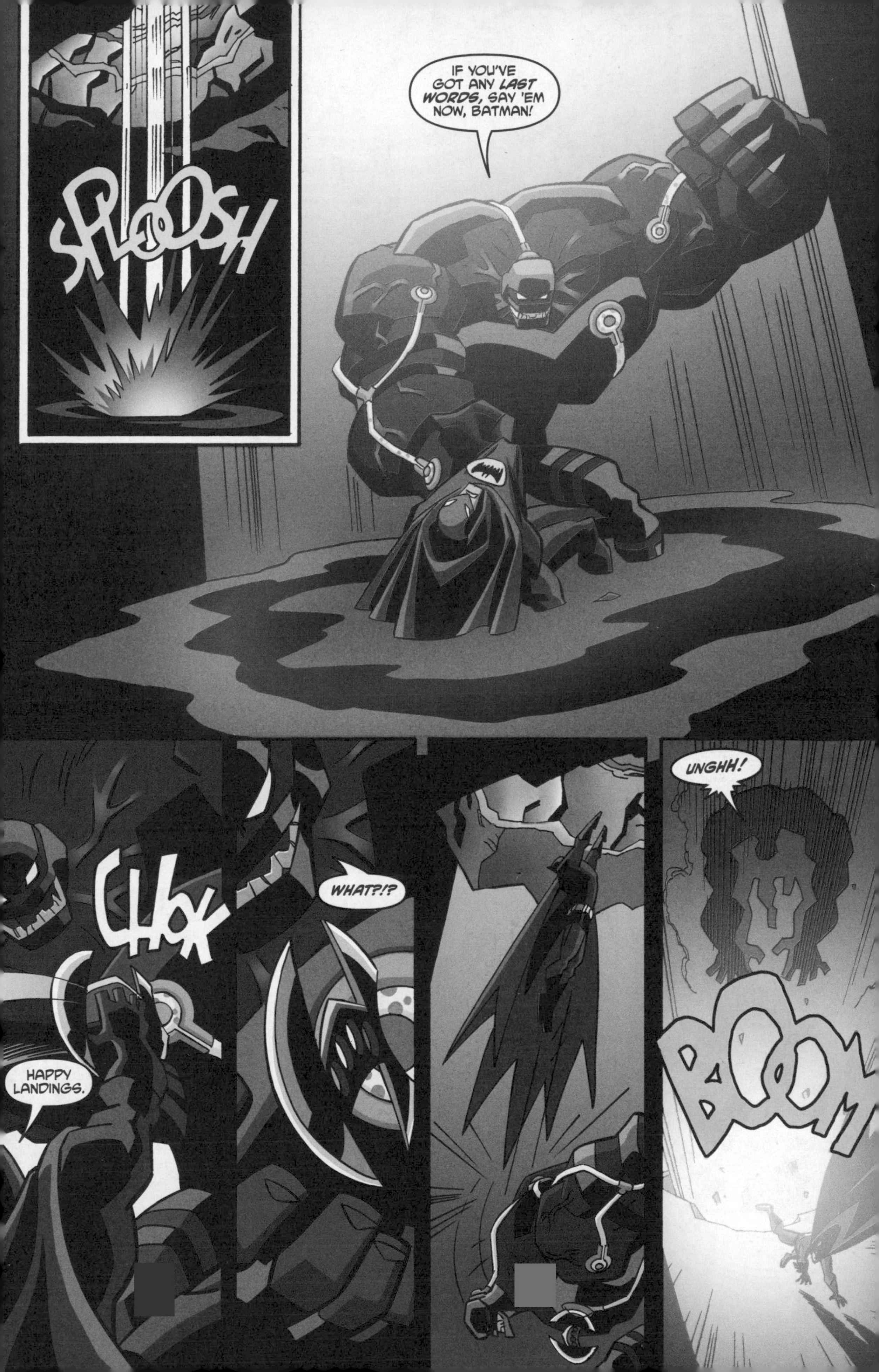
SPLOOSH
IF YOU'VE GOT ANY *LAST WORDS*, SAY 'EM NOW, BATMAN!
CHOK
HAPPY LANDINGS.
WHAT?!?
UNGHH!
BOOM

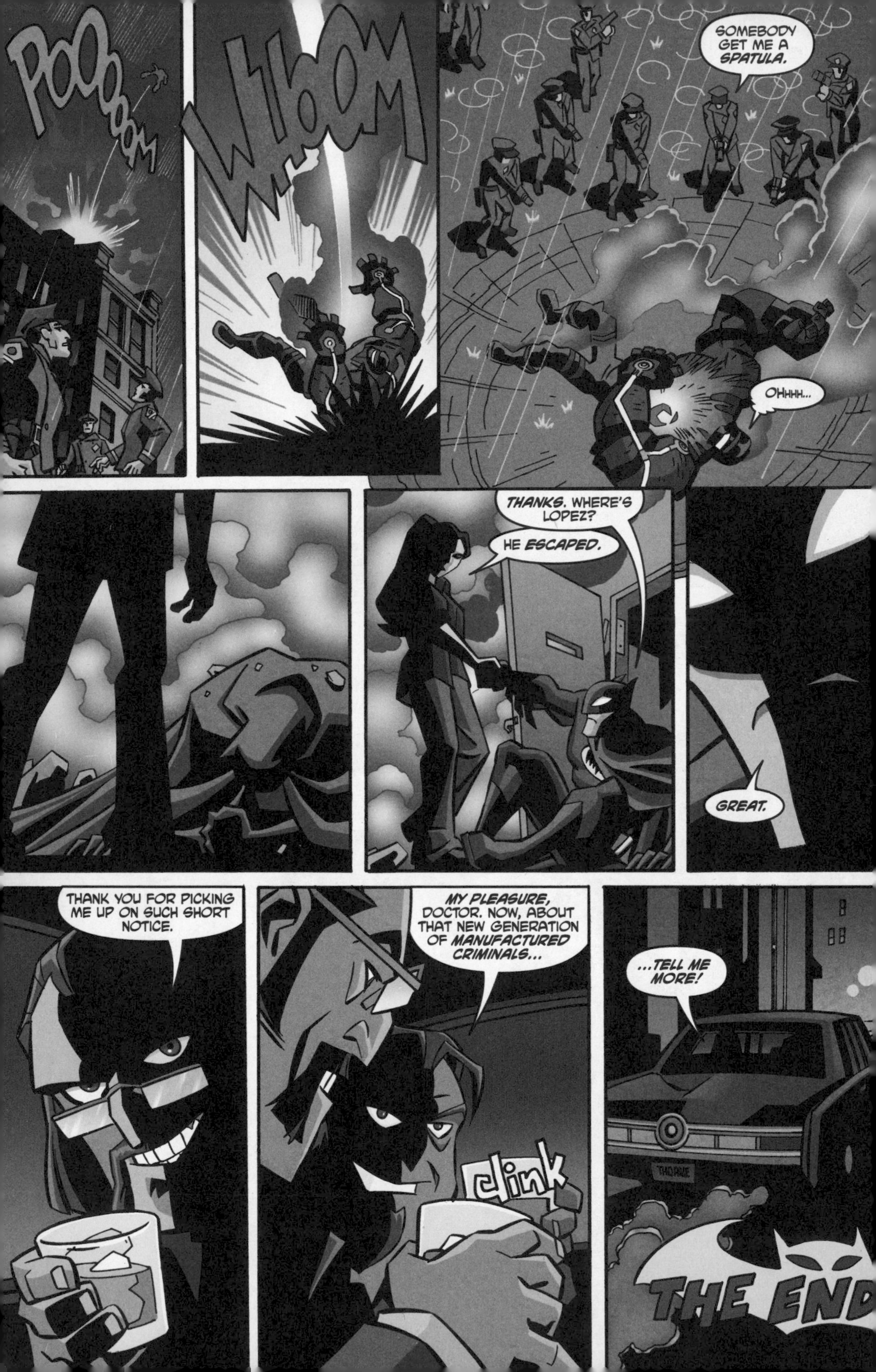
POOOOOOM
WHOOM
SOMEBODY GET ME A SPATULA.
OHHHH...
THANKS. WHERE'S LOPEZ?
HE ESCAPED.
GREAT.
THANK YOU FOR PICKING ME UP ON SUCH SHORT NOTICE.
MY PLEASURE, DOCTOR. NOW, ABOUT THAT NEW GENERATION OF MANUFACTURED CRIMINALS...
clink
...TELL ME MORE!
THE END

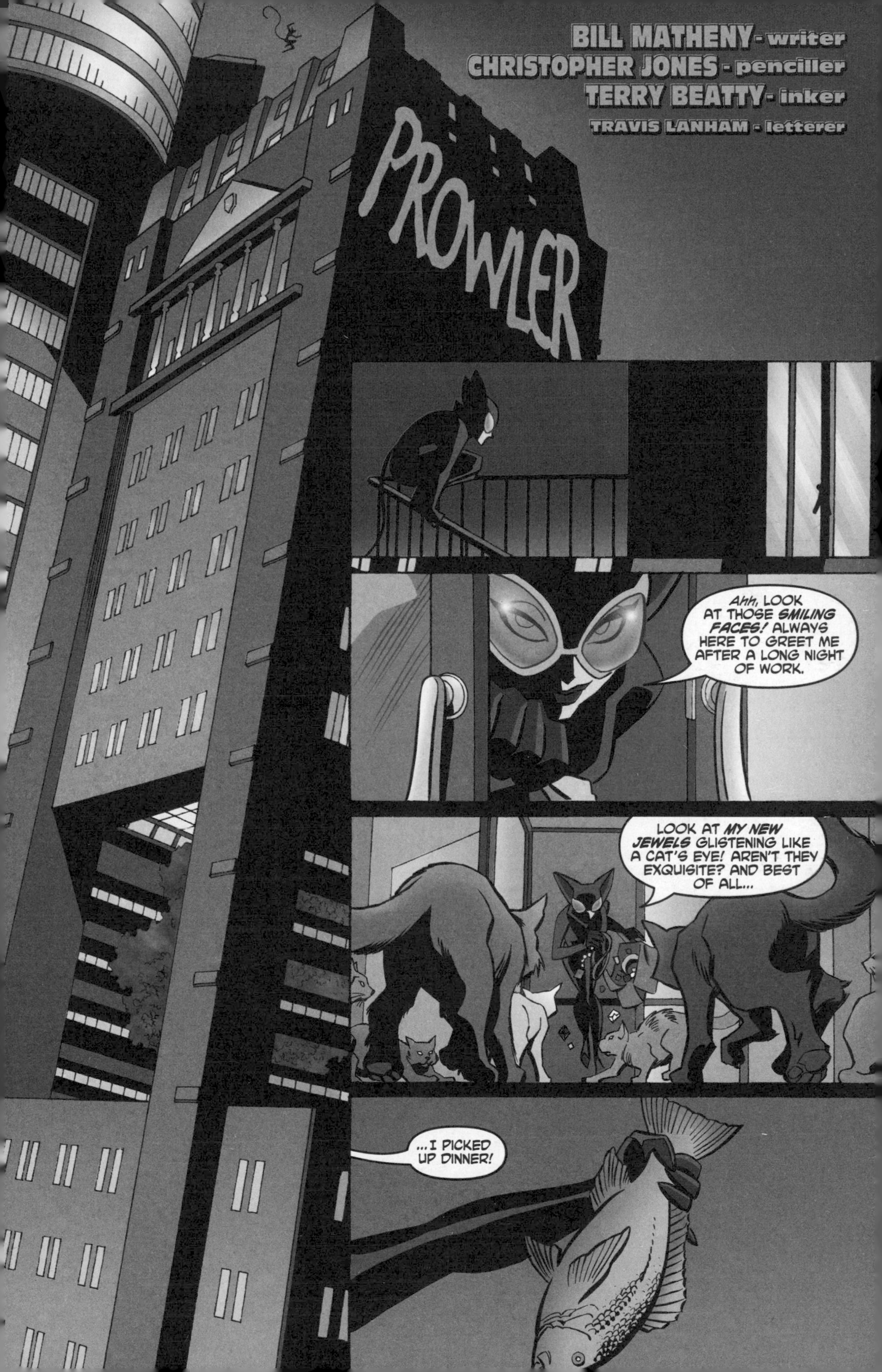
BILL MATHENY - writer
CHRISTOPHER JONES - penciller
TERRY BEATTY - inker
TRAVIS LANHAM - letterer
PROWLER
Ahh, LOOK AT THOSE SMILING FACES! ALWAYS HERE TO GREET ME AFTER A LONG NIGHT OF WORK.
LOOK AT MY NEW JEWELS GLISTENING LIKE A CAT'S EYE! AREN'T THEY EXQUISITE? AND BEST OF ALL...
...I PICKED UP DINNER!

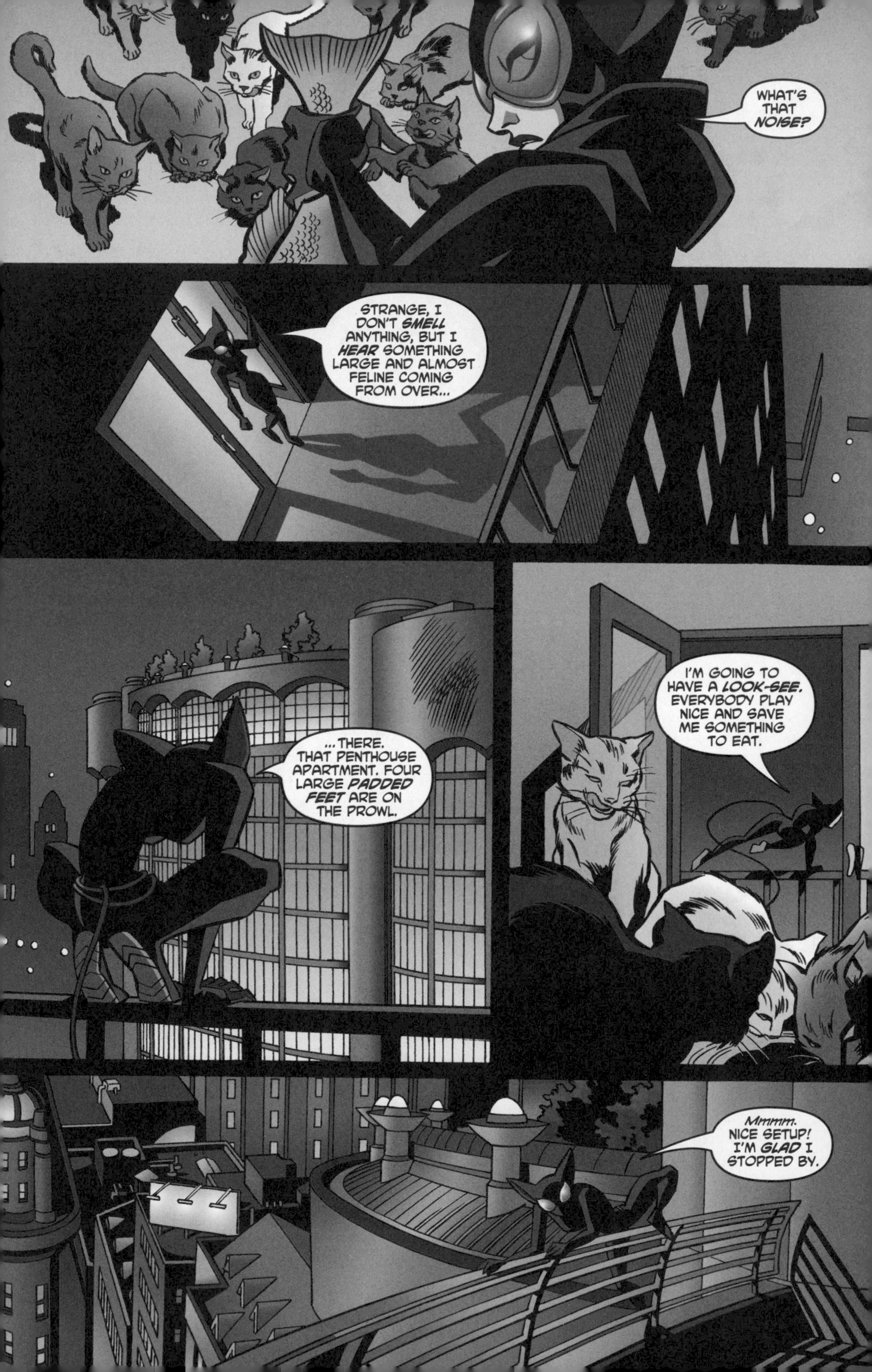
WHAT'S THAT NOISE?
STRANGE, I DON'T SMELL ANYTHING, BUT I HEAR SOMETHING LARGE AND ALMOST FELINE COMING FROM OVER...
...THERE. THAT PENTHOUSE APARTMENT. FOUR LARGE PADDED FEET ARE ON THE PROWL.
I'M GOING TO HAVE A LOOK-SEE. EVERYBODY PLAY NICE AND SAVE ME SOMETHING TO EAT.
Mmmm. NICE SETUP! I'M GLAD I STOPPED BY.

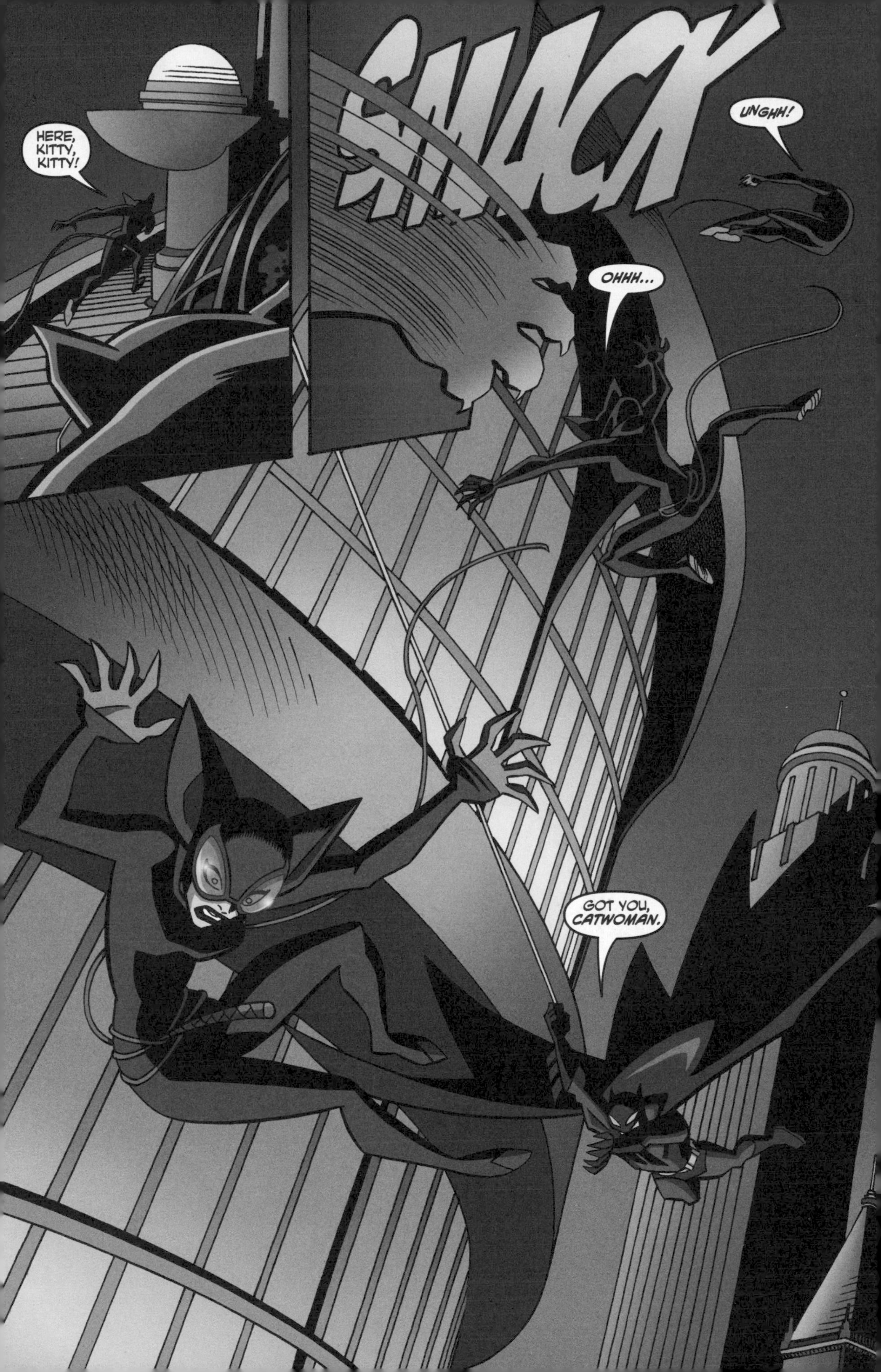
HERE, KITTY, KITTY!
SMACK
UNGHH!
OHHH...
GOT YOU, CATWOMAN.

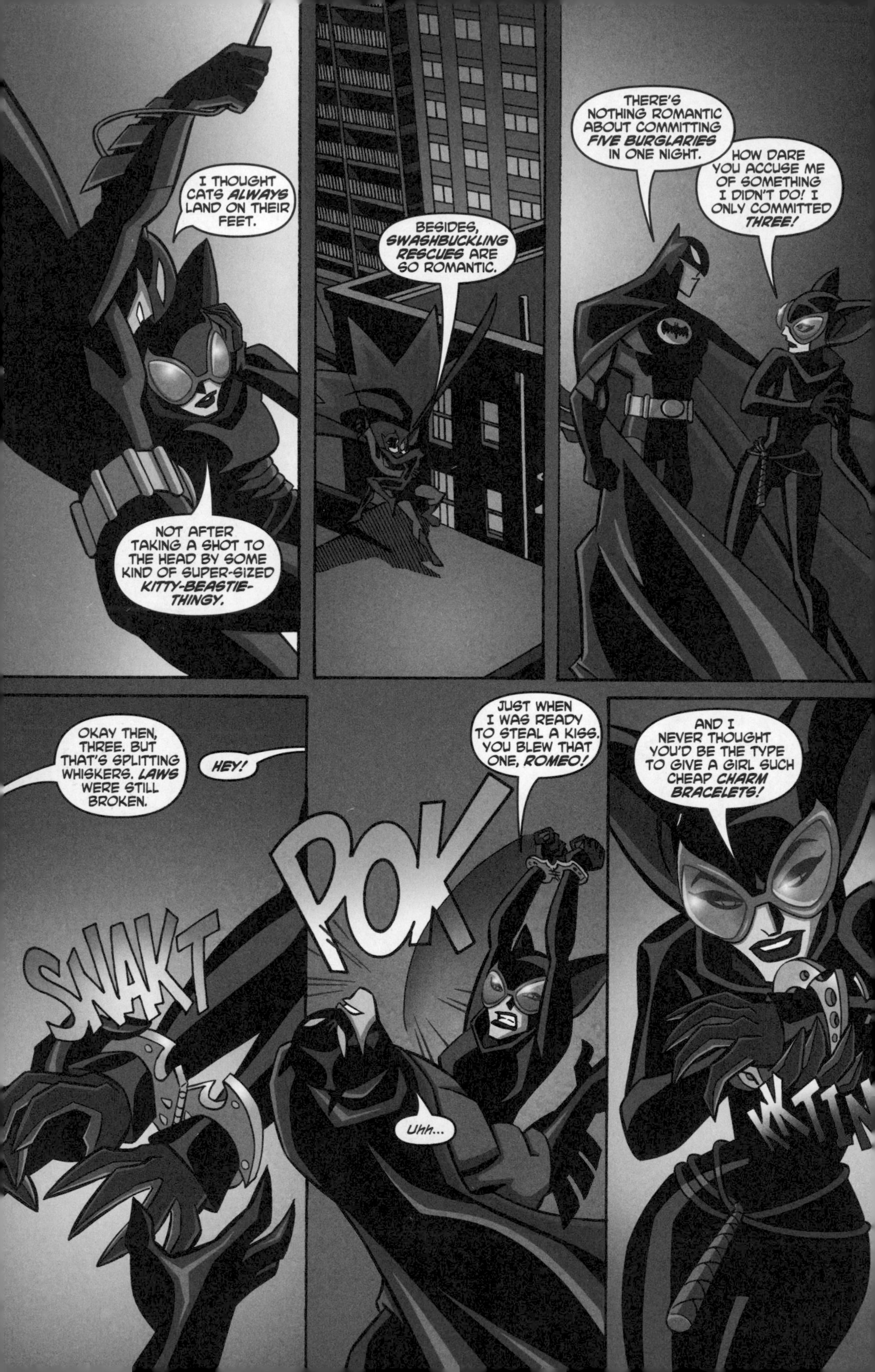
I THOUGHT CATS *ALWAYS* LAND ON THEIR FEET.
NOT AFTER TAKING A SHOT TO THE HEAD BY SOME KIND OF SUPER-SIZED *KITTY-BEASTIE-THINGY*.
BESIDES, *SWASHBUCKLING RESCUES* ARE SO ROMANTIC.
THERE'S NOTHING ROMANTIC ABOUT COMMITTING *FIVE BURGLARIES* IN ONE NIGHT.
HOW DARE YOU ACCUSE ME OF SOMETHING I DIDN'T DO! I ONLY COMMITTED *THREE!*
OKAY THEN, THREE. BUT THAT'S SPLITTING WHISKERS. *LAWS* WERE STILL BROKEN.
HEY!
SNAKT
JUST WHEN I WAS READY TO STEAL A KISS. YOU BLEW THAT ONE, *ROMEO!*
POK
Uhh...
AND I NEVER THOUGHT YOU'D BE THE TYPE TO GIVE A GIRL SUCH CHEAP *CHARM BRACELETS!*

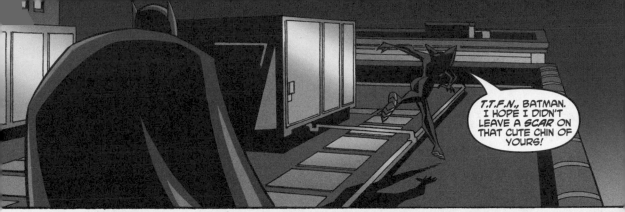

T.T.F.N,, BATMAN. I HOPE I DIDN'T LEAVE A *SCAR* ON THAT CUTE CHIN OF YOURS!

DO ME A FAVOR...

...LET'S END THIS PEACEFULLY. THE *HUMANE SOCIETY* WILL FROWN UPON MY INVOLVEMENT IN A CATFIGHT.

NOT ME, CUTIE! I LOVE A MAN WHO'S NOT AFRAID TO STAND HIS GROUND.

EVEN IF HIS LADY FRIEND HAS A LEG UP ON HIM!

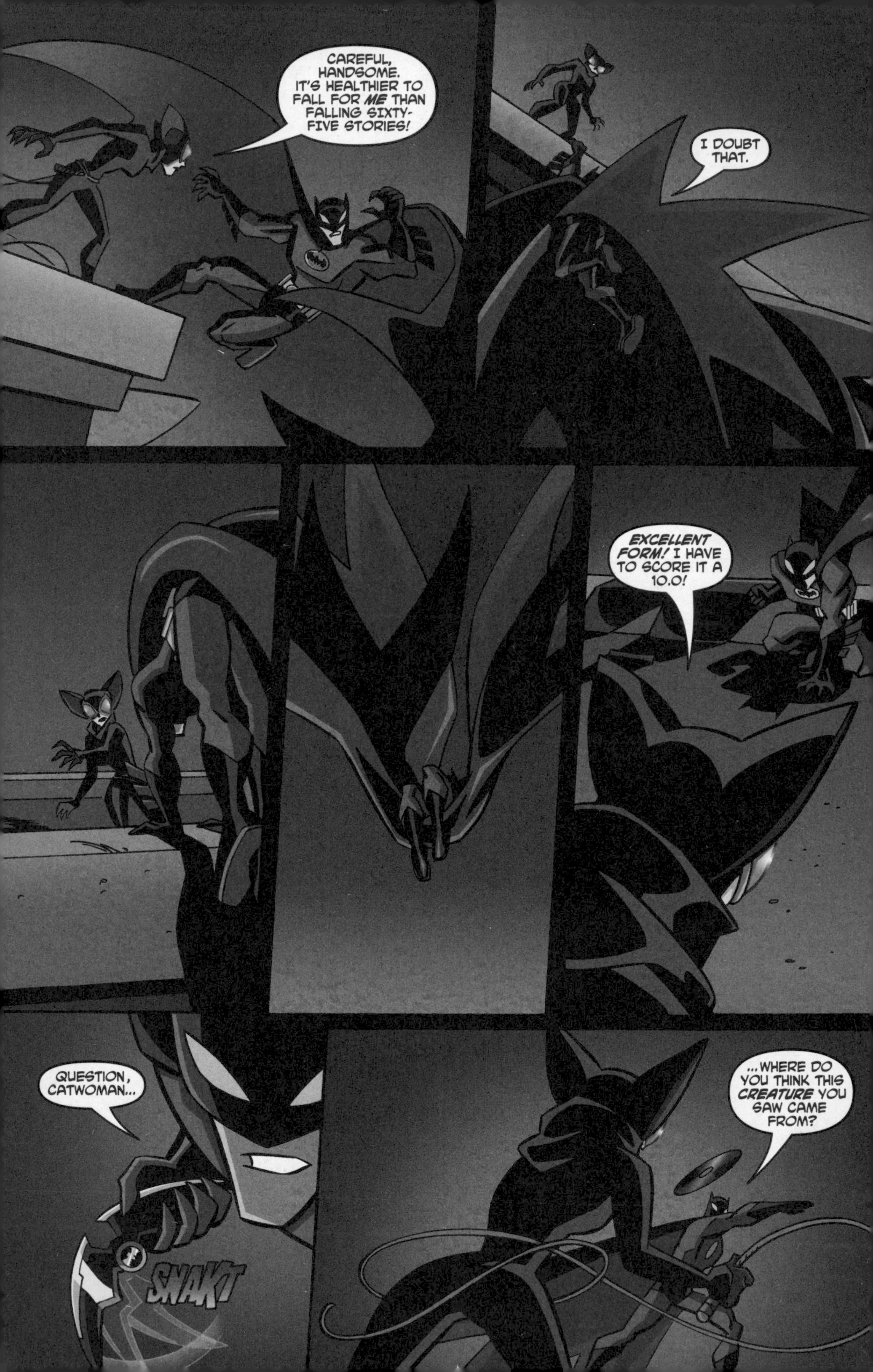
CAREFUL, HANDSOME. IT'S HEALTHIER TO FALL FOR *ME* THAN FALLING SIXTY-FIVE STORIES!
I DOUBT THAT.
EXCELLENT FORM! I HAVE TO SCORE IT A 10.0!
QUESTION, CATWOMAN...
SNAKT
...WHERE DO YOU THINK THIS *CREATURE* YOU SAW CAME FROM?

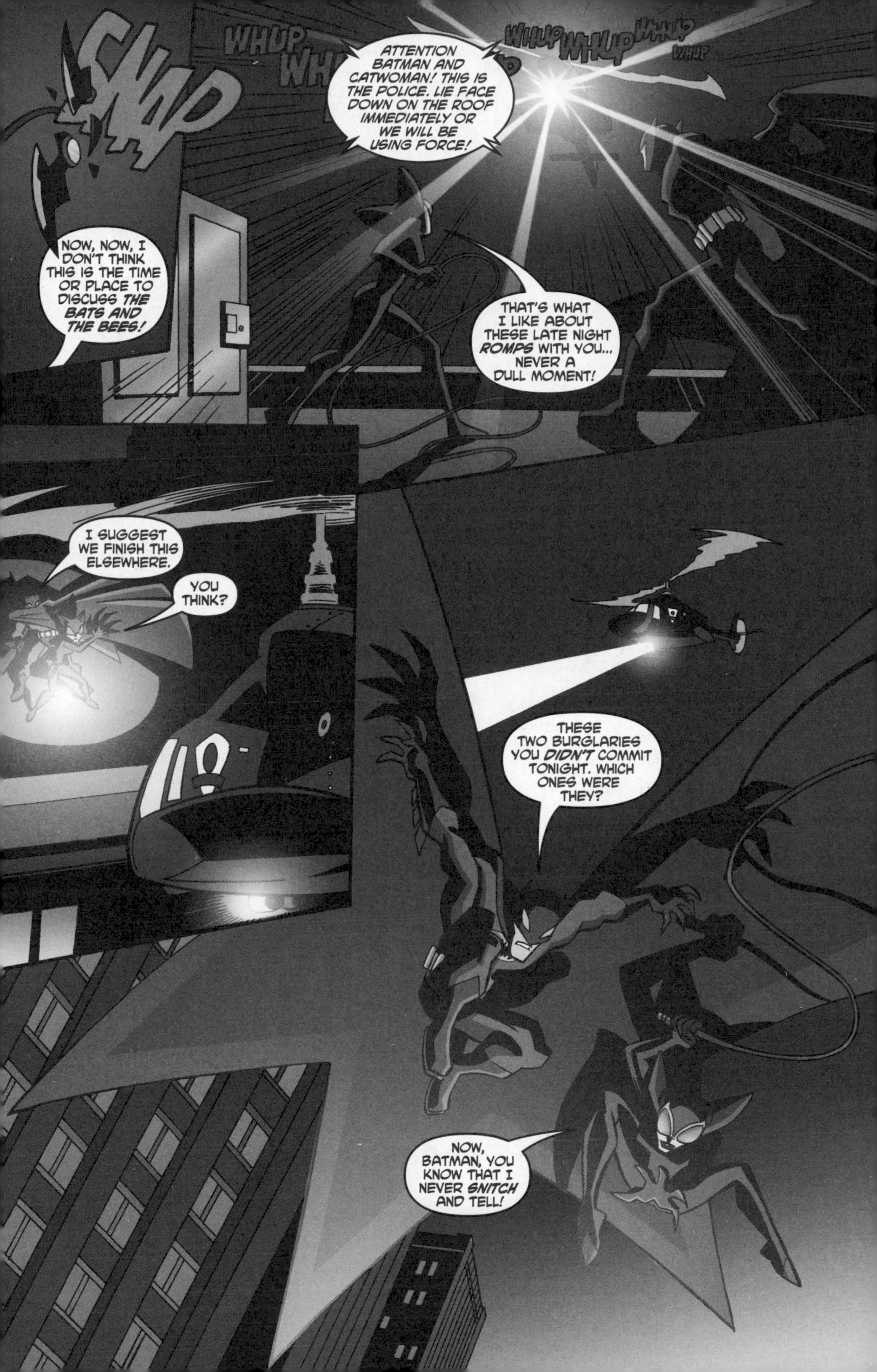
SNAP
WHUP WHUP
ATTENTION BATMAN AND CATWOMAN! THIS IS THE POLICE. LIE FACE DOWN ON THE ROOF IMMEDIATELY OR WE WILL BE USING FORCE!
WHUP WHUP WHUP WHUP
NOW, NOW, I DON'T THINK THIS IS THE TIME OR PLACE TO DISCUSS THE BATS AND THE BEES!
THAT'S WHAT I LIKE ABOUT THESE LATE NIGHT ROMPS WITH YOU... NEVER A DULL MOMENT!
I SUGGEST WE FINISH THIS ELSEWHERE.
YOU THINK?
THESE TWO BURGLARIES YOU DIDN'T COMMIT TONIGHT. WHICH ONES WERE THEY?
NOW, BATMAN, YOU KNOW THAT I NEVER SNITCH AND TELL!

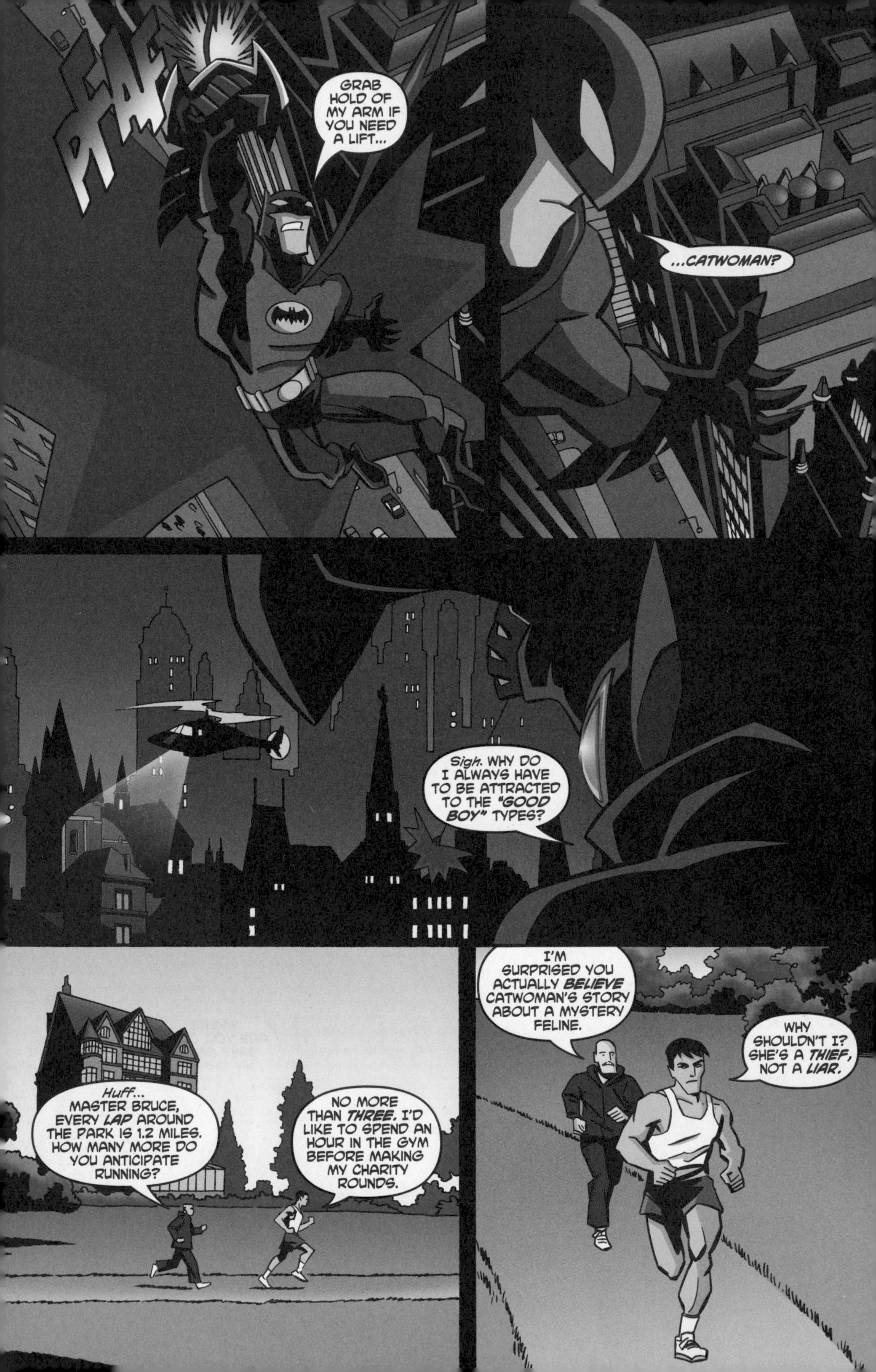
THPAF
GRAB HOLD OF MY ARM IF YOU NEED A LIFT...
...CATWOMAN?
Sigh. WHY DO I ALWAYS HAVE TO BE ATTRACTED TO THE "GOOD BOY" TYPES?
Huff... MASTER BRUCE, EVERY LAP AROUND THE PARK IS 1.2 MILES. HOW MANY MORE DO YOU ANTICIPATE RUNNING?
NO MORE THAN THREE. I'D LIKE TO SPEND AN HOUR IN THE GYM BEFORE MAKING MY CHARITY ROUNDS.
I'M SURPRISED YOU ACTUALLY BELIEVE CATWOMAN'S STORY ABOUT A MYSTERY FELINE.
WHY SHOULDN'T I? SHE'S A THIEF, NOT A LIAR.

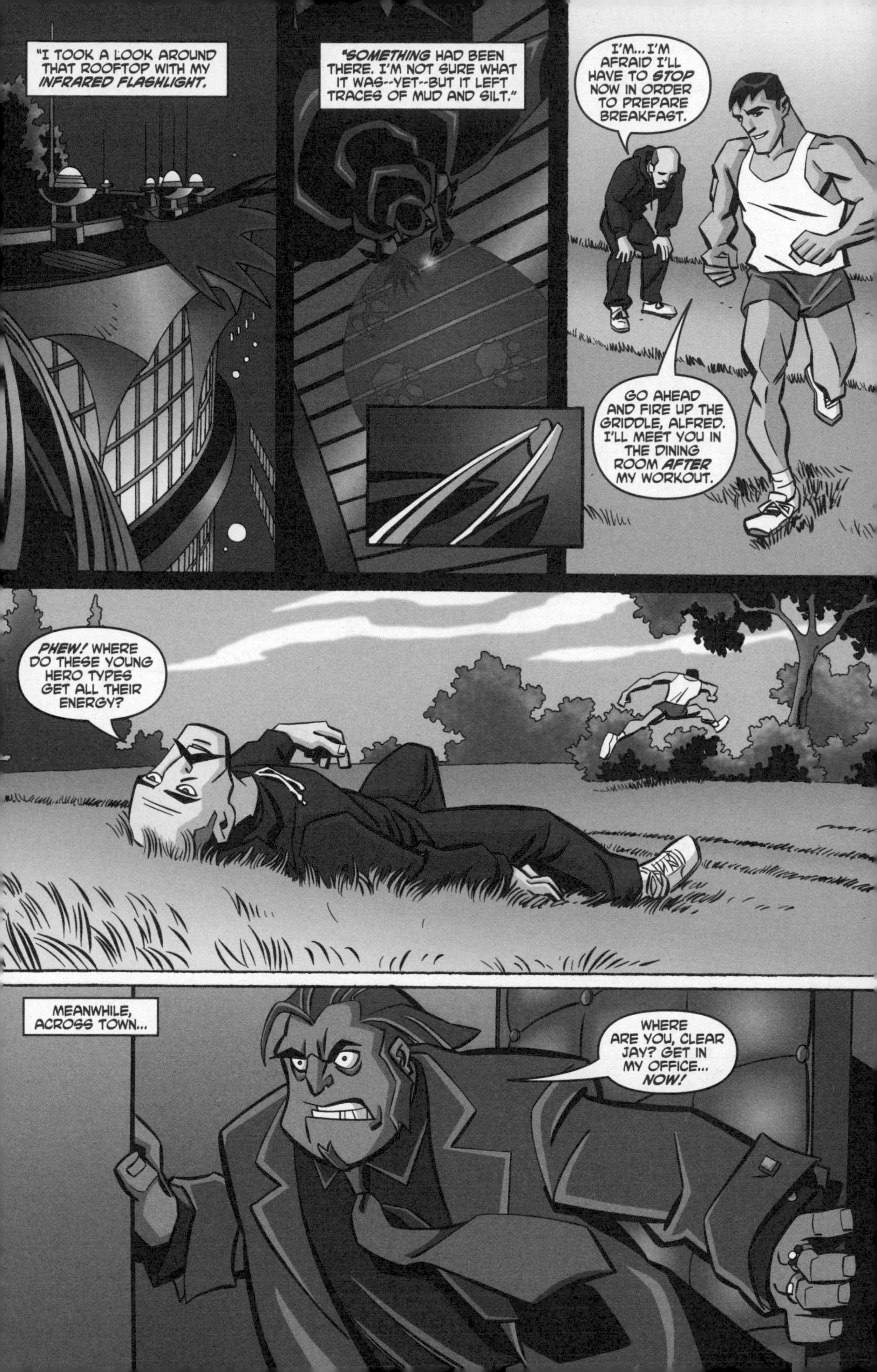
"I TOOK A LOOK AROUND THAT ROOFTOP WITH MY *INFRARED FLASHLIGHT.*
"*SOMETHING* HAD BEEN THERE. I'M NOT SURE WHAT IT WAS--YET--BUT IT LEFT TRACES OF MUD AND SILT."
I'M... I'M AFRAID I'LL HAVE TO *STOP* NOW IN ORDER TO PREPARE BREAKFAST.
GO AHEAD AND FIRE UP THE GRIDDLE, ALFRED. I'LL MEET YOU IN THE DINING ROOM *AFTER* MY WORKOUT.
PHEW! WHERE DO THESE YOUNG HERO TYPES GET ALL THEIR ENERGY?
MEANWHILE, ACROSS TOWN...
WHERE ARE YOU, CLEAR JAY? GET IN MY OFFICE... *NOW!*

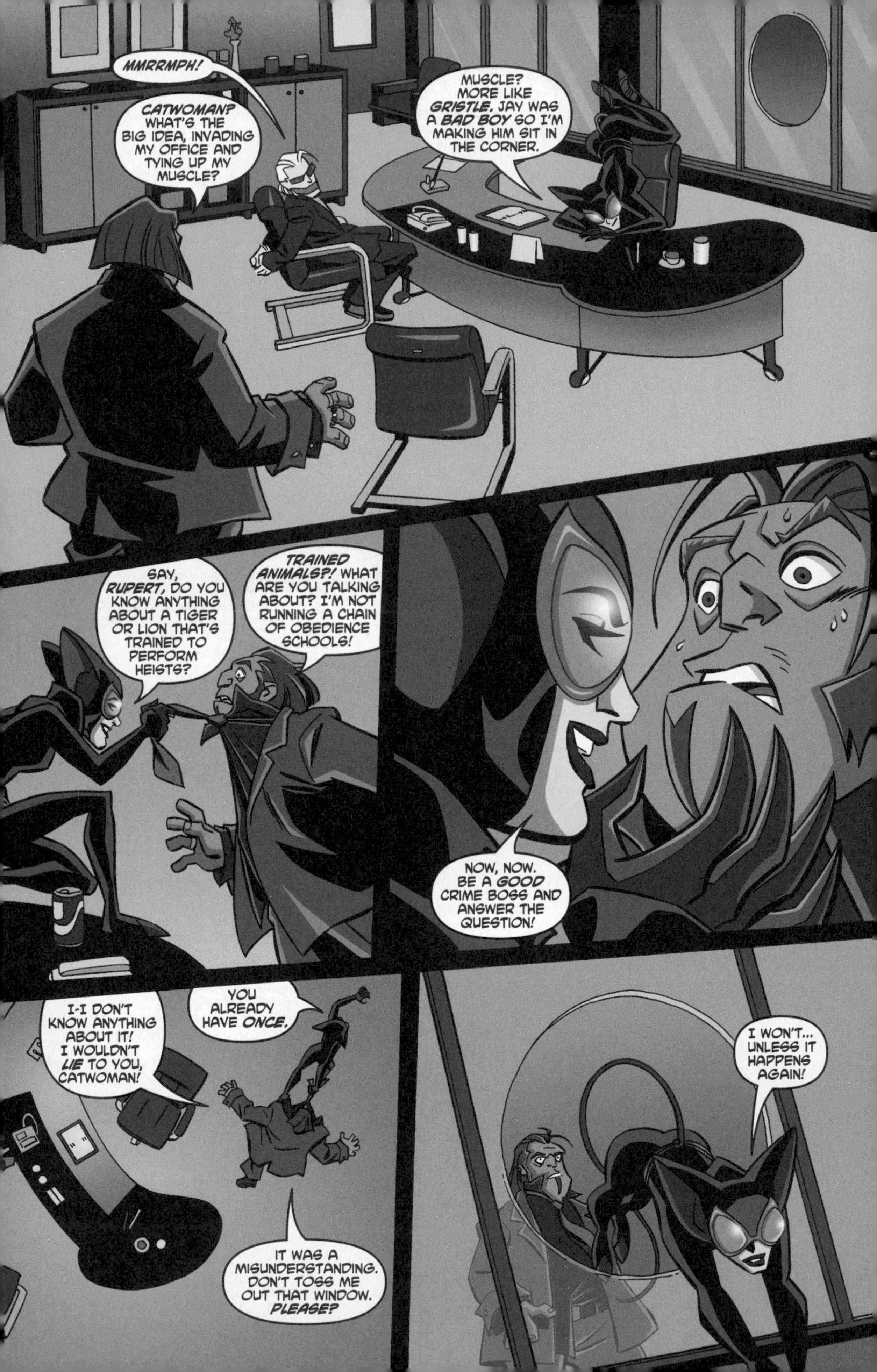
MMRRMPH!
CATWOMAN? WHAT'S THE BIG IDEA, INVADING MY OFFICE AND TYING UP MY MUSCLE?
MUSCLE? MORE LIKE GRISTLE. JAY WAS A BAD BOY SO I'M MAKING HIM SIT IN THE CORNER.
SAY, RUPERT, DO YOU KNOW ANYTHING ABOUT A TIGER OR LION THAT'S TRAINED TO PERFORM HEISTS?
TRAINED ANIMALS?! WHAT ARE YOU TALKING ABOUT? I'M NOT RUNNING A CHAIN OF OBEDIENCE SCHOOLS!
NOW, NOW. BE A GOOD CRIME BOSS AND ANSWER THE QUESTION!
I-I DON'T KNOW ANYTHING ABOUT IT! I WOULDN'T LIE TO YOU, CATWOMAN!
YOU ALREADY HAVE ONCE.
IT WAS A MISUNDERSTANDING. DON'T TOSS ME OUT THAT WINDOW. PLEASE?
I WON'T... UNLESS IT HAPPENS AGAIN!

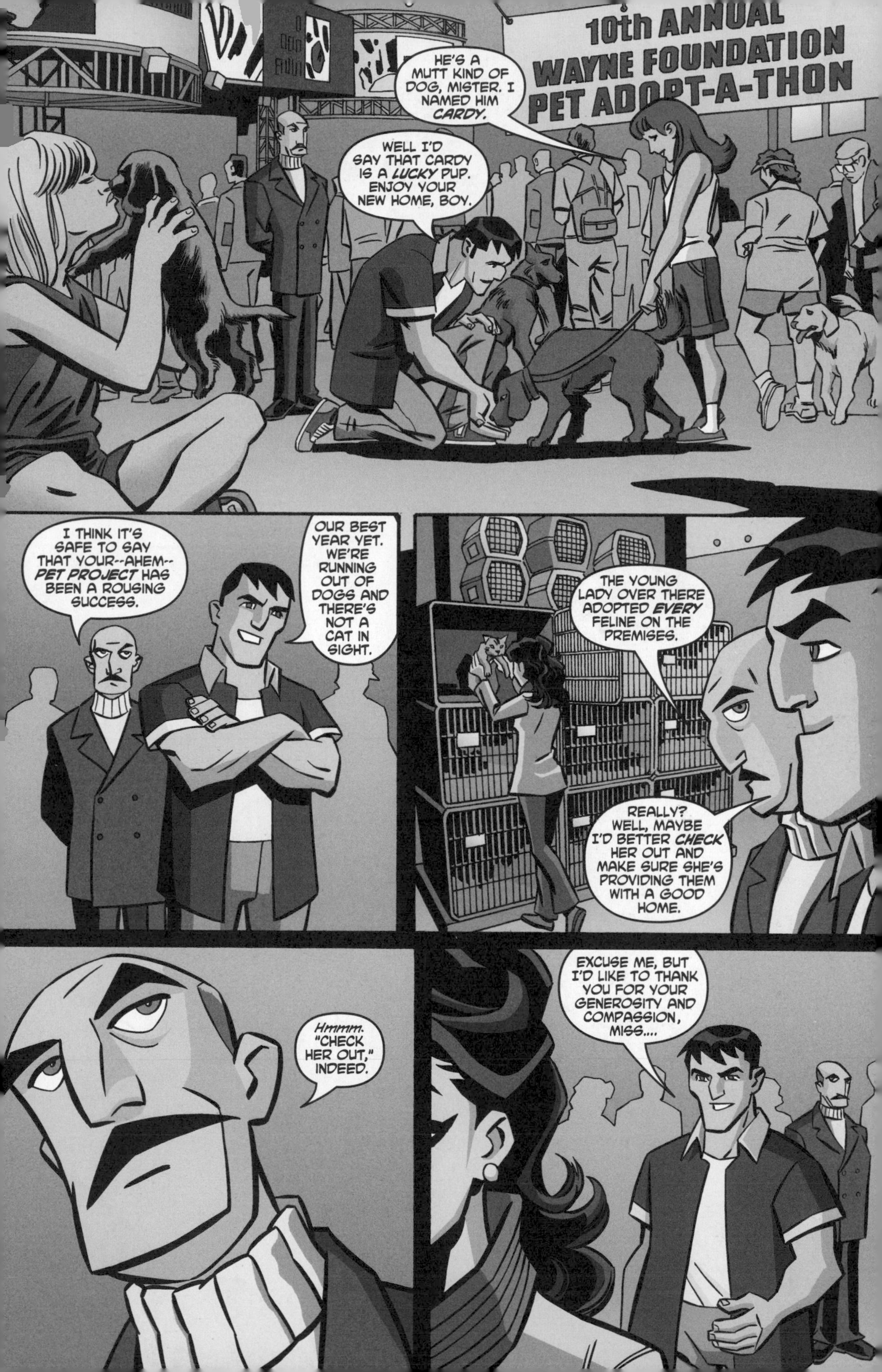
10th ANNUAL WAYNE FOUNDATION PET ADOPT-A-THON
HE'S A MUTT KIND OF DOG, MISTER. I NAMED HIM *CARDY.*
WELL I'D SAY THAT CARDY IS A *LUCKY* PUP. ENJOY YOUR NEW HOME, BOY.
I THINK IT'S SAFE TO SAY THAT YOUR--AHEM-- *PET PROJECT* HAS BEEN A ROUSING SUCCESS.
OUR BEST YEAR YET. WE'RE RUNNING OUT OF DOGS AND THERE'S NOT A CAT IN SIGHT.
THE YOUNG LADY OVER THERE ADOPTED *EVERY* FELINE ON THE PREMISES.
REALLY? WELL, MAYBE I'D BETTER *CHECK* HER OUT AND MAKE SURE SHE'S PROVIDING THEM WITH A GOOD HOME.
Hmmm. "CHECK HER OUT," INDEED.
EXCUSE ME, BUT I'D LIKE TO THANK YOU FOR YOUR GENEROSITY AND COMPASSION, MISS....

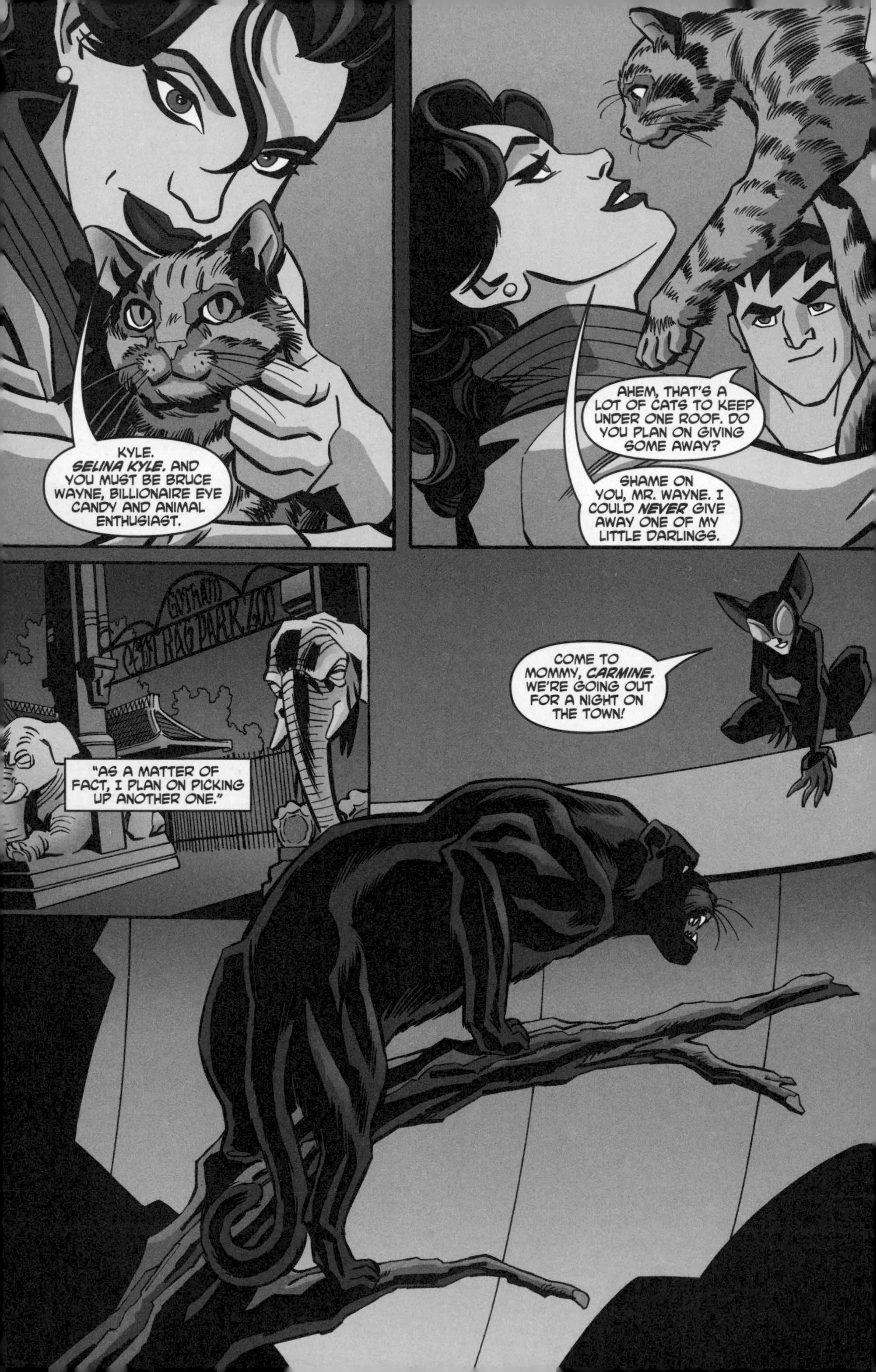
KYLE. SELINA KYLE. AND YOU MUST BE BRUCE WAYNE, BILLIONAIRE EYE CANDY AND ANIMAL ENTHUSIAST.
AHEM, THAT'S A LOT OF CATS TO KEEP UNDER ONE ROOF. DO YOU PLAN ON GIVING SOME AWAY?
SHAME ON YOU, MR. WAYNE. I COULD NEVER GIVE AWAY ONE OF MY LITTLE DARLINGS.
"AS A MATTER OF FACT, I PLAN ON PICKING UP ANOTHER ONE."
COME TO MOMMY, CARMINE. WE'RE GOING OUT FOR A NIGHT ON THE TOWN!

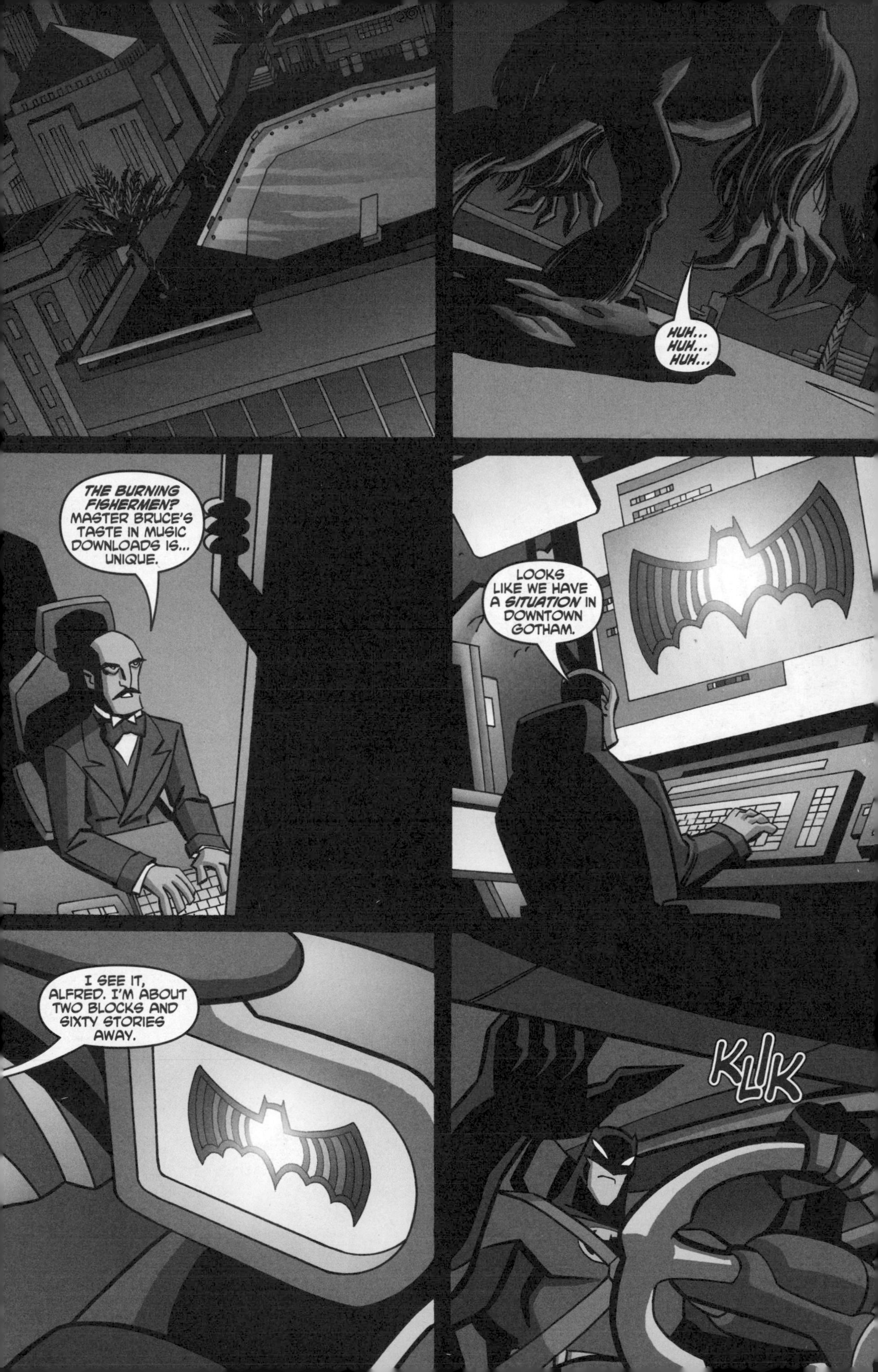
HUH... HUH... HUH...
THE BURNING FISHERMEN? MASTER BRUCE'S TASTE IN MUSIC DOWNLOADS IS... UNIQUE.
LOOKS LIKE WE HAVE A SITUATION IN DOWNTOWN GOTHAM.
I SEE IT, ALFRED. I'M ABOUT TWO BLOCKS AND SIXTY STORIES AWAY.
KLIK

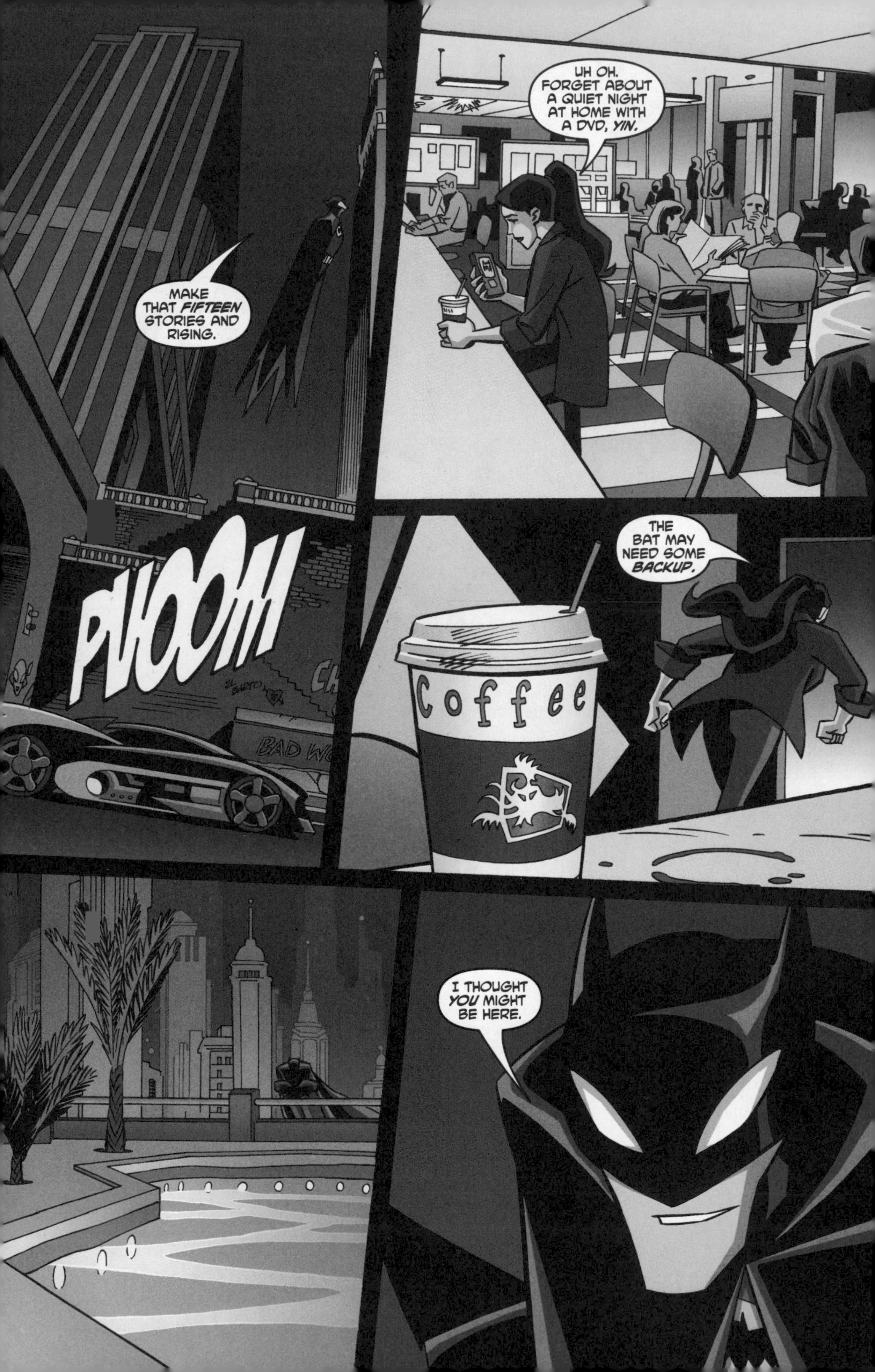
MAKE THAT *FIFTEEN* STORIES AND RISING.
UH OH. FORGET ABOUT A QUIET NIGHT AT HOME WITH A DVD, *YIN.*
PVOOM
BAD WO
Coffee
THE BAT MAY NEED SOME *BACKUP.*
I THOUGHT *YOU* MIGHT BE HERE.

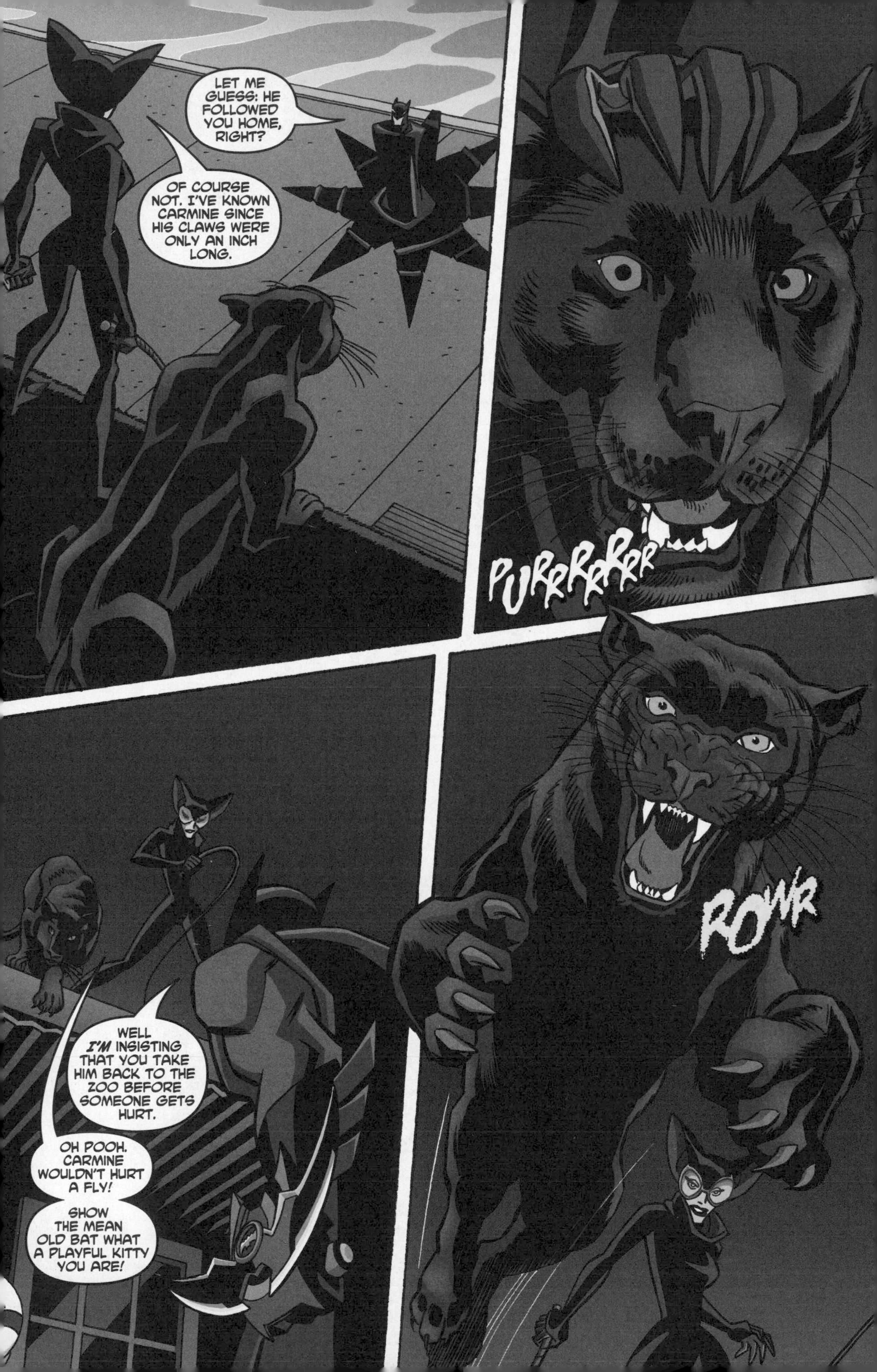
LET ME GUESS: HE FOLLOWED YOU HOME, RIGHT?
OF COURSE NOT. I'VE KNOWN CARMINE SINCE HIS CLAWS WERE ONLY AN INCH LONG.
PURRRRRRR
WELL *I'M* INSISTING THAT YOU TAKE HIM BACK TO THE ZOO BEFORE SOMEONE GETS HURT.
OH POOH. CARMINE WOULDN'T HURT A FLY!
SHOW THE MEAN OLD BAT WHAT A PLAYFUL KITTY YOU ARE!
ROWR

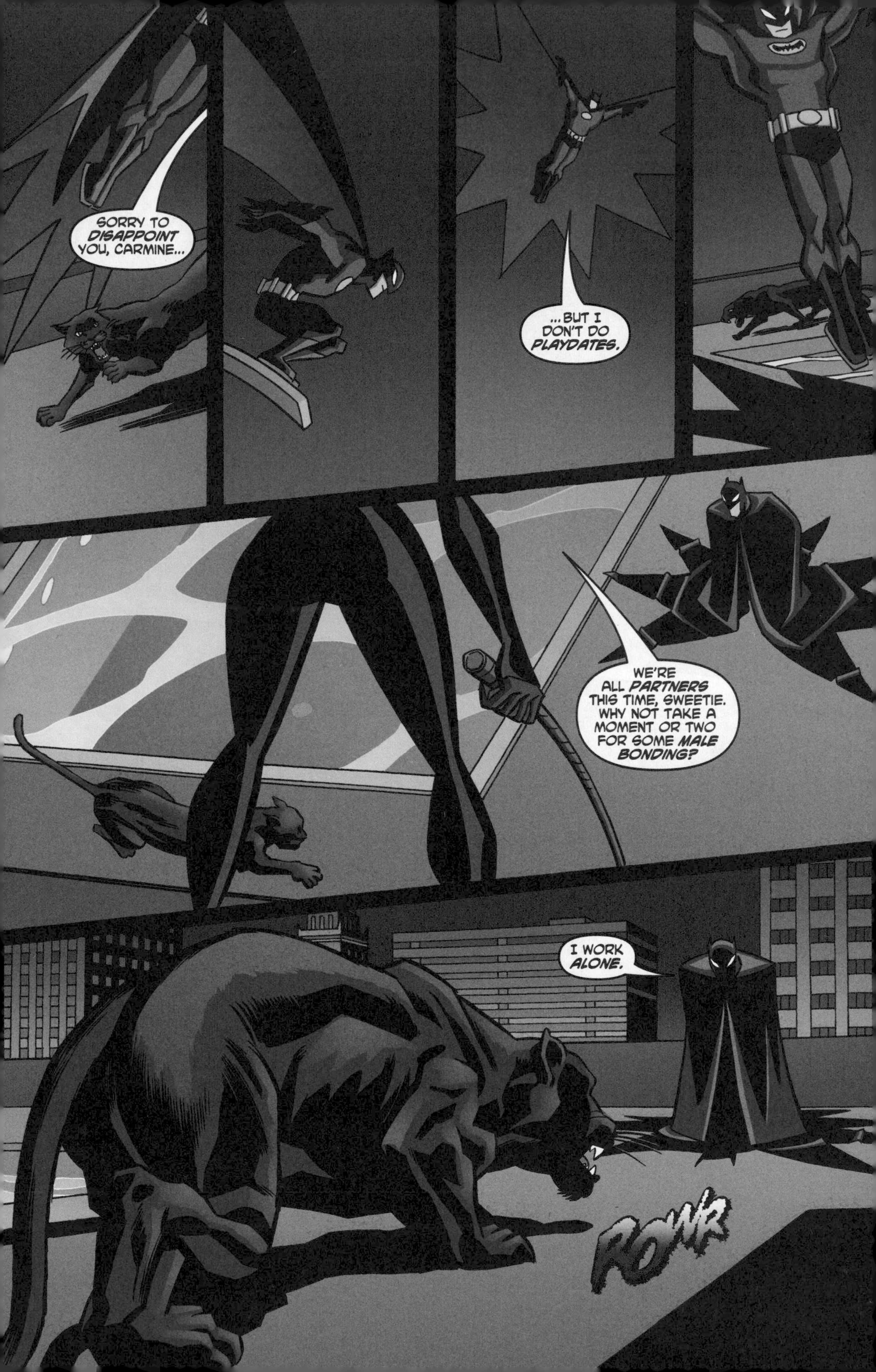
SORRY TO DISAPPOINT YOU, CARMINE...
...BUT I DON'T DO PLAYDATES.
WE'RE ALL PARTNERS THIS TIME, SWEETIE. WHY NOT TAKE A MOMENT OR TWO FOR SOME MALE BONDING?
I WORK ALONE.
ROWR

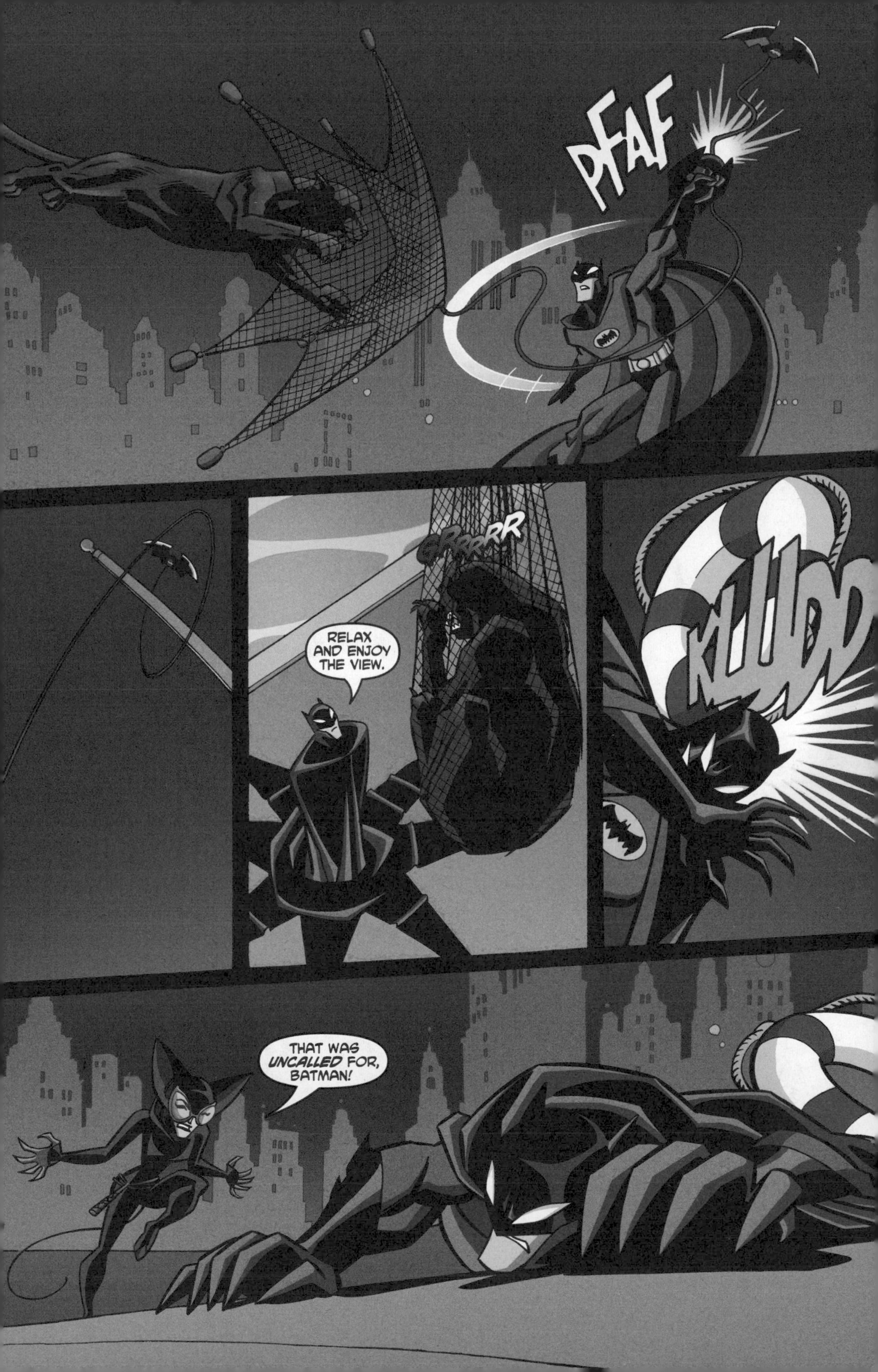
PFAF
GRRRRR
RELAX AND ENJOY THE VIEW.
KLUDD
THAT WAS *UNCALLED* FOR, BATMAN!

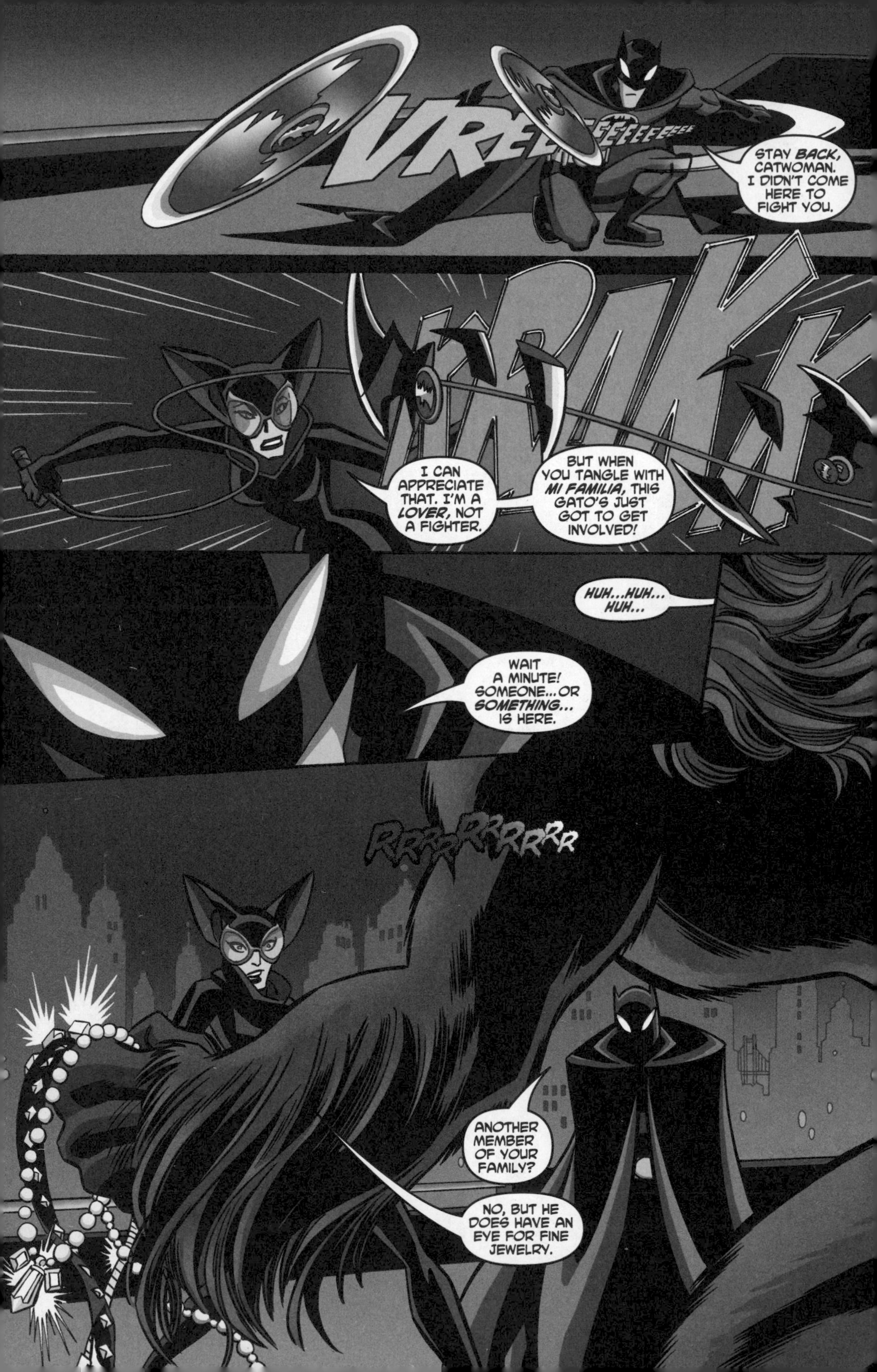
VREEEEEEEEEEEE
STAY BACK, CATWOMAN. I DIDN'T COME HERE TO FIGHT YOU.
I CAN APPRECIATE THAT. I'M A LOVER, NOT A FIGHTER.
BUT WHEN YOU TANGLE WITH MI FAMILIA, THIS GATO'S JUST GOT TO GET INVOLVED!
HUH...HUH... HUH...
WAIT A MINUTE! SOMEONE...OR SOMETHING... IS HERE.
RRRRRRRRRR
ANOTHER MEMBER OF YOUR FAMILY?
NO, BUT HE DOES HAVE AN EYE FOR FINE JEWELRY.

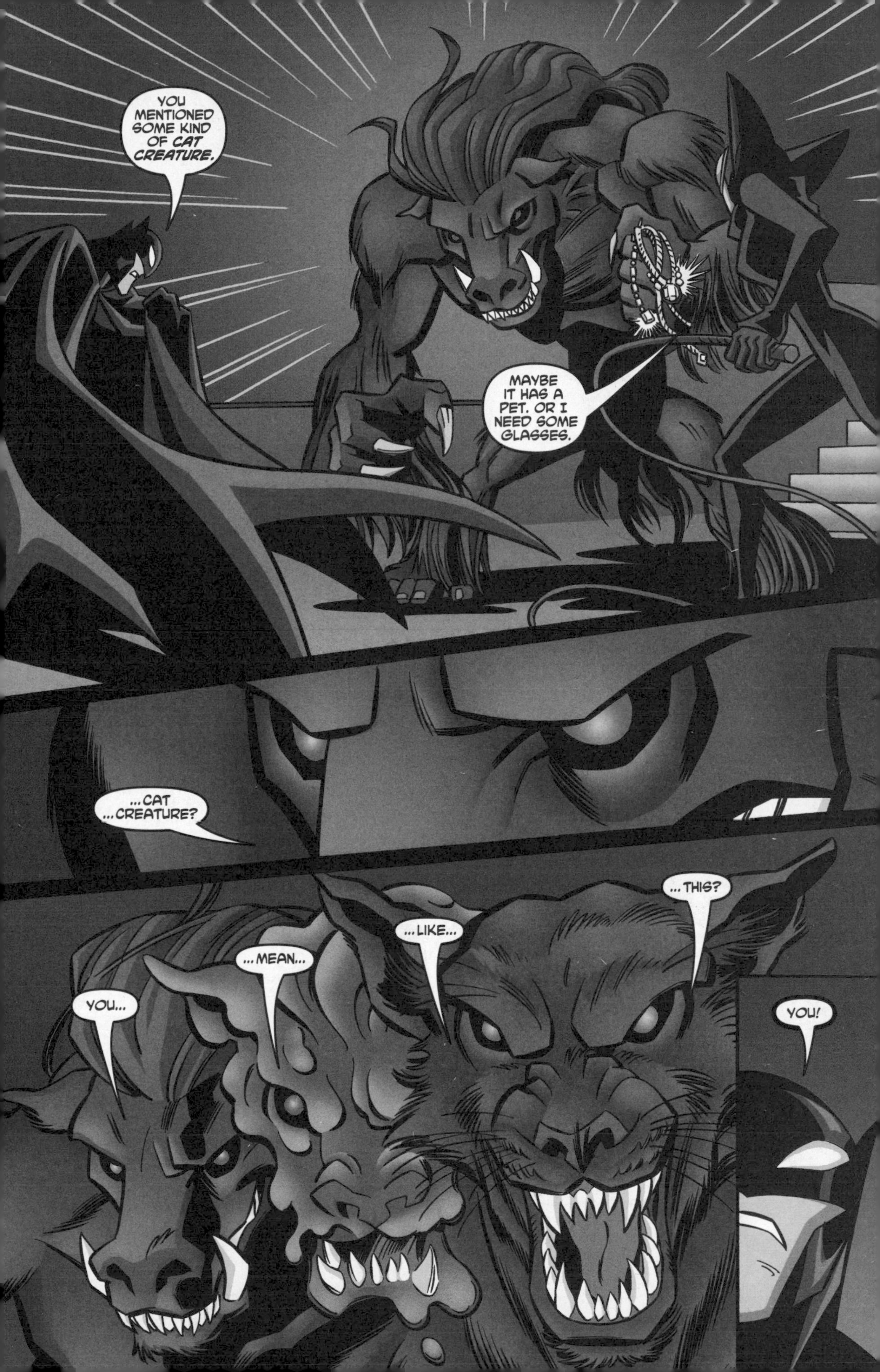
YOU MENTIONED SOME KIND OF CAT CREATURE.
MAYBE IT HAS A PET. OR I NEED SOME GLASSES.
...CAT ...CREATURE?
YOU...
...MEAN...
...LIKE...
...THIS?
YOU!

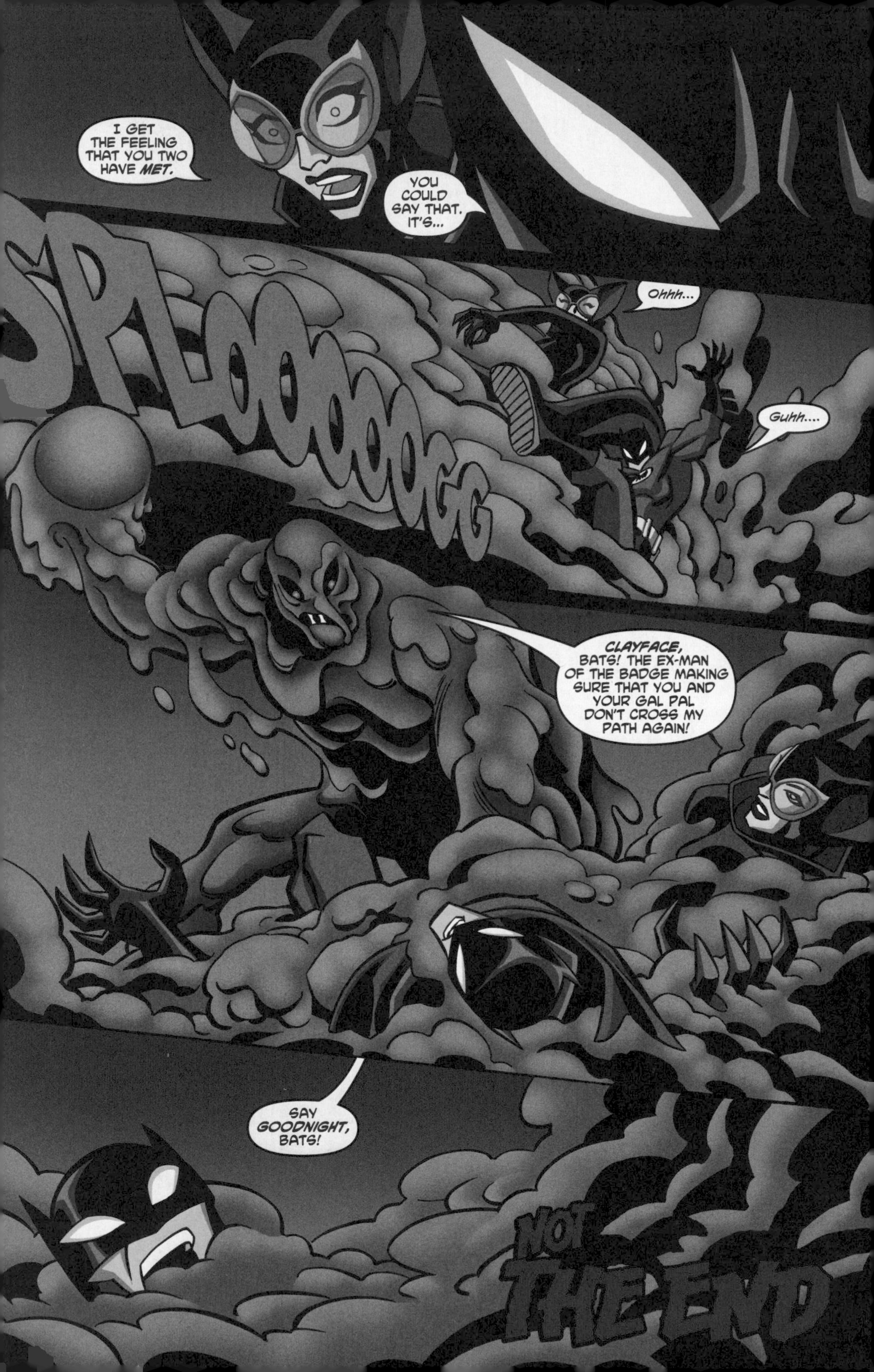
I GET THE FEELING THAT YOU TWO HAVE *MET.*
YOU COULD SAY THAT. IT'S...
SPLOOOOOOGG
Ohhh...
Guhh....
CLAYFACE, BATS! THE EX-MAN OF THE BADGE MAKING SURE THAT YOU AND YOUR GAL PAL DON'T CROSS MY PATH AGAIN!
SAY *GOODNIGHT,* BATS!
NOT THE END

ETHAN... NO...!

SAVE YOUR BREATH, BATS. *ETHAN BENNETT* HAS LEFT THE BUILDING AND CLAYFACE IS CALLING THE SHOTS! YOU AND THE *CATLADY* WON'T BE DIGGING YOUR WAY OUT OF THIS ONE!

SANDS OF TIME

BILL MATHENY – WRITER
CHRISTOPHER JONES – PENCILLER
TERRY BEATTY – INKER
TRAVIS LANHAM – LETTERER

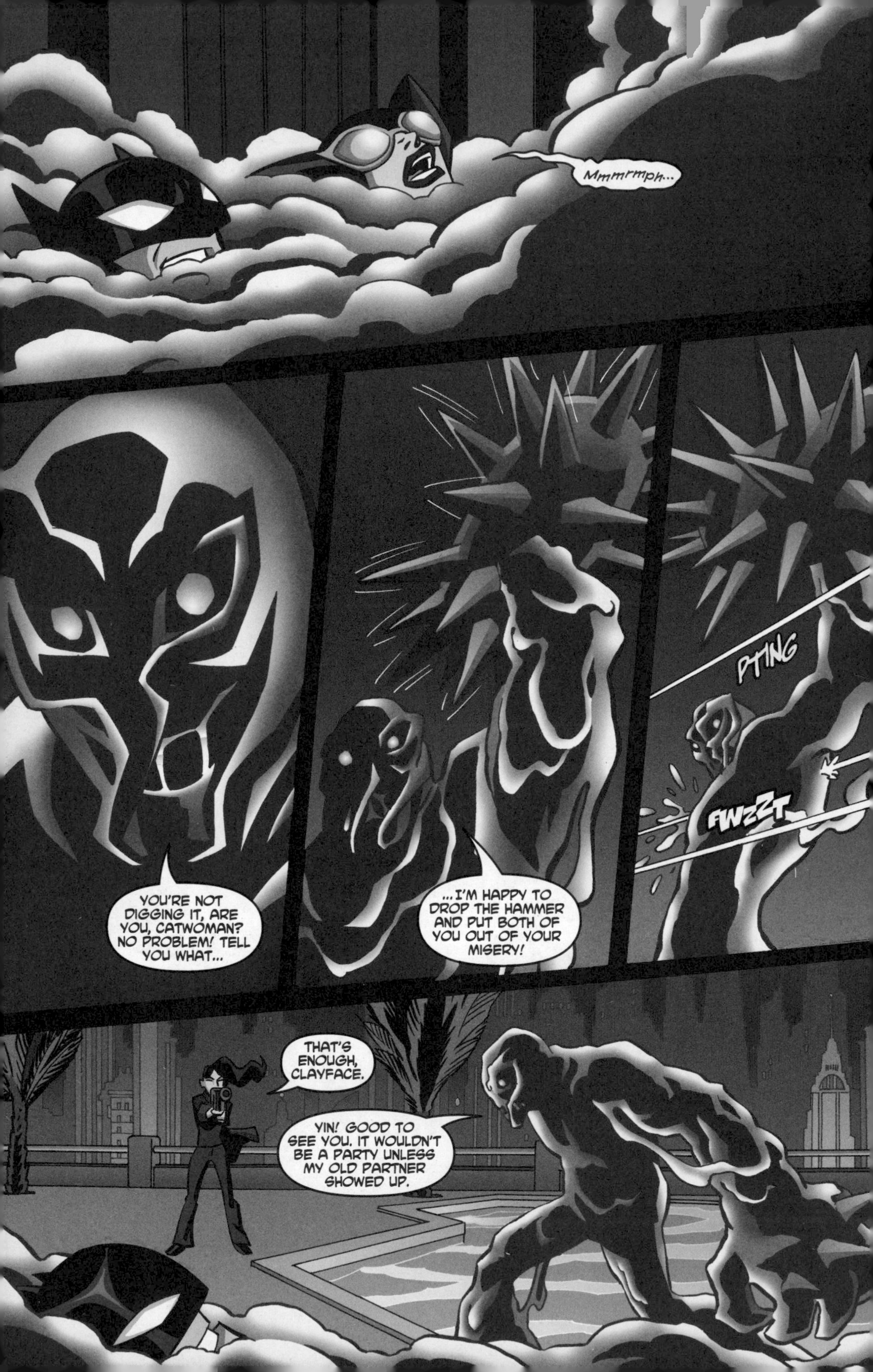

Mmmrmph...
YOU'RE NOT DIGGING IT, ARE YOU, CATWOMAN? NO PROBLEM! TELL YOU WHAT...
...I'M HAPPY TO DROP THE HAMMER AND PUT BOTH OF YOU OUT OF YOUR MISERY!
PTING
FWZZT
THAT'S ENOUGH, CLAYFACE.
YIN! GOOD TO SEE YOU. IT WOULDN'T BE A PARTY UNLESS MY OLD PARTNER SHOWED UP.

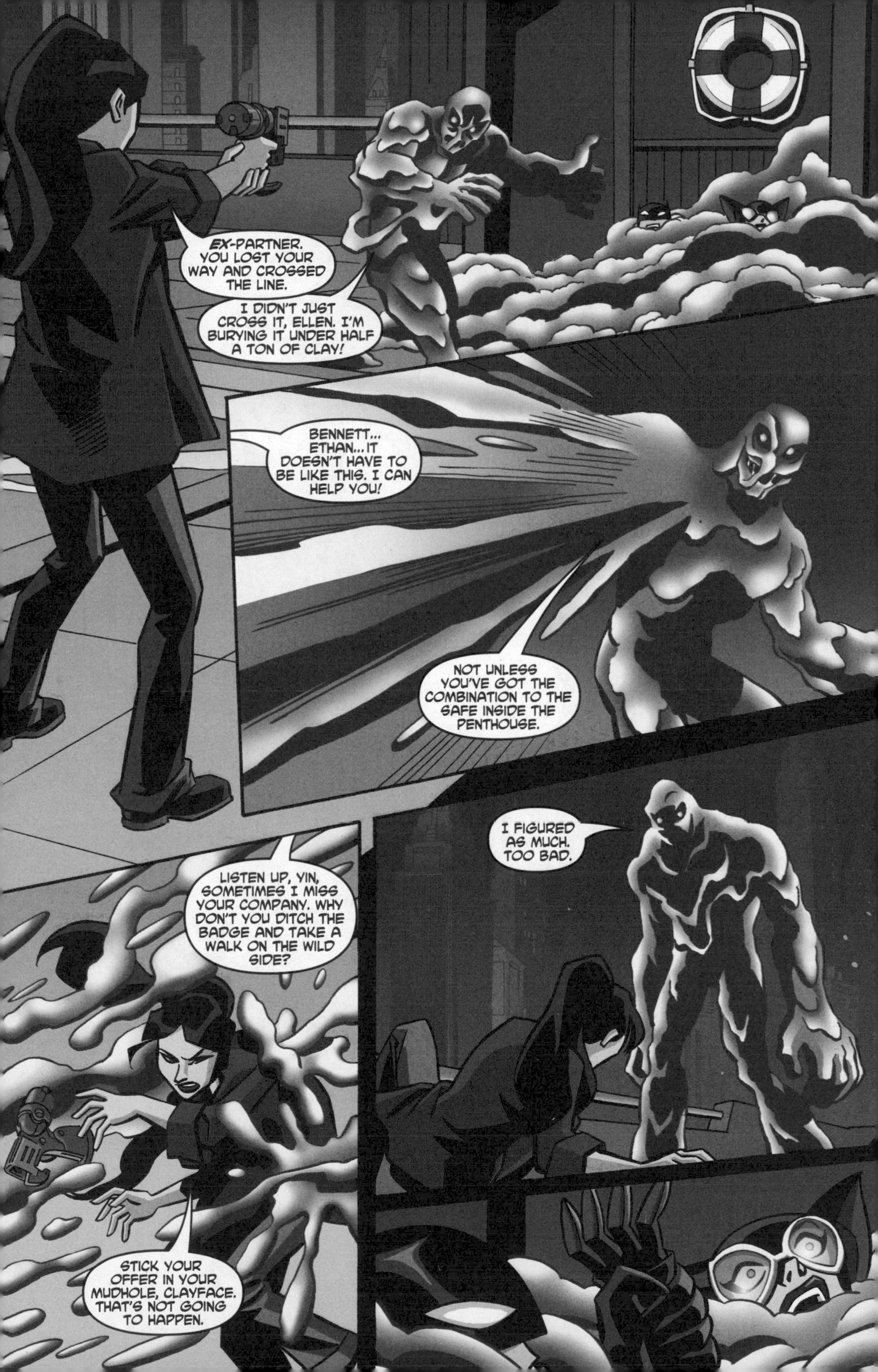
EX-PARTNER. YOU LOST YOUR WAY AND CROSSED THE LINE.
I DIDN'T JUST CROSS IT, ELLEN. I'M BURYING IT UNDER HALF A TON OF CLAY!
BENNETT... ETHAN... IT DOESN'T HAVE TO BE LIKE THIS. I CAN HELP YOU!
NOT UNLESS YOU'VE GOT THE COMBINATION TO THE SAFE INSIDE THE PENTHOUSE.
LISTEN UP, YIN, SOMETIMES I MISS YOUR COMPANY. WHY DON'T YOU DITCH THE BADGE AND TAKE A WALK ON THE WILD SIDE?
STICK YOUR OFFER IN YOUR MUDHOLE, CLAYFACE. THAT'S NOT GOING TO HAPPEN.
I FIGURED AS MUCH. TOO BAD.

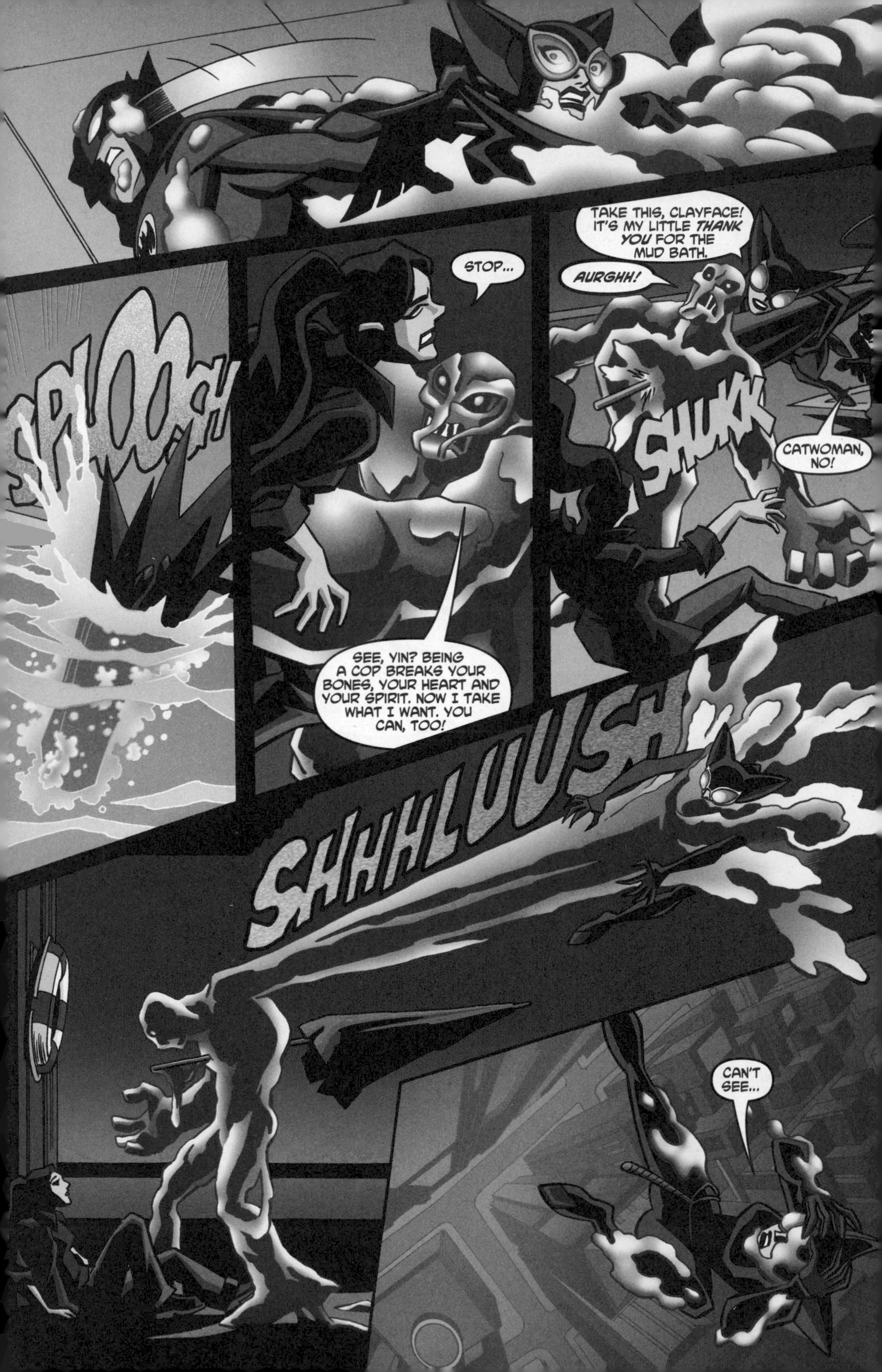
SPLOOOSH
STOP...
SEE, YIN? BEING A COP BREAKS YOUR BONES, YOUR HEART AND YOUR SPIRIT. NOW I TAKE WHAT I WANT. YOU CAN, TOO!
TAKE THIS, CLAYFACE! IT'S MY LITTLE *THANK YOU* FOR THE MUD BATH.
AURGHH!
SHUKK
CATWOMAN, NO!
SHHHLUUSH
CAN'T SEE...

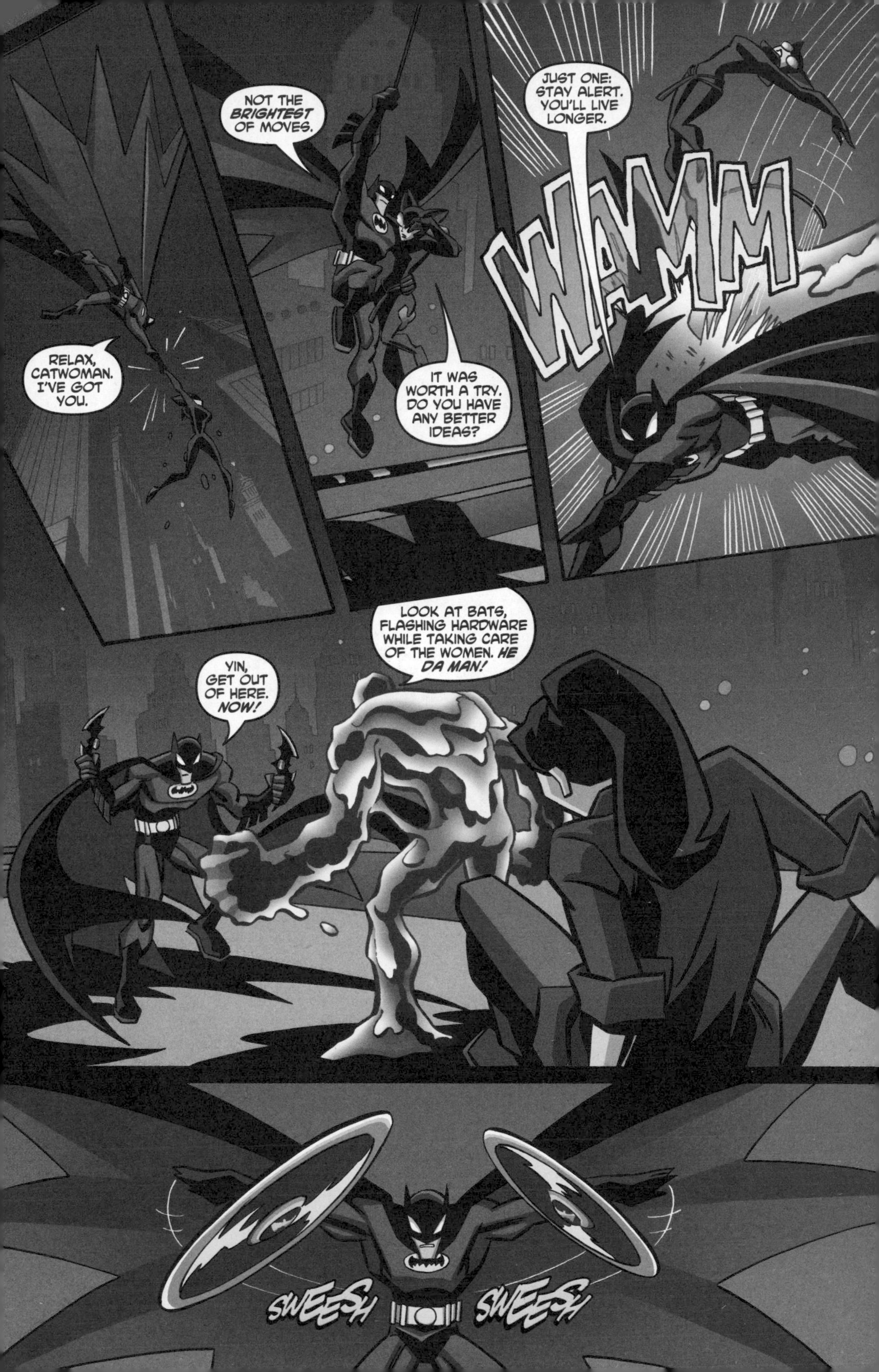
RELAX, CATWOMAN. I'VE GOT YOU.
NOT THE BRIGHTEST OF MOVES.
IT WAS WORTH A TRY. DO YOU HAVE ANY BETTER IDEAS?
JUST ONE: STAY ALERT. YOU'LL LIVE LONGER.
WAMM
LOOK AT BATS, FLASHING HARDWARE WHILE TAKING CARE OF THE WOMEN. HE DA MAN!
YIN, GET OUT OF HERE. NOW!
SWEESH
SWEESH

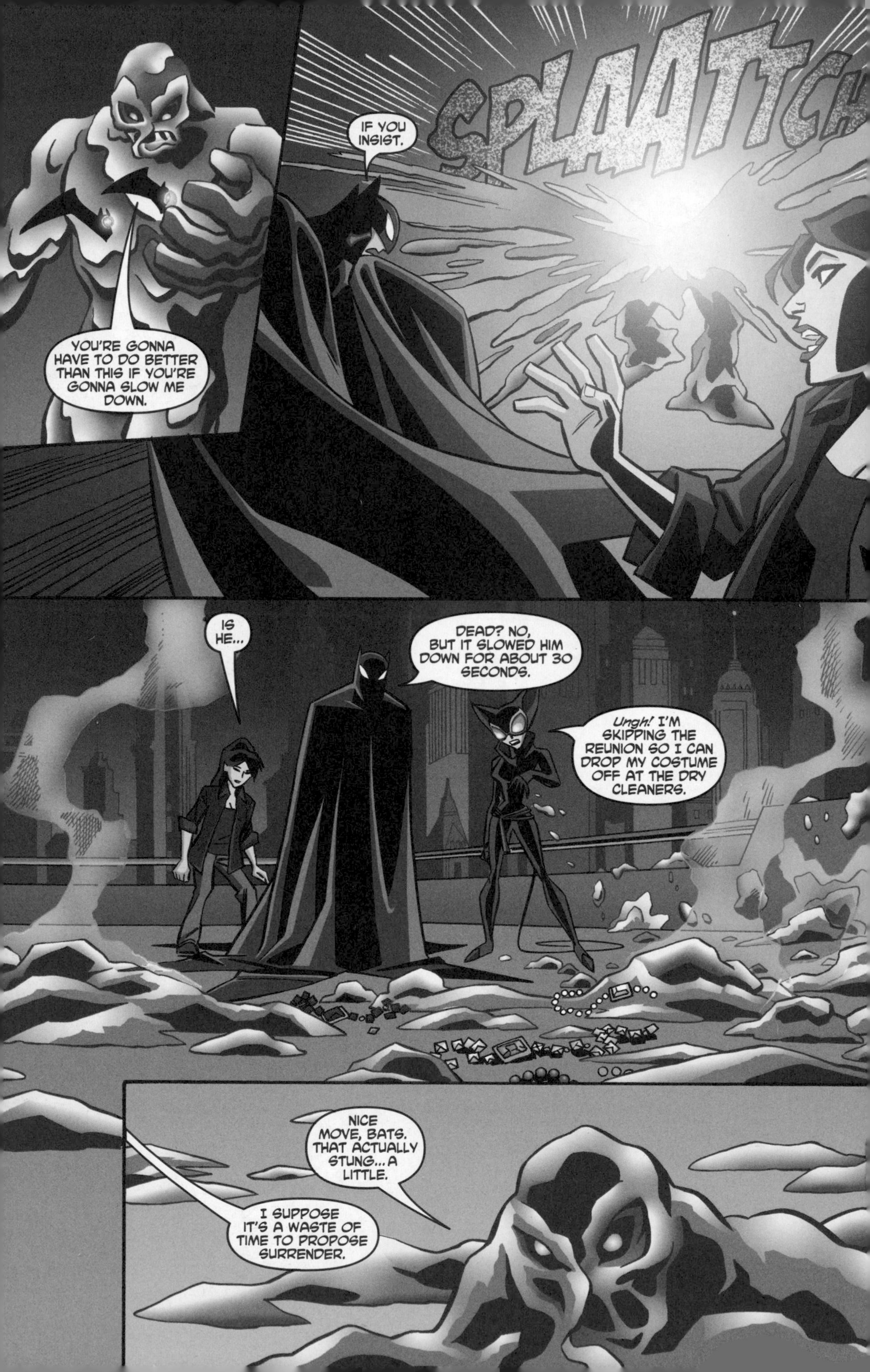
YOU'RE GONNA HAVE TO DO BETTER THAN THIS IF YOU'RE GONNA SLOW ME DOWN.
IF YOU INSIST.
SPLAATTCH
IS HE...
DEAD? NO, BUT IT SLOWED HIM DOWN FOR ABOUT 30 SECONDS.
Ungh! I'M SKIPPING THE REUNION SO I CAN DROP MY COSTUME OFF AT THE DRY CLEANERS.
NICE MOVE, BATS. THAT ACTUALLY STUNG... A LITTLE.
I SUPPOSE IT'S A WASTE OF TIME TO PROPOSE SURRENDER.

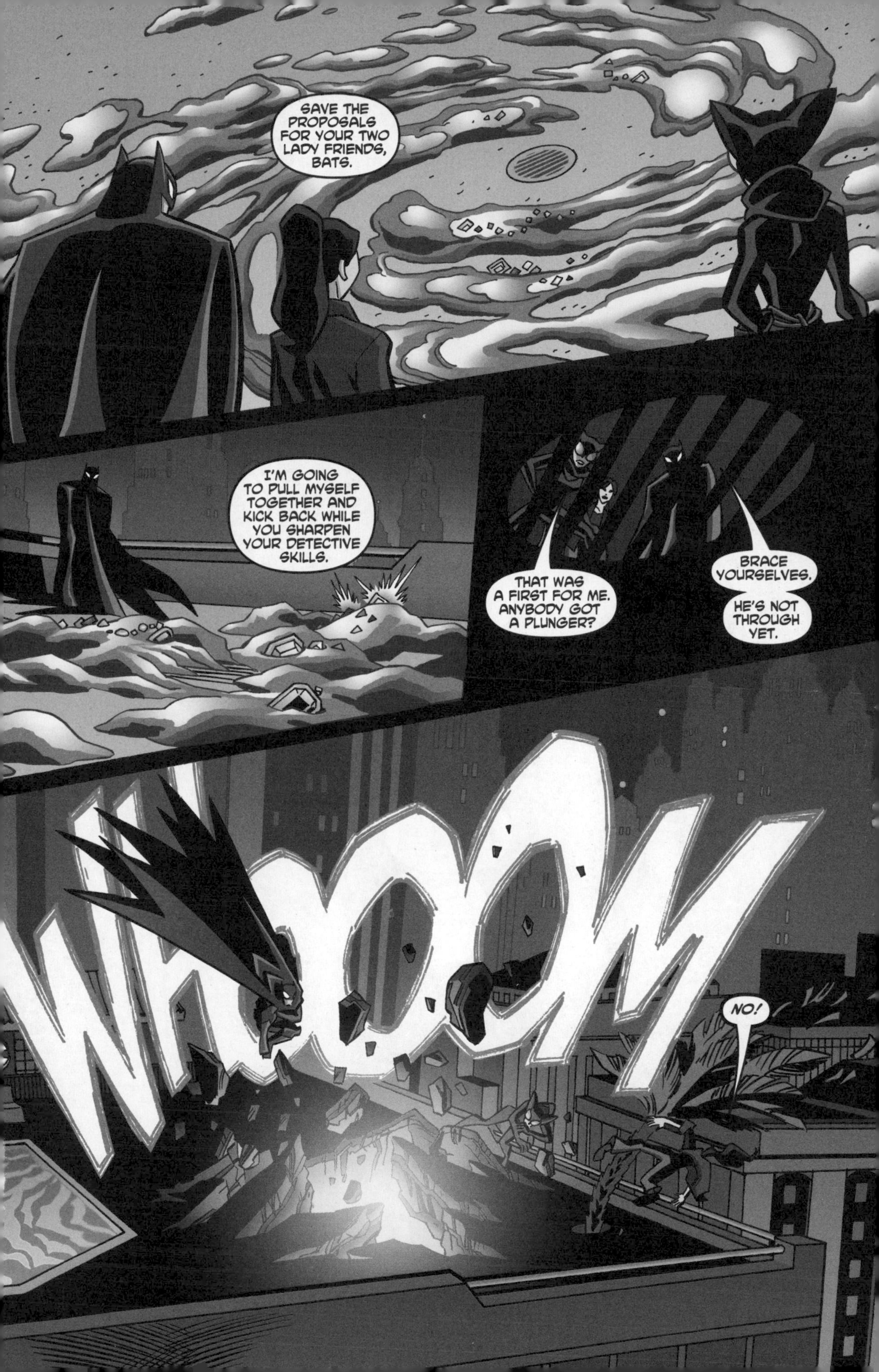
SAVE THE PROPOSALS FOR YOUR TWO LADY FRIENDS, BATS.
I'M GOING TO PULL MYSELF TOGETHER AND KICK BACK WHILE YOU SHARPEN YOUR DETECTIVE SKILLS.
THAT WAS A FIRST FOR ME. ANYBODY GOT A PLUNGER?
BRACE YOURSELVES.
HE'S NOT THROUGH YET.
WHOOOM
NO!

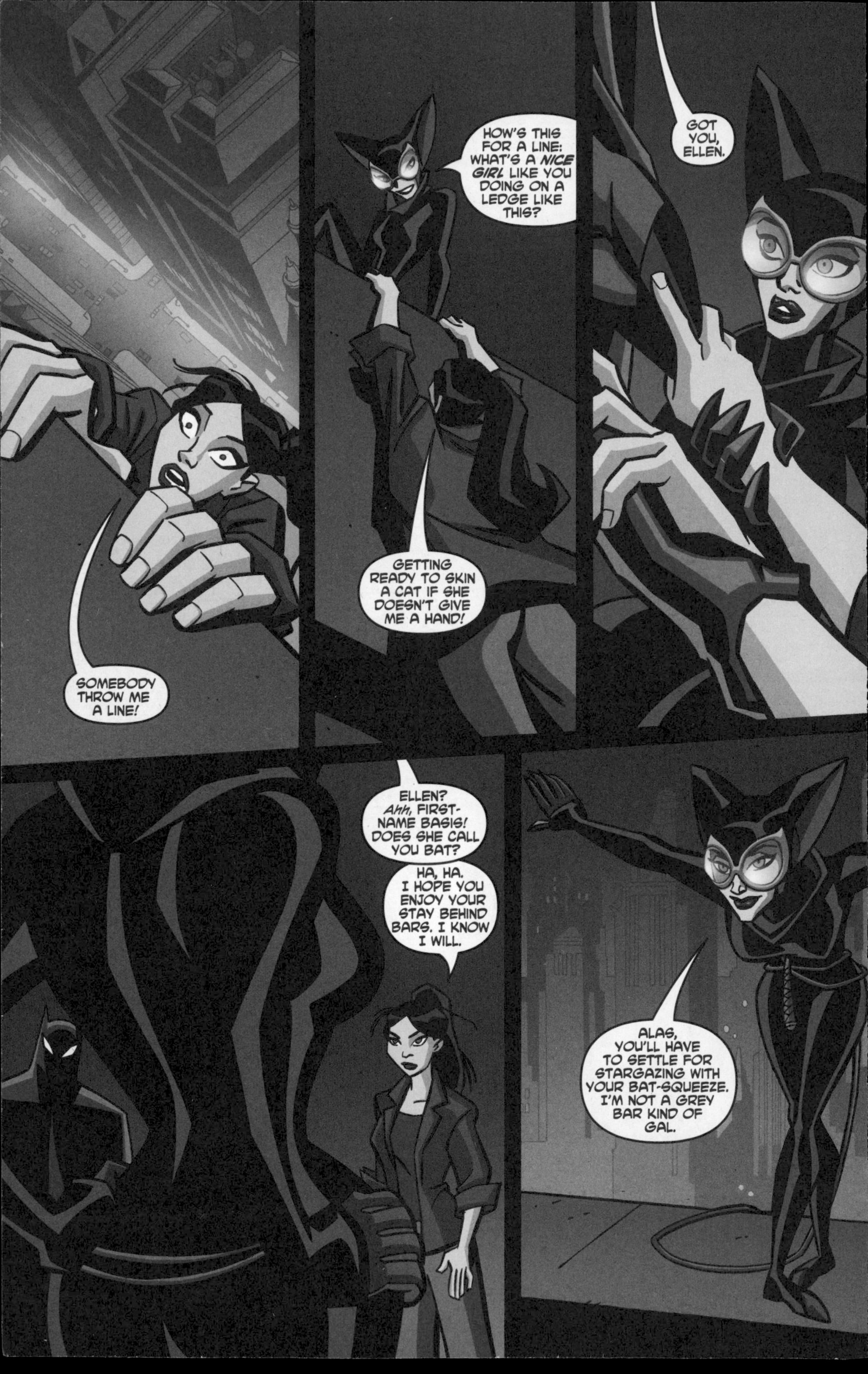
SOMEBODY THROW ME A LINE!
HOW'S THIS FOR A LINE: WHAT'S A *NICE GIRL* LIKE YOU DOING ON A LEDGE LIKE THIS?
GETTING READY TO SKIN A CAT IF SHE DOESN'T GIVE ME A HAND!
GOT YOU, ELLEN.
ELLEN? *AHH*, FIRST-NAME BASIS! DOES SHE CALL YOU BAT?
HA, HA. I HOPE YOU ENJOY YOUR STAY BEHIND BARS. I KNOW I WILL.
ALAS, YOU'LL HAVE TO SETTLE FOR STARGAZING WITH YOUR BAT-SQUEEZE. I'M NOT A GREY BAR KIND OF GAL.

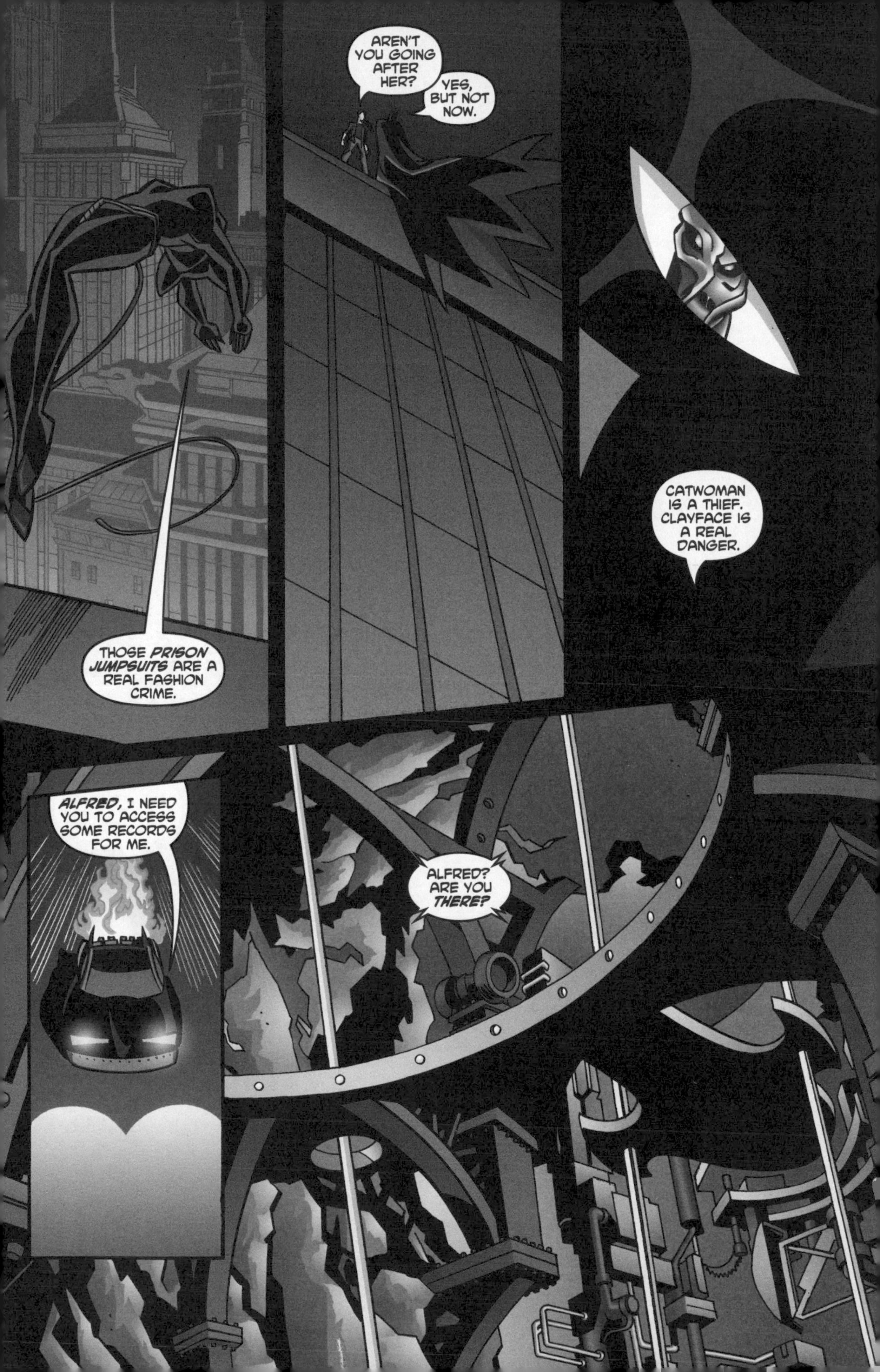
THOSE *PRISON JUMPSUITS* ARE A REAL FASHION CRIME.
AREN'T YOU GOING AFTER HER?
YES, BUT NOT NOW.
CATWOMAN IS A THIEF. CLAYFACE IS A REAL DANGER.
ALFRED, I NEED YOU TO ACCESS SOME RECORDS FOR ME.
ALFRED? ARE YOU *THERE?*

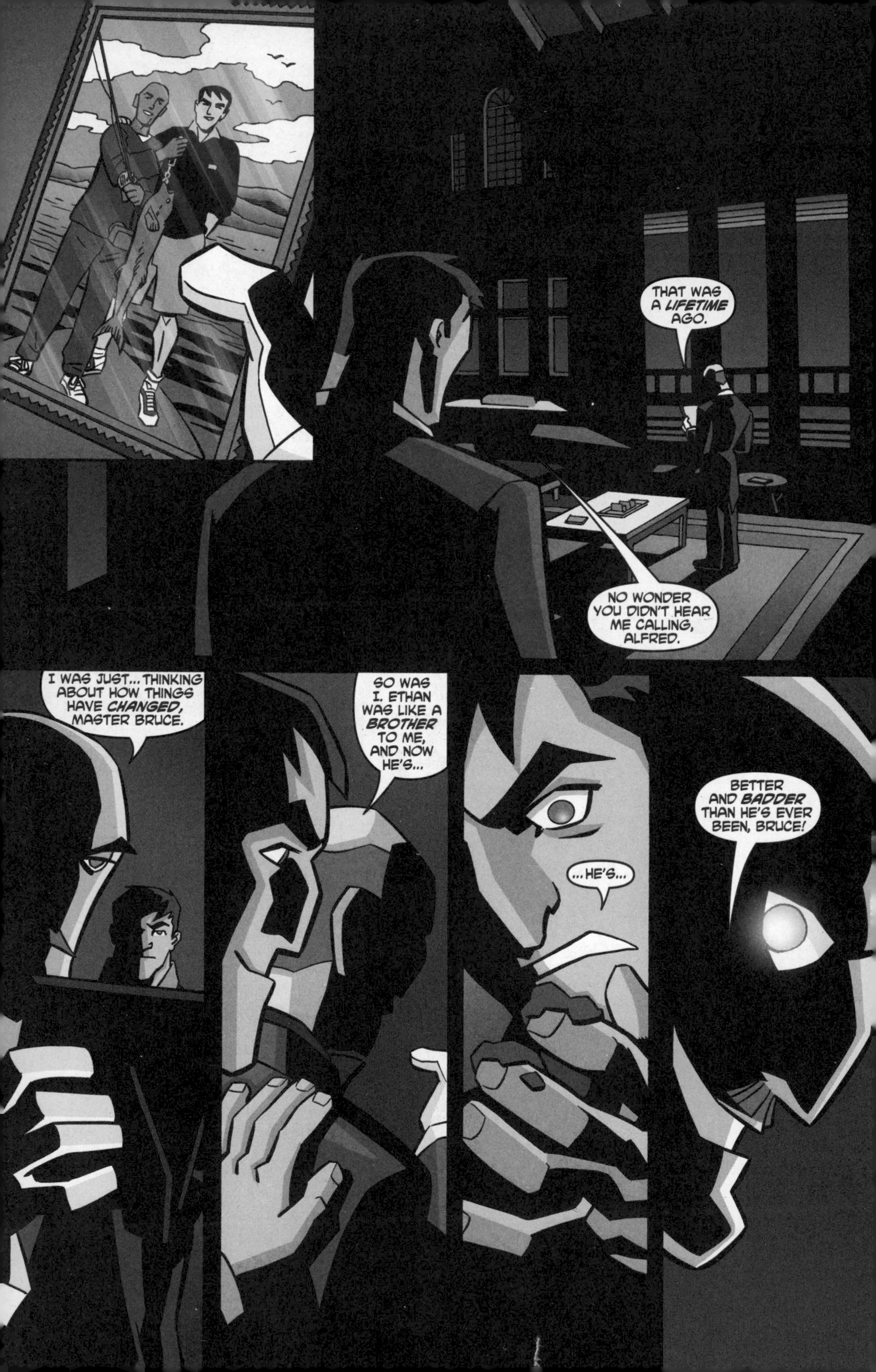
THAT WAS A *LIFETIME* AGO.
NO WONDER YOU DIDN'T HEAR ME CALLING, ALFRED.
I WAS JUST... THINKING ABOUT HOW THINGS HAVE *CHANGED*, MASTER BRUCE.
SO WAS I. ETHAN WAS LIKE A *BROTHER* TO ME, AND NOW HE'S...
...HE'S...
BETTER AND *BADDER* THAN HE'S EVER BEEN, BRUCE!

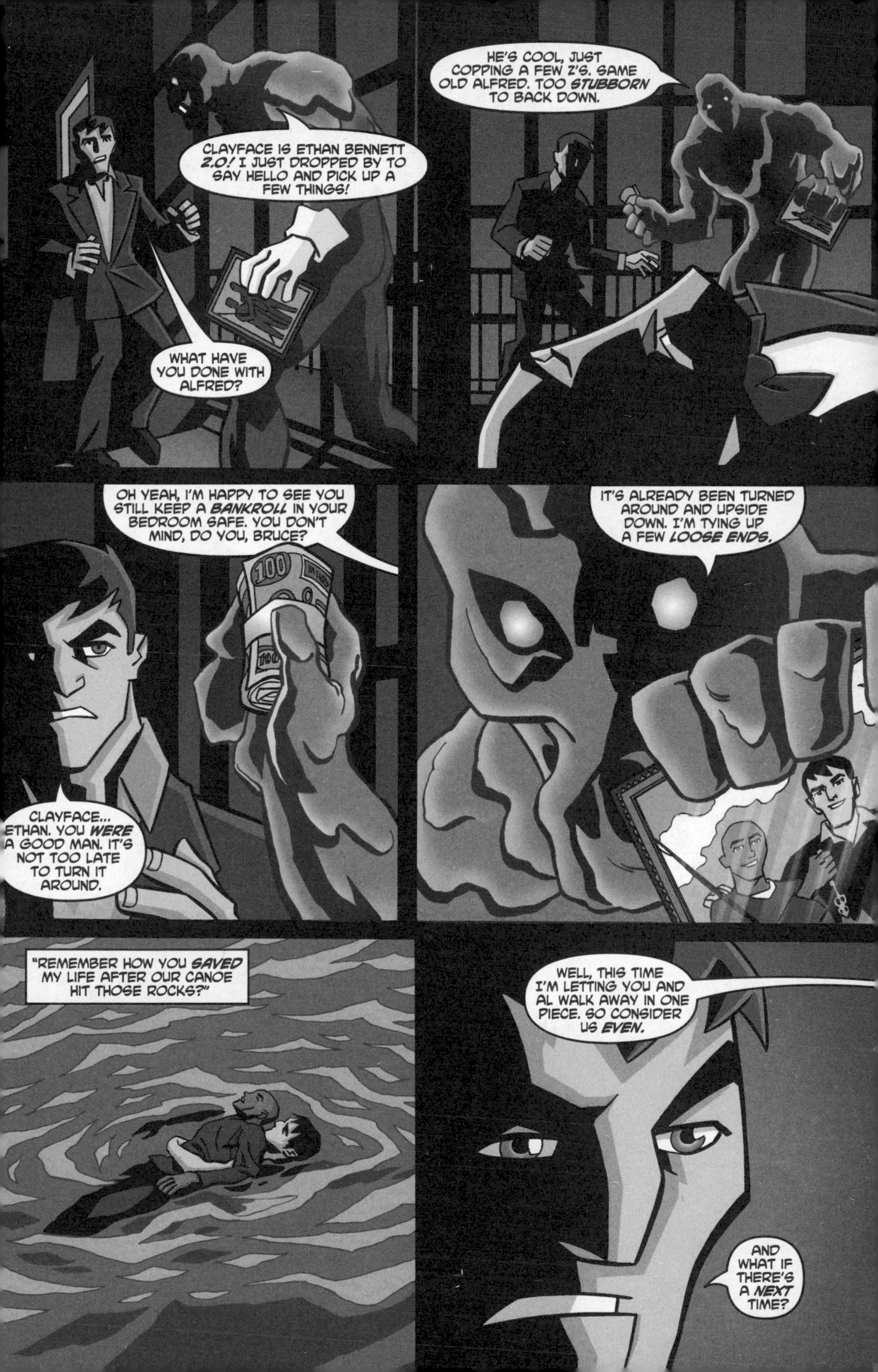
CLAYFACE IS ETHAN BENNETT 2.0! I JUST DROPPED BY TO SAY HELLO AND PICK UP A FEW THINGS!
WHAT HAVE YOU DONE WITH ALFRED?
HE'S COOL, JUST COPPING A FEW Z'S. SAME OLD ALFRED. TOO STUBBORN TO BACK DOWN.
OH YEAH, I'M HAPPY TO SEE YOU STILL KEEP A BANKROLL IN YOUR BEDROOM SAFE. YOU DON'T MIND, DO YOU, BRUCE?
CLAYFACE... ETHAN. YOU WERE A GOOD MAN. IT'S NOT TOO LATE TO TURN IT AROUND.
IT'S ALREADY BEEN TURNED AROUND AND UPSIDE DOWN. I'M TYING UP A FEW LOOSE ENDS.
"REMEMBER HOW YOU SAVED MY LIFE AFTER OUR CANOE HIT THOSE ROCKS?"
WELL, THIS TIME I'M LETTING YOU AND AL WALK AWAY IN ONE PIECE. SO CONSIDER US EVEN.
AND WHAT IF THERE'S A NEXT TIME?

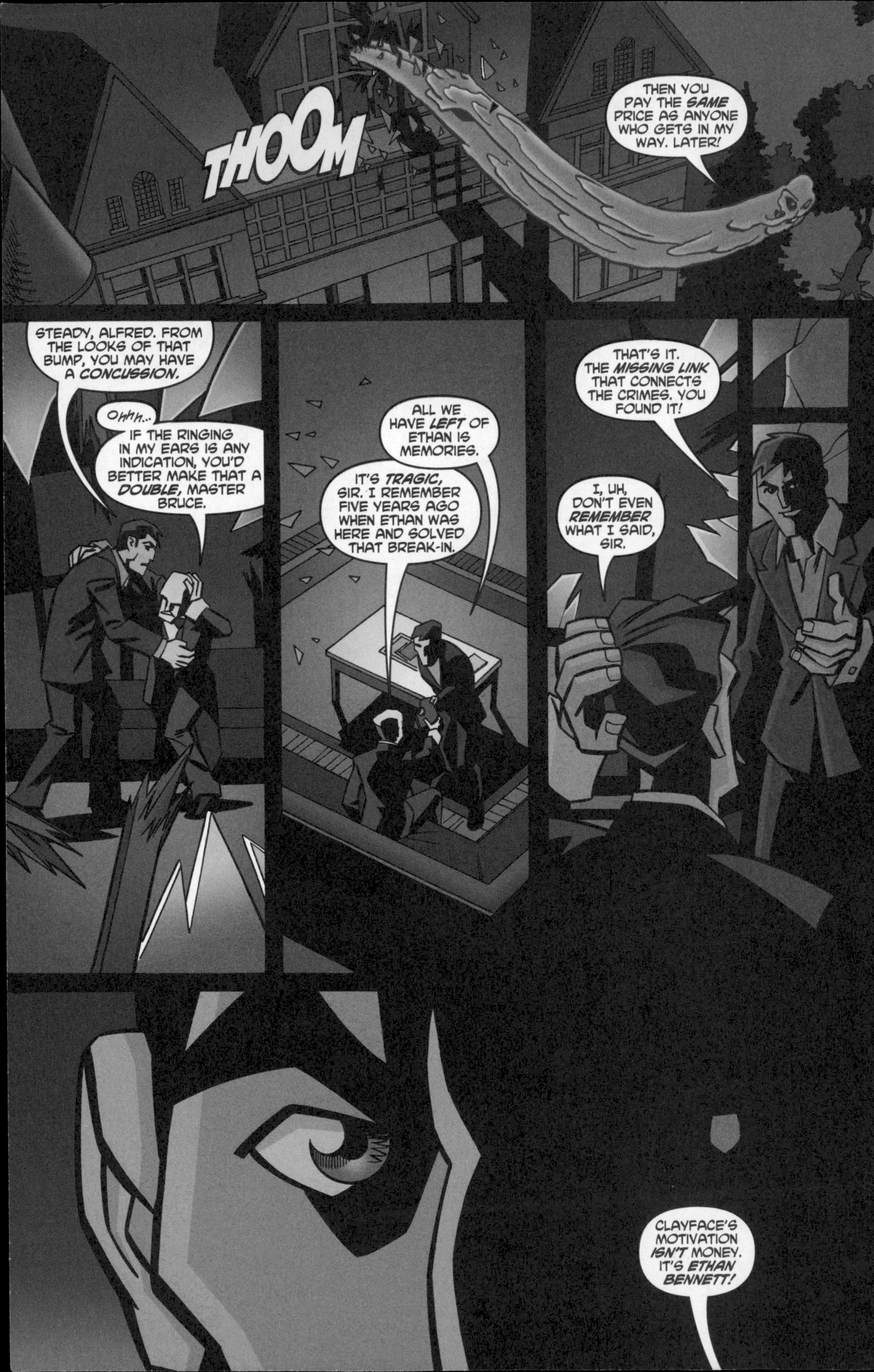
THOOM
THEN YOU PAY THE SAME PRICE AS ANYONE WHO GETS IN MY WAY. LATER!
STEADY, ALFRED. FROM THE LOOKS OF THAT BUMP, YOU MAY HAVE A CONCUSSION.
Ohhh...
IF THE RINGING IN MY EARS IS ANY INDICATION, YOU'D BETTER MAKE THAT A DOUBLE, MASTER BRUCE.
ALL WE HAVE LEFT OF ETHAN IS MEMORIES.
IT'S TRAGIC, SIR. I REMEMBER FIVE YEARS AGO WHEN ETHAN WAS HERE AND SOLVED THAT BREAK-IN.
THAT'S IT. THE MISSING LINK THAT CONNECTS THE CRIMES. YOU FOUND IT!
I, UH, DON'T EVEN REMEMBER WHAT I SAID, SIR.
CLAYFACE'S MOTIVATION ISN'T MONEY. IT'S ETHAN BENNETT!

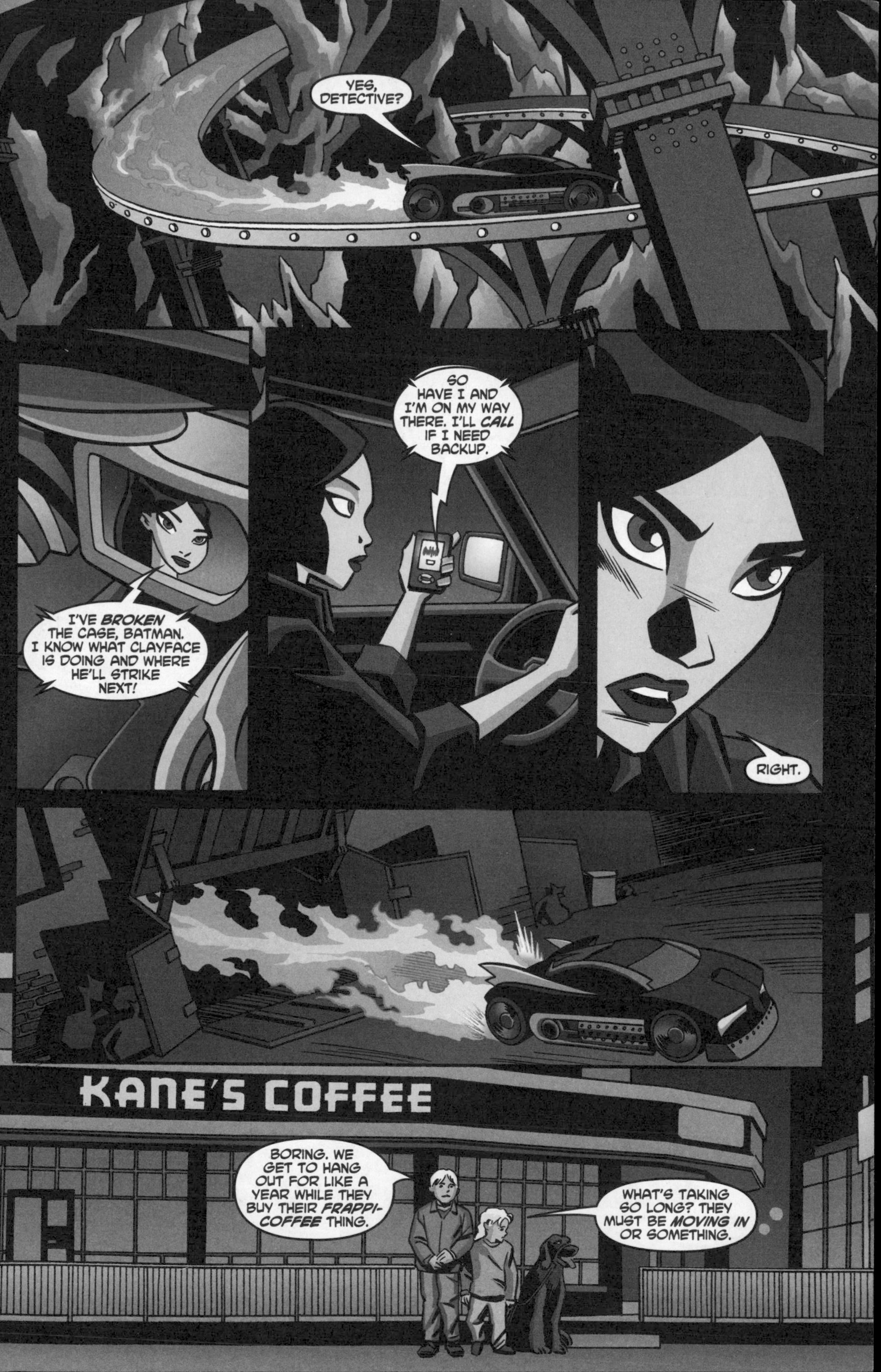
YES, DETECTIVE?
I'VE *BROKEN* THE CASE, BATMAN. I KNOW WHAT CLAYFACE IS DOING AND WHERE HE'LL STRIKE NEXT!
SO HAVE I AND I'M ON MY WAY THERE. I'LL *CALL* IF I NEED BACKUP.
RIGHT.
KANE'S COFFEE
BORING. WE GET TO HANG OUT FOR LIKE A YEAR WHILE THEY BUY THEIR *FRAPPI-COFFEE* THING.
WHAT'S TAKING SO LONG? THEY MUST BE *MOVING IN* OR SOMETHING.

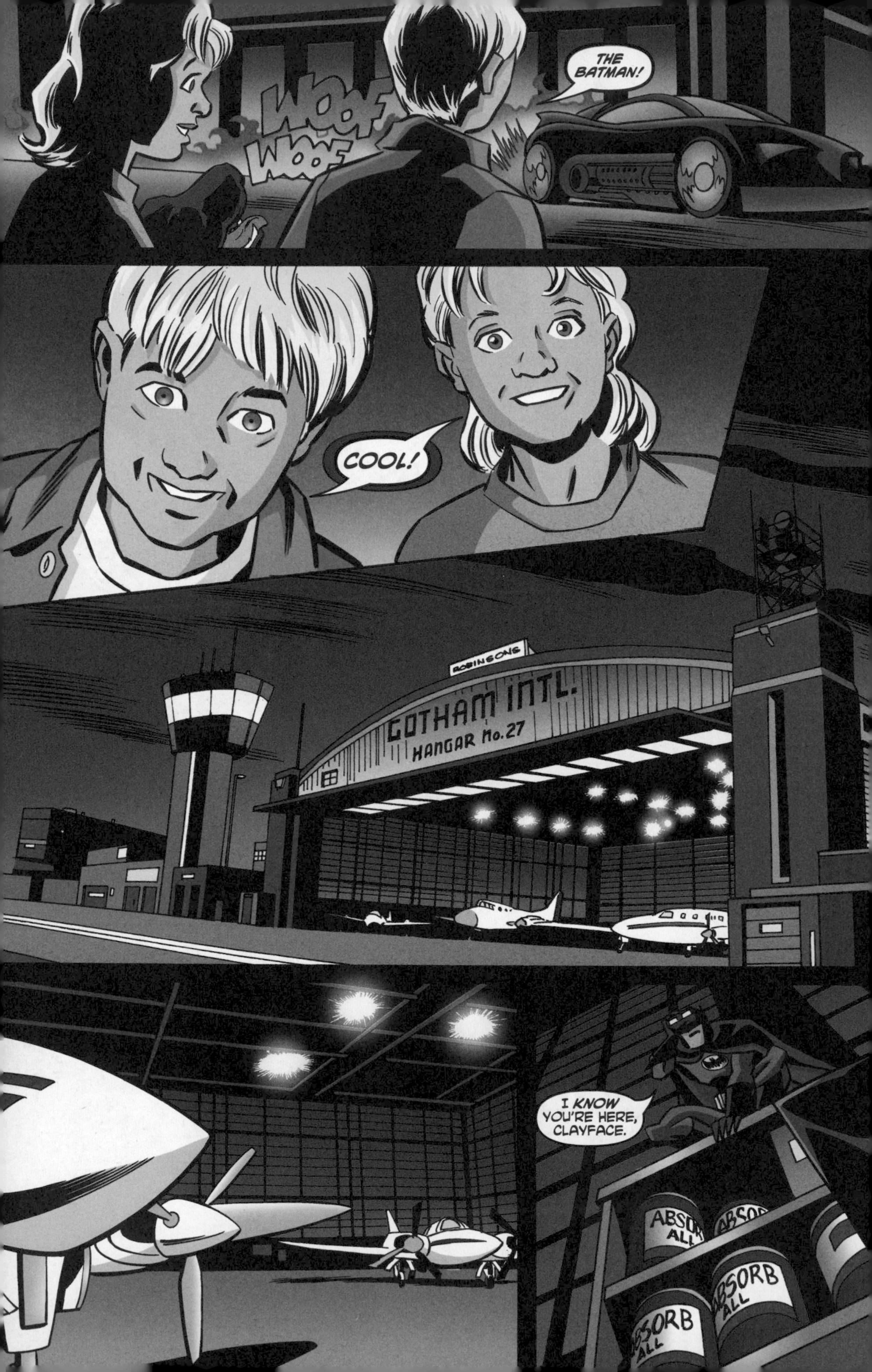
WOOF
WOOF
THE BATMAN!
COOL!
ROBINSONS
GOTHAM INTL.
HANGAR No. 27
I KNOW YOU'RE HERE, CLAYFACE.
ABSORB ALL
ABSORB ALL
ABSORB ALL

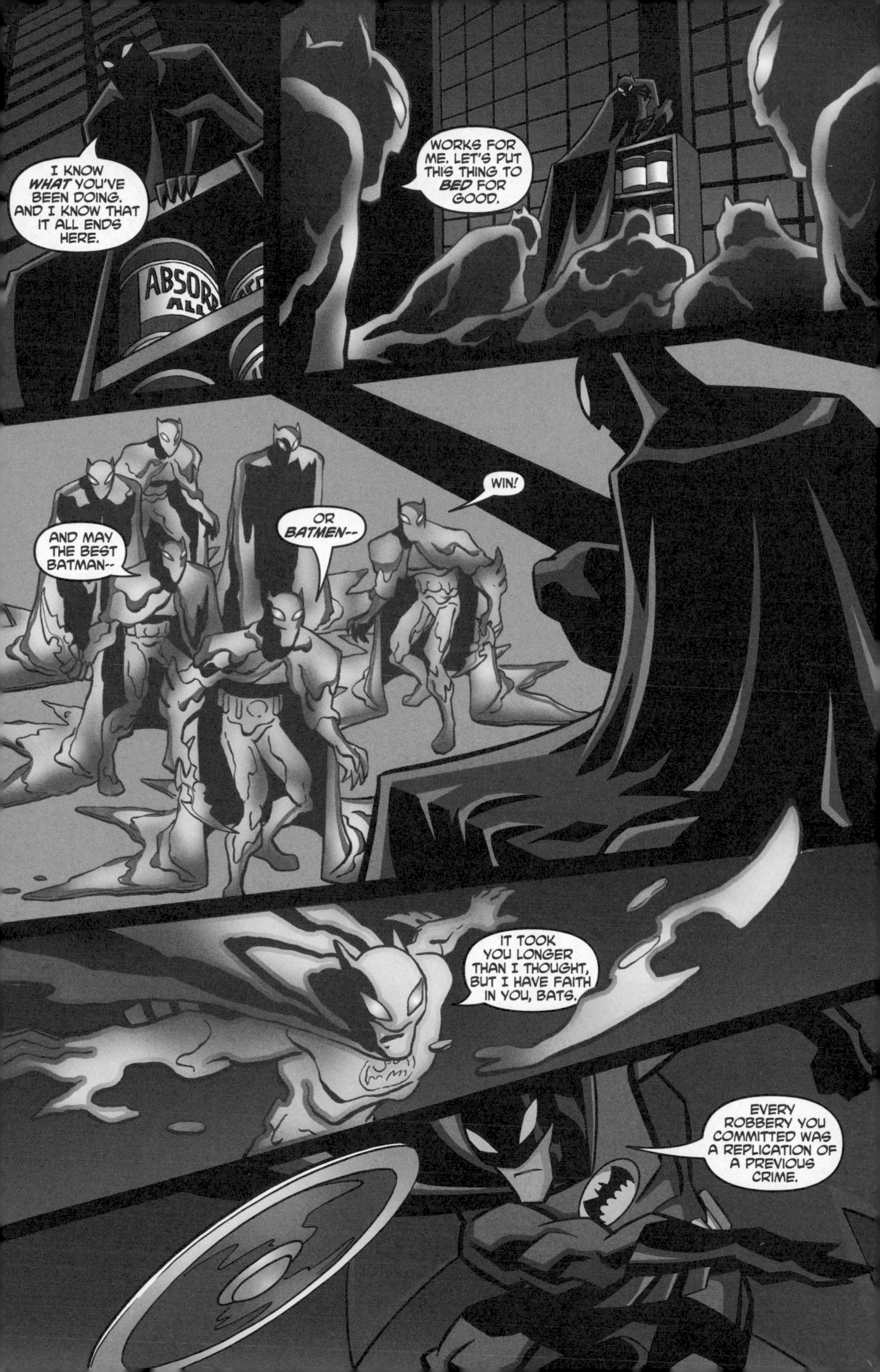

I KNOW *WHAT* YOU'VE BEEN DOING. AND I KNOW THAT IT ALL ENDS HERE.
ABSORB ALL
WORKS FOR ME. LET'S PUT THIS THING TO *BED* FOR GOOD.
AND MAY THE BEST BATMAN--
OR *BATMEN*--
WIN!
IT TOOK YOU LONGER THAN I THOUGHT, BUT I HAVE FAITH IN YOU, BATS.
EVERY ROBBERY YOU COMMITTED WAS A REPLICATION OF A PREVIOUS CRIME.

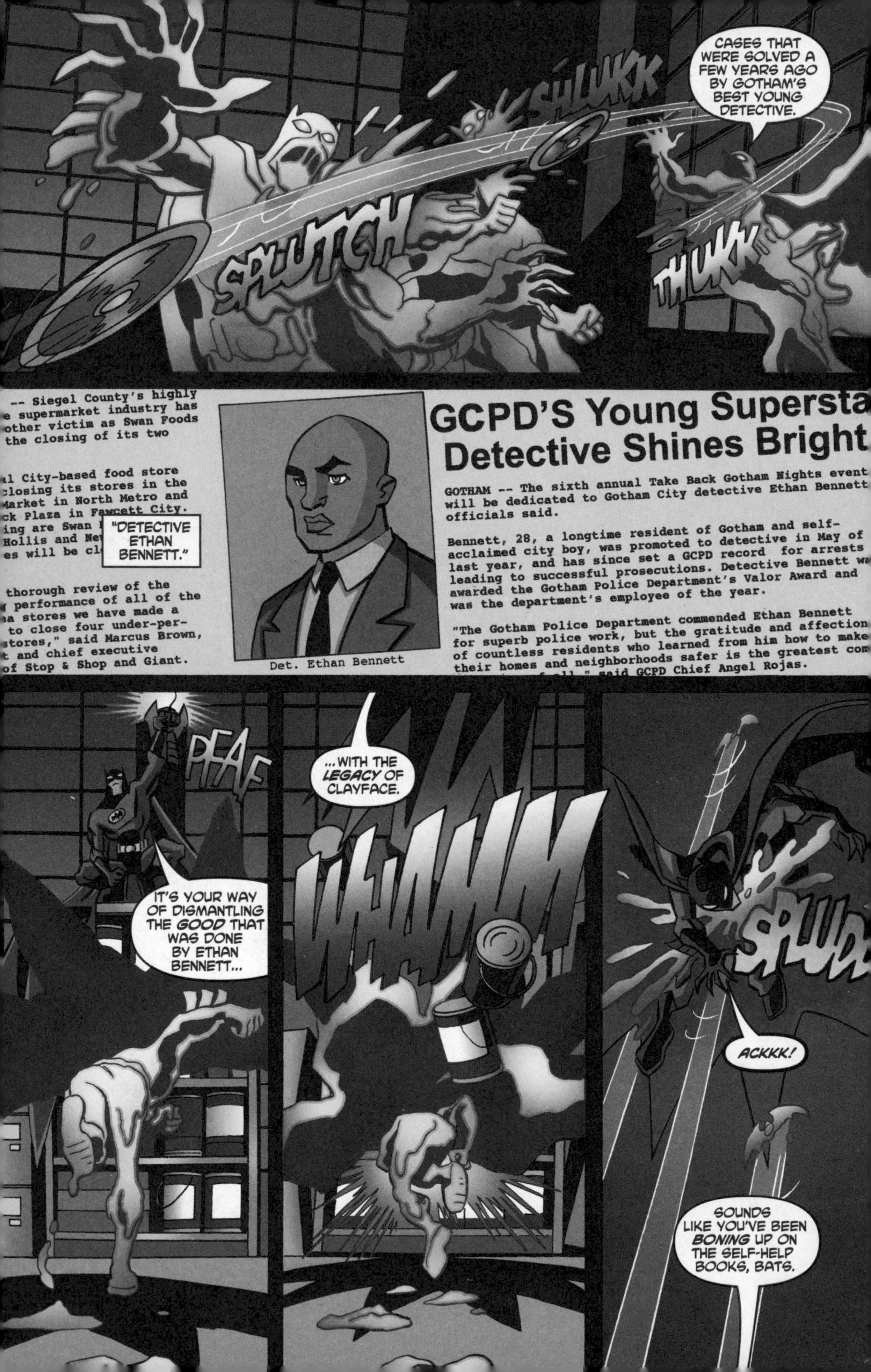
CASES THAT WERE SOLVED A FEW YEARS AGO BY GOTHAM'S BEST YOUNG DETECTIVE.
SHLUKK
SPLUTCH
THUKK
GCPD'S Young Supersta
Detective Shines Bright
GOTHAM -- The sixth annual Take Back Gotham Nights event will be dedicated to Gotham City detective Ethan Bennett officials said.
Bennett, 28, a longtime resident of Gotham and self-acclaimed city boy, was promoted to detective in May of last year, and has since set a GCPD record for arrests leading to successful prosecutions. Detective Bennett wa awarded the Gotham Police Department's Valor Award and was the department's employee of the year.
"The Gotham Police Department commended Ethan Bennett for superb police work, but the gratitude and affection of countless residents who learned from him how to make their homes and neighborhoods safer is the greatest com
Det. Ethan Bennett
-- Siegel County's highly
e supermarket industry has
other victim as Swan Foods
the closing of its two
al City-based food store
closing its stores in the
Market in North Metro and
ck Plaza in Fawcett City.
thorough review of the
performance of all of the
a stores we have made a
to close four under-per-
stores," said Marcus Brown,
t and chief executive
of Stop & Shop and Giant.
"DETECTIVE ETHAN BENNETT."
PFAF
IT'S YOUR WAY OF DISMANTLING THE GOOD THAT WAS DONE BY ETHAN BENNETT...
...WITH THE LEGACY OF CLAYFACE.
WHAMM
SPLUD
ACKKK!
SOUNDS LIKE YOU'VE BEEN BONING UP ON THE SELF-HELP BOOKS, BATS.

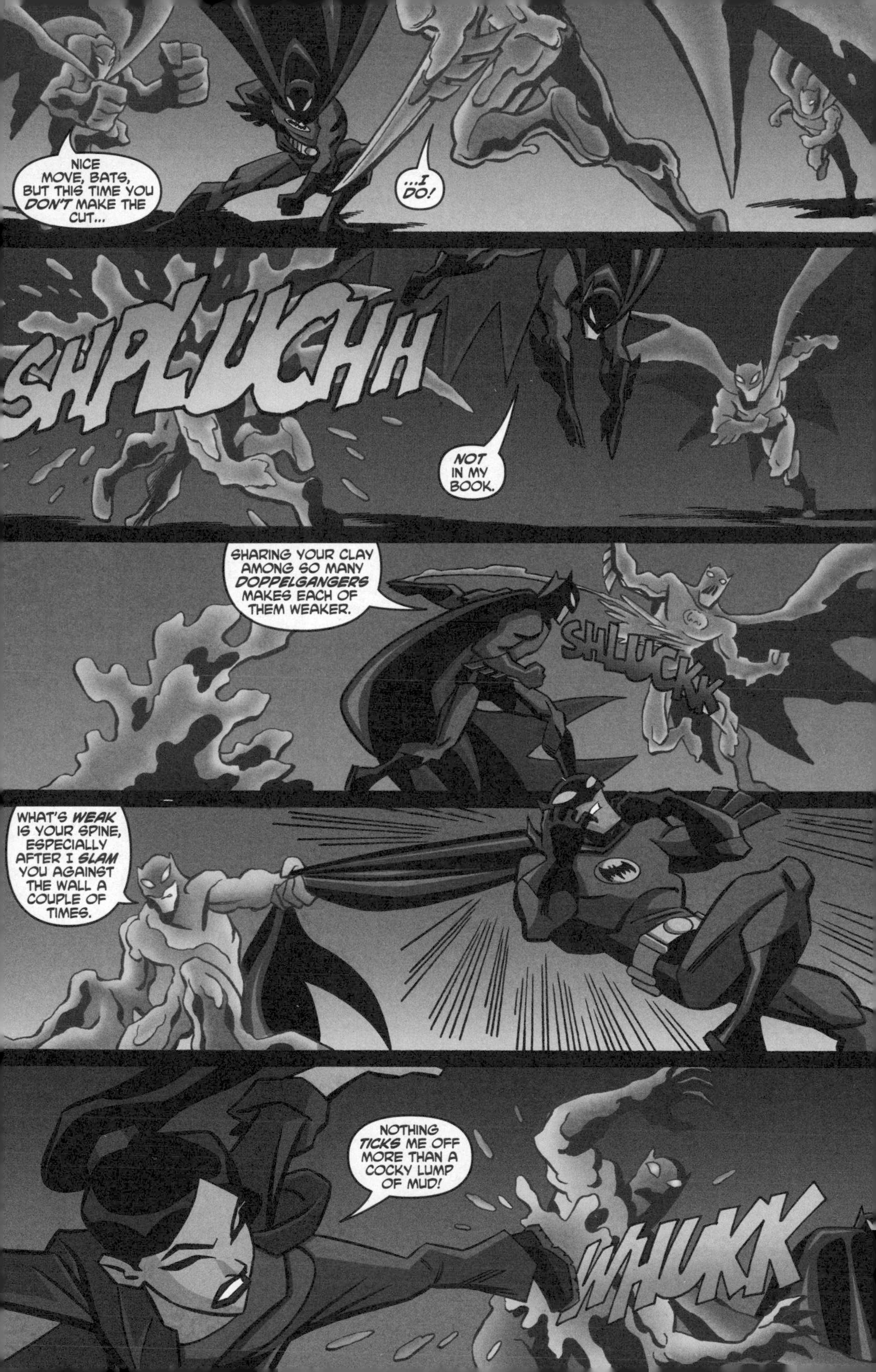
NICE MOVE, BATS, BUT THIS TIME YOU *DON'T* MAKE THE CUT...
...*I DO!*
SHPLUCHA
NOT IN MY BOOK.
SHARING YOUR CLAY AMONG SO MANY *DOPPELGANGERS* MAKES EACH OF THEM WEAKER.
SHLUCKK
WHAT'S *WEAK* IS YOUR SPINE, ESPECIALLY AFTER I *SLAM* YOU AGAINST THE WALL A COUPLE OF TIMES.
NOTHING *TICKS* ME OFF MORE THAN A COCKY LUMP OF MUD!
WHUKK

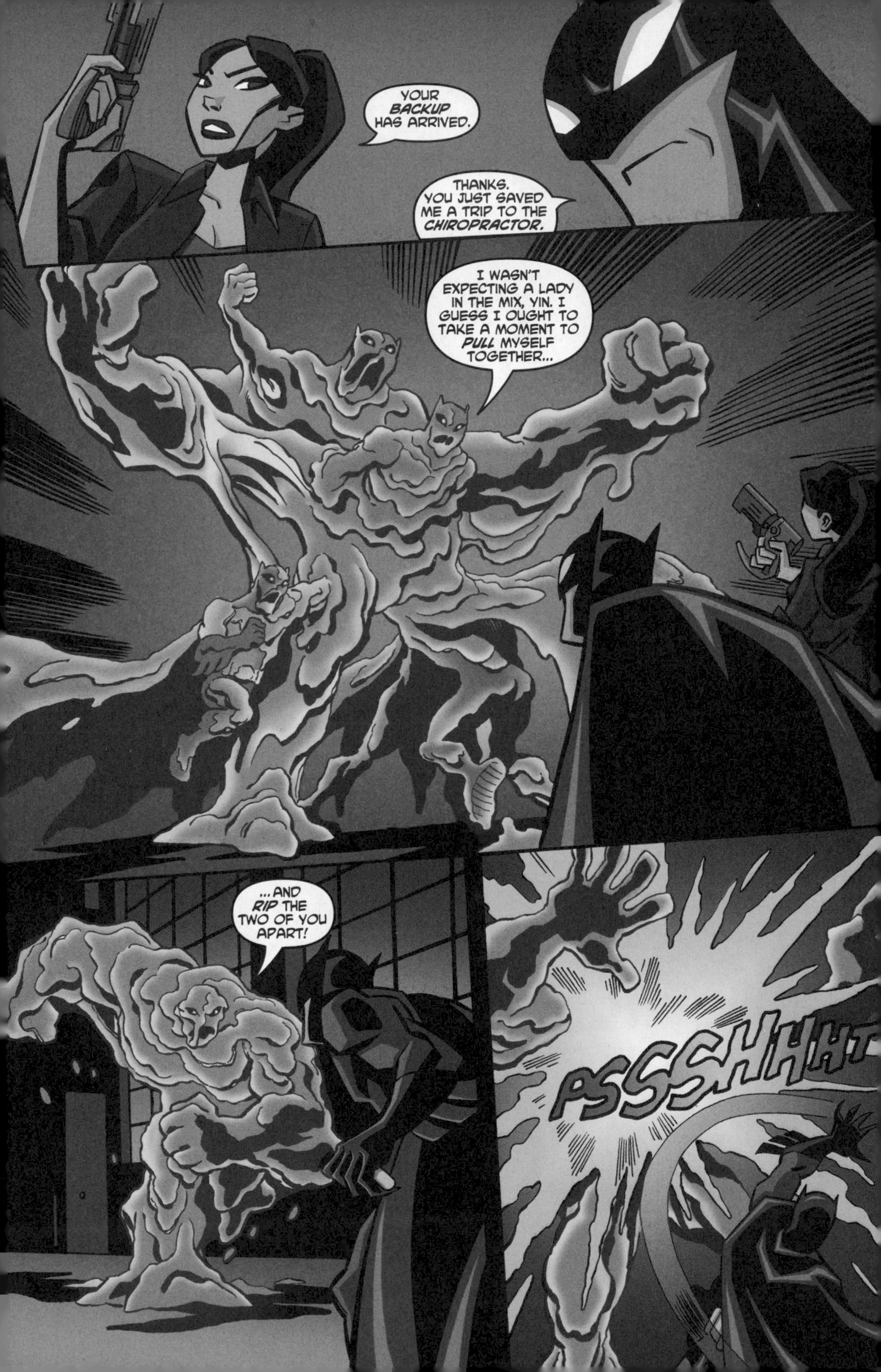
YOUR BACKUP HAS ARRIVED.
THANKS. YOU JUST SAVED ME A TRIP TO THE CHIROPRACTOR.
I WASN'T EXPECTING A LADY IN THE MIX, YIN. I GUESS I OUGHT TO TAKE A MOMENT TO PULL MYSELF TOGETHER...
...AND RIP THE TWO OF YOU APART!
PSSSHHHT

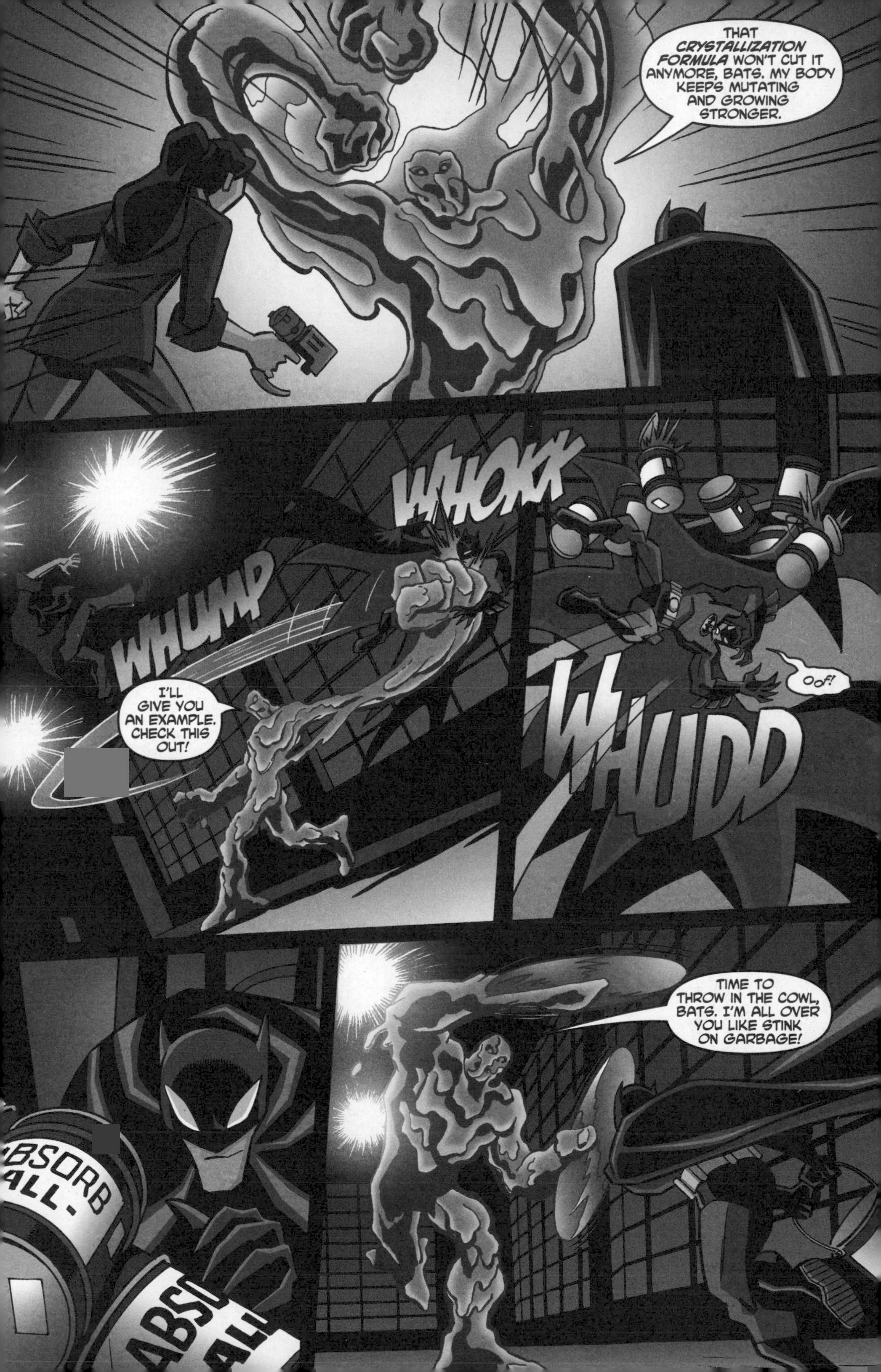
THAT CRYSTALLIZATION FORMULA WON'T CUT IT ANYMORE, BATS. MY BODY KEEPS MUTATING AND GROWING STRONGER.
WHOKK
WHUMP
I'LL GIVE YOU AN EXAMPLE. CHECK THIS OUT!
WHUDD
Oof!
TIME TO THROW IN THE COWL, BATS. I'M ALL OVER YOU LIKE STINK ON GARBAGE!

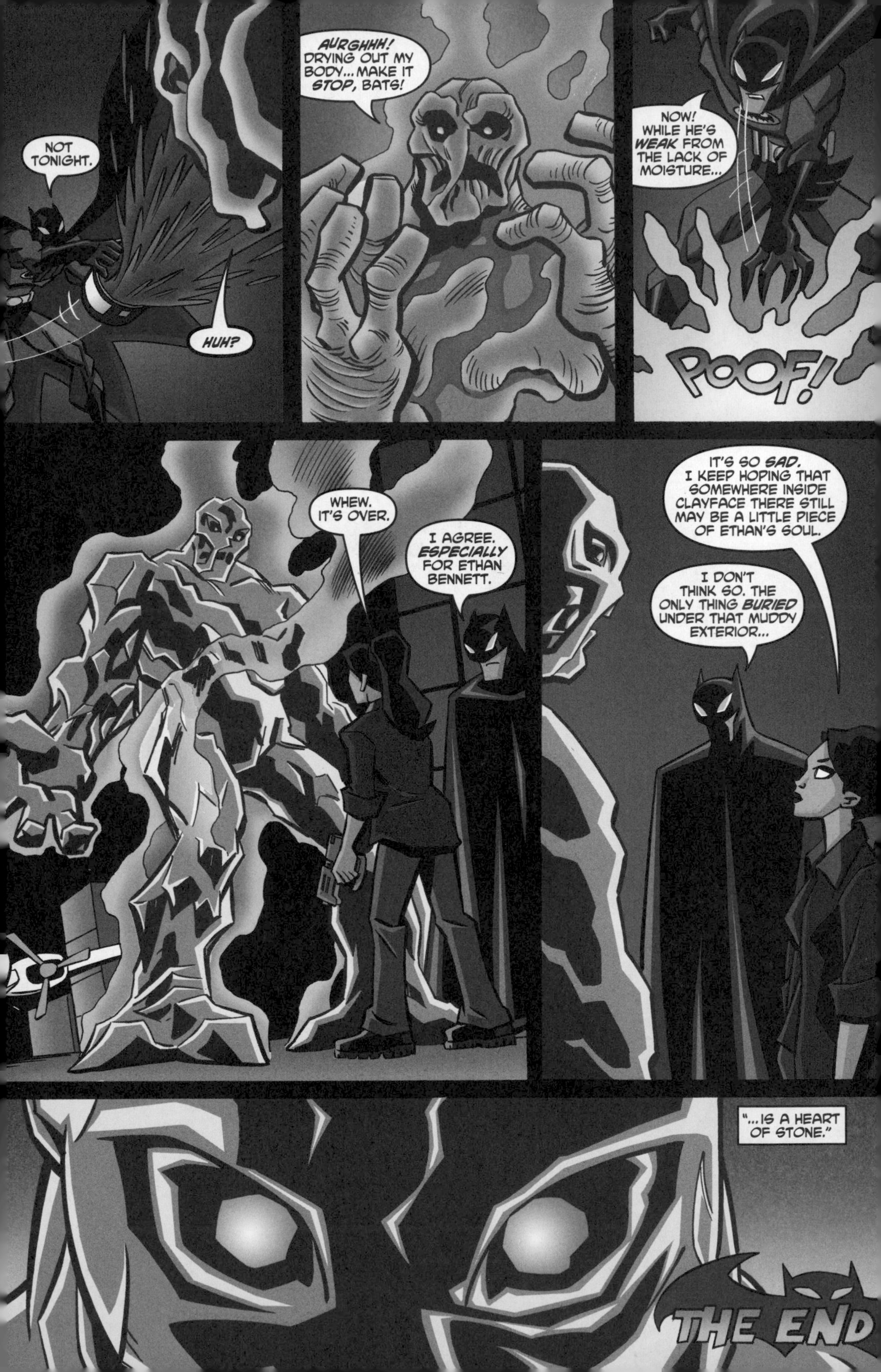
NOT TONIGHT.
HUH?
AURGHHH! DRYING OUT MY BODY... MAKE IT STOP, BATS!
NOW! WHILE HE'S WEAK FROM THE LACK OF MOISTURE...
POOF!
WHEW. IT'S OVER.
I AGREE. ESPECIALLY FOR ETHAN BENNETT.
IT'S SO SAD. I KEEP HOPING THAT SOMEWHERE INSIDE CLAYFACE THERE STILL MAY BE A LITTLE PIECE OF ETHAN'S SOUL.
I DON'T THINK SO. THE ONLY THING BURIED UNDER THAT MUDDY EXTERIOR...
"...IS A HEART OF STONE."
THE END

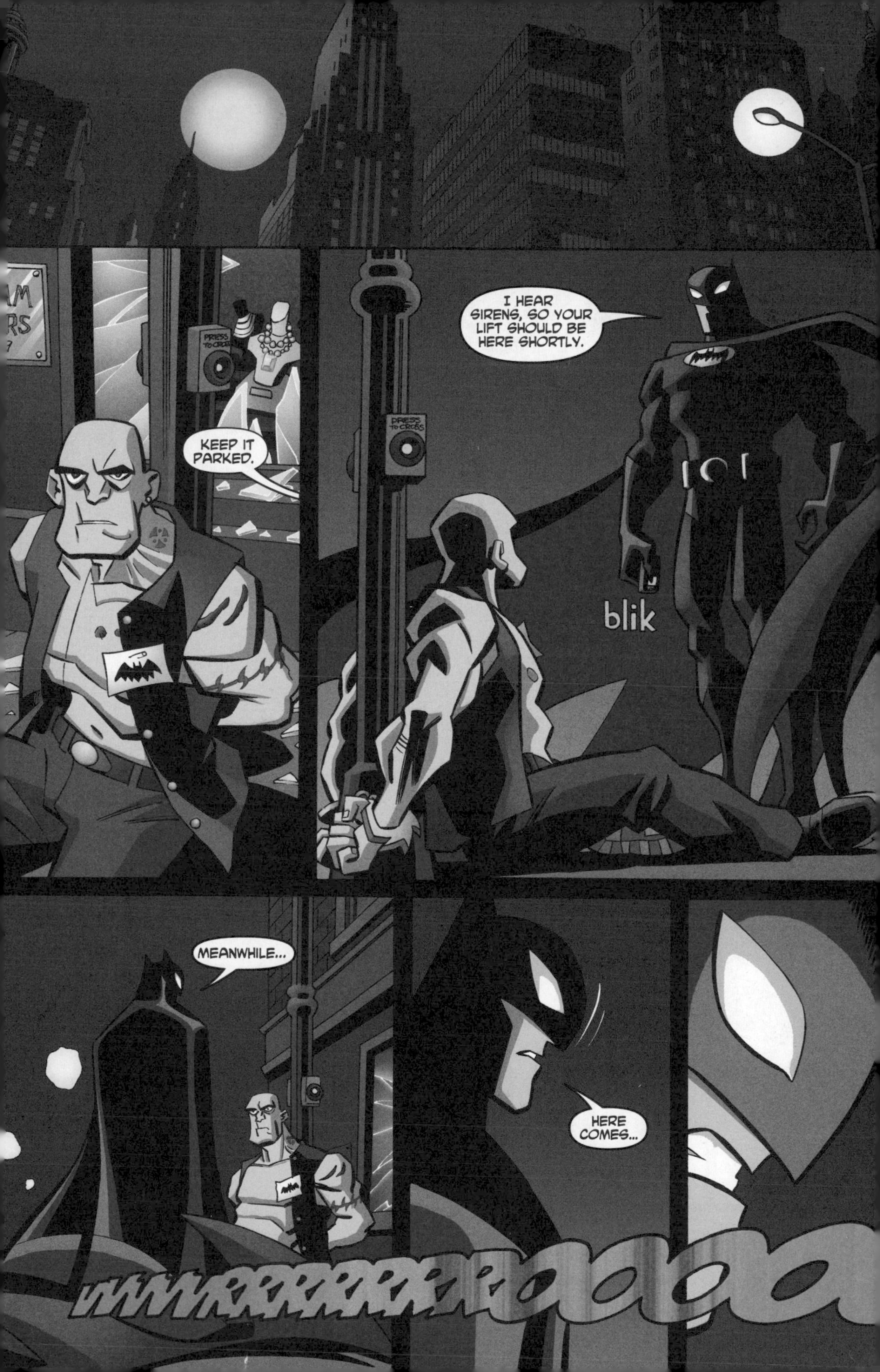
KEEP IT PARKED.
I HEAR SIRENS, SO YOUR LIFT SHOULD BE HERE SHORTLY.
blik
MEANWHILE...
HERE COMES...
VMMMRRRRRRRRRRAAAAA

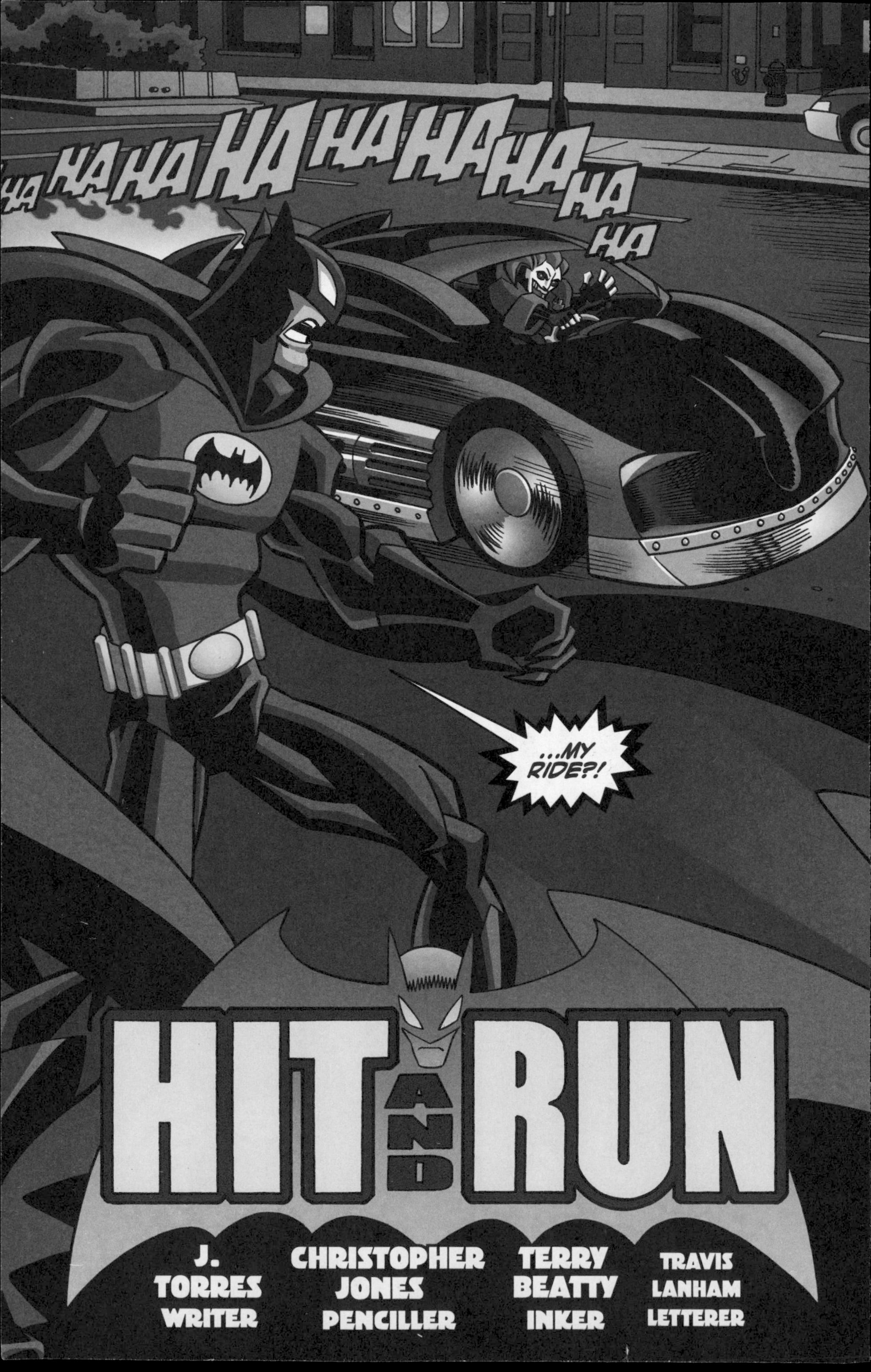
HA HA HA HA HA HA HA HA HA HA HA HA
...MY RIDE?!
HIT AND RUN
J. TORRES WRITER
CHRISTOPHER JONES PENCILLER
TERRY BEATTY INKER
TRAVIS LANHAM LETTERER

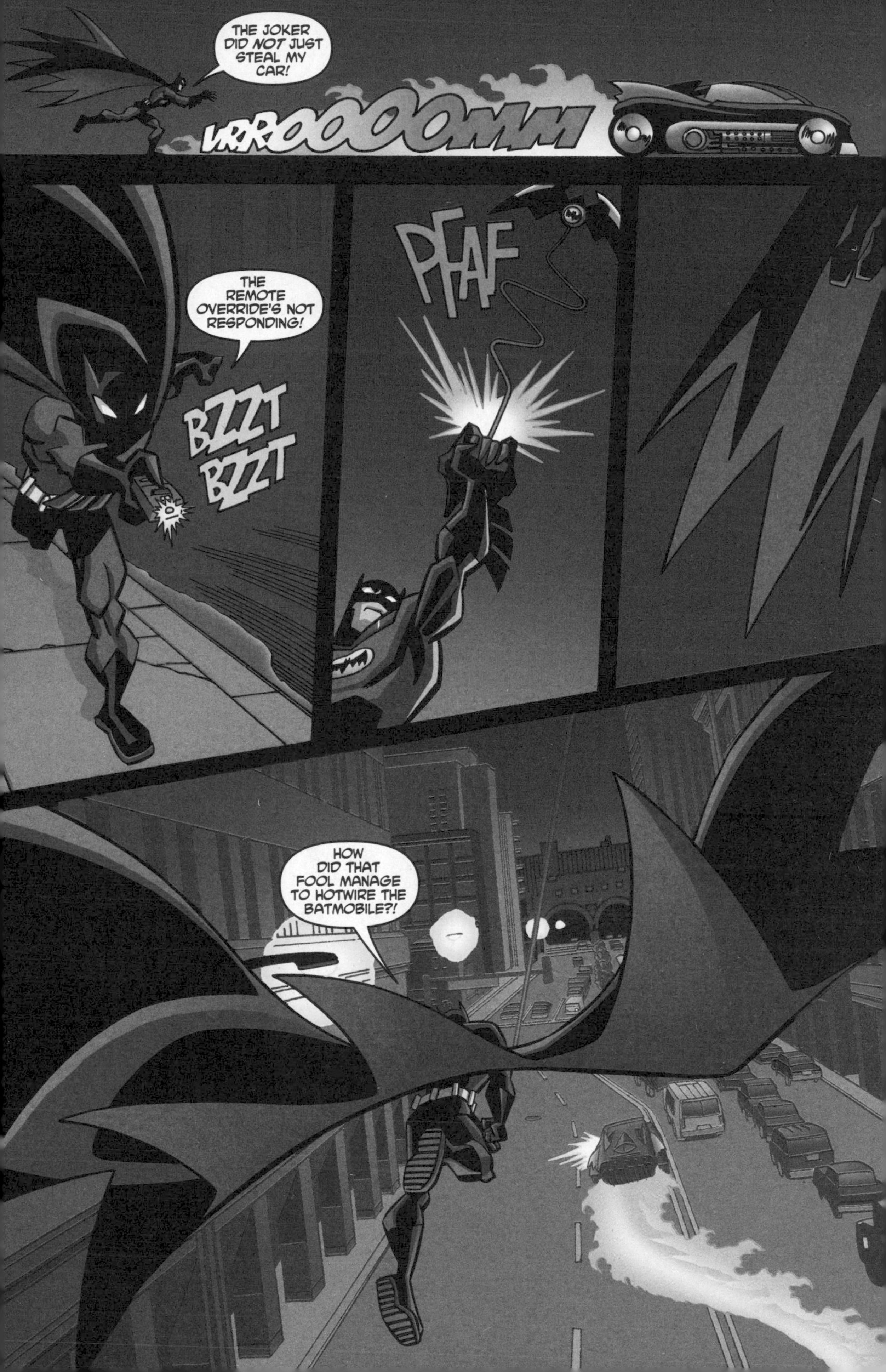
THE JOKER DID *NOT* JUST STEAL MY CAR!
VRRROOOOOMMM
THE REMOTE OVERRIDE'S NOT RESPONDING!
BZZT BZZT
PFAF
HOW DID THAT FOOL MANAGE TO HOTWIRE THE BATMOBILE?!

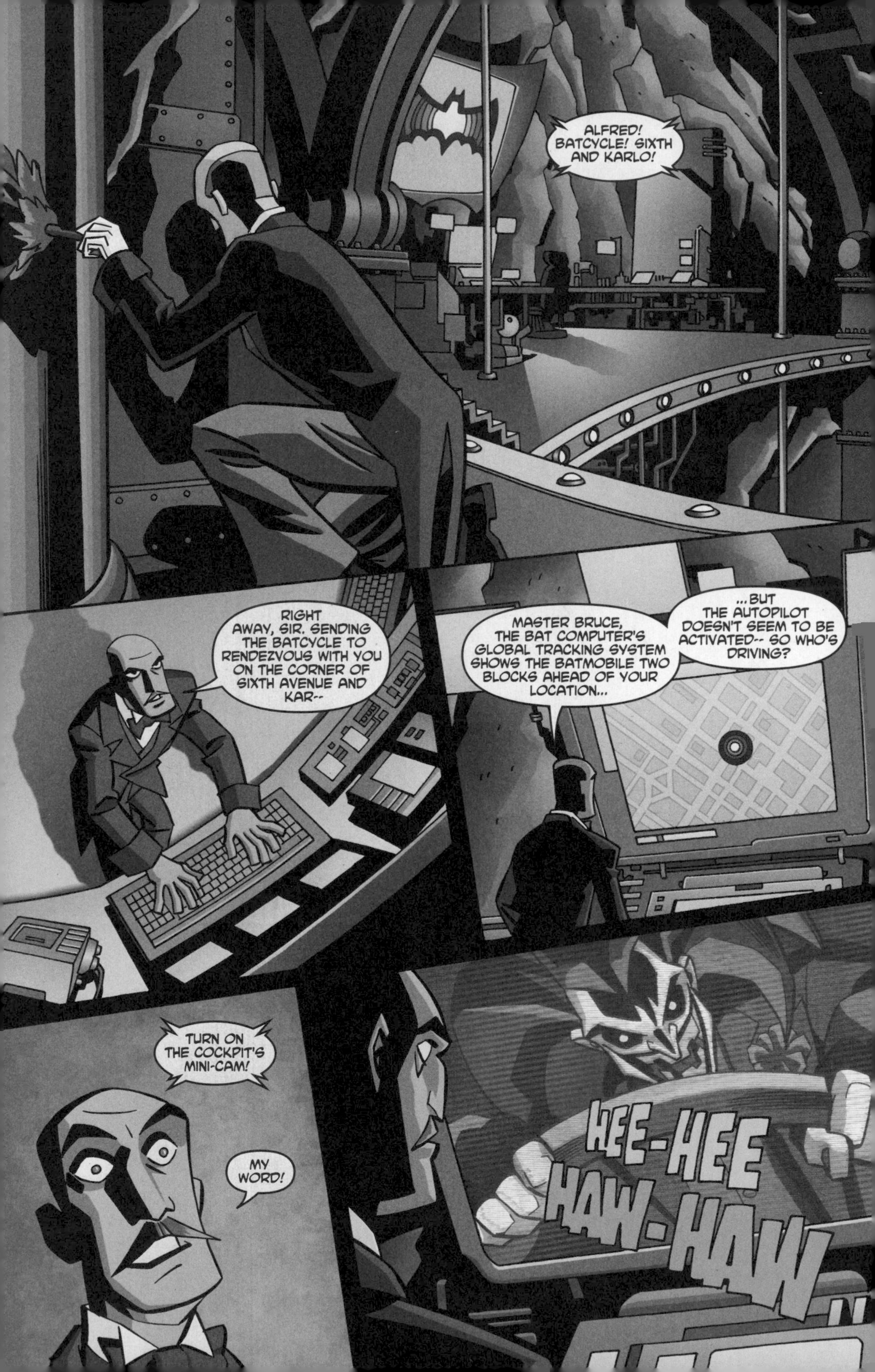
ALFRED! BATCYCLE! SIXTH AND KARLO!
RIGHT AWAY, SIR. SENDING THE BATCYCLE TO RENDEZVOUS WITH YOU ON THE CORNER OF SIXTH AVENUE AND KAR--
MASTER BRUCE, THE BAT COMPUTER'S GLOBAL TRACKING SYSTEM SHOWS THE BATMOBILE TWO BLOCKS AHEAD OF YOUR LOCATION...
...BUT THE AUTOPILOT DOESN'T SEEM TO BE ACTIVATED-- SO WHO'S DRIVING?
TURN ON THE COCKPIT'S MINI-CAM!
MY WORD!
HEE-HEE
HAW-HAW

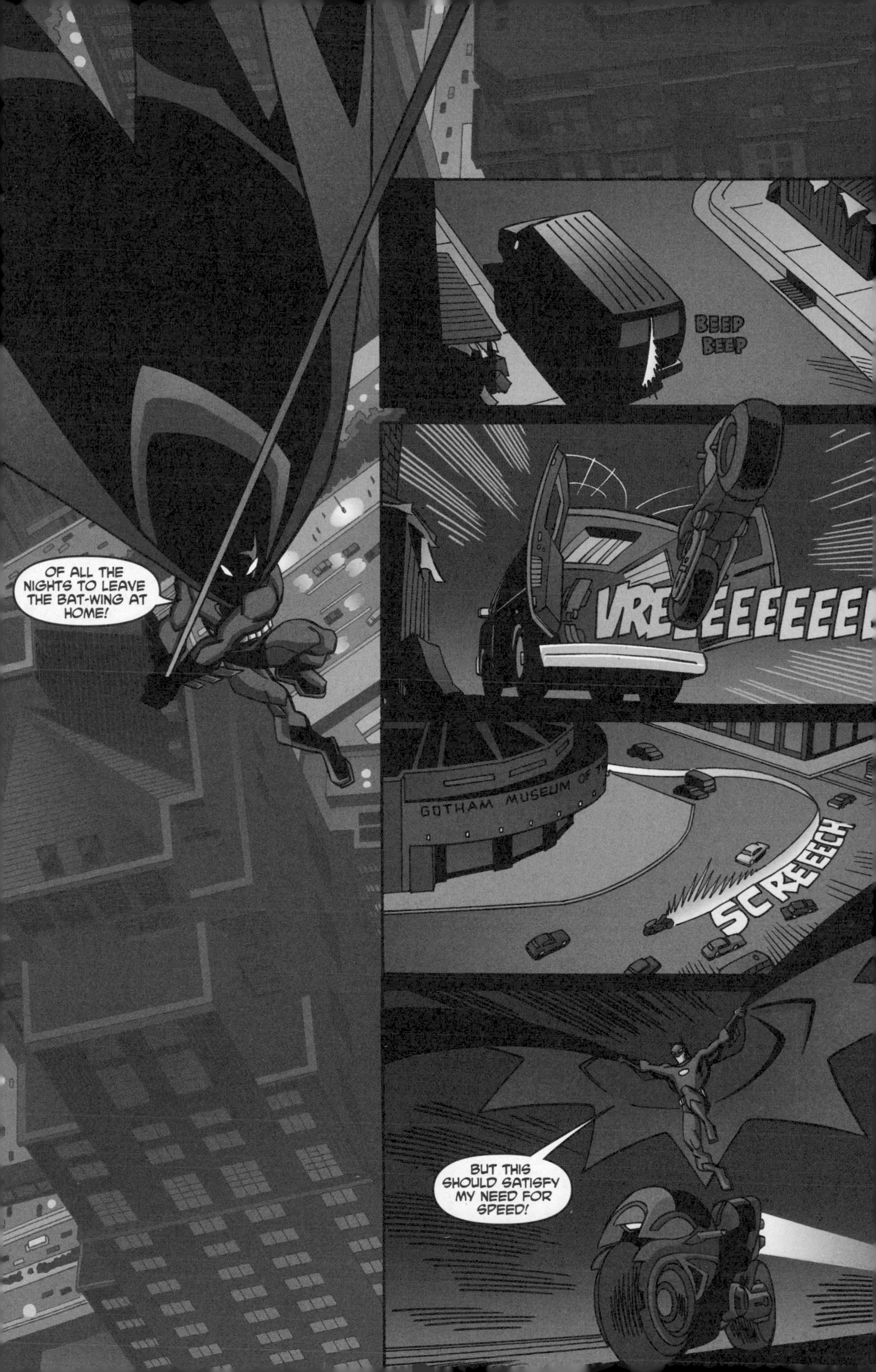

OF ALL THE NIGHTS TO LEAVE THE BAT-WING AT HOME!
BEEP BEEP
VREEEEEEEEE
GOTHAM MUSEUM OF
SCREEECH
BUT THIS SHOULD SATISFY MY NEED FOR SPEED!

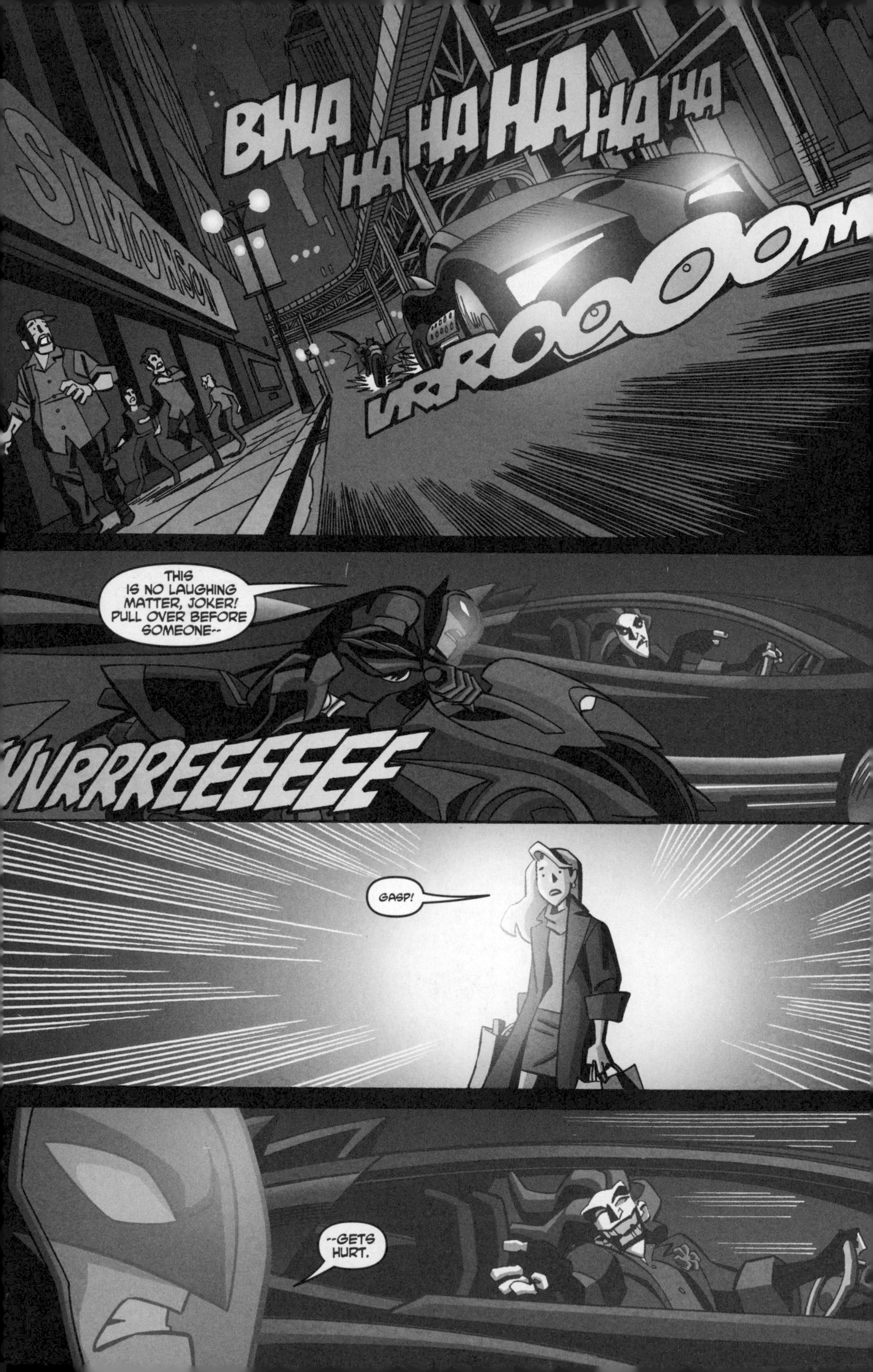
SIMONSON
BWA HA HA HA HA HA HA
VRROOOOOOOM
THIS IS NO LAUGHING MATTER, JOKER! PULL OVER BEFORE SOMEONE--
VVRRREEEEEEE
GASP!
--GETS HURT.

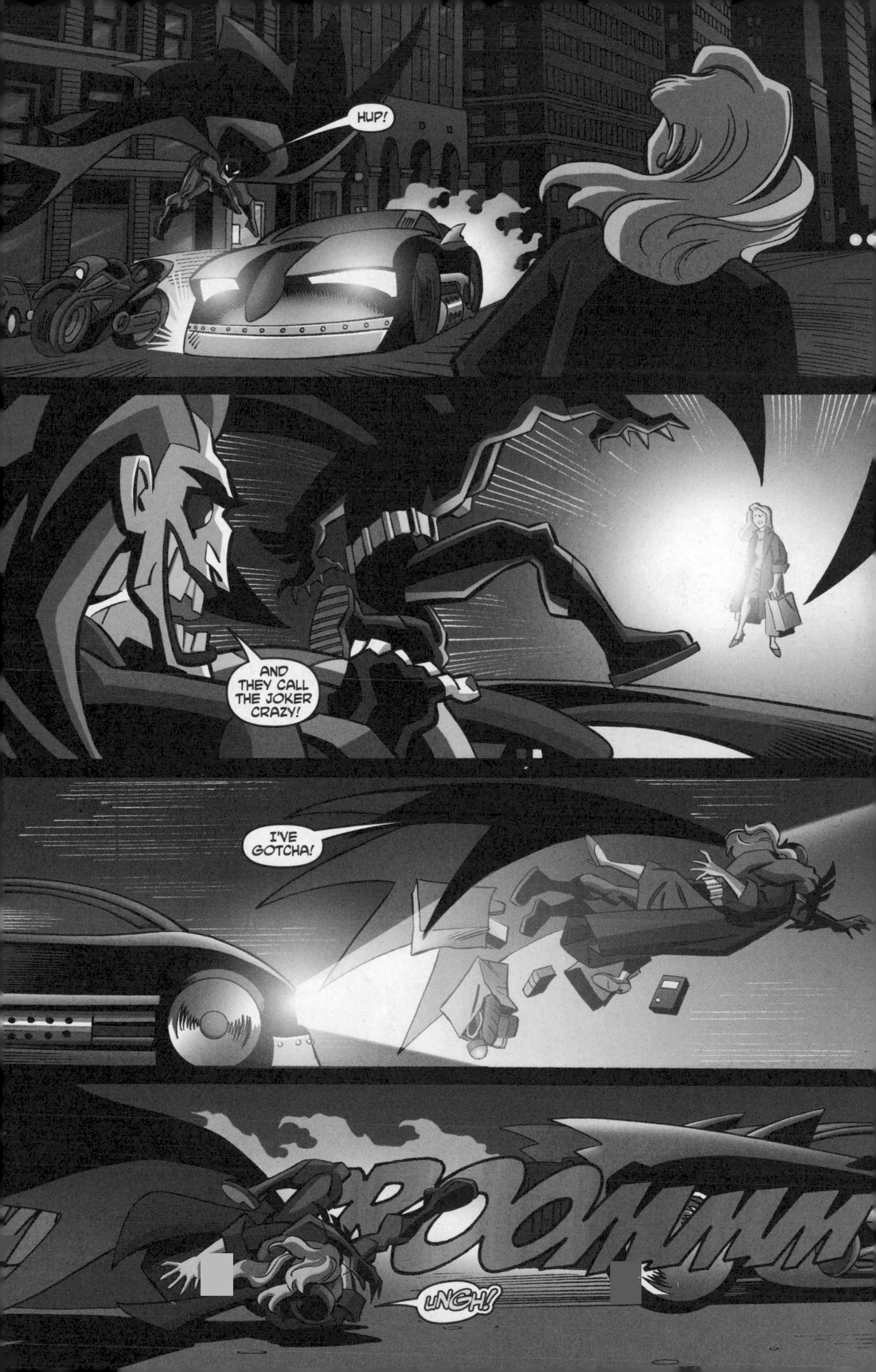
HUP!
AND THEY CALL THE JOKER CRAZY!
I'VE GOTCHA!
UNCH!

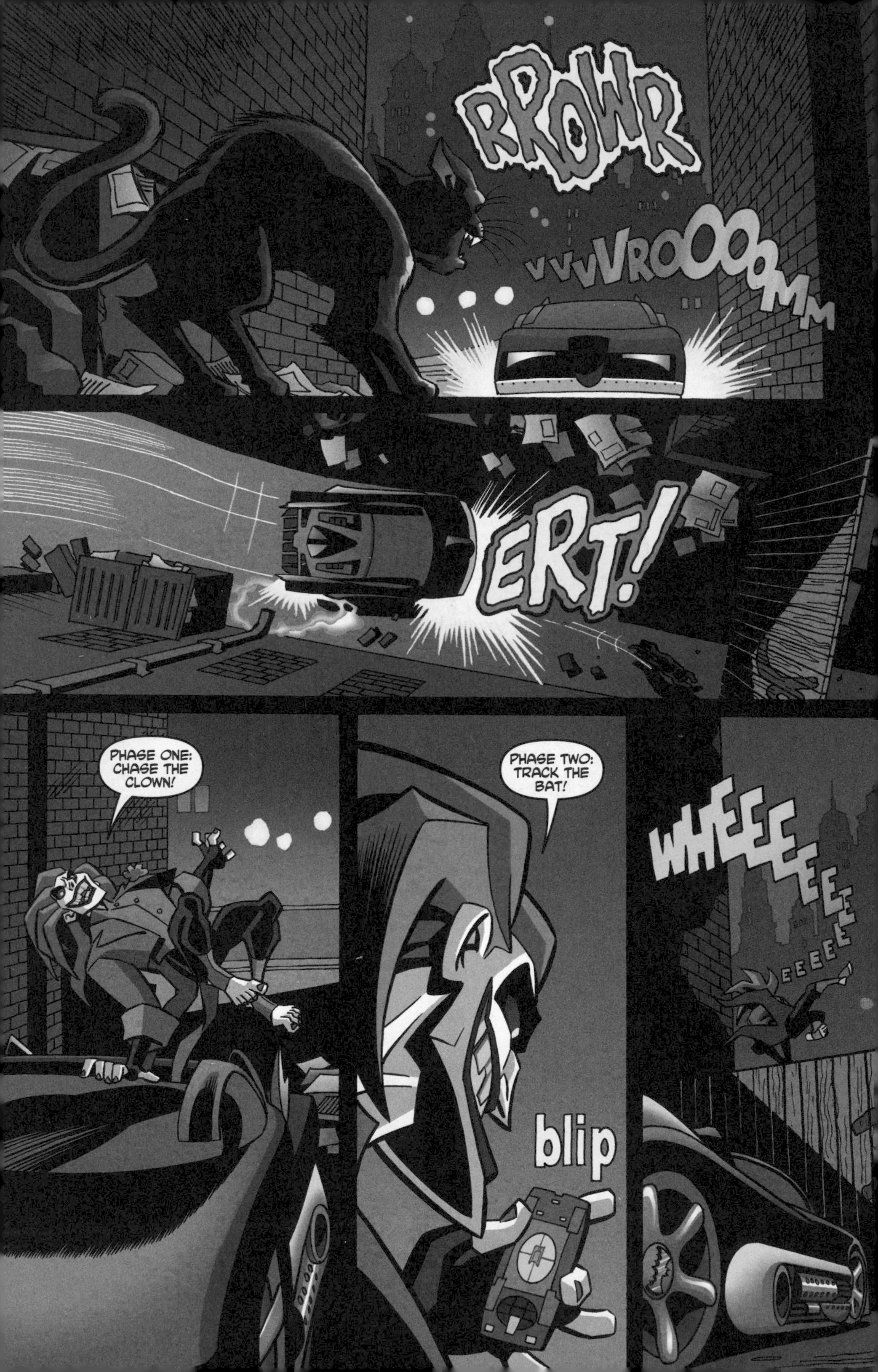
RROWR
VVVVROOOOOMMM
ERT!
PHASE ONE: CHASE THE CLOWN!
PHASE TWO: TRACK THE BAT!
blip
WHEEEEEEEEEEEE

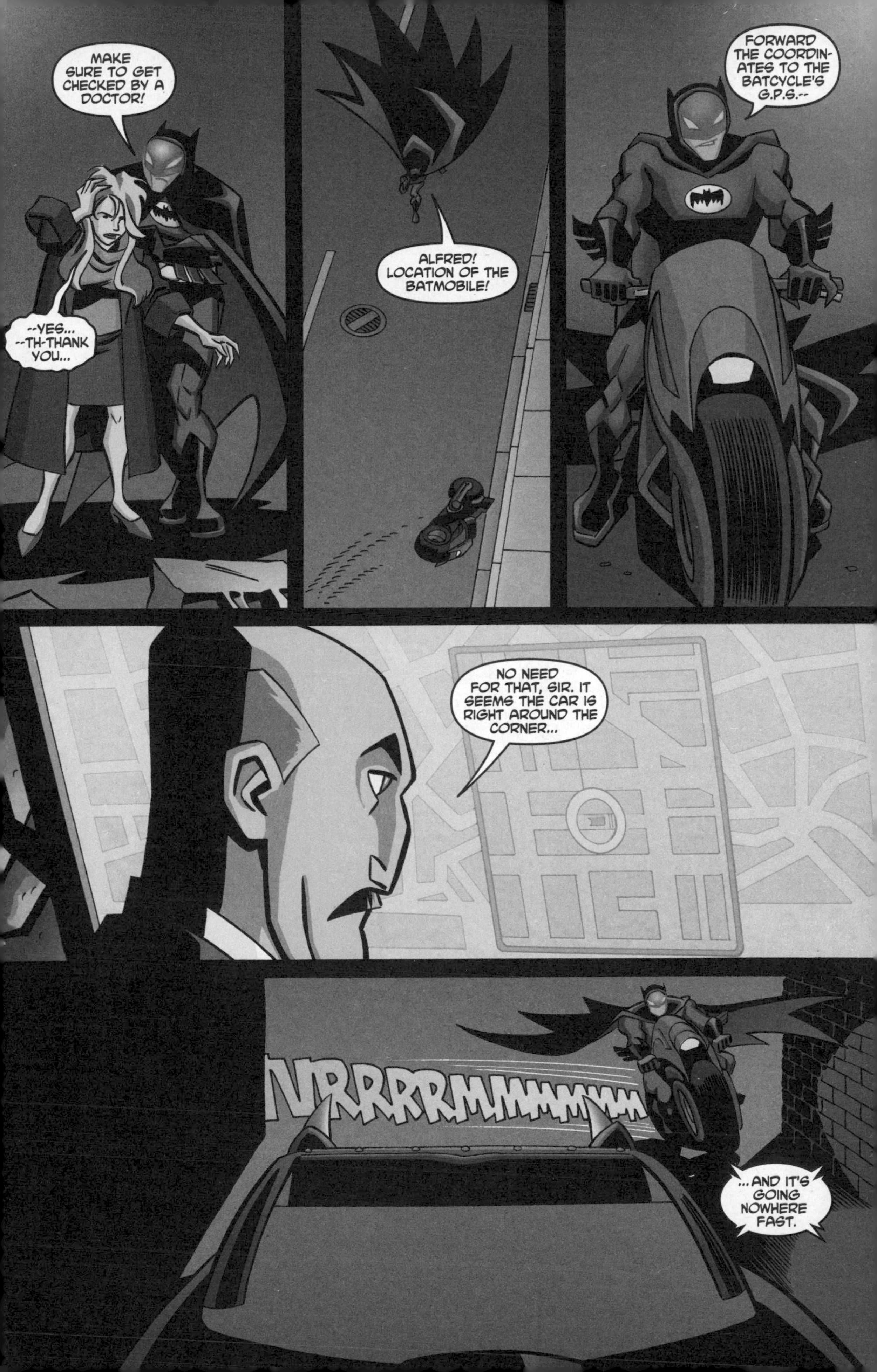
MAKE SURE TO GET CHECKED BY A DOCTOR!
--YES... --TH-THANK YOU...
ALFRED! LOCATION OF THE BATMOBILE!
FORWARD THE COORDIN-ATES TO THE BATCYCLE'S G.P.S.--
NO NEED FOR THAT, SIR. IT SEEMS THE CAR IS RIGHT AROUND THE CORNER...
NRRRRMMMMMMM
...AND IT'S GOING NOWHERE FAST.

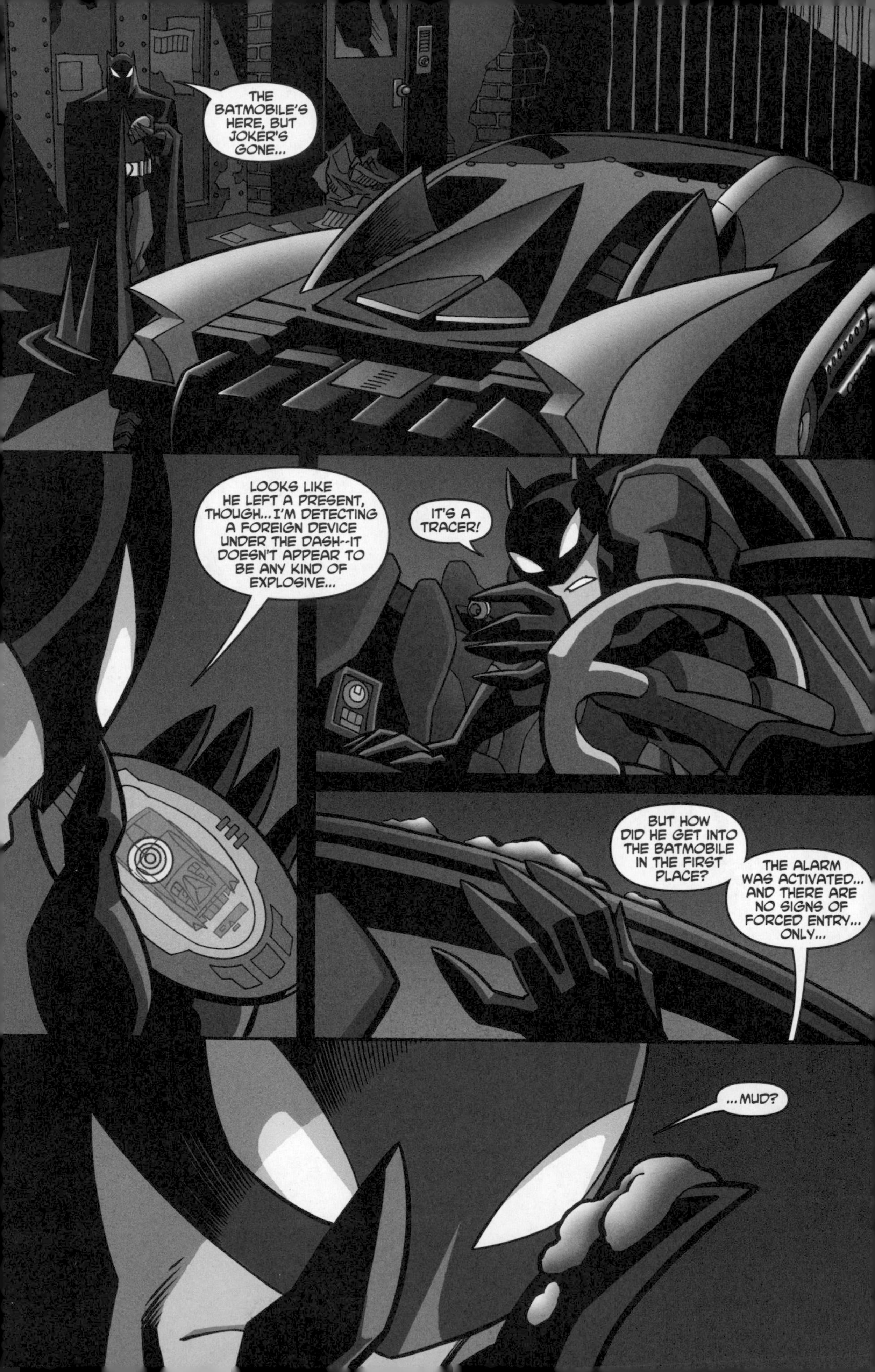
THE BATMOBILE'S HERE, BUT JOKER'S GONE...
LOOKS LIKE HE LEFT A PRESENT, THOUGH... I'M DETECTING A FOREIGN DEVICE UNDER THE DASH--IT DOESN'T APPEAR TO BE ANY KIND OF EXPLOSIVE...
IT'S A TRACER!
BUT HOW DID HE GET INTO THE BATMOBILE IN THE FIRST PLACE?
THE ALARM WAS ACTIVATED... AND THERE ARE NO SIGNS OF FORCED ENTRY... ONLY...
...MUD?

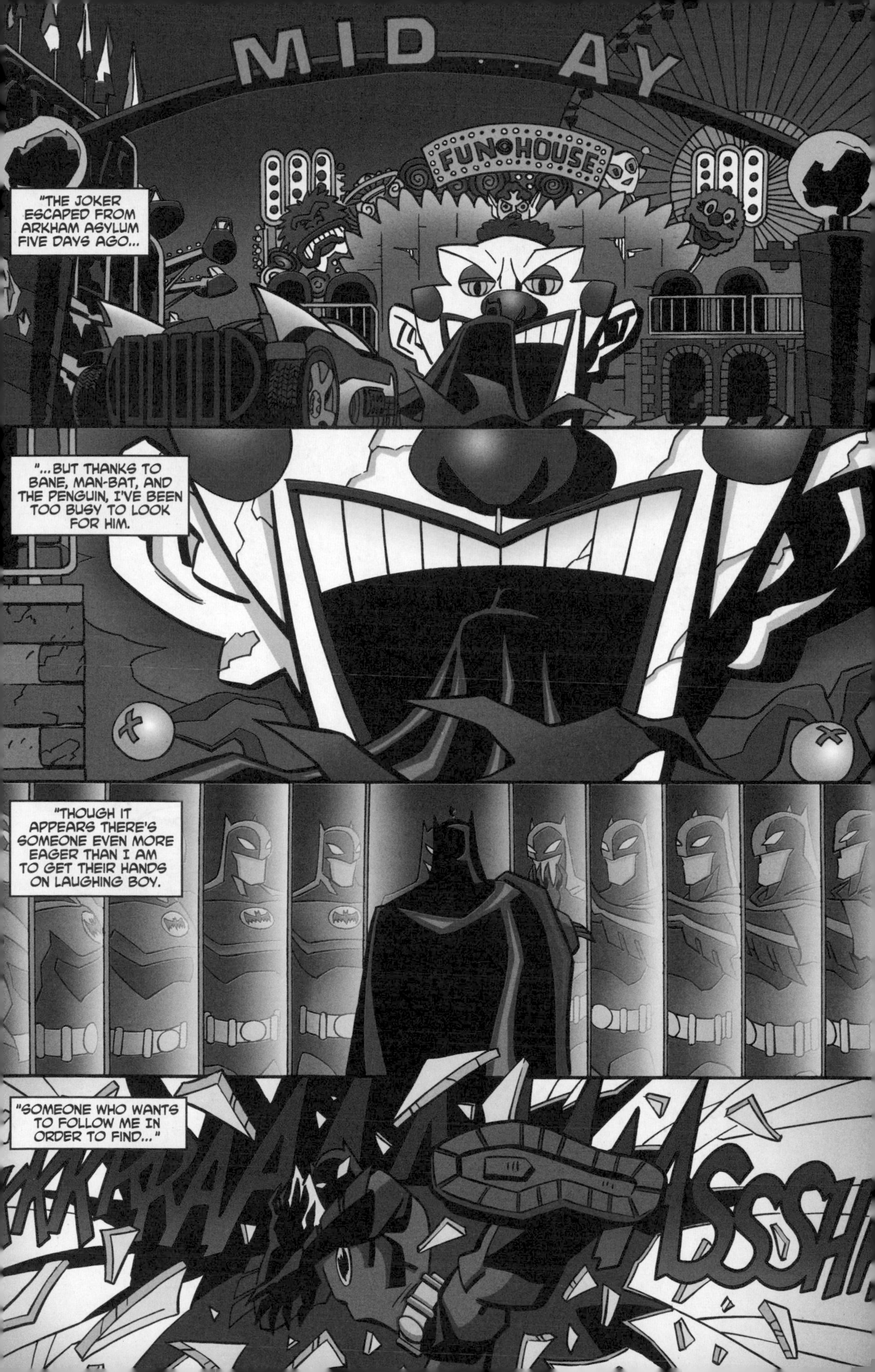
MID AY
FUN HOUSE
"THE JOKER ESCAPED FROM ARKHAM ASYLUM FIVE DAYS AGO...
"...BUT THANKS TO BANE, MAN-BAT, AND THE PENGUIN, I'VE BEEN TOO BUSY TO LOOK FOR HIM.
"THOUGH IT APPEARS THERE'S SOMEONE EVEN MORE EAGER THAN I AM TO GET THEIR HANDS ON LAUGHING BOY.
"SOMEONE WHO WANTS TO FOLLOW ME IN ORDER TO FIND..."

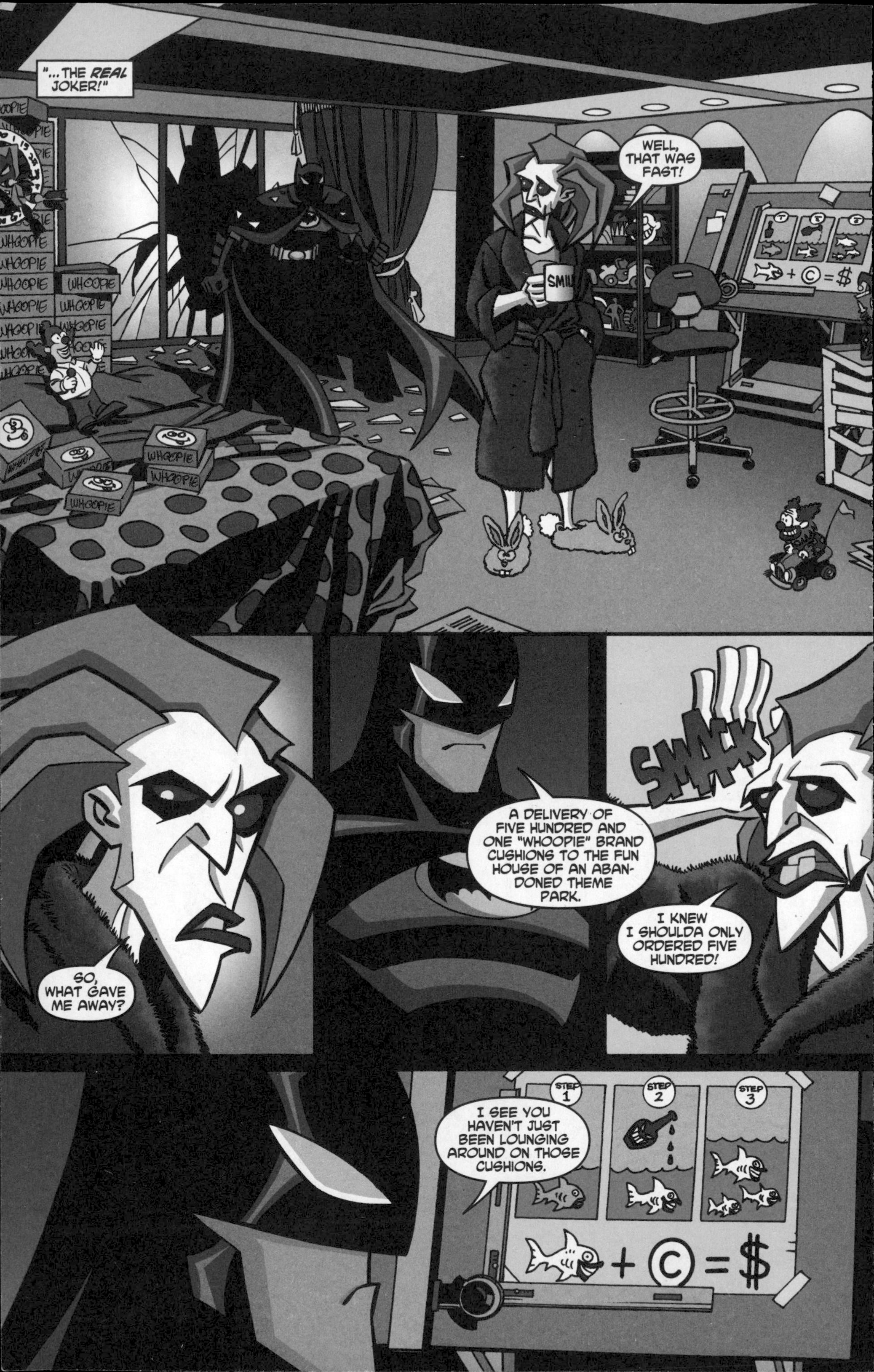
"...THE *REAL* JOKER!"
WELL, THAT WAS FAST!
SO, WHAT GAVE ME AWAY?
A DELIVERY OF FIVE HUNDRED AND ONE "WHOOPIE" BRAND CUSHIONS TO THE FUN HOUSE OF AN ABANDONED THEME PARK.
SMACK
I KNEW I SHOULDA ONLY ORDERED FIVE HUNDRED!
I SEE YOU HAVEN'T JUST BEEN LOUNGING AROUND ON THOSE CUSHIONS.
STEP 1
STEP 2
STEP 3
+ © = $

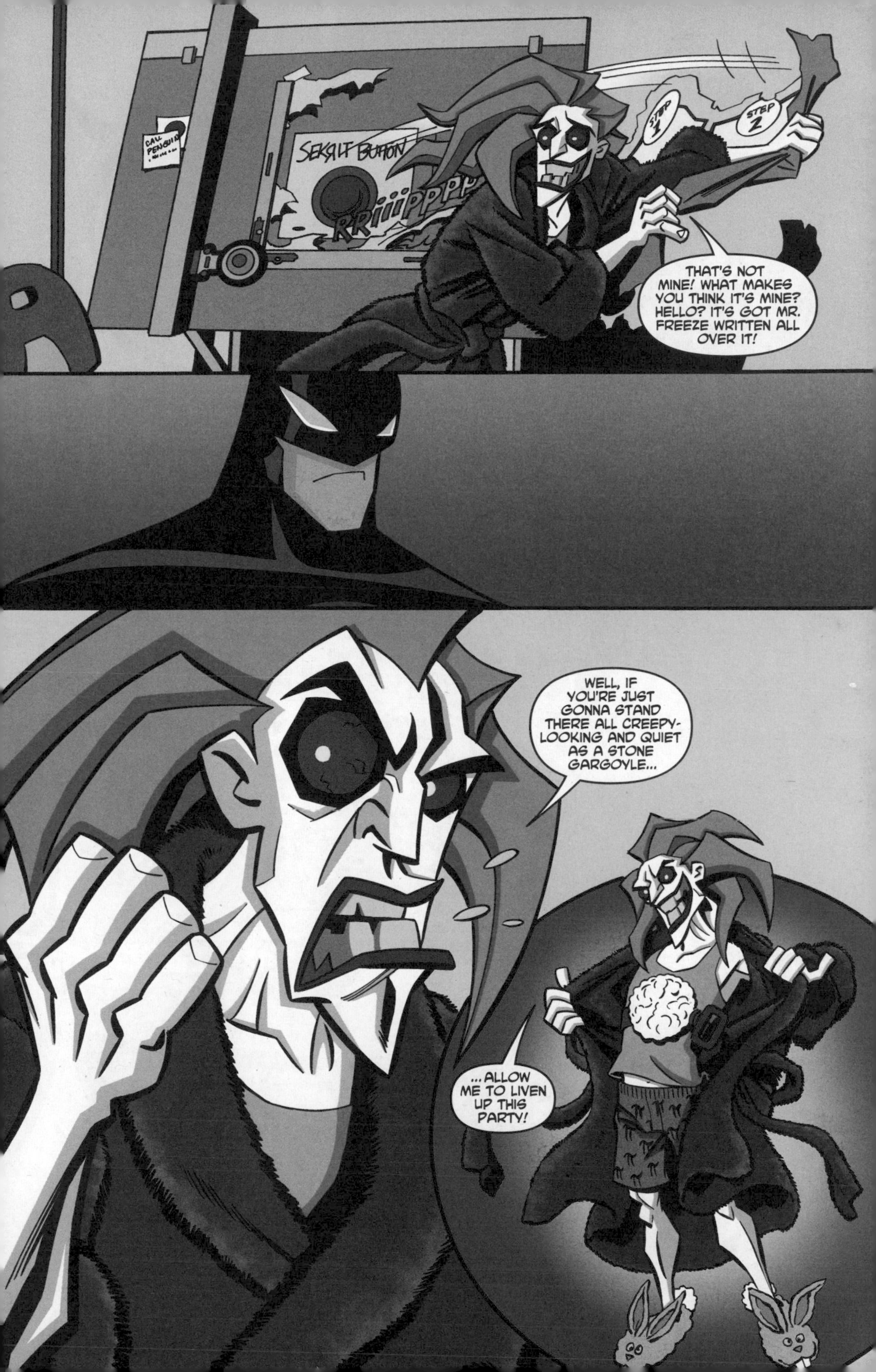
SEKRIT BUTTON
CALL PENGUIN
STEP 1
STEP 2
RRIIIPPPP
THAT'S NOT MINE! WHAT MAKES YOU THINK IT'S MINE? HELLO? IT'S GOT MR. FREEZE WRITTEN ALL OVER IT!
WELL, IF YOU'RE JUST GONNA STAND THERE ALL CREEPY-LOOKING AND QUIET AS A STONE GARGOYLE...
...ALLOW ME TO LIVEN UP THIS PARTY!

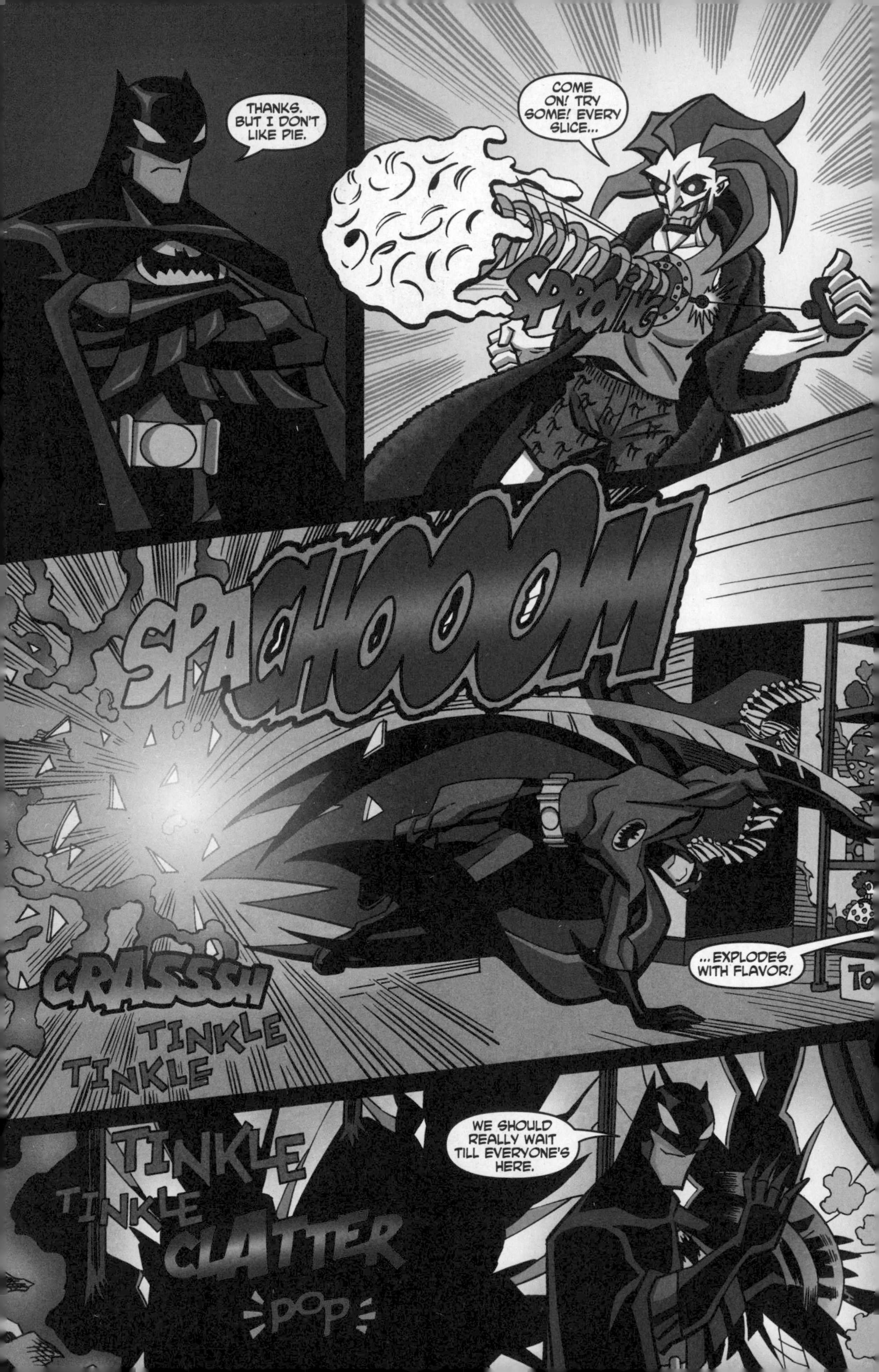
THANKS. BUT I DON'T LIKE PIE.
COME ON! TRY SOME! EVERY SLICE...
SPROING
SPACHOOOM
...EXPLODES WITH FLAVOR!
CRASSSH
TINKLE TINKLE
TINKLE TINKLE CLATTER
POP
WE SHOULD REALLY WAIT TILL EVERYONE'S HERE.

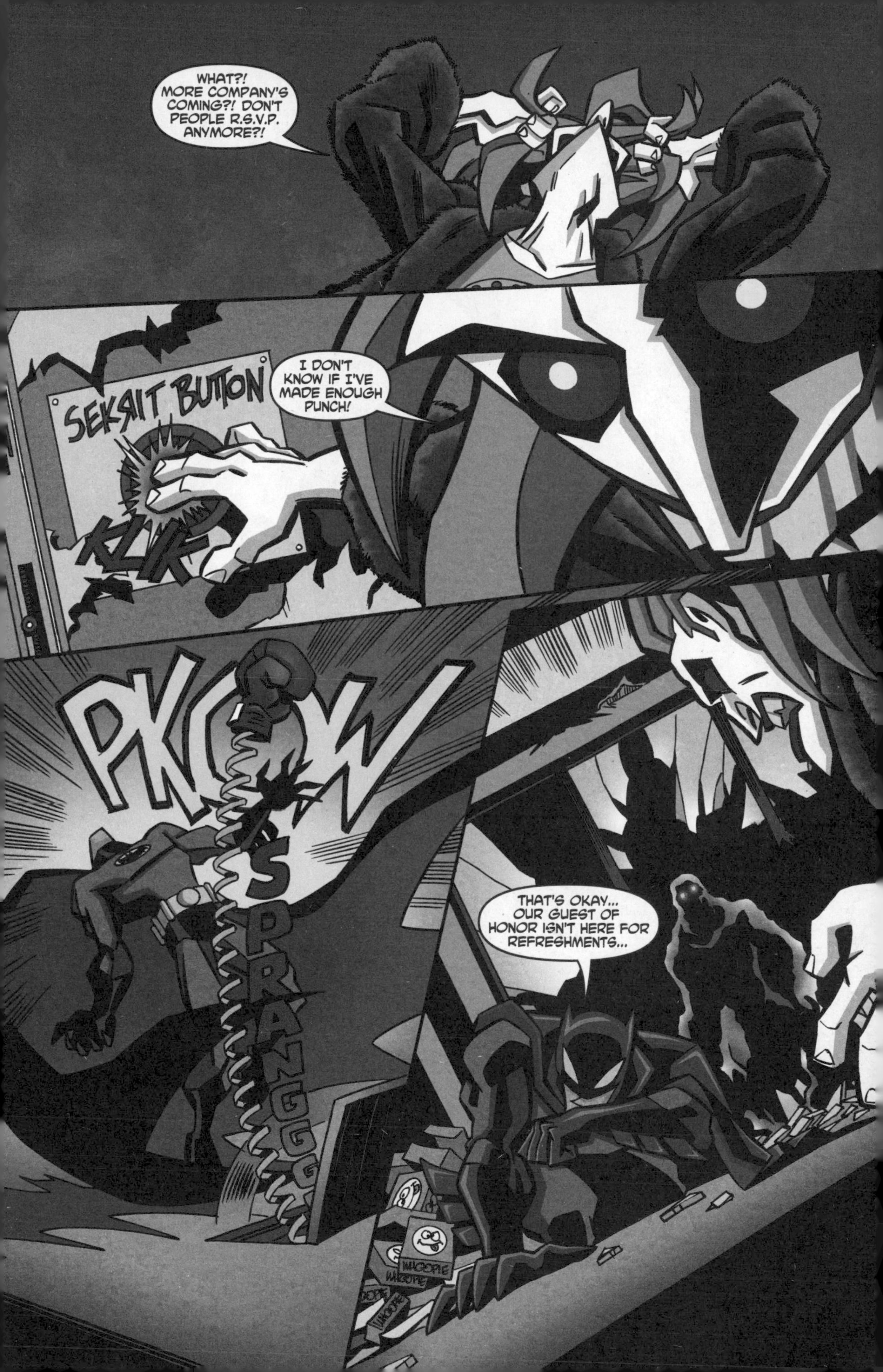
WHAT?! MORE COMPANY'S COMING?! DON'T PEOPLE R.S.V.P. ANYMORE?!
SEKRIT BUTTON
I DON'T KNOW IF I'VE MADE ENOUGH PUNCH!
KLIK
PKOW
SPRANGGG
THAT'S OKAY... OUR GUEST OF HONOR ISN'T HERE FOR REFRESHMENTS...

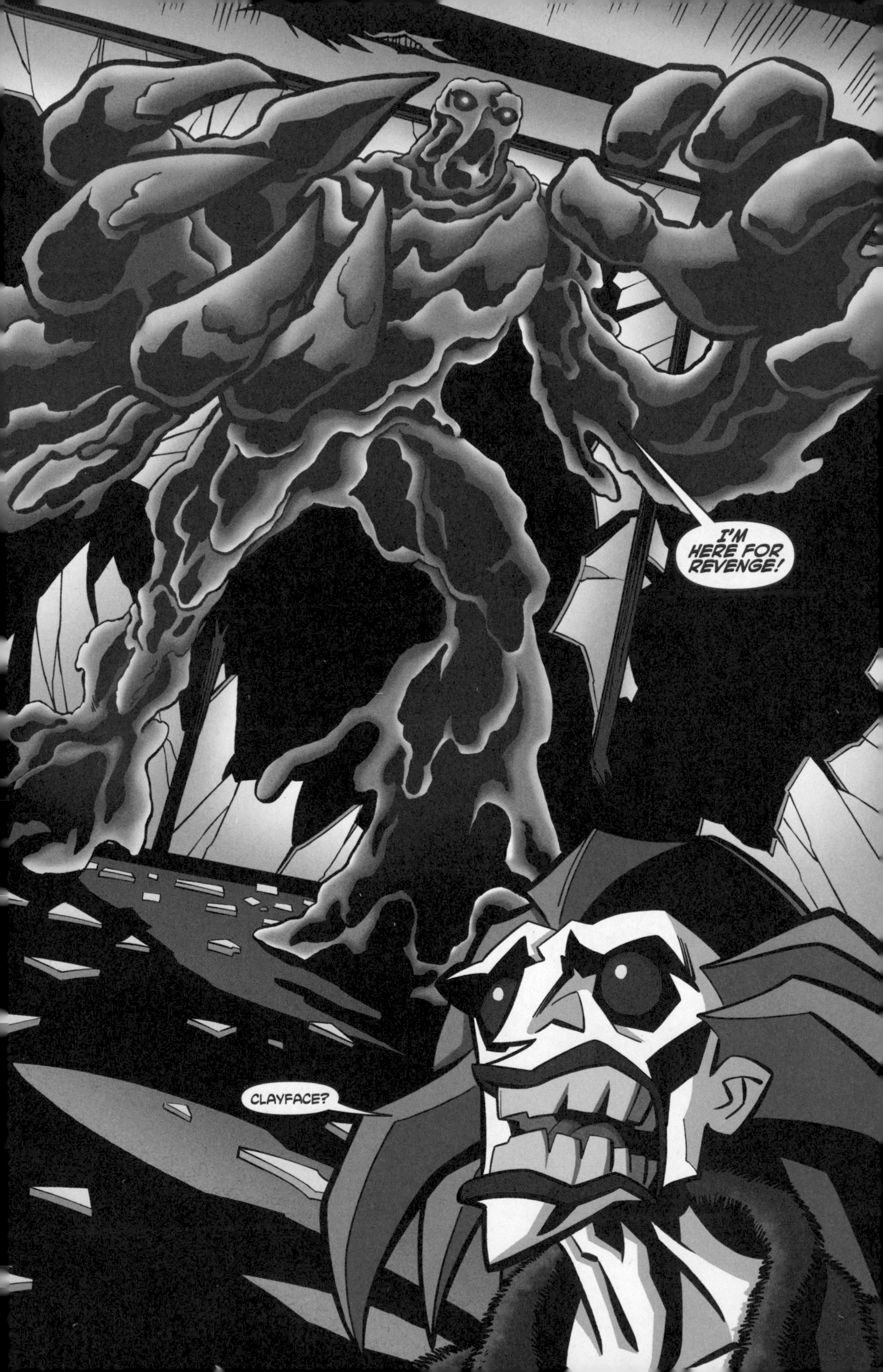
I'M HERE FOR REVENGE!
CLAYFACE?

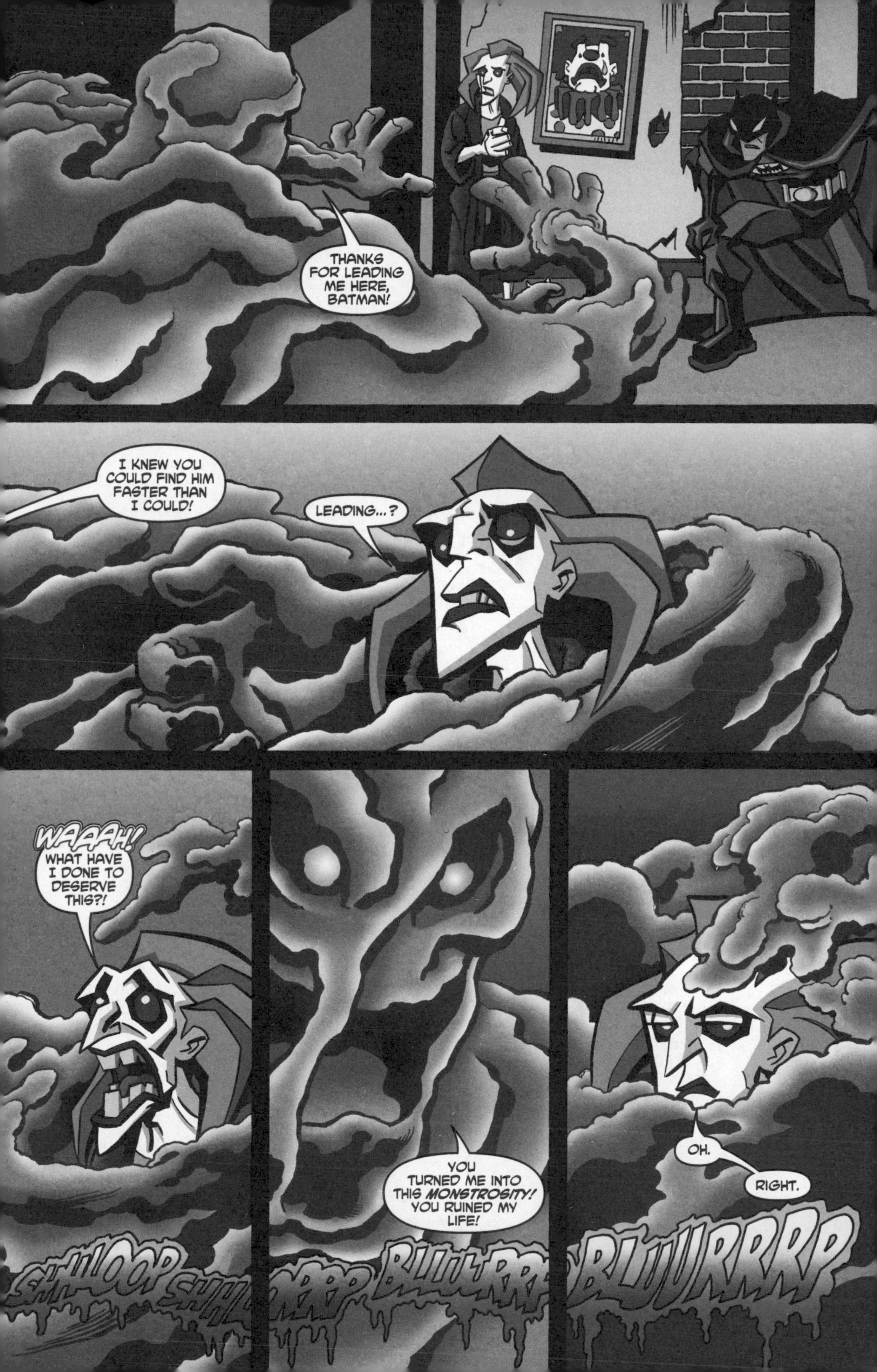
THANKS FOR LEADING ME HERE, BATMAN!
I KNEW YOU COULD FIND HIM FASTER THAN I COULD!
LEADING...?
WAAAH!
WHAT HAVE I DONE TO DESERVE THIS?!
YOU TURNED ME INTO THIS MONSTROSITY! YOU RUINED MY LIFE!
OH.
RIGHT.
SHLOOP SHLURRP BLUURRP BLUURRRP

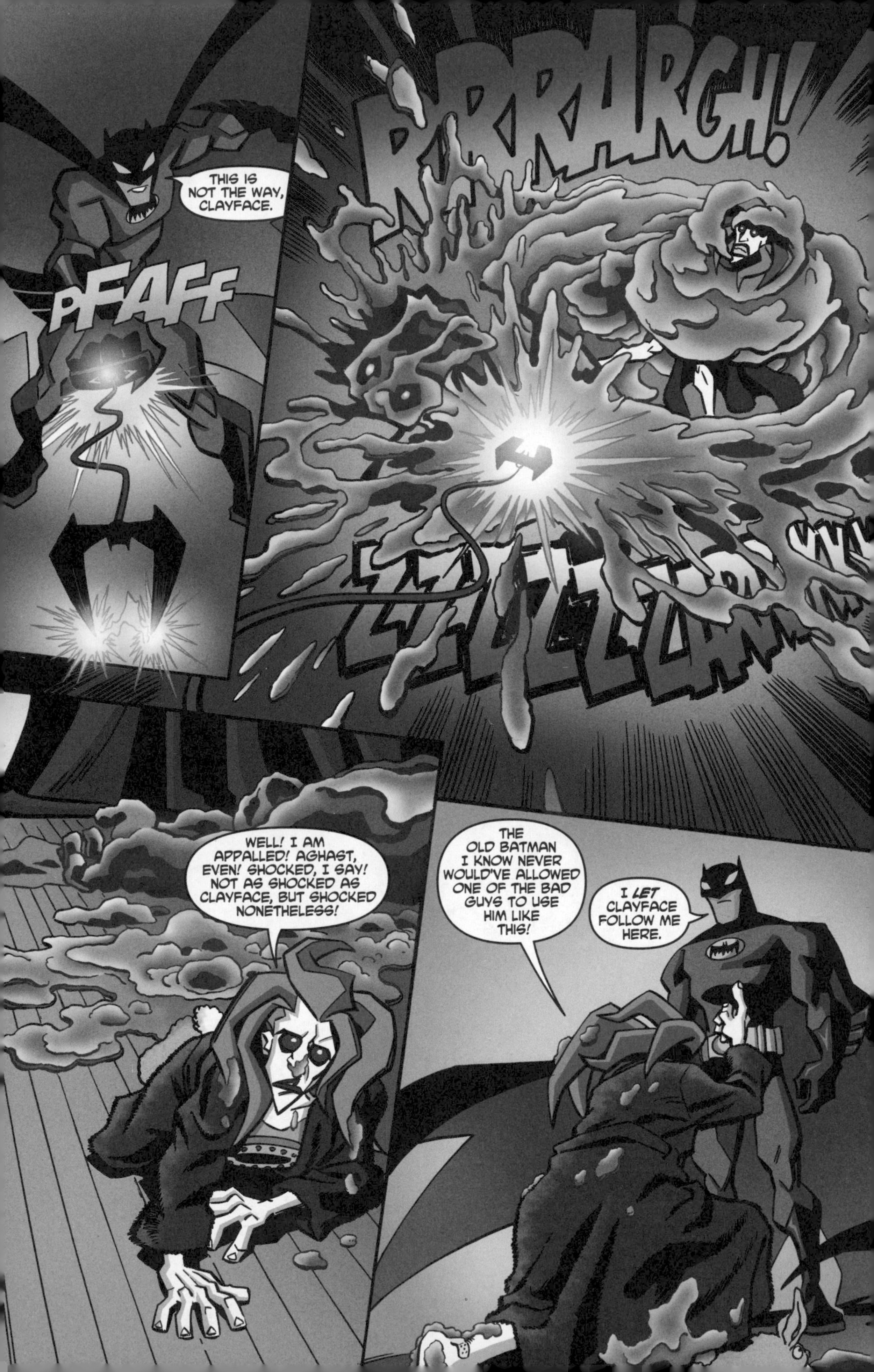
THIS IS NOT THE WAY, CLAYFACE.
PFAFF
RRRRARGH!
ZZZZZZAMMM
WELL! I AM APPALLED! AGHAST, EVEN! SHOCKED, I SAY! NOT AS SHOCKED AS CLAYFACE, BUT SHOCKED NONETHELESS!
THE OLD BATMAN I KNOW NEVER WOULD'VE ALLOWED ONE OF THE BAD GUYS TO USE HIM LIKE THIS!
I LET CLAYFACE FOLLOW ME HERE.

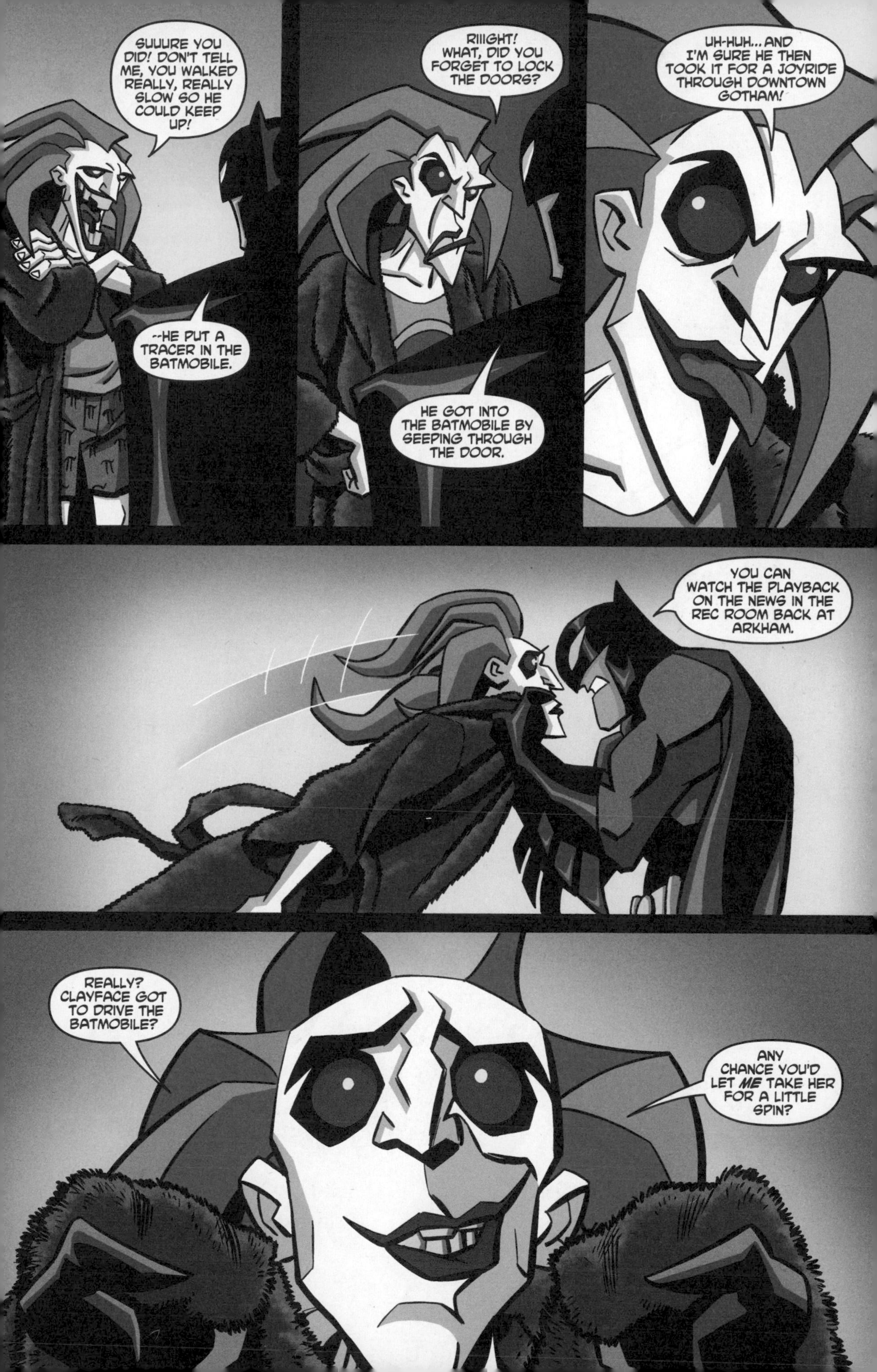
SUUURE YOU DID! DON'T TELL ME, YOU WALKED REALLY, REALLY SLOW SO HE COULD KEEP UP!
--HE PUT A TRACER IN THE BATMOBILE.
RIIIGHT! WHAT, DID YOU FORGET TO LOCK THE DOORS?
HE GOT INTO THE BATMOBILE BY SEEPING THROUGH THE DOOR.
UH-HUH... AND I'M SURE HE THEN TOOK IT FOR A JOYRIDE THROUGH DOWNTOWN GOTHAM!
YOU CAN WATCH THE PLAYBACK ON THE NEWS IN THE REC ROOM BACK AT ARKHAM.
REALLY? CLAYFACE GOT TO DRIVE THE BATMOBILE?
ANY CHANCE YOU'D LET *ME* TAKE HER FOR A LITTLE SPIN?

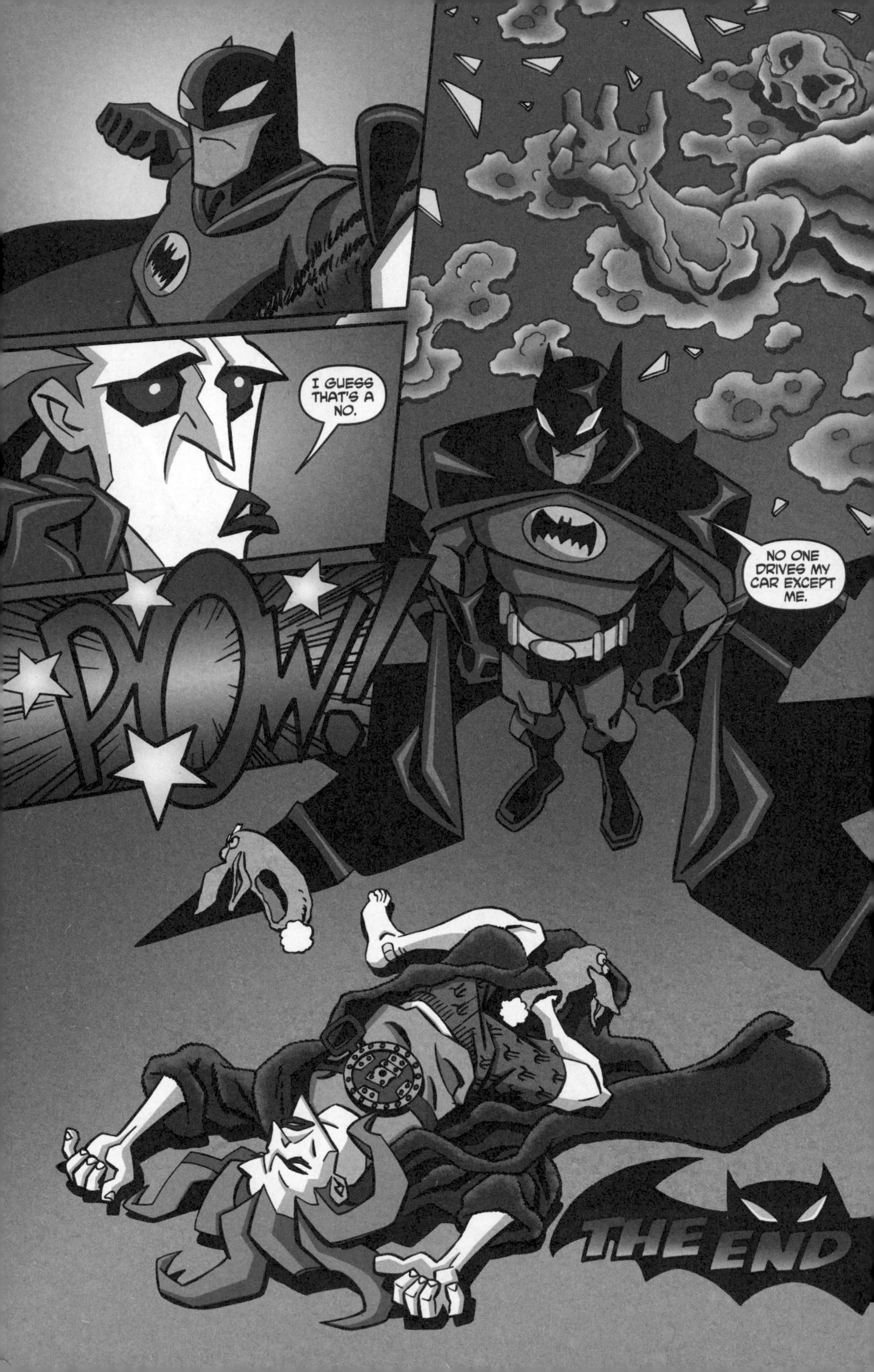
I GUESS THAT'S A NO.
POW!
NO ONE DRIVES MY CAR EXCEPT ME.
THE END

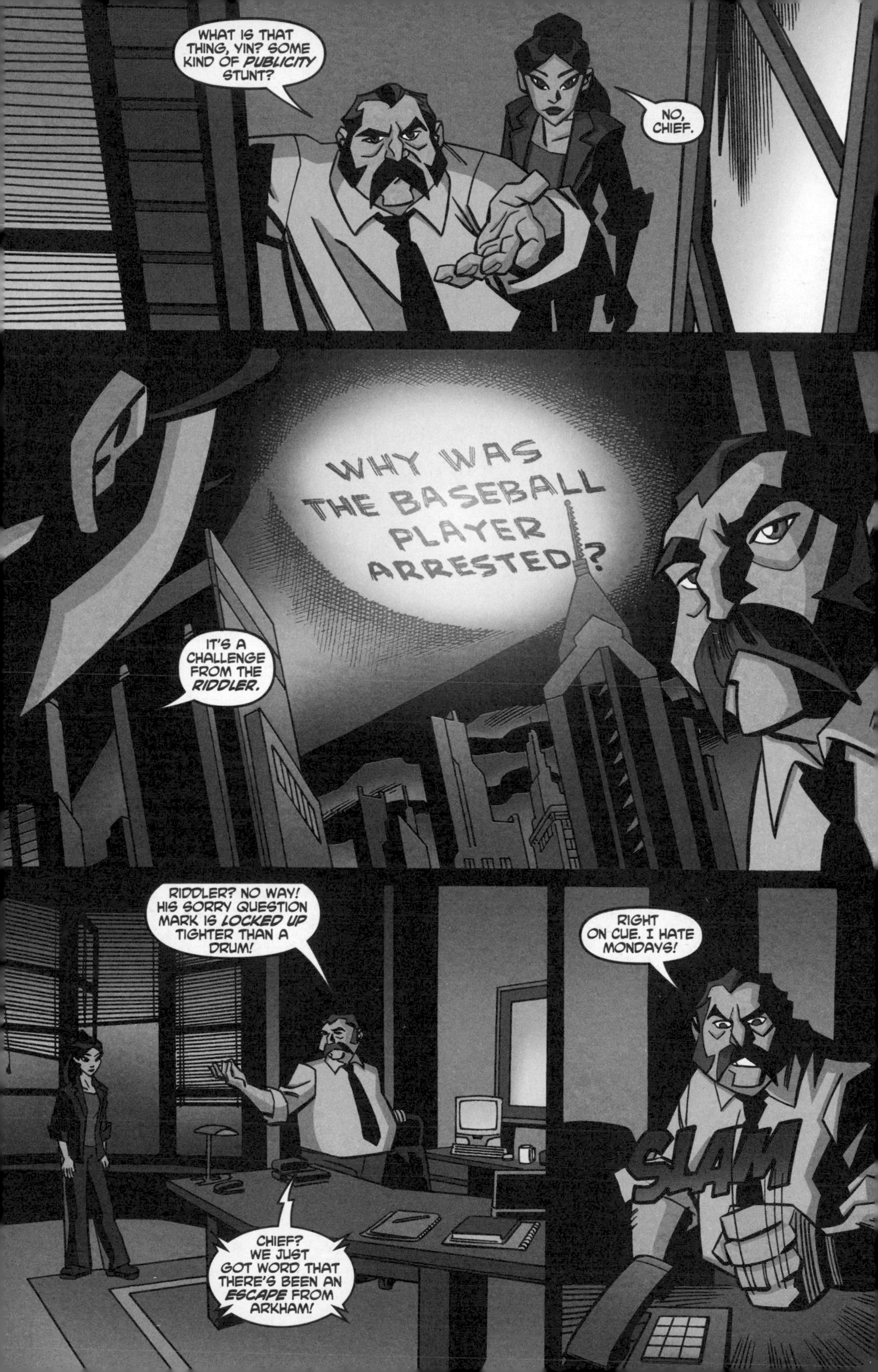
WHAT IS THAT THING, YIN? SOME KIND OF *PUBLICITY* STUNT?
NO, CHIEF.
WHY WAS THE BASEBALL PLAYER ARRESTED?
IT'S A CHALLENGE FROM THE *RIDDLER.*
RIDDLER? NO WAY! HIS SORRY QUESTION MARK IS *LOCKED UP* TIGHTER THAN A DRUM!
CHIEF? WE JUST GOT WORD THAT THERE'S BEEN AN *ESCAPE* FROM ARKHAM!
RIGHT ON CUE. I HATE MONDAYS!
SLAM

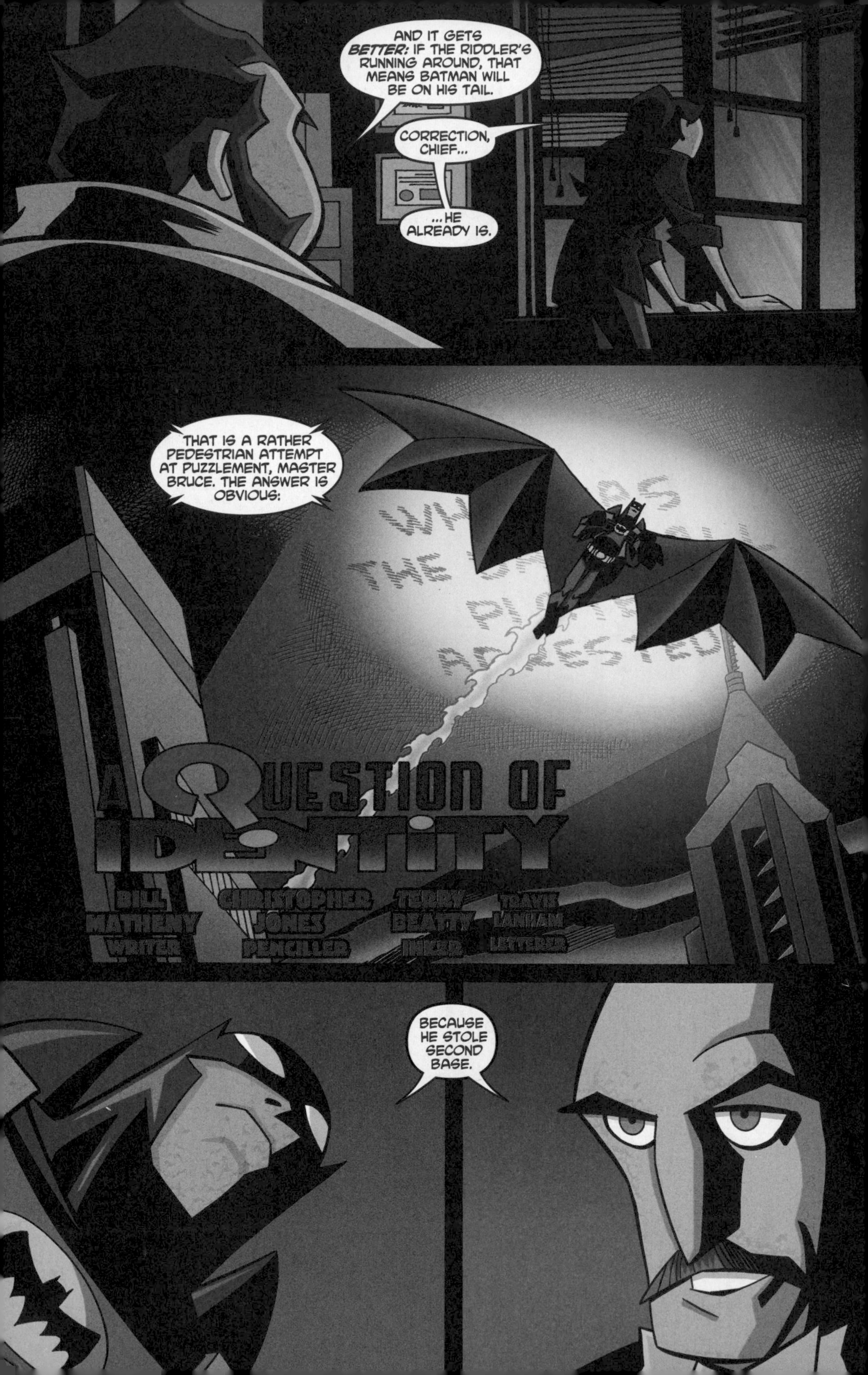
AND IT GETS *BETTER:* IF THE RIDDLER'S RUNNING AROUND, THAT MEANS BATMAN WILL BE ON HIS TAIL.
CORRECTION, CHIEF...
...HE ALREADY IS.
THAT IS A RATHER PEDESTRIAN ATTEMPT AT PUZZLEMENT, MASTER BRUCE. THE ANSWER IS OBVIOUS:
A QUESTION OF IDENTITY
BILL MATHENY WRITER
CHRISTOPHER JONES PENCILLER
TERRY BEATTY INKER
TRAVIS LANHAM LETTERER
BECAUSE HE STOLE SECOND BASE.

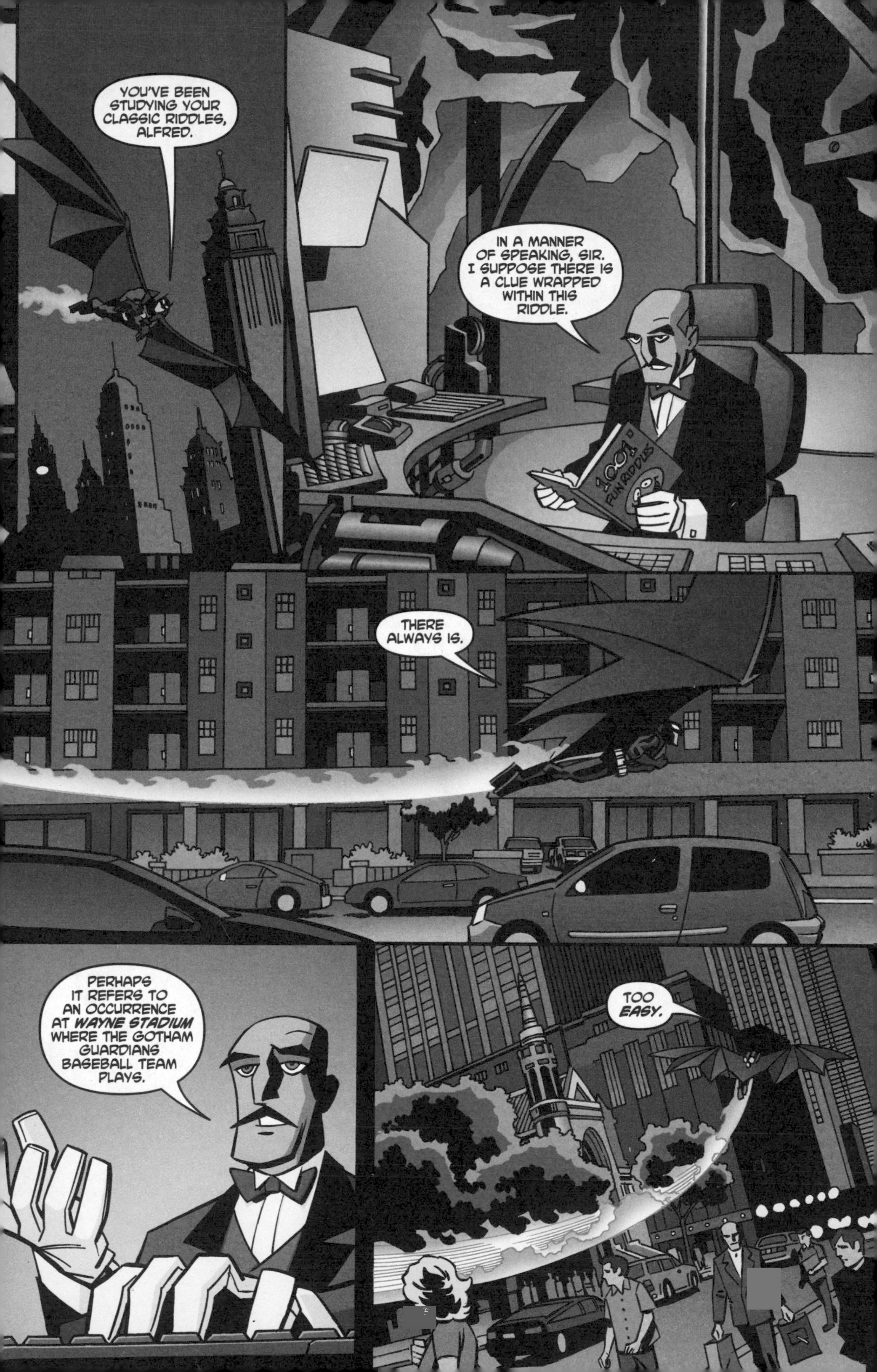
YOU'VE BEEN STUDYING YOUR CLASSIC RIDDLES, ALFRED.
IN A MANNER OF SPEAKING, SIR. I SUPPOSE THERE IS A CLUE WRAPPED WITHIN THIS RIDDLE.
1001 FUN RIDDLES
THERE ALWAYS IS.
PERHAPS IT REFERS TO AN OCCURRENCE AT *WAYNE STADIUM* WHERE THE GOTHAM GUARDIANS BASEBALL TEAM PLAYS.
TOO *EASY.*

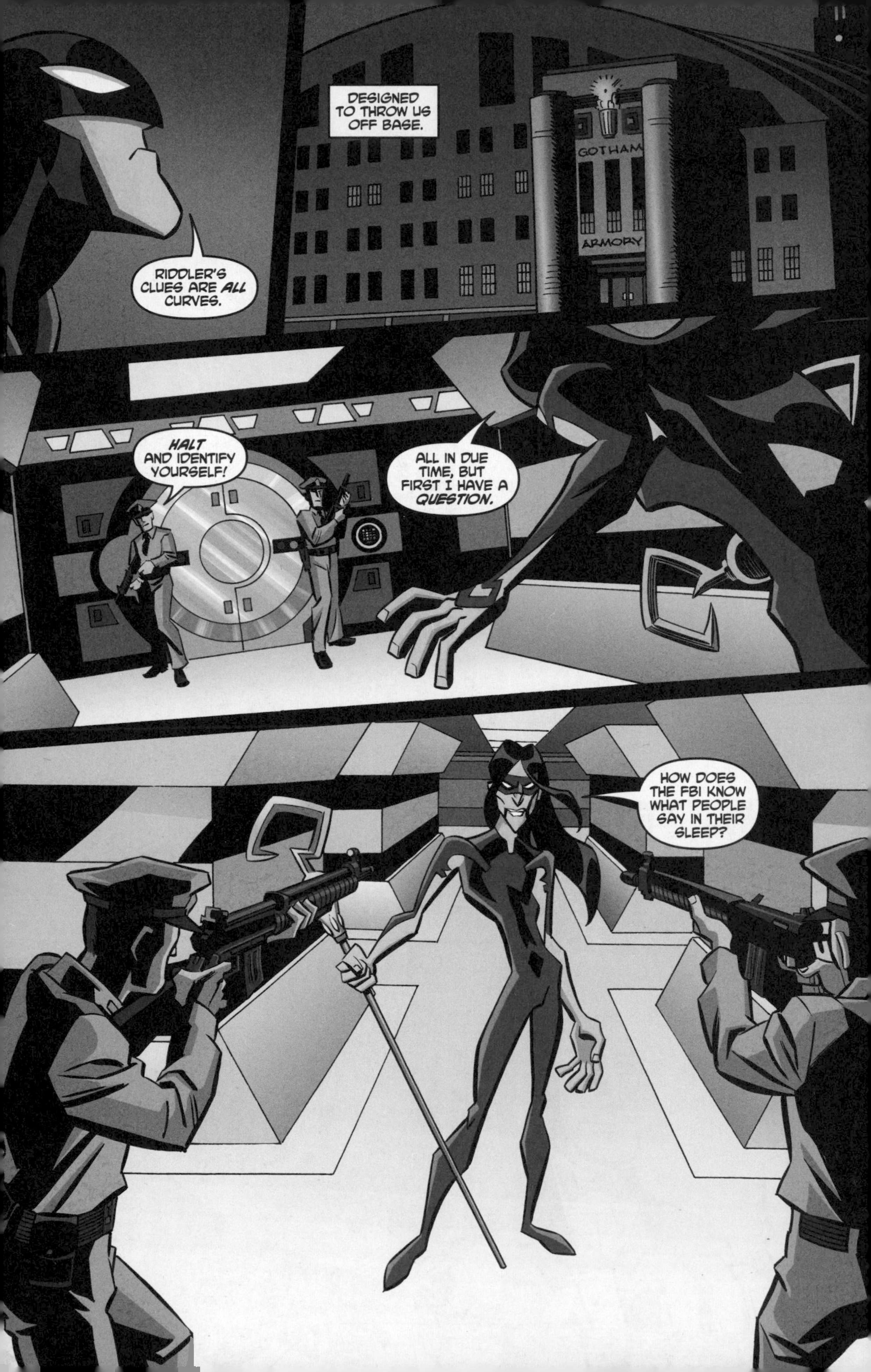
DESIGNED TO THROW US OFF BASE.
RIDDLER'S CLUES ARE *ALL* CURVES.
GOTHAM
ARMORY
HALT AND IDENTIFY YOURSELF!
ALL IN DUE TIME, BUT FIRST I HAVE A *QUESTION*.
HOW DOES THE FBI KNOW WHAT PEOPLE SAY IN THEIR SLEEP?

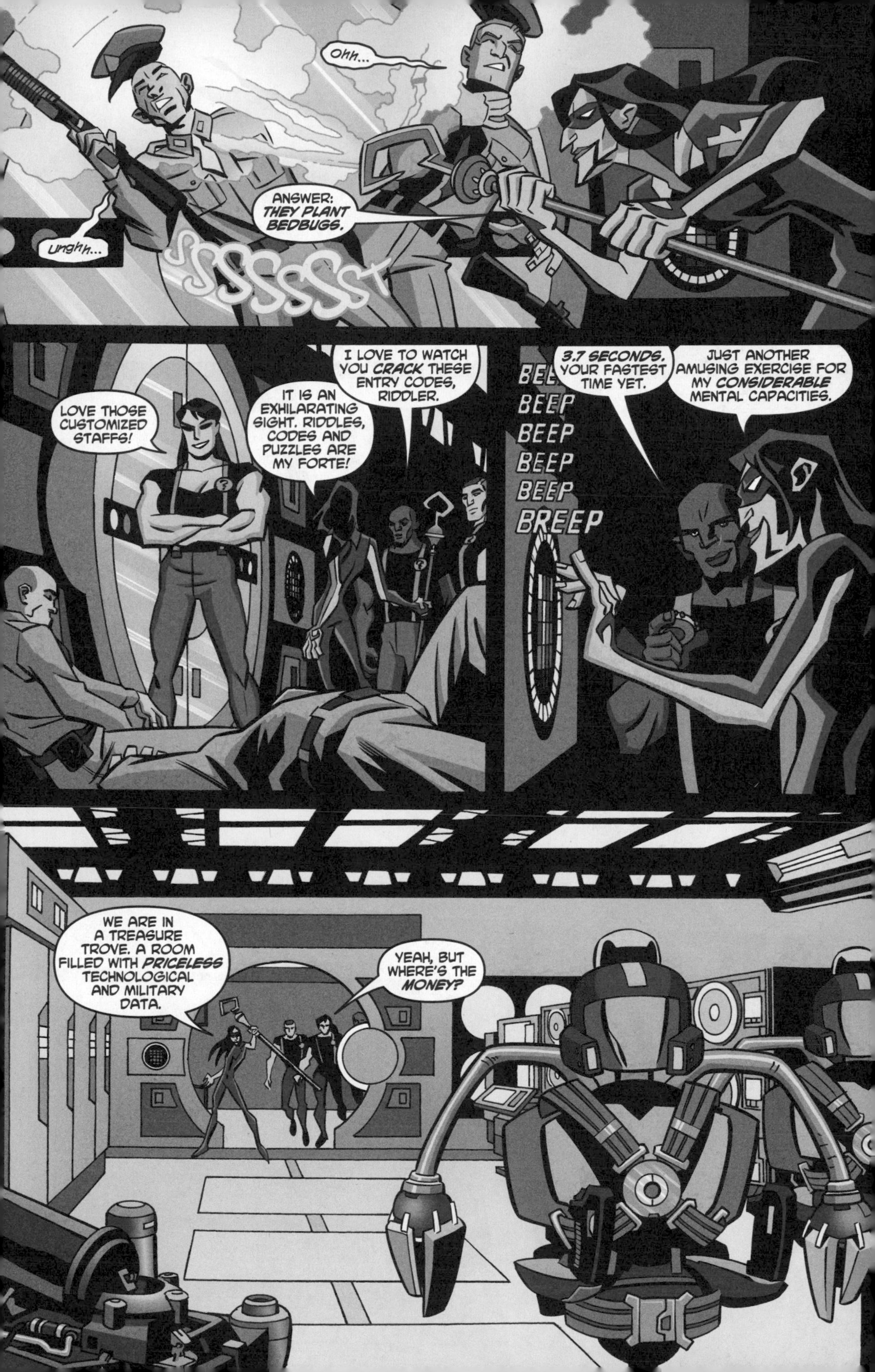
Ohh...
ANSWER: THEY PLANT BEDBUGS.
Unghh...
SSSSSST
LOVE THOSE CUSTOMIZED STAFFS!
IT IS AN EXHILARATING SIGHT. RIDDLES, CODES AND PUZZLES ARE MY FORTE!
I LOVE TO WATCH YOU CRACK THESE ENTRY CODES, RIDDLER.
BEEP
BEEP
BEEP
BEEP
BEEP
BREEP
3.7 SECONDS. YOUR FASTEST TIME YET.
JUST ANOTHER AMUSING EXERCISE FOR MY CONSIDERABLE MENTAL CAPACITIES.
WE ARE IN A TREASURE TROVE. A ROOM FILLED WITH PRICELESS TECHNOLOGICAL AND MILITARY DATA.
YEAH, BUT WHERE'S THE MONEY?

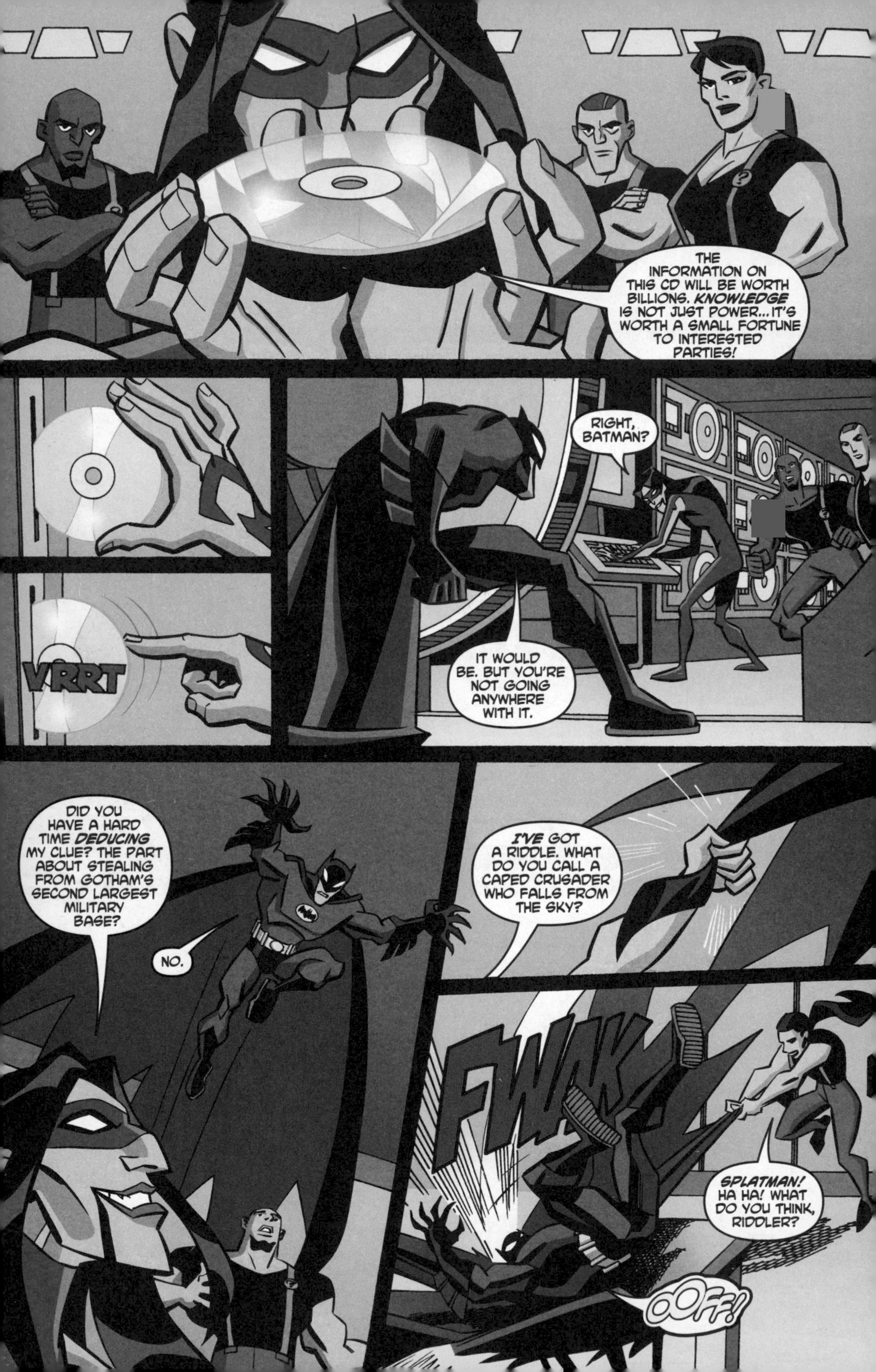
THE INFORMATION ON THIS CD WILL BE WORTH BILLIONS. KNOWLEDGE IS NOT JUST POWER... IT'S WORTH A SMALL FORTUNE TO INTERESTED PARTIES!
VRRT
RIGHT, BATMAN?
IT WOULD BE. BUT YOU'RE NOT GOING ANYWHERE WITH IT.
DID YOU HAVE A HARD TIME DEDUCING MY CLUE? THE PART ABOUT STEALING FROM GOTHAM'S SECOND LARGEST MILITARY BASE?
NO.
I'VE GOT A RIDDLE. WHAT DO YOU CALL A CAPED CRUSADER WHO FALLS FROM THE SKY?
FWAK
SPLATMAN! HA HA! WHAT DO YOU THINK, RIDDLER?
OOFF!

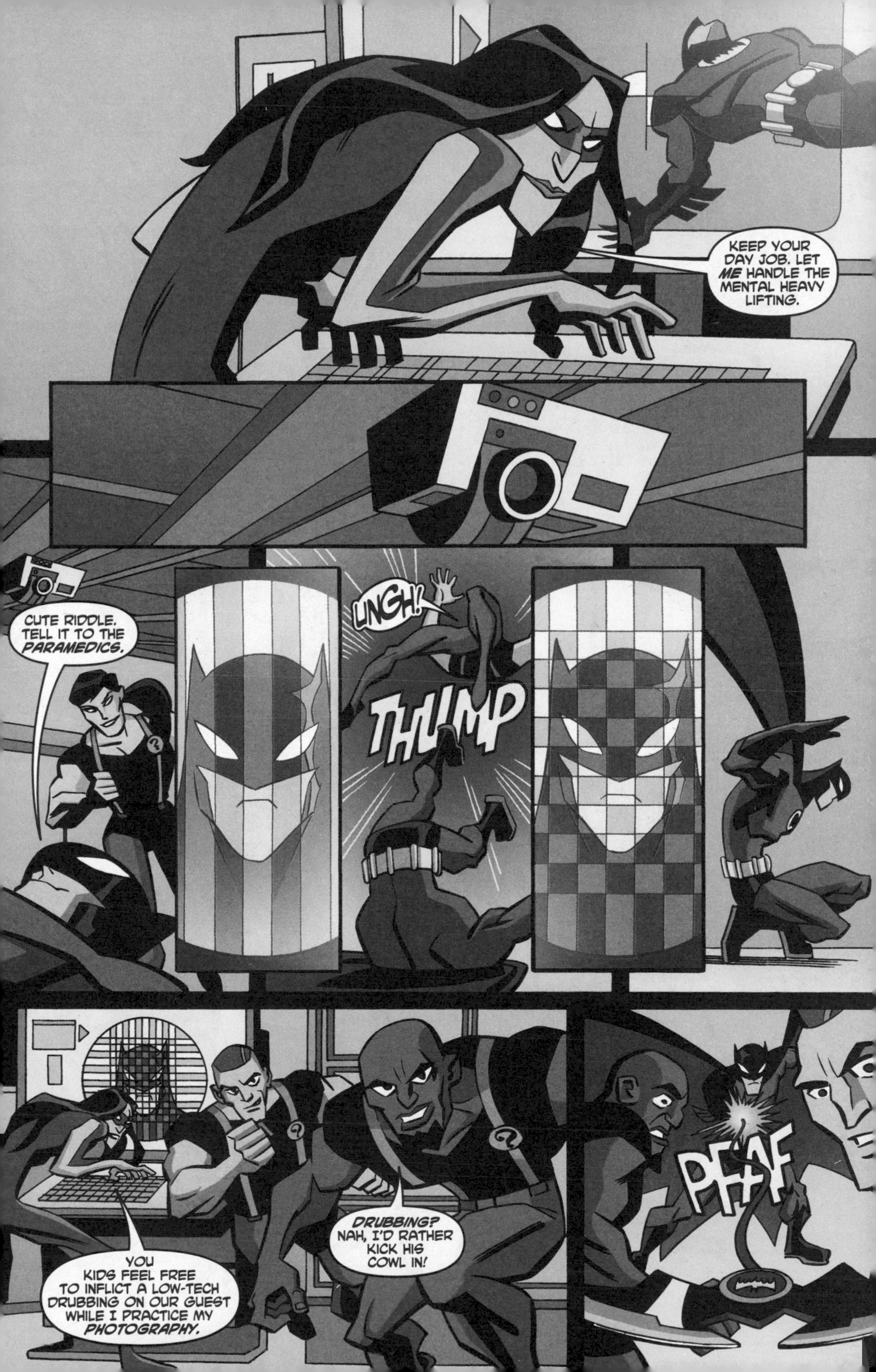
KEEP YOUR DAY JOB. LET ME HANDLE THE MENTAL HEAVY LIFTING.
CUTE RIDDLE. TELL IT TO THE PARAMEDICS.
UNGH!
THUMP
YOU KIDS FEEL FREE TO INFLICT A LOW-TECH DRUBBING ON OUR GUEST WHILE I PRACTICE MY PHOTOGRAPHY.
DRUBBING? NAH, I'D RATHER KICK HIS COWL IN!
PFAF

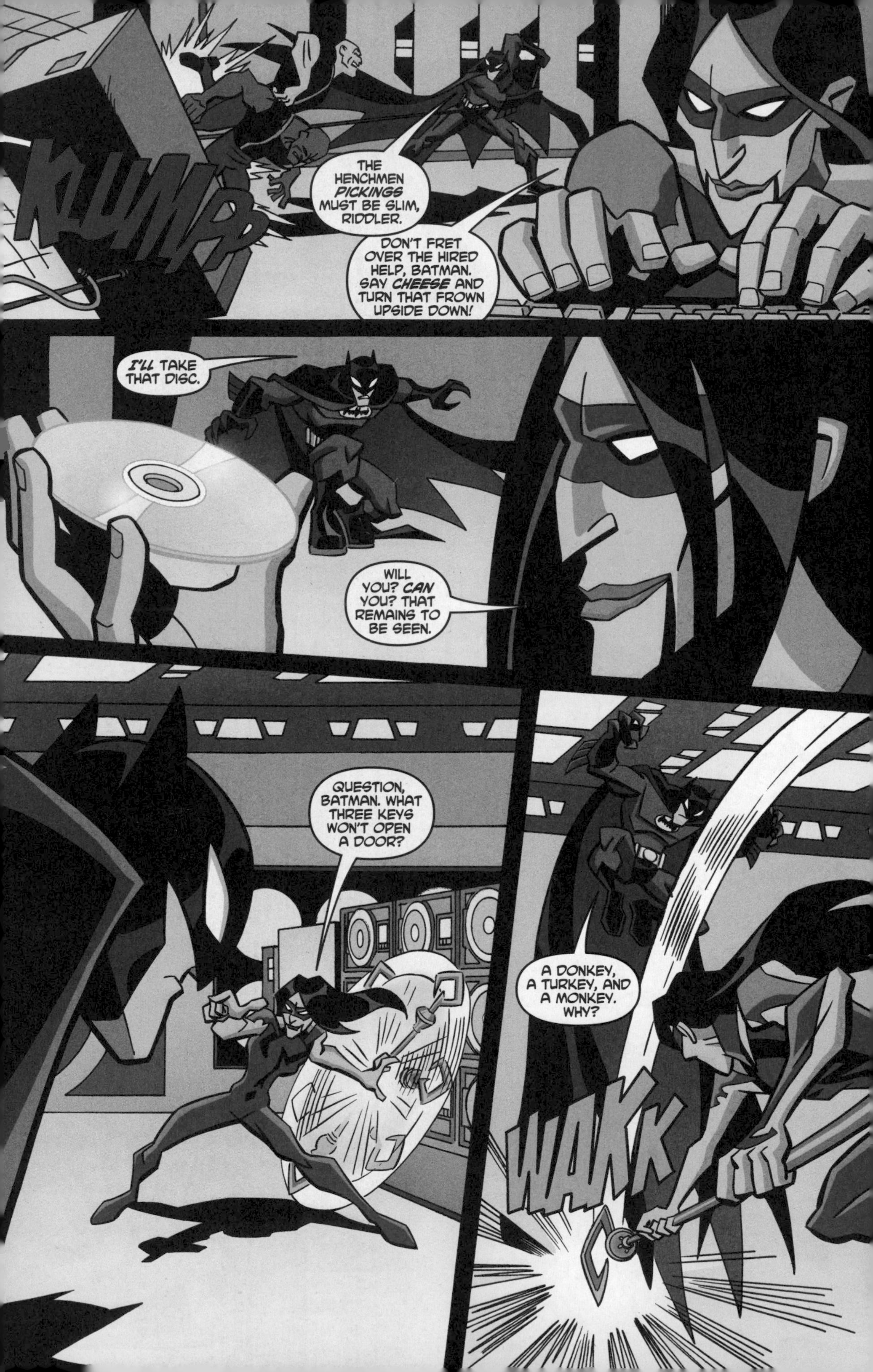
KLUMP
THE HENCHMEN PICKINGS MUST BE SLIM, RIDDLER.
DON'T FRET OVER THE HIRED HELP, BATMAN. SAY CHEESE AND TURN THAT FROWN UPSIDE DOWN!
I'LL TAKE THAT DISC.
WILL YOU? CAN YOU? THAT REMAINS TO BE SEEN.
QUESTION, BATMAN. WHAT THREE KEYS WON'T OPEN A DOOR?
A DONKEY, A TURKEY, AND A MONKEY. WHY?
WAKK

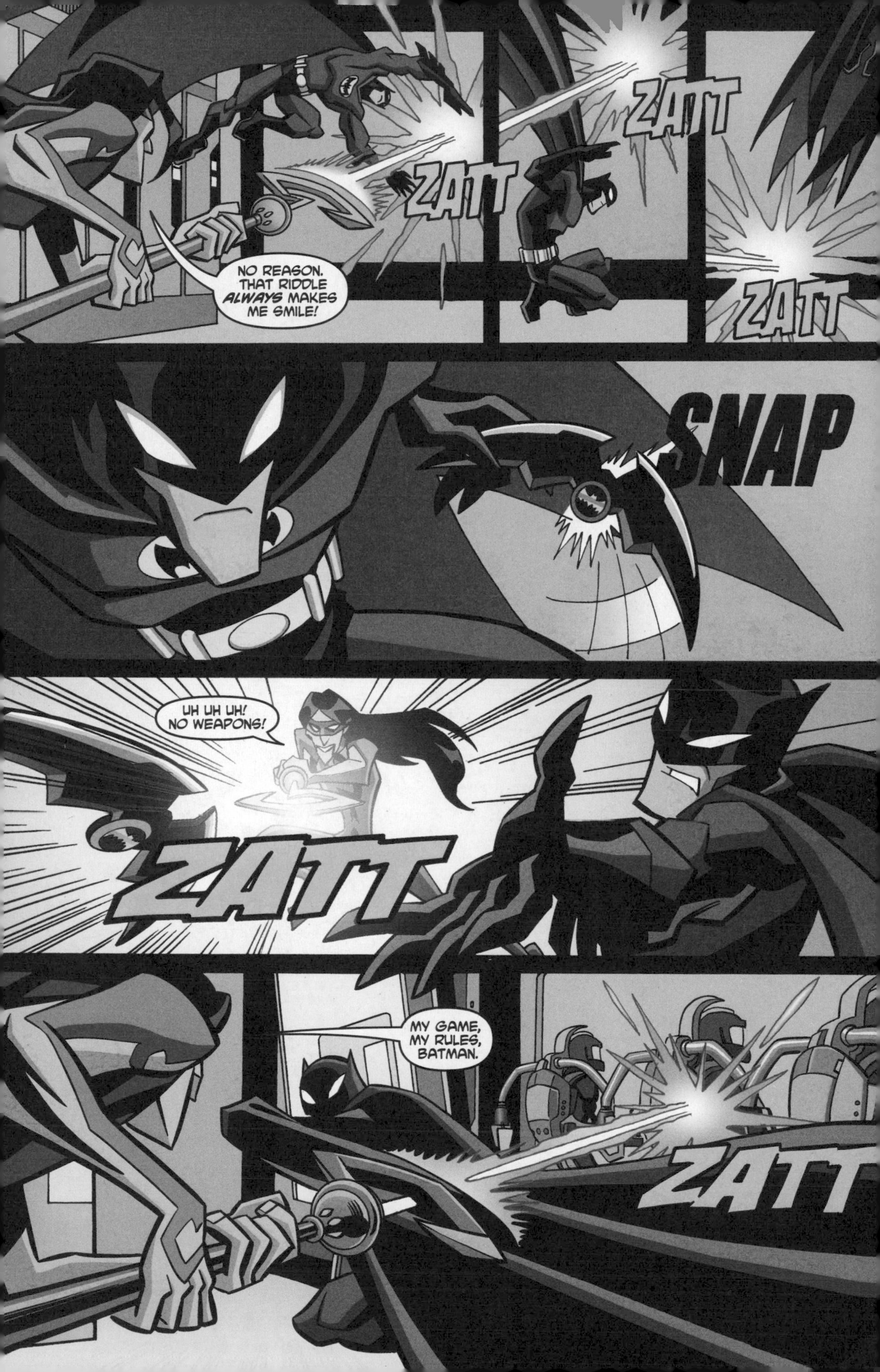
NO REASON. THAT RIDDLE ALWAYS MAKES ME SMILE!
ZATT
ZATT
ZATT
SNAP
UH UH UH! NO WEAPONS!
ZATT
MY GAME, MY RULES, BATMAN.
ZATT

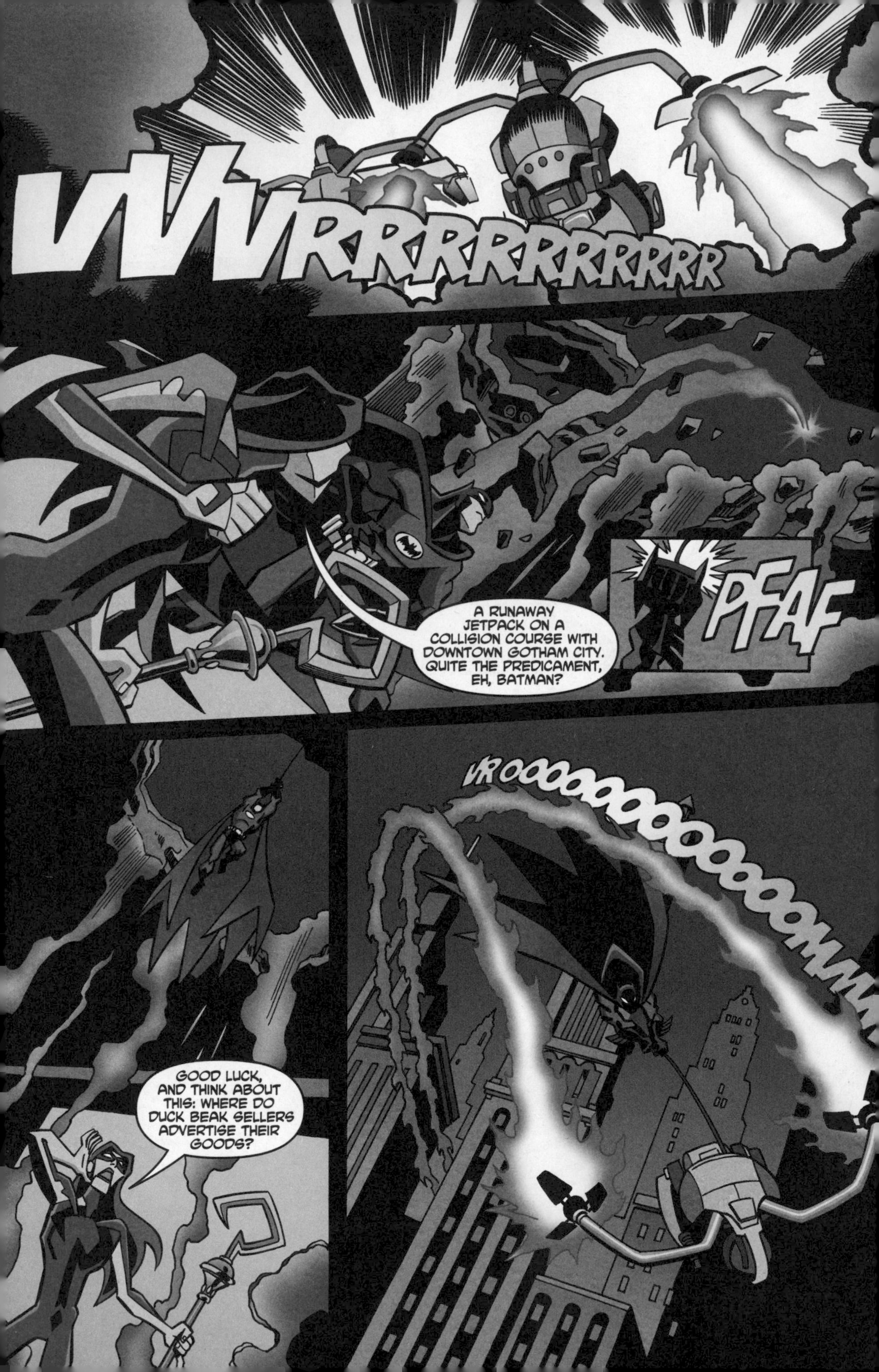
VVVRRRRRRRRRRRR
A RUNAWAY JETPACK ON A COLLISION COURSE WITH DOWNTOWN GOTHAM CITY. QUITE THE PREDICAMENT, EH, BATMAN?
PFAF
GOOD LUCK, AND THINK ABOUT THIS: WHERE DO DUCK BEAK SELLERS ADVERTISE THEIR GOODS?
VROOOOOOOOOOOOOOOOMMMM

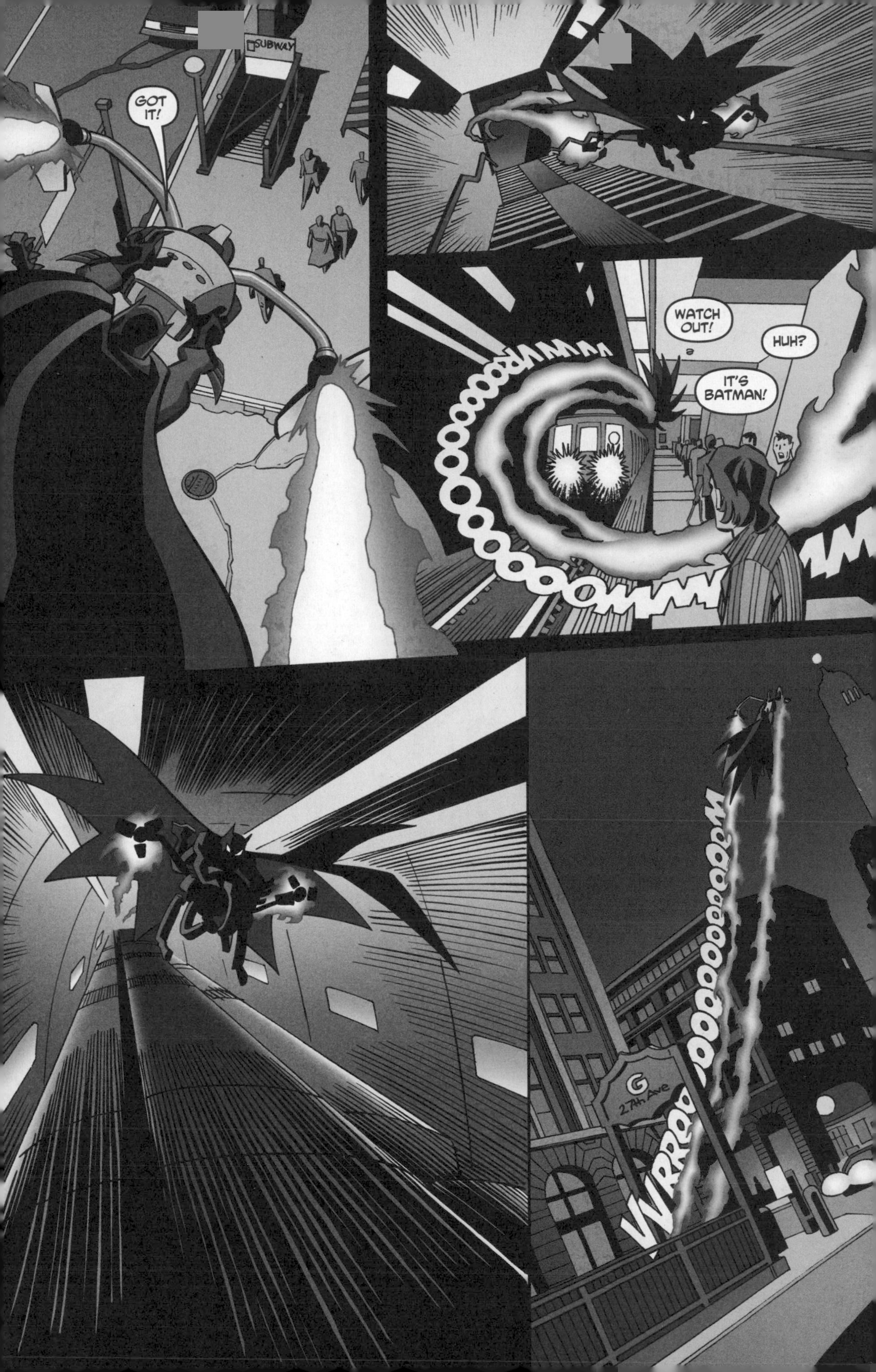
SUBWAY
GOT IT!
VVRROOOOOOOOOOOOOOMMMMM
WATCH OUT!
HUH?
IT'S BATMAN!
27th Ave
VVRROOOOOOOOOOOOOOOOM

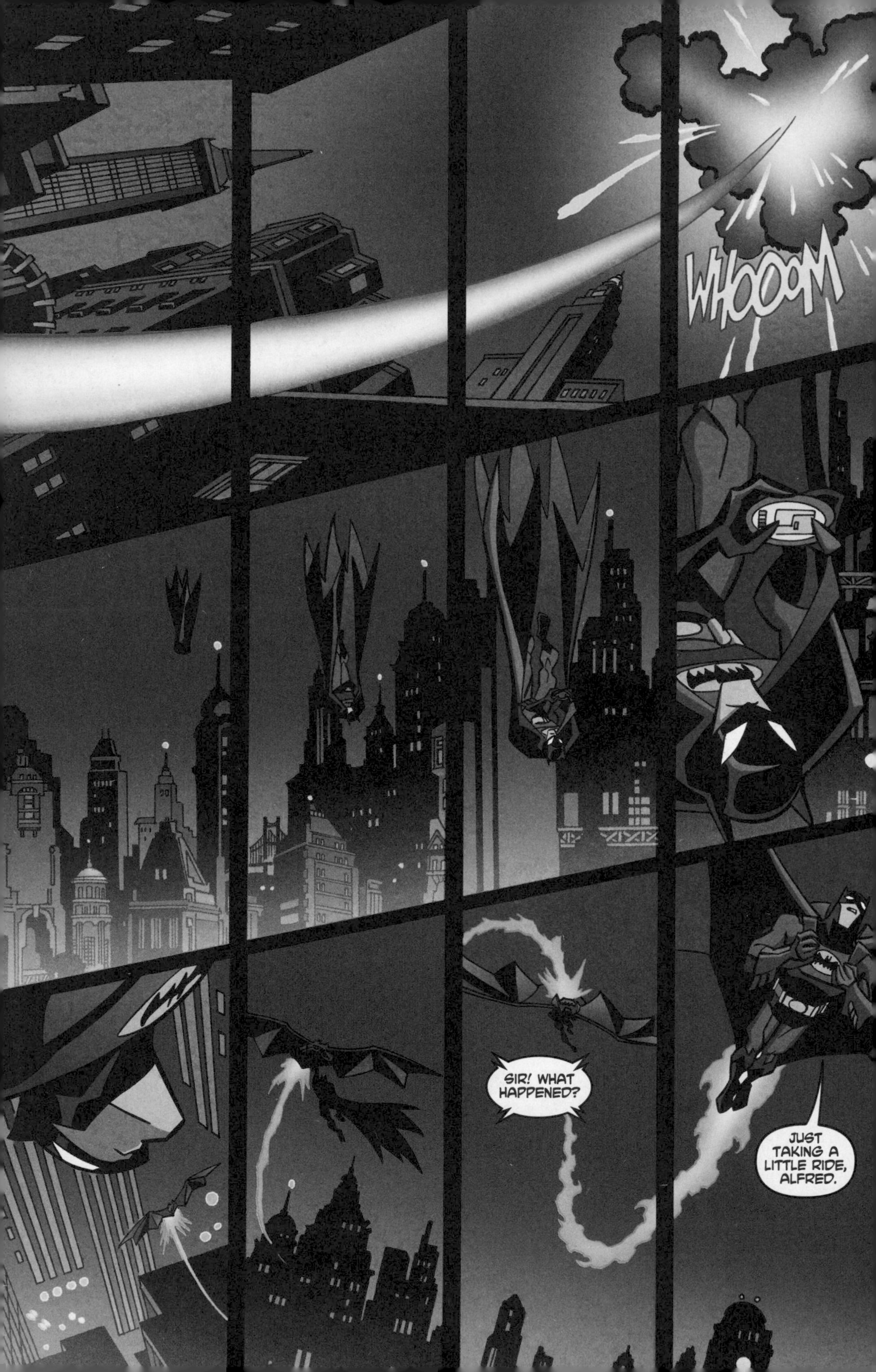
WHOOOM
SIR! WHAT HAPPENED?
JUST TAKING A LITTLE RIDE, ALFRED.

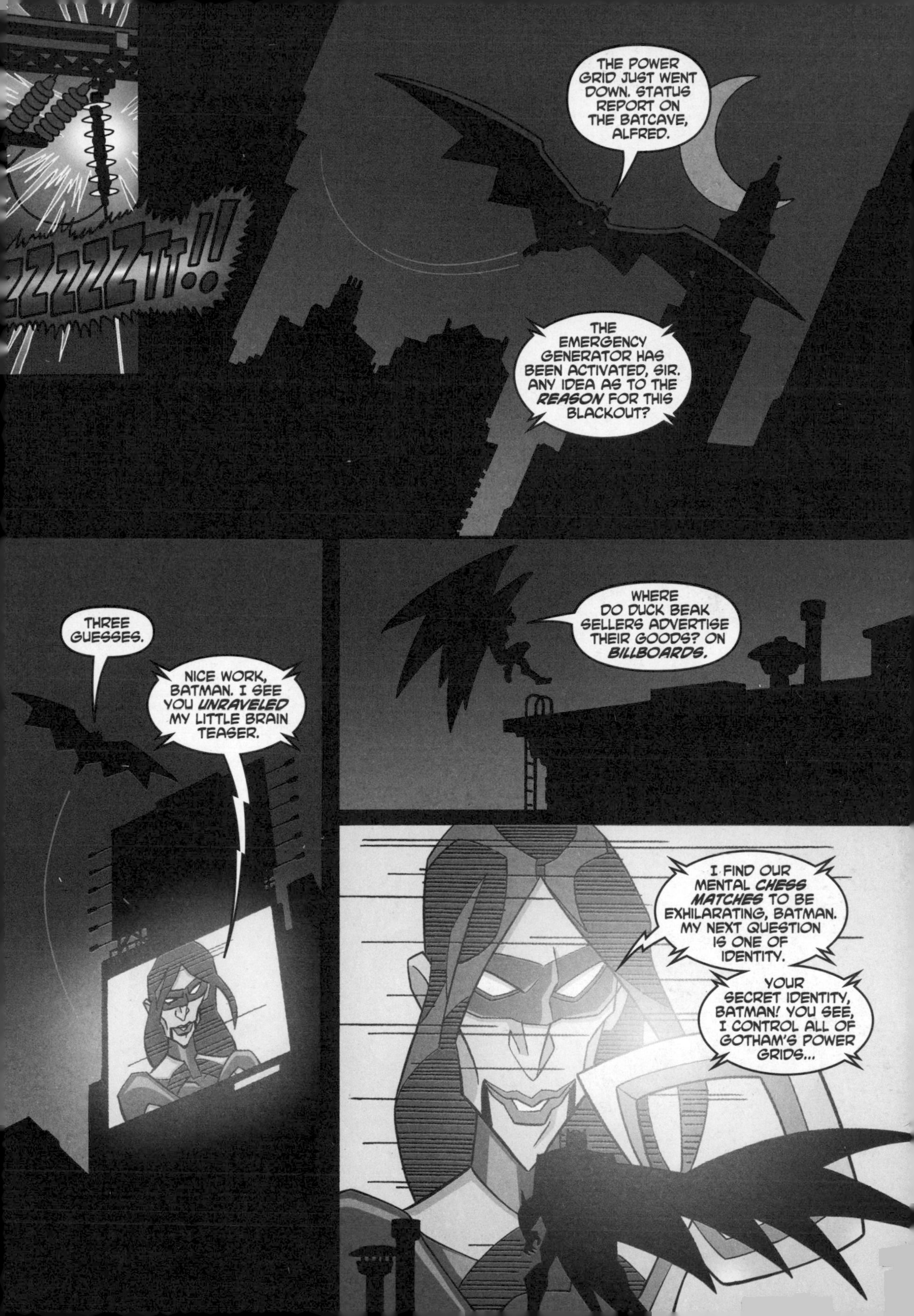
ZZZZZZTT!!
THE POWER GRID JUST WENT DOWN. STATUS REPORT ON THE BATCAVE, ALFRED.
THE EMERGENCY GENERATOR HAS BEEN ACTIVATED, SIR. ANY IDEA AS TO THE *REASON* FOR THIS BLACKOUT?
THREE GUESSES.
WHERE DO DUCK BEAK SELLERS ADVERTISE THEIR GOODS? ON *BILLBOARDS.*
NICE WORK, BATMAN. I SEE YOU *UNRAVELED* MY LITTLE BRAIN TEASER.
I FIND OUR MENTAL *CHESS MATCHES* TO BE EXHILARATING, BATMAN. MY NEXT QUESTION IS ONE OF IDENTITY.
YOUR SECRET IDENTITY, BATMAN! YOU SEE, I CONTROL ALL OF GOTHAM'S POWER GRIDS...

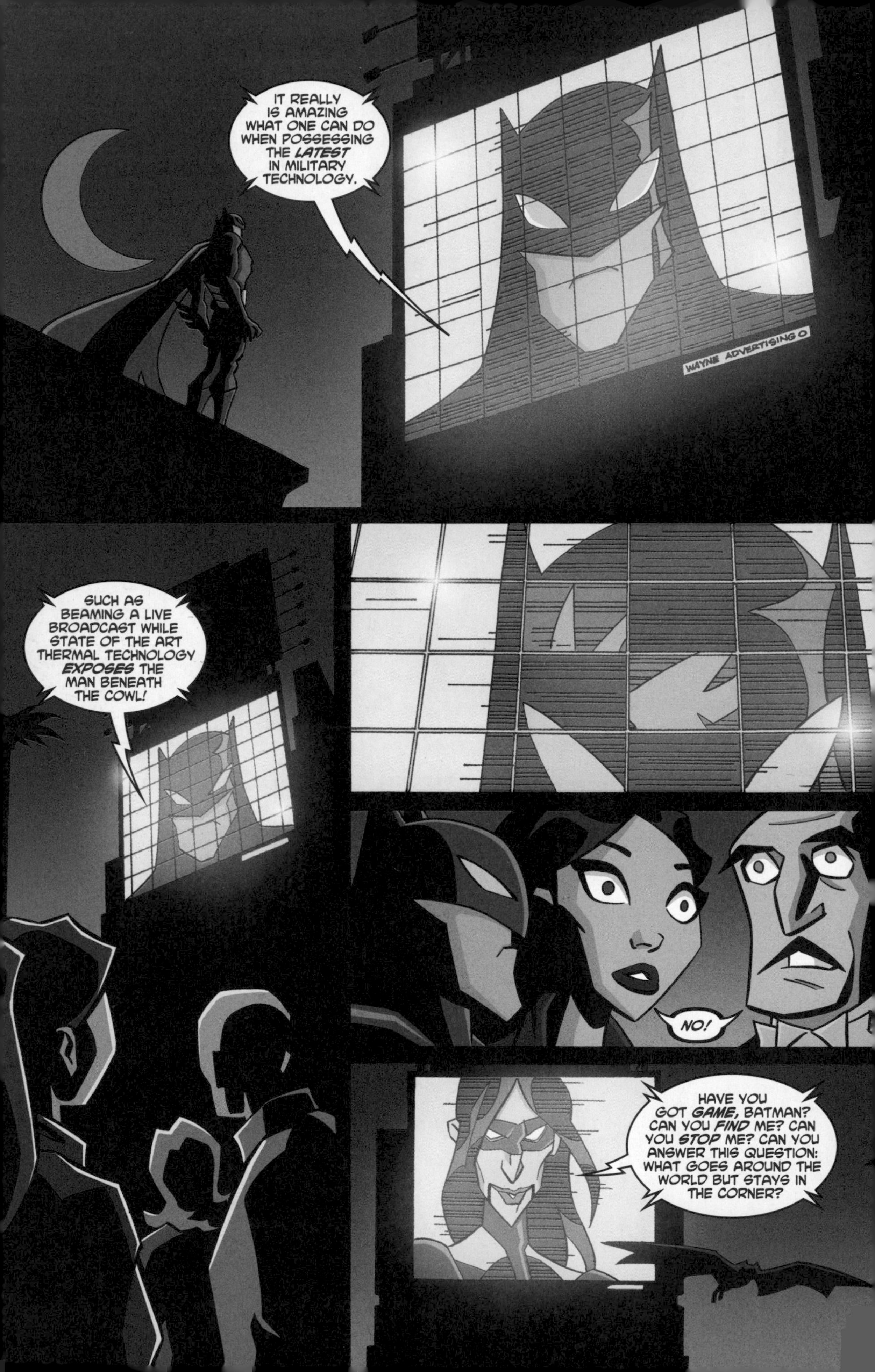
IT REALLY IS AMAZING WHAT ONE CAN DO WHEN POSSESSING THE *LATEST* IN MILITARY TECHNOLOGY.
WAYNE ADVERTISING
SUCH AS BEAMING A LIVE BROADCAST WHILE STATE OF THE ART THERMAL TECHNOLOGY *EXPOSES* THE MAN BENEATH THE COWL!
NO!
HAVE YOU GOT *GAME,* BATMAN? CAN YOU *FIND* ME? CAN YOU *STOP* ME? CAN YOU ANSWER THIS QUESTION: WHAT GOES AROUND THE WORLD BUT STAYS IN THE CORNER?

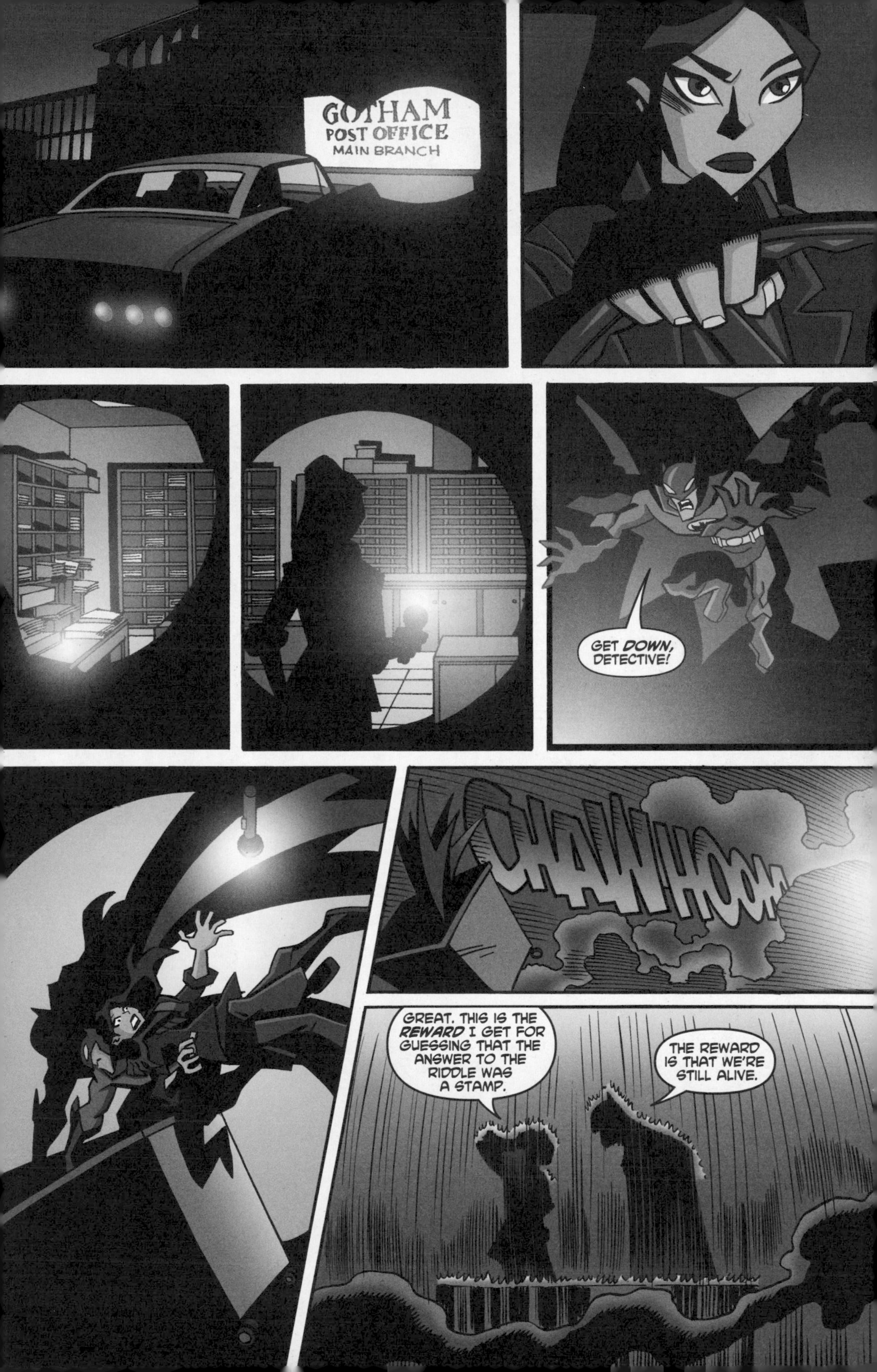
GOTHAM
POST OFFICE
MAIN BRANCH
GET DOWN, DETECTIVE!
CHAWHOOM
GREAT. THIS IS THE REWARD I GET FOR GUESSING THAT THE ANSWER TO THE RIDDLE WAS A STAMP.
THE REWARD IS THAT WE'RE STILL ALIVE.

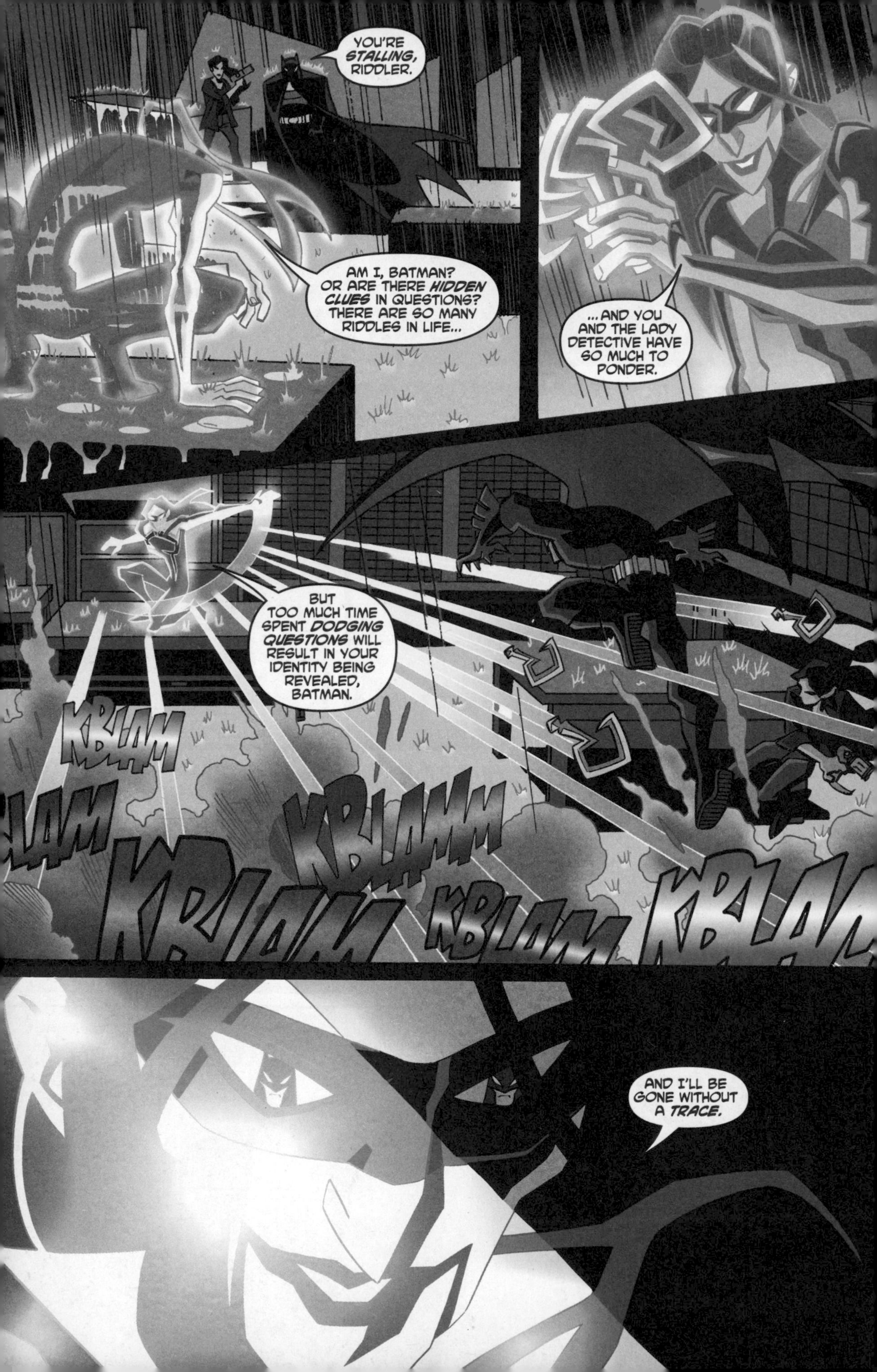
YOU'RE STALLING, RIDDLER.
AM I, BATMAN? OR ARE THERE HIDDEN CLUES IN QUESTIONS? THERE ARE SO MANY RIDDLES IN LIFE...
...AND YOU AND THE LADY DETECTIVE HAVE SO MUCH TO PONDER.
BUT TOO MUCH TIME SPENT DODGING QUESTIONS WILL RESULT IN YOUR IDENTITY BEING REVEALED, BATMAN.
KBLAM
KBLAMM
KBLAM
KBLAM
AND I'LL BE GONE WITHOUT A TRACE.

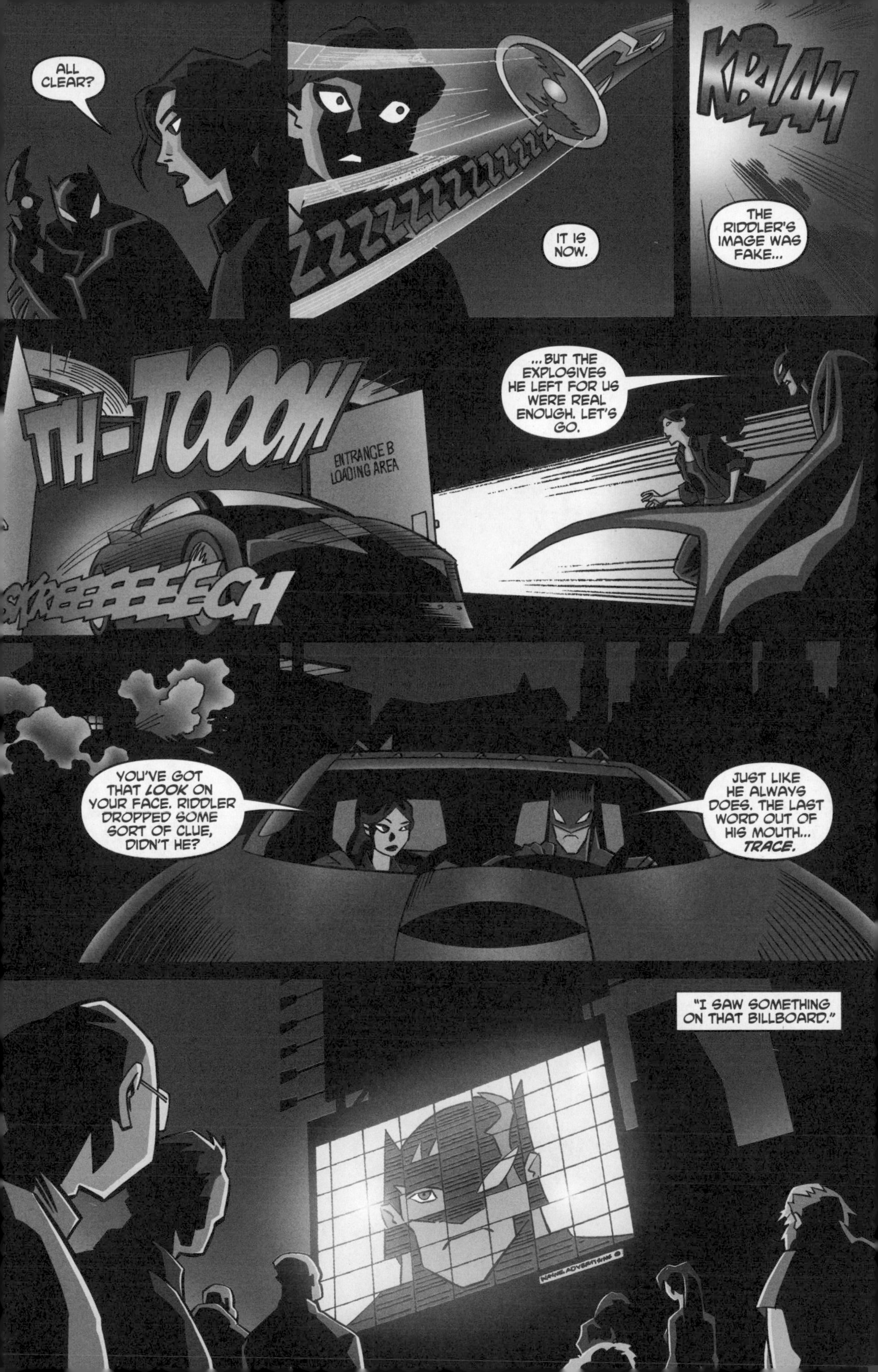

ALL CLEAR?
ZZZZZZZZZZZZZZZZ
IT IS NOW.
KBLAM
THE RIDDLER'S IMAGE WAS FAKE...
TH-TOOOM
ENTRANCE B LOADING AREA
SKREEEEEEECH
...BUT THE EXPLOSIVES HE LEFT FOR US WERE REAL ENOUGH. LET'S GO.
YOU'VE GOT THAT *LOOK* ON YOUR FACE. RIDDLER DROPPED SOME SORT OF CLUE, DIDN'T HE?
JUST LIKE HE ALWAYS DOES. THE LAST WORD OUT OF HIS MOUTH... ***TRACE.***
"I SAW SOMETHING ON THAT BILLBOARD."

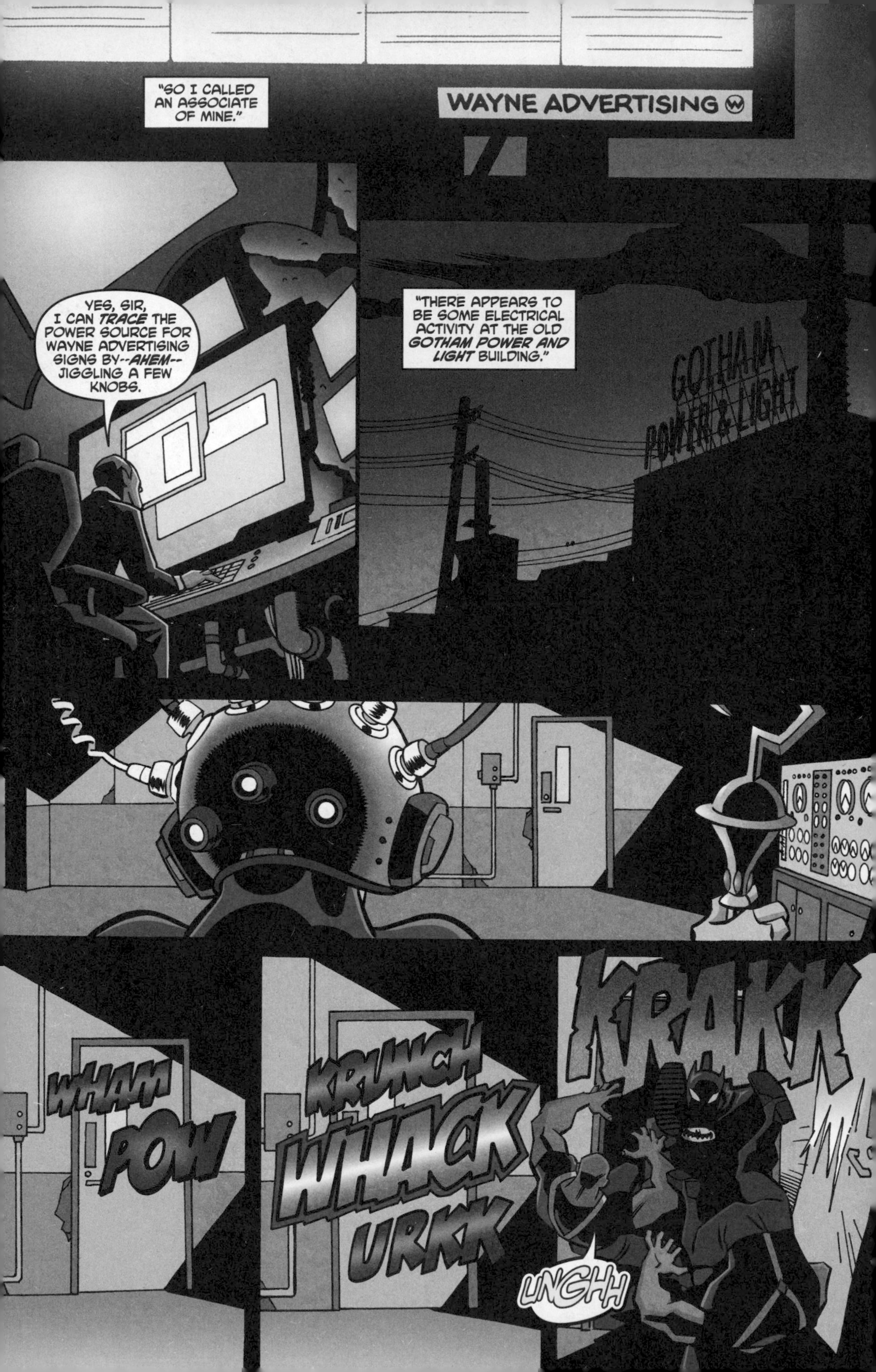
"SO I CALLED AN ASSOCIATE OF MINE."
WAYNE ADVERTISING
YES, SIR, I CAN *TRACE* THE POWER SOURCE FOR WAYNE ADVERTISING SIGNS BY--*AHEM*--JIGGLING A FEW KNOBS.
"THERE APPEARS TO BE SOME ELECTRICAL ACTIVITY AT THE OLD *GOTHAM POWER AND LIGHT* BUILDING."
GOTHAM POWER & LIGHT
WHAM
POW
KRUNCH
WHACK
URKK
KRAKK
UNGHH

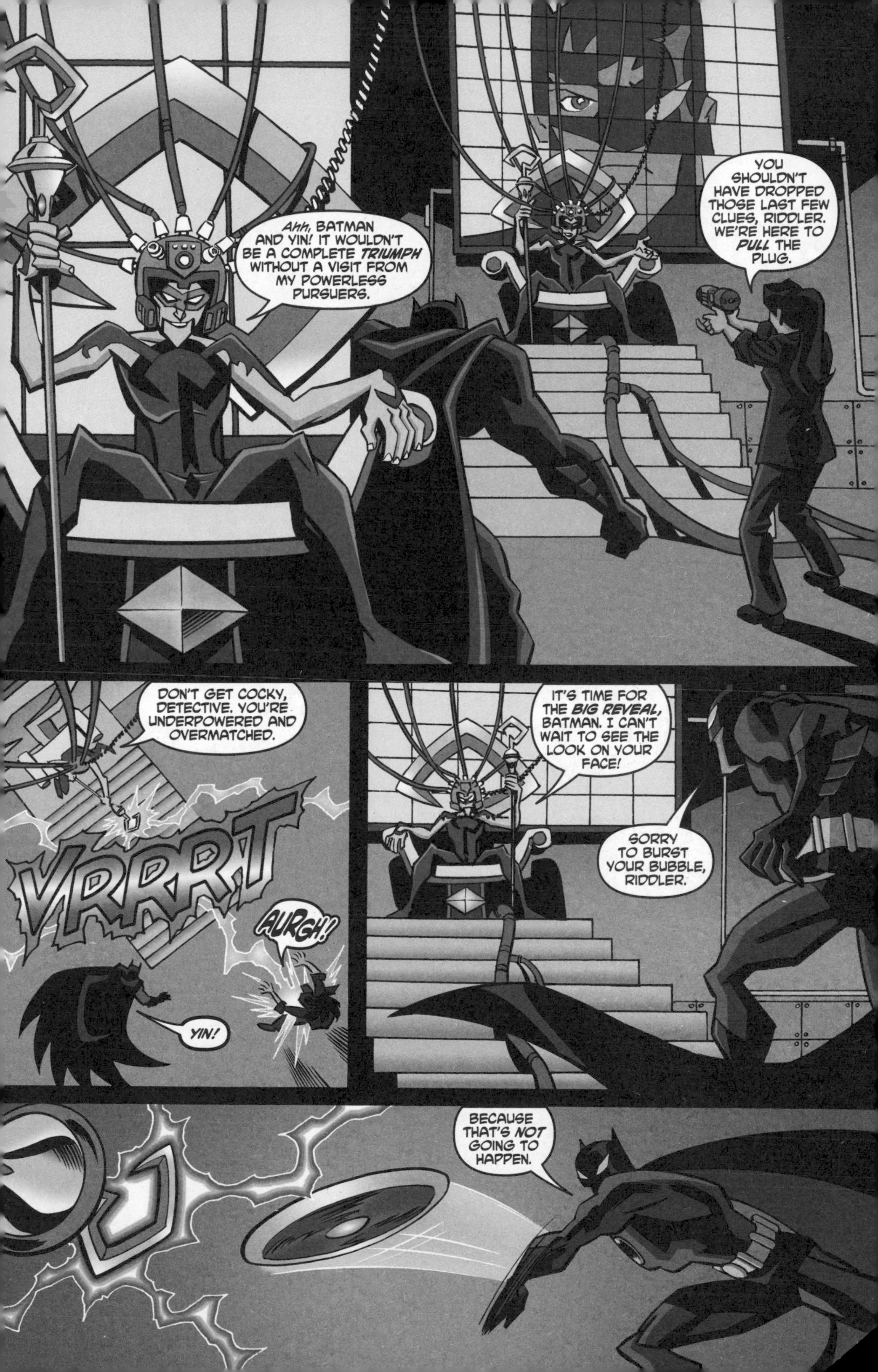

Ahh, BATMAN AND YIN! IT WOULDN'T BE A COMPLETE *TRIUMPH* WITHOUT A VISIT FROM MY POWERLESS PURSUERS.
YOU SHOULDN'T HAVE DROPPED THOSE LAST FEW CLUES, RIDDLER. WE'RE HERE TO *PULL* THE PLUG.
DON'T GET COCKY, DETECTIVE. YOU'RE UNDERPOWERED AND OVERMATCHED.
VRRRT
AURGH!
YIN!
IT'S TIME FOR THE *BIG REVEAL,* BATMAN. I CAN'T WAIT TO SEE THE LOOK ON YOUR FACE!
SORRY TO BURST YOUR BUBBLE, RIDDLER.
BECAUSE THAT'S *NOT* GOING TO HAPPEN.

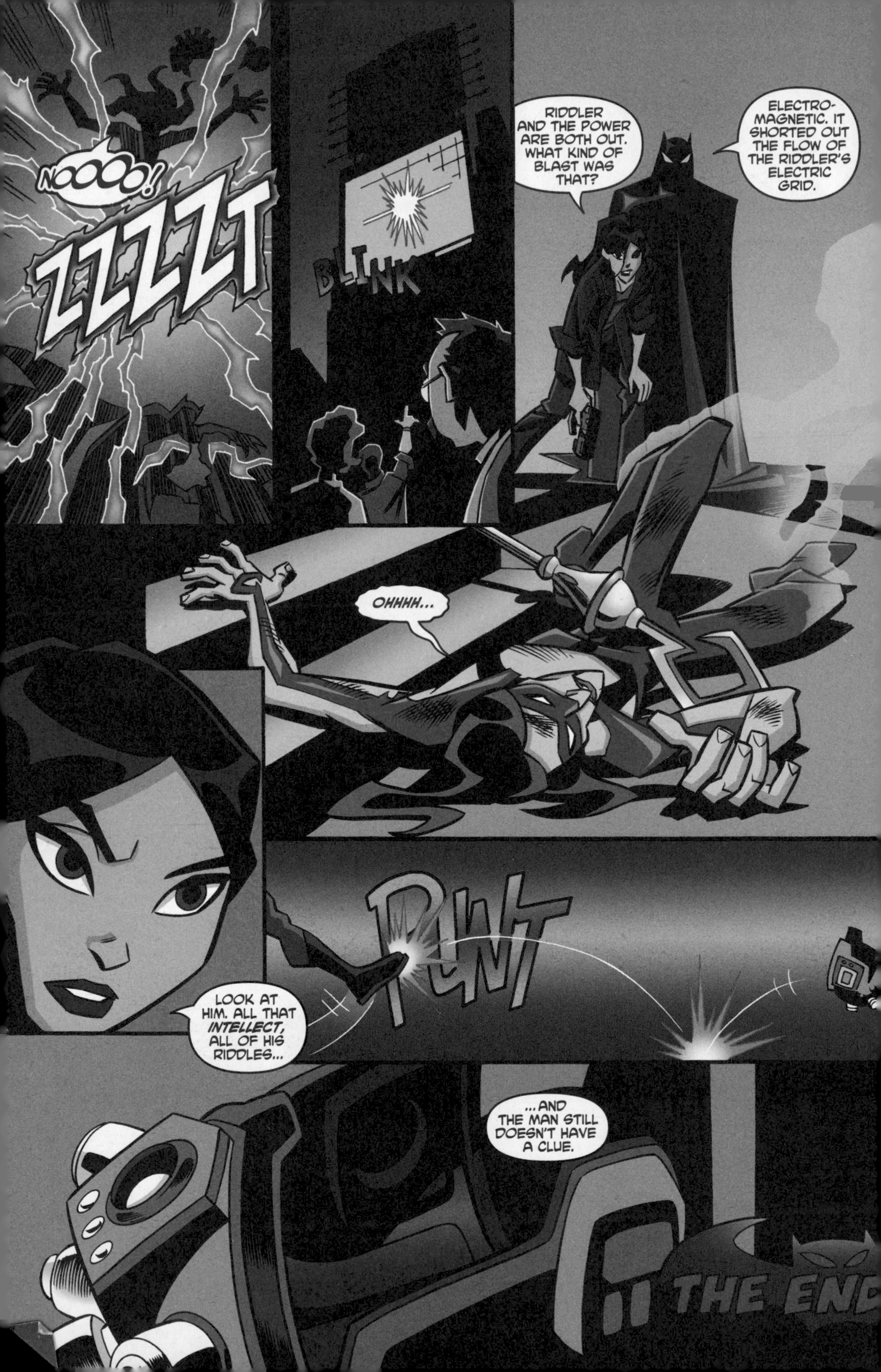
NOOOO!
ZZZZZT
BLINK
RIDDLER AND THE POWER ARE BOTH OUT. WHAT KIND OF BLAST WAS THAT?
ELECTRO-MAGNETIC. IT SHORTED OUT THE FLOW OF THE RIDDLER'S ELECTRIC GRID.
OHHHH...
PUNT
LOOK AT HIM. ALL THAT INTELLECT, ALL OF HIS RIDDLES...
...AND THE MAN STILL DOESN'T HAVE A CLUE.
THE END

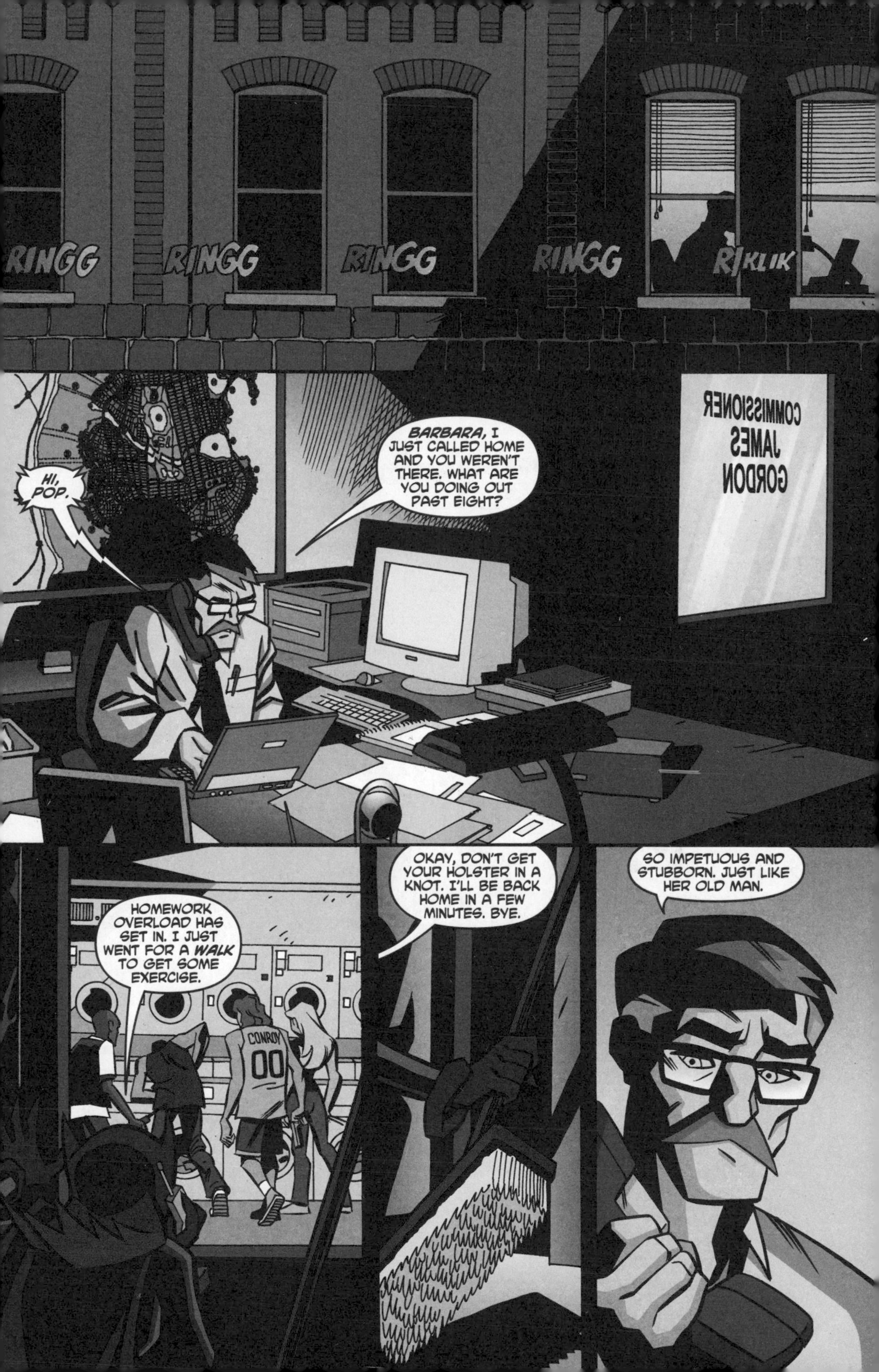
RINGG
RINGG
RINGG
RINGG
RIKLIK
HI, POP.
BARBARA, I JUST CALLED HOME AND YOU WEREN'T THERE. WHAT ARE YOU DOING OUT PAST EIGHT?
COMMISSIONER JAMES GORDON
HOMEWORK OVERLOAD HAS SET IN. I JUST WENT FOR A WALK TO GET SOME EXERCISE.
CONROY 00
OKAY, DON'T GET YOUR HOLSTER IN A KNOT. I'LL BE BACK HOME IN A FEW MINUTES. BYE.
SO IMPETUOUS AND STUBBORN. JUST LIKE HER OLD MAN.

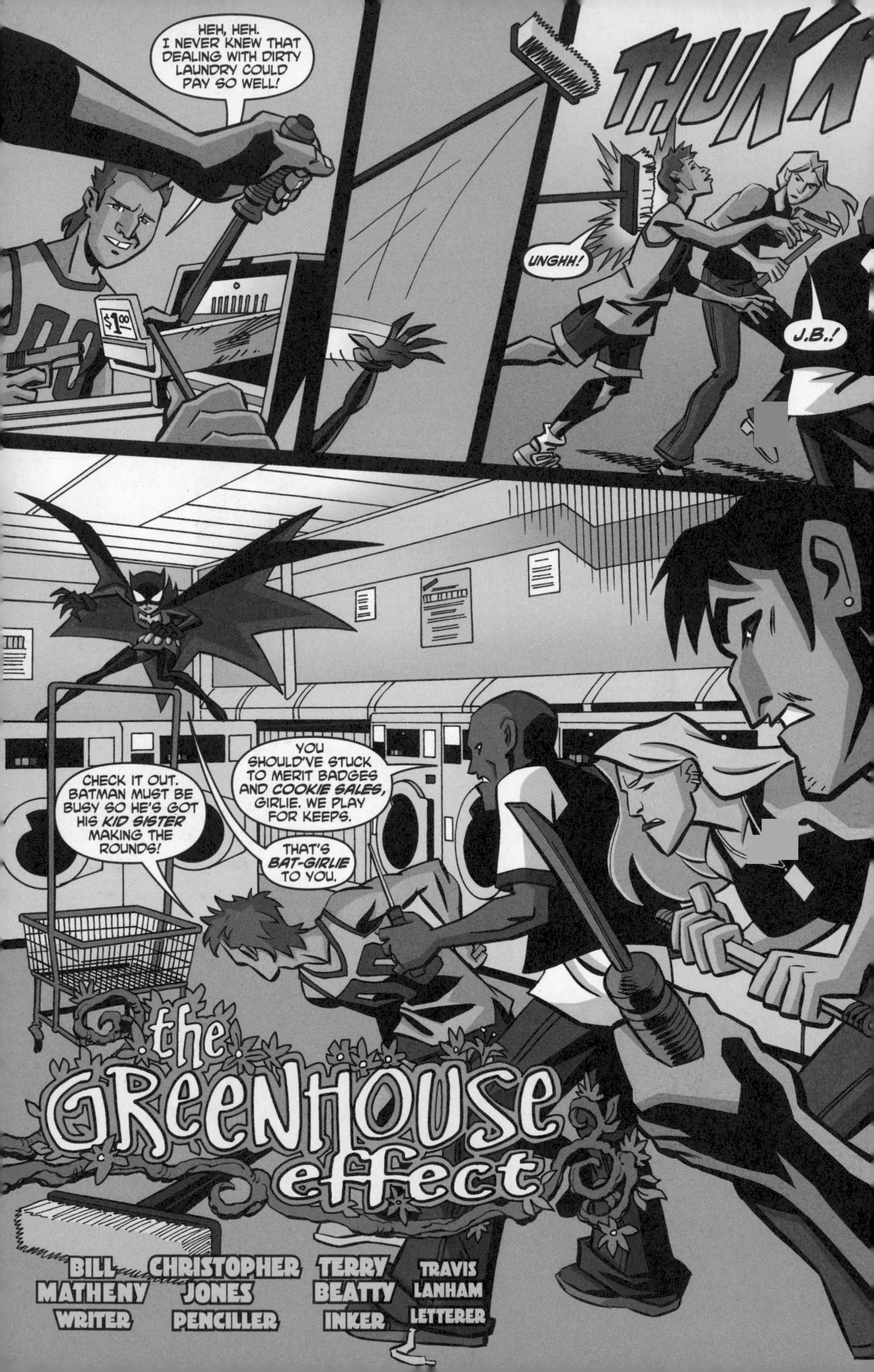

HEH, HEH. I NEVER KNEW THAT DEALING WITH DIRTY LAUNDRY COULD PAY SO WELL!
$1.00
THUKK
UNGHH!
J.B.!
CHECK IT OUT. BATMAN MUST BE BUSY SO HE'S GOT HIS KID SISTER MAKING THE ROUNDS!
YOU SHOULD'VE STUCK TO MERIT BADGES AND COOKIE SALES, GIRLIE. WE PLAY FOR KEEPS.
THAT'S BAT-GIRLIE TO YOU.
the GREENHOUSE effect
BILL MATHENY WRITER
CHRISTOPHER JONES PENCILLER
TERRY BEATTY INKER
TRAVIS LANHAM LETTERER

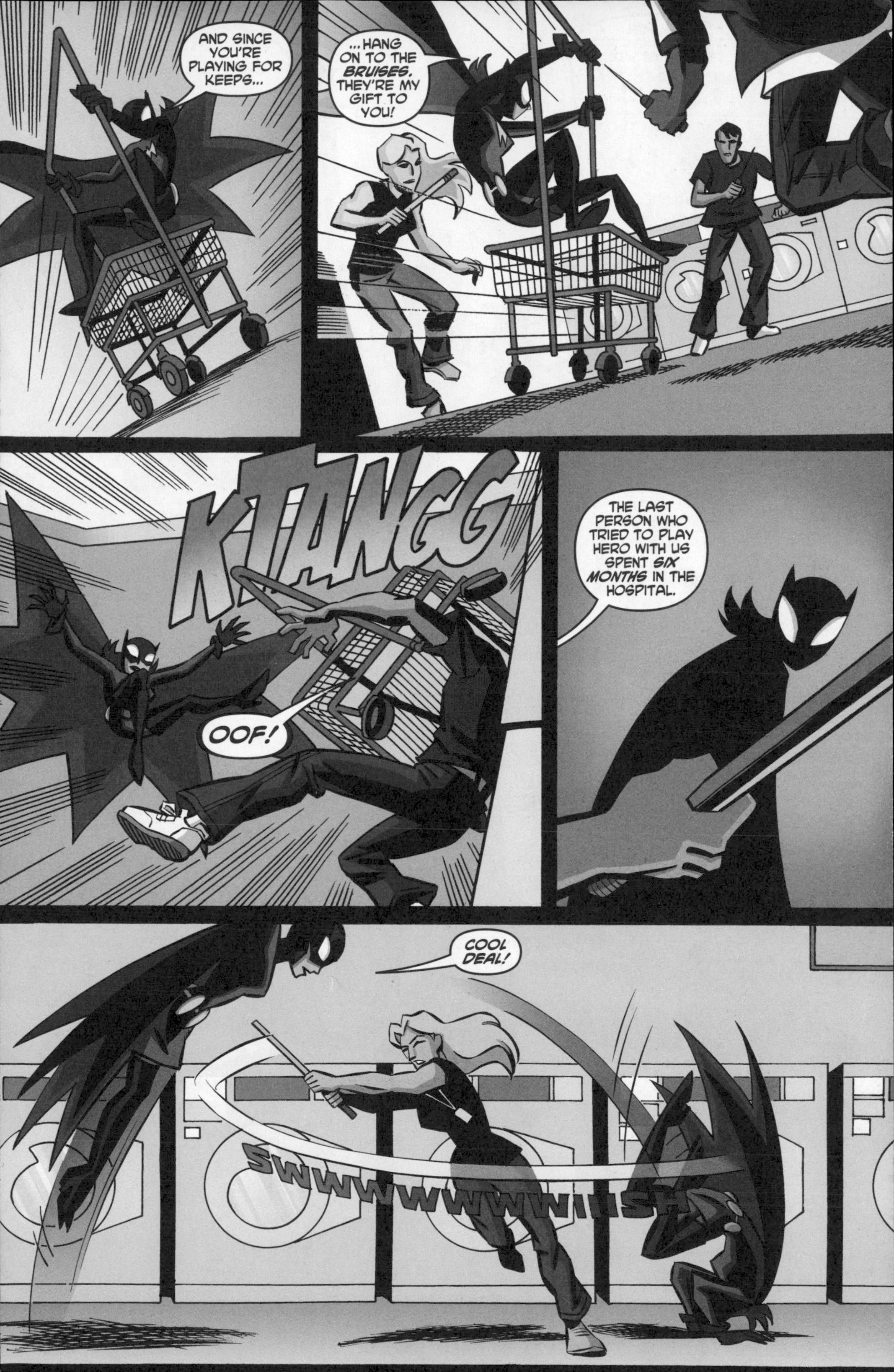
AND SINCE YOU'RE PLAYING FOR KEEPS...
...HANG ON TO THE BRUISES. THEY'RE MY GIFT TO YOU!
KTANGG
OOF!
THE LAST PERSON WHO TRIED TO PLAY HERO WITH US SPENT SIX MONTHS IN THE HOSPITAL.
COOL DEAL!
SWWWWWWWWIIISH

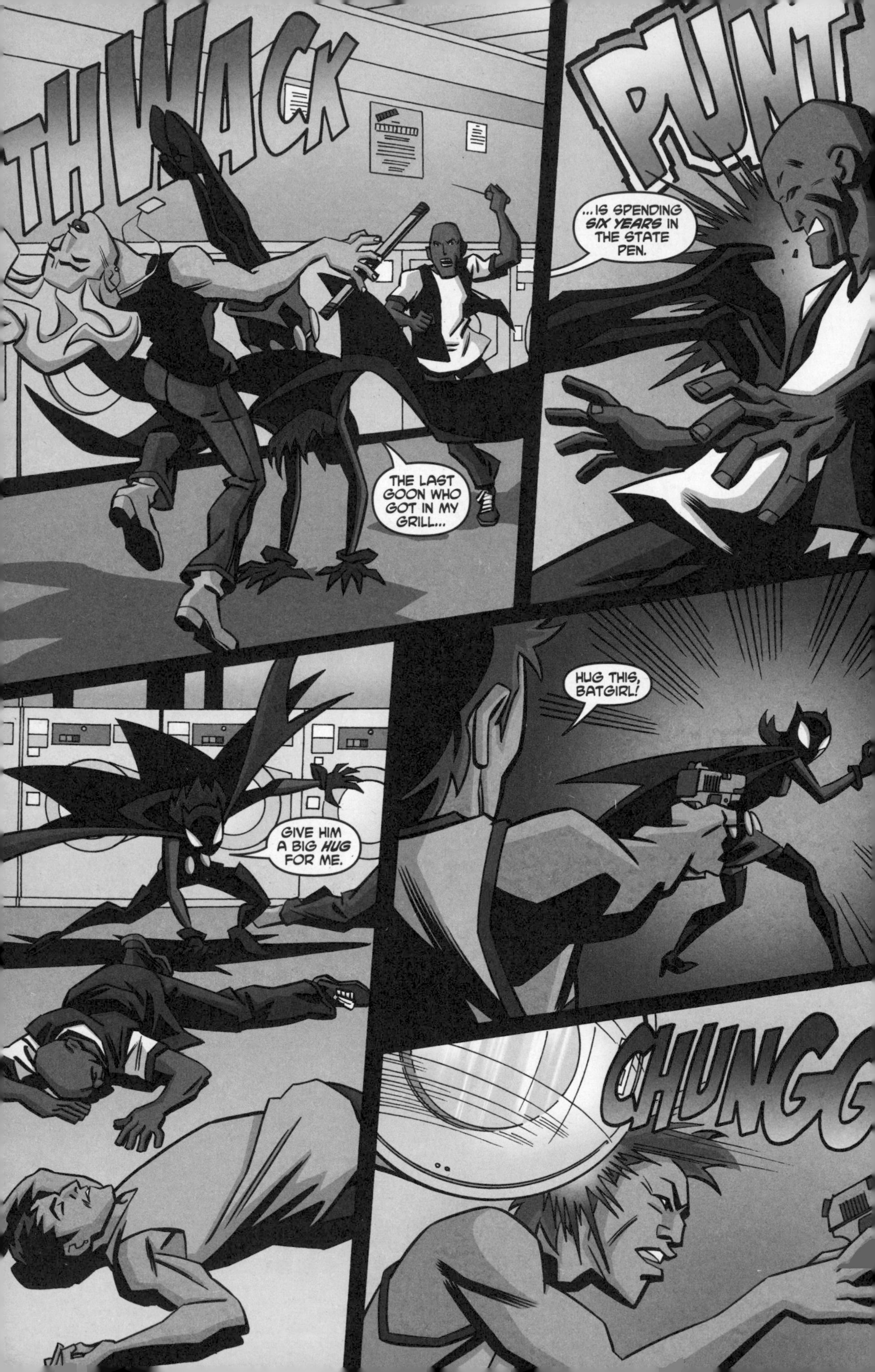
THWACK
THE LAST GOON WHO GOT IN MY GRILL...
PUNT
...IS SPENDING SIX YEARS IN THE STATE PEN.
GIVE HIM A BIG HUG FOR ME.
HUG THIS, BATGIRL!
CHUNGG

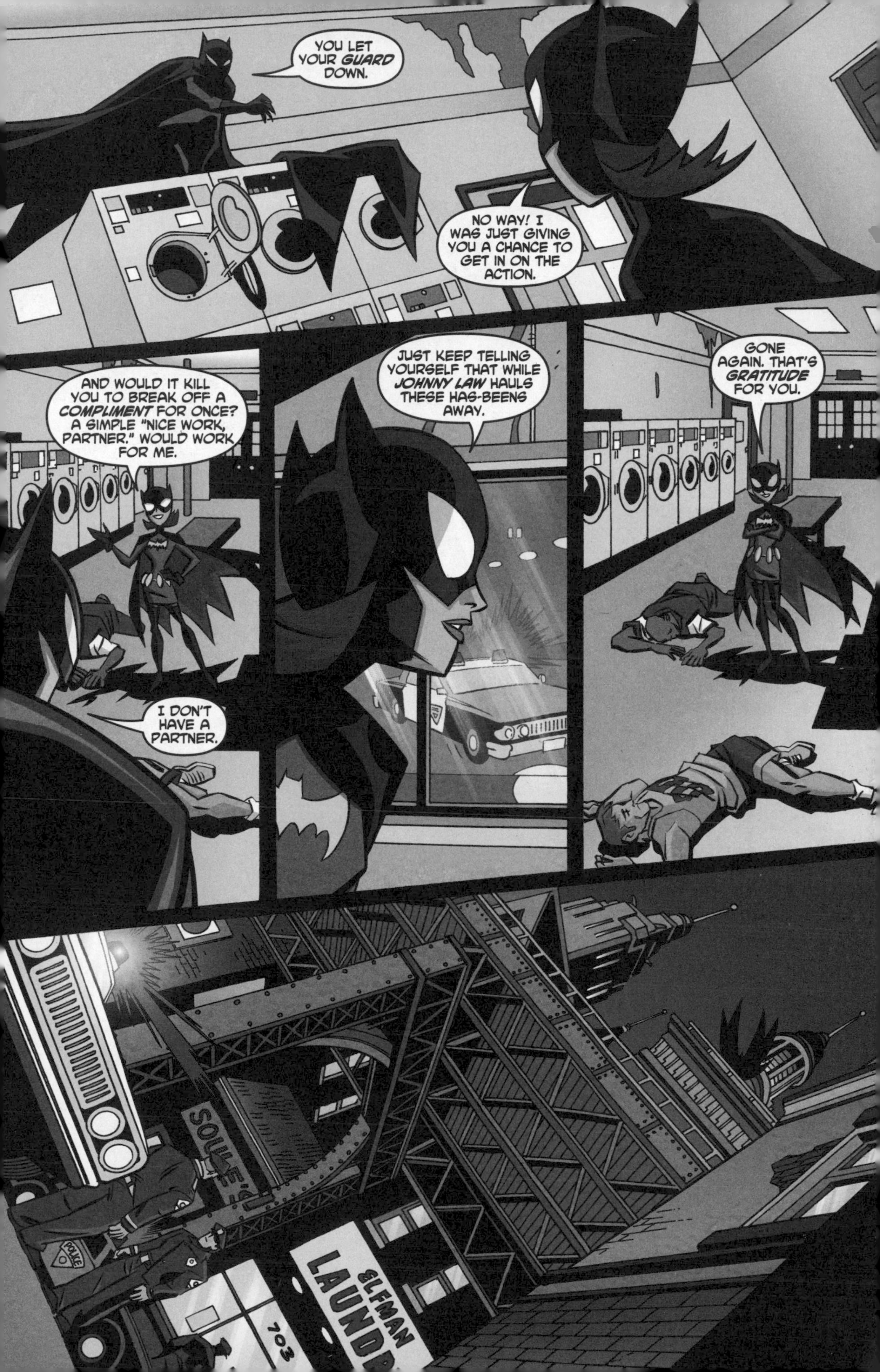
YOU LET YOUR *GUARD* DOWN.
NO WAY! I WAS JUST GIVING YOU A CHANCE TO GET IN ON THE ACTION.
AND WOULD IT KILL YOU TO BREAK OFF A *COMPLIMENT* FOR ONCE? A SIMPLE "NICE WORK, PARTNER." WOULD WORK FOR ME.
I DON'T HAVE A PARTNER.
JUST KEEP TELLING YOURSELF THAT WHILE *JOHNNY LAW* HAULS THESE HAS-BEENS AWAY.
GONE AGAIN. THAT'S *GRATITUDE* FOR YOU.
ELFMAN
703

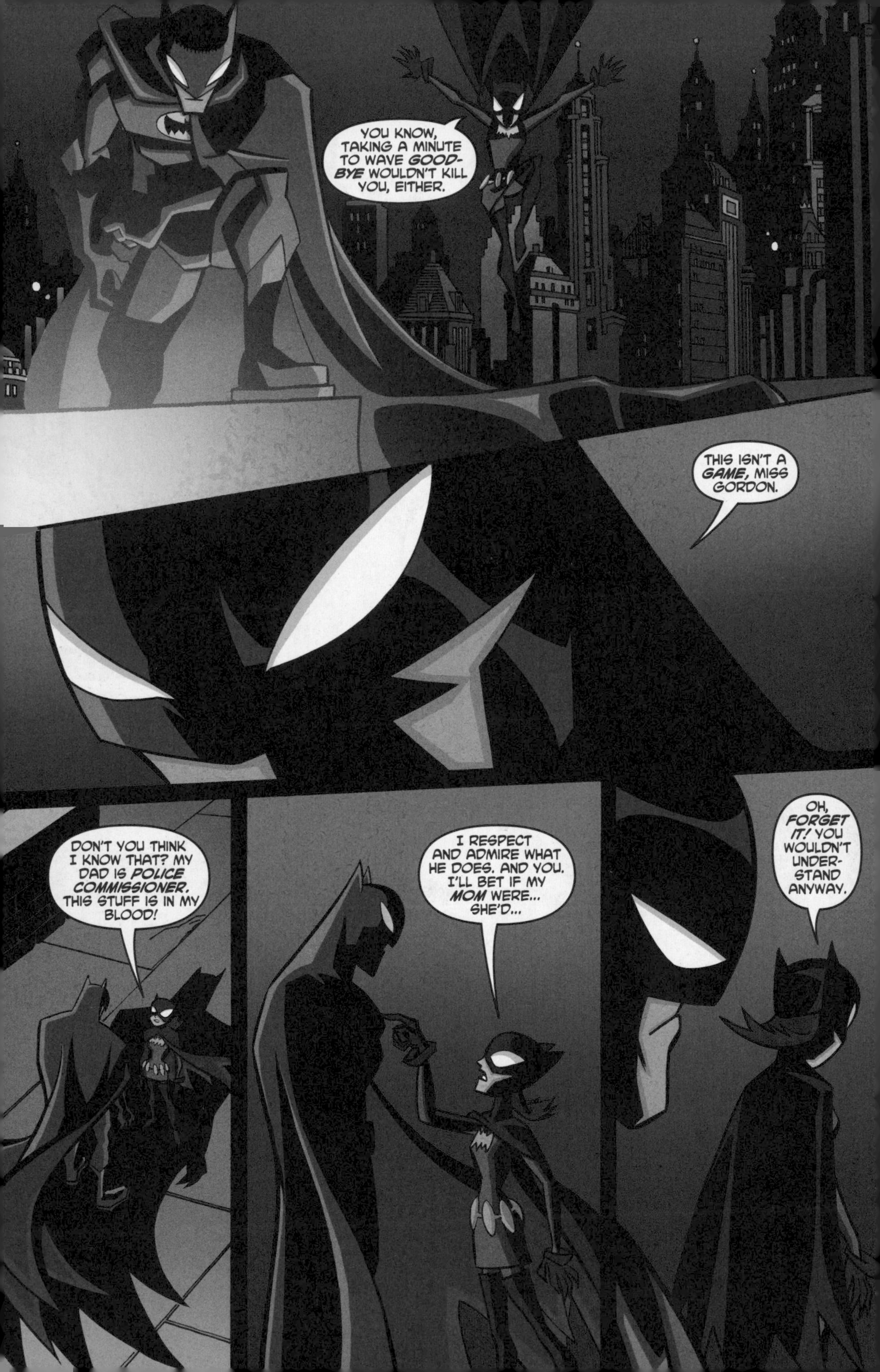
YOU KNOW, TAKING A MINUTE TO WAVE GOOD-BYE WOULDN'T KILL YOU, EITHER.
THIS ISN'T A GAME, MISS GORDON.
DON'T YOU THINK I KNOW THAT? MY DAD IS POLICE COMMISSIONER. THIS STUFF IS IN MY BLOOD!
I RESPECT AND ADMIRE WHAT HE DOES. AND YOU. I'LL BET IF MY MOM WERE... SHE'D...
OH, FORGET IT! YOU WOULDN'T UNDER-STAND ANYWAY.

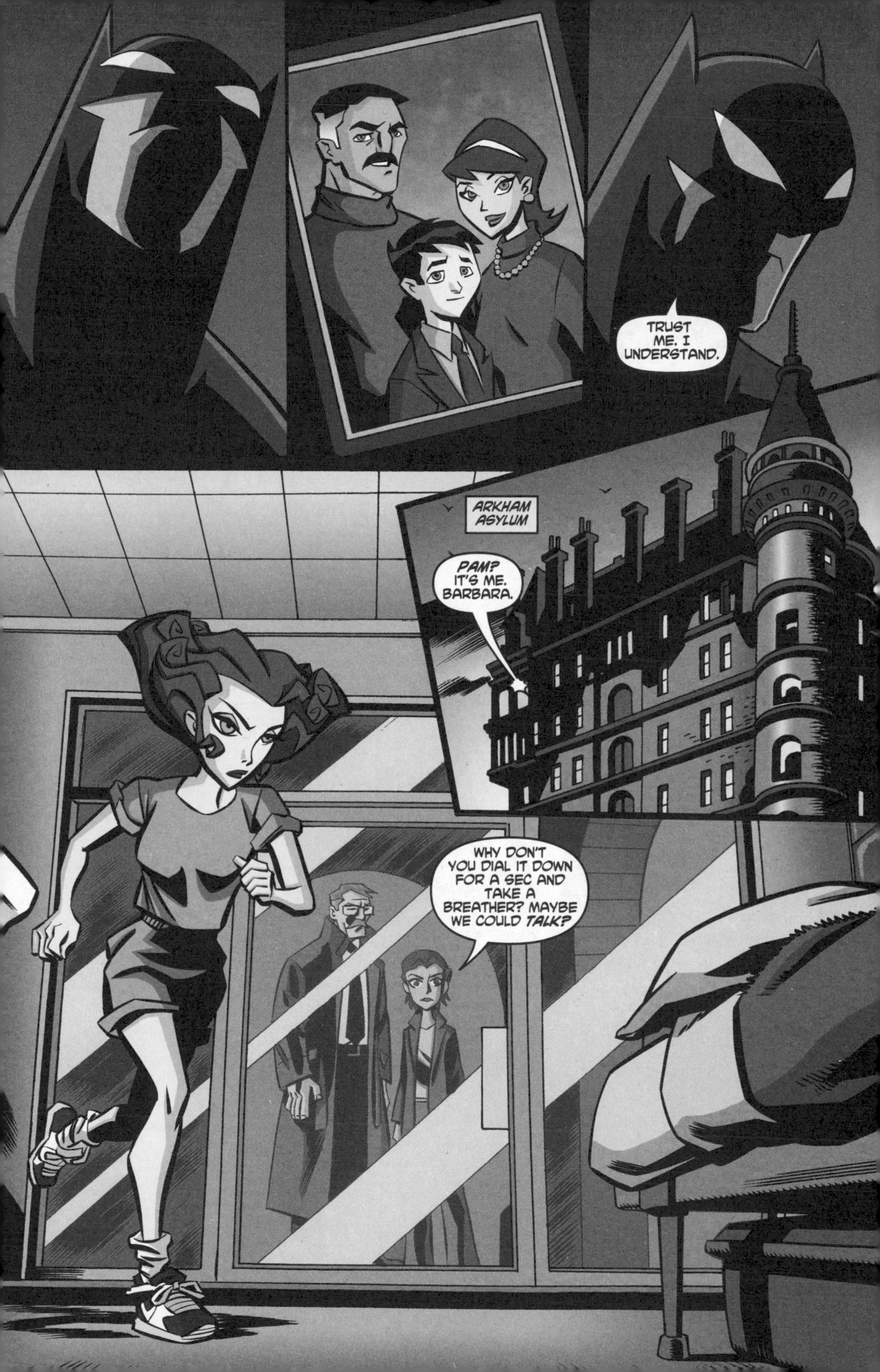
TRUST ME. I UNDERSTAND.
ARKHAM ASYLUM
PAM? IT'S ME. BARBARA.
WHY DON'T YOU DIAL IT DOWN FOR A SEC AND TAKE A BREATHER? MAYBE WE COULD TALK?

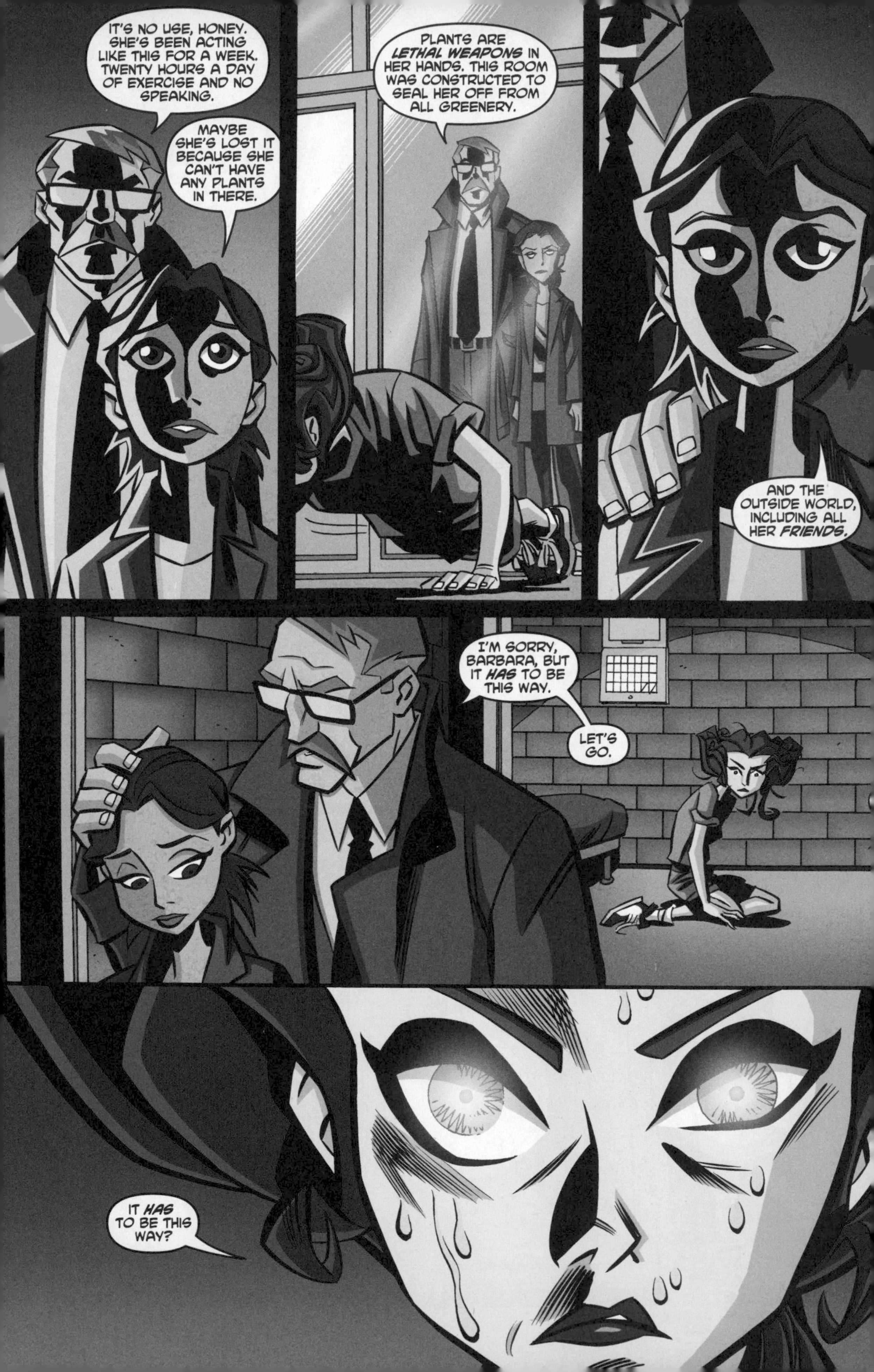
IT'S NO USE, HONEY. SHE'S BEEN ACTING LIKE THIS FOR A WEEK. TWENTY HOURS A DAY OF EXERCISE AND NO SPEAKING.
MAYBE SHE'S LOST IT BECAUSE SHE CAN'T HAVE ANY PLANTS IN THERE.
PLANTS ARE ***LETHAL WEAPONS*** IN HER HANDS. THIS ROOM WAS CONSTRUCTED TO SEAL HER OFF FROM ALL GREENERY.
AND THE OUTSIDE WORLD, INCLUDING ALL HER ***FRIENDS***.
I'M SORRY, BARBARA, BUT IT ***HAS*** TO BE THIS WAY.
LET'S GO.
IT ***HAS*** TO BE THIS WAY?

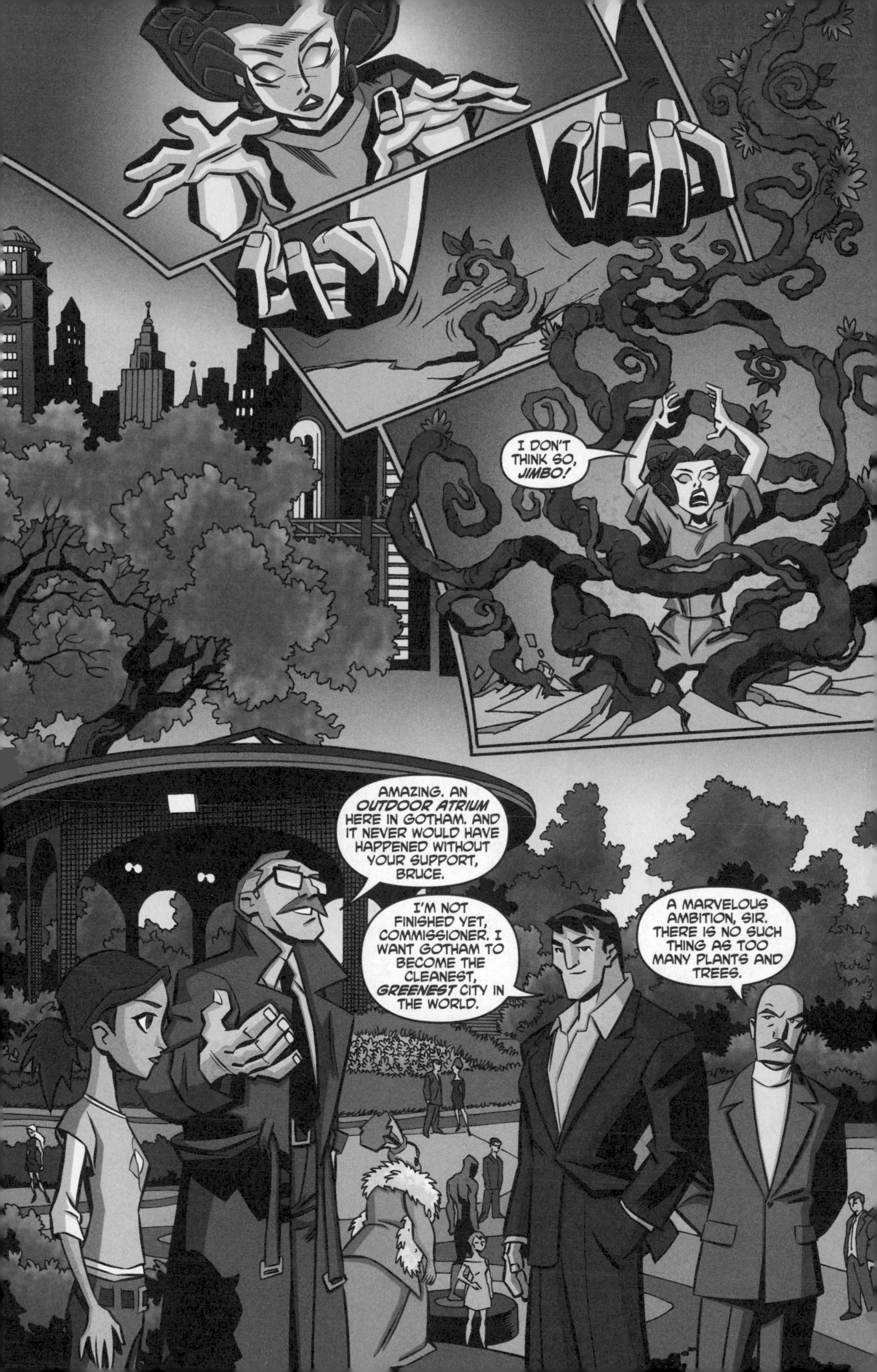
I DON'T THINK SO, JIMBO!
AMAZING. AN OUTDOOR ATRIUM HERE IN GOTHAM. AND IT NEVER WOULD HAVE HAPPENED WITHOUT YOUR SUPPORT, BRUCE.
I'M NOT FINISHED YET, COMMISSIONER. I WANT GOTHAM TO BECOME THE CLEANEST, GREENEST CITY IN THE WORLD.
A MARVELOUS AMBITION, SIR. THERE IS NO SUCH THING AS TOO MANY PLANTS AND TREES.

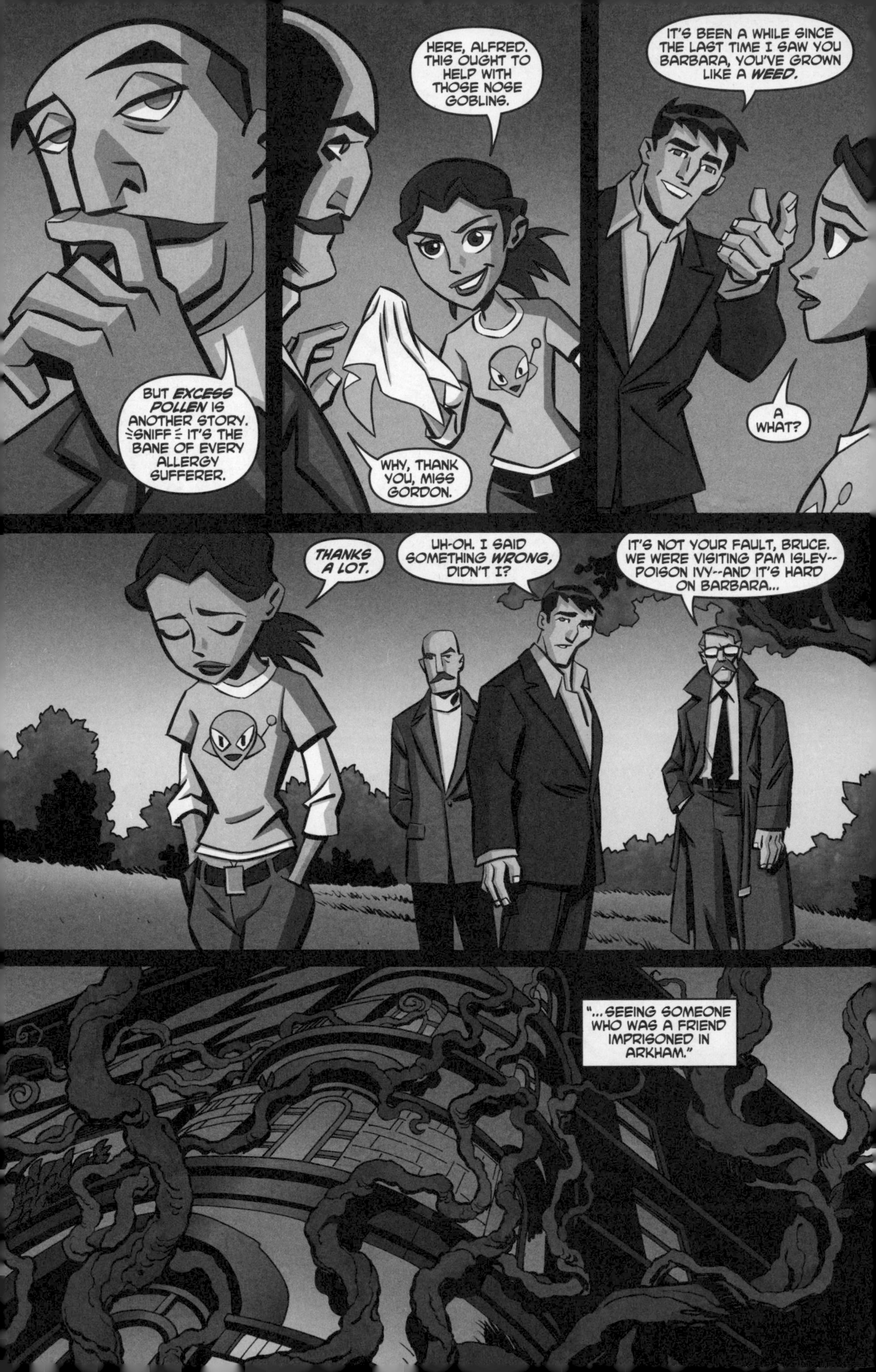

BUT EXCESS POLLEN IS ANOTHER STORY. SNIFF IT'S THE BANE OF EVERY ALLERGY SUFFERER.
HERE, ALFRED. THIS OUGHT TO HELP WITH THOSE NOSE GOBLINS.
WHY, THANK YOU, MISS GORDON.
IT'S BEEN A WHILE SINCE THE LAST TIME I SAW YOU BARBARA, YOU'VE GROWN LIKE A WEED.
A WHAT?
THANKS A LOT.
UH-OH. I SAID SOMETHING WRONG, DIDN'T I?
IT'S NOT YOUR FAULT, BRUCE. WE WERE VISITING PAM ISLEY--POISON IVY--AND IT'S HARD ON BARBARA...
"...SEEING SOMEONE WHO WAS A FRIEND IMPRISONED IN ARKHAM."

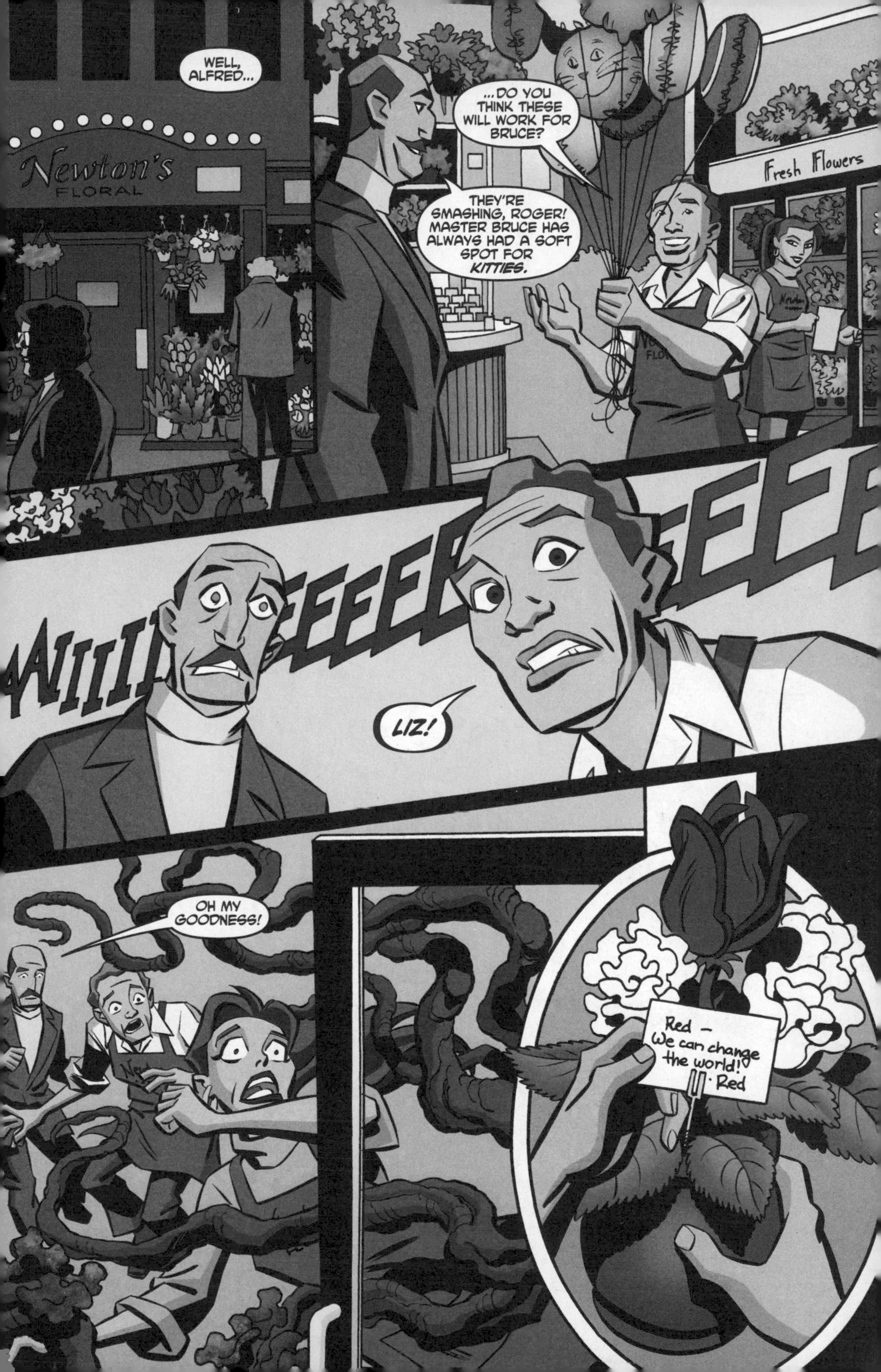
WELL, ALFRED...
Newton's FLORAL
...DO YOU THINK THESE WILL WORK FOR BRUCE?
Fresh Flowers
THEY'RE SMASHING, ROGER! MASTER BRUCE HAS ALWAYS HAD A SOFT SPOT FOR KITTIES.
AIIIIEEEEEEEEEEE
LIZ!
OH MY GOODNESS!
Red - We can change the world! - Red

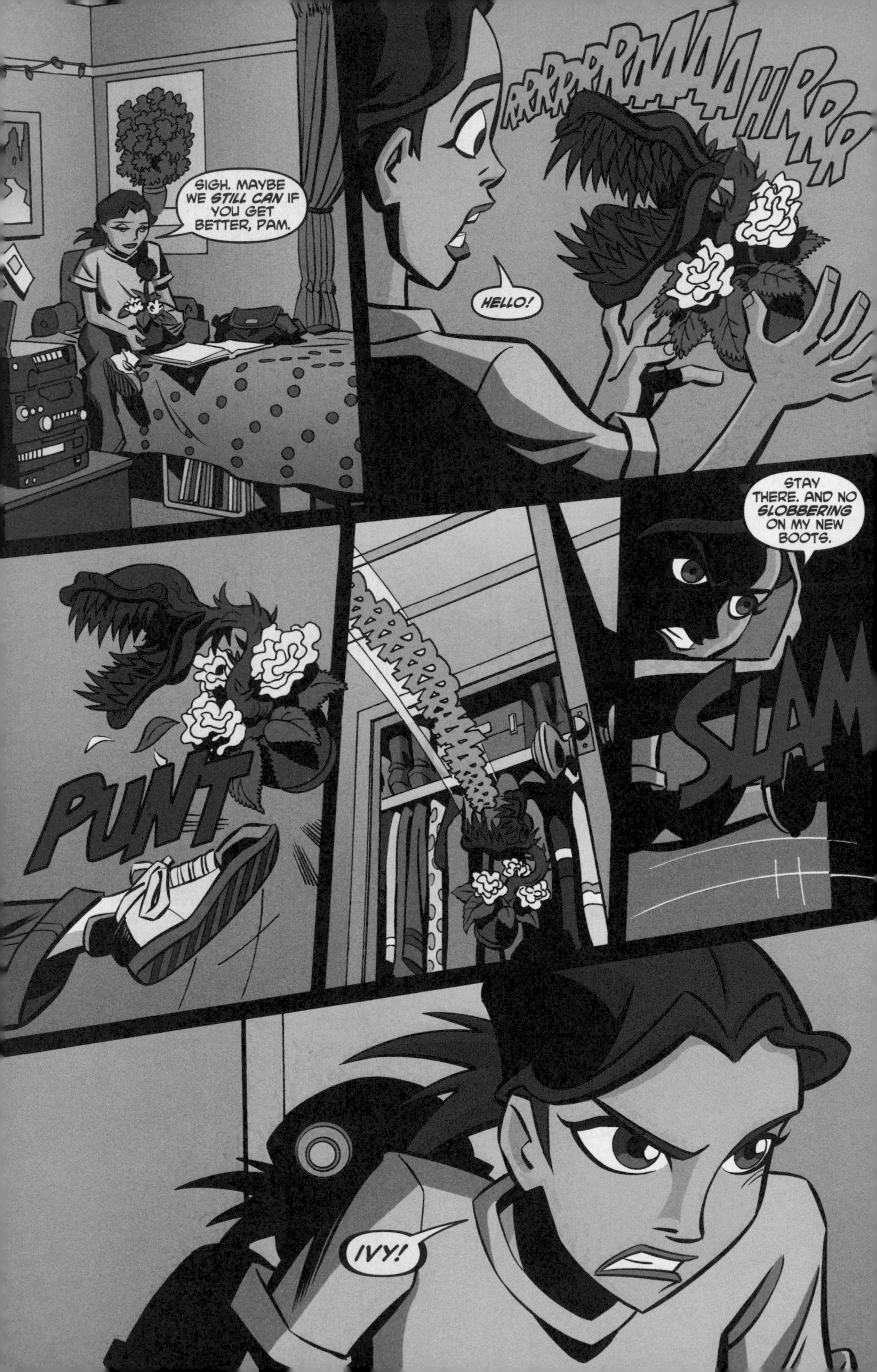
SIGH. MAYBE WE *STILL CAN* IF YOU GET BETTER, PAM.
RRRRRRRAAAAHRRR
HELLO!
PUNT
STAY THERE. AND NO *SLOBBERING* ON MY NEW BOOTS.
SLAM
IVY!

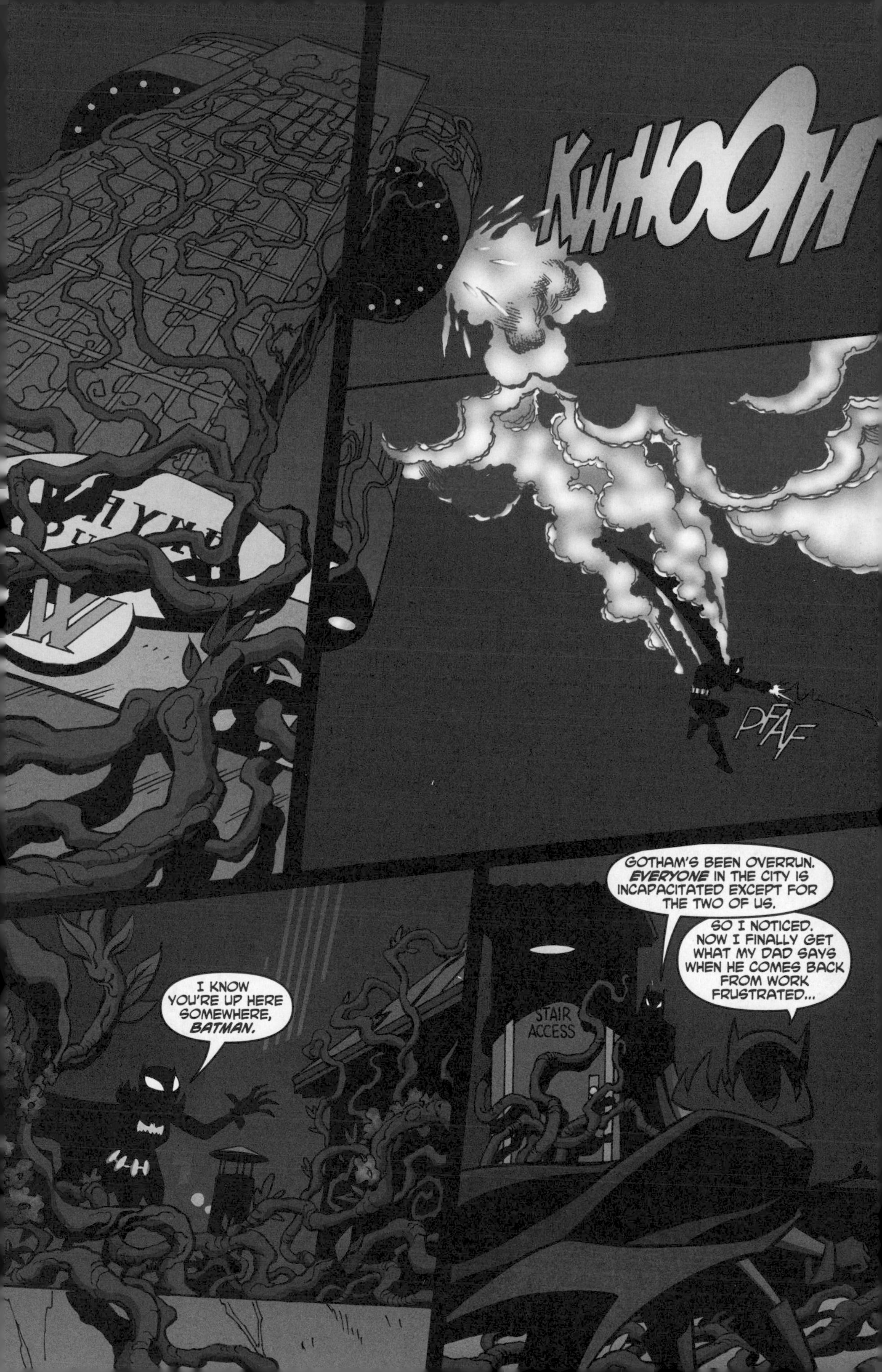
KWHOOM
PFAF
I KNOW YOU'RE UP HERE SOMEWHERE, BATMAN.
GOTHAM'S BEEN OVERRUN. EVERYONE IN THE CITY IS INCAPACITATED EXCEPT FOR THE TWO OF US.
SO I NOTICED. NOW I FINALLY GET WHAT MY DAD SAYS WHEN HE COMES BACK FROM WORK FRUSTRATED...
STAIR ACCESS

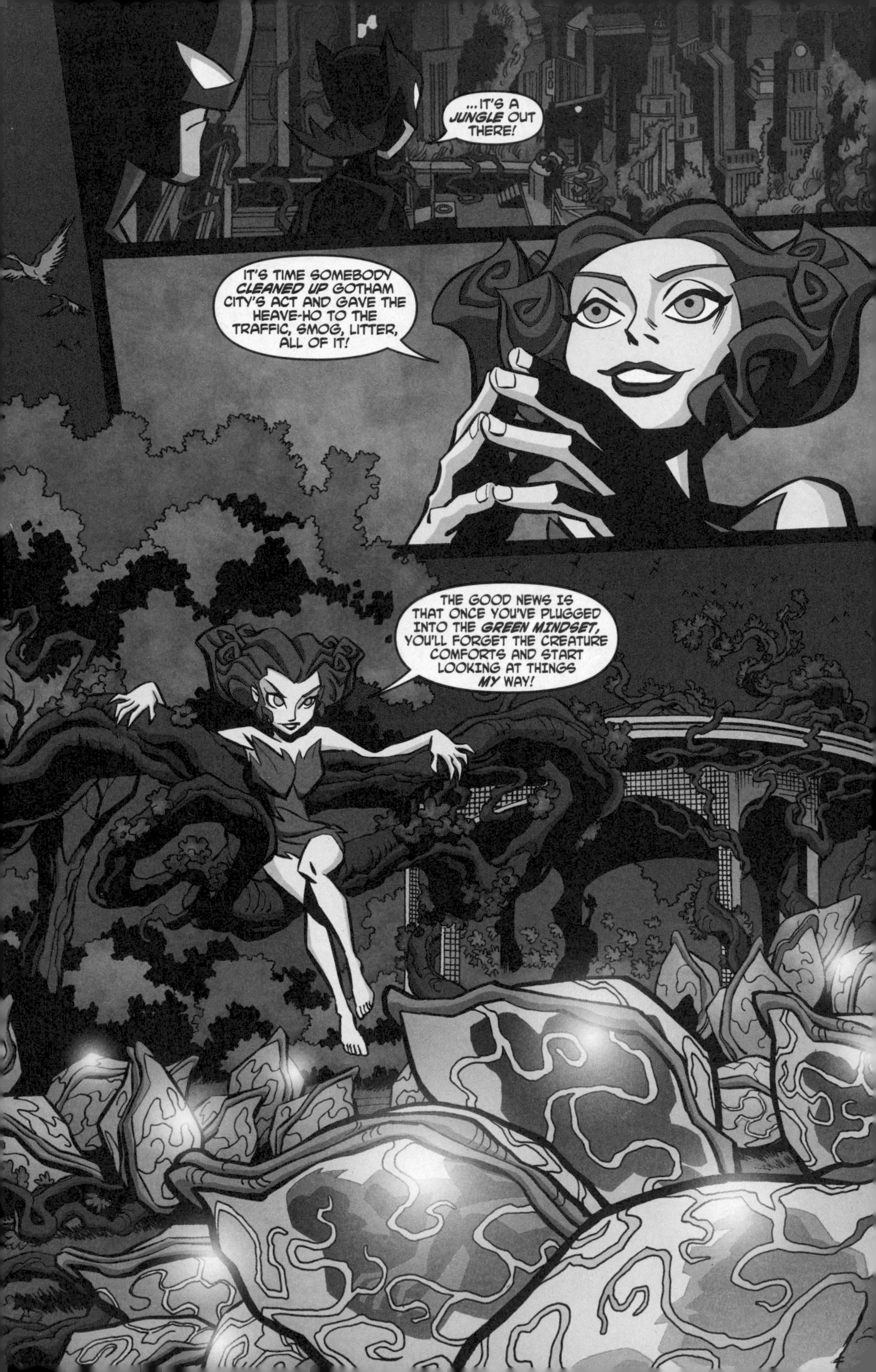
...IT'S A JUNGLE OUT THERE!
IT'S TIME SOMEBODY CLEANED UP GOTHAM CITY'S ACT AND GAVE THE HEAVE-HO TO THE TRAFFIC, SMOG, LITTER, ALL OF IT!
THE GOOD NEWS IS THAT ONCE YOU'VE PLUGGED INTO THE GREEN MINDSET, YOU'LL FORGET THE CREATURE COMFORTS AND START LOOKING AT THINGS MY WAY!

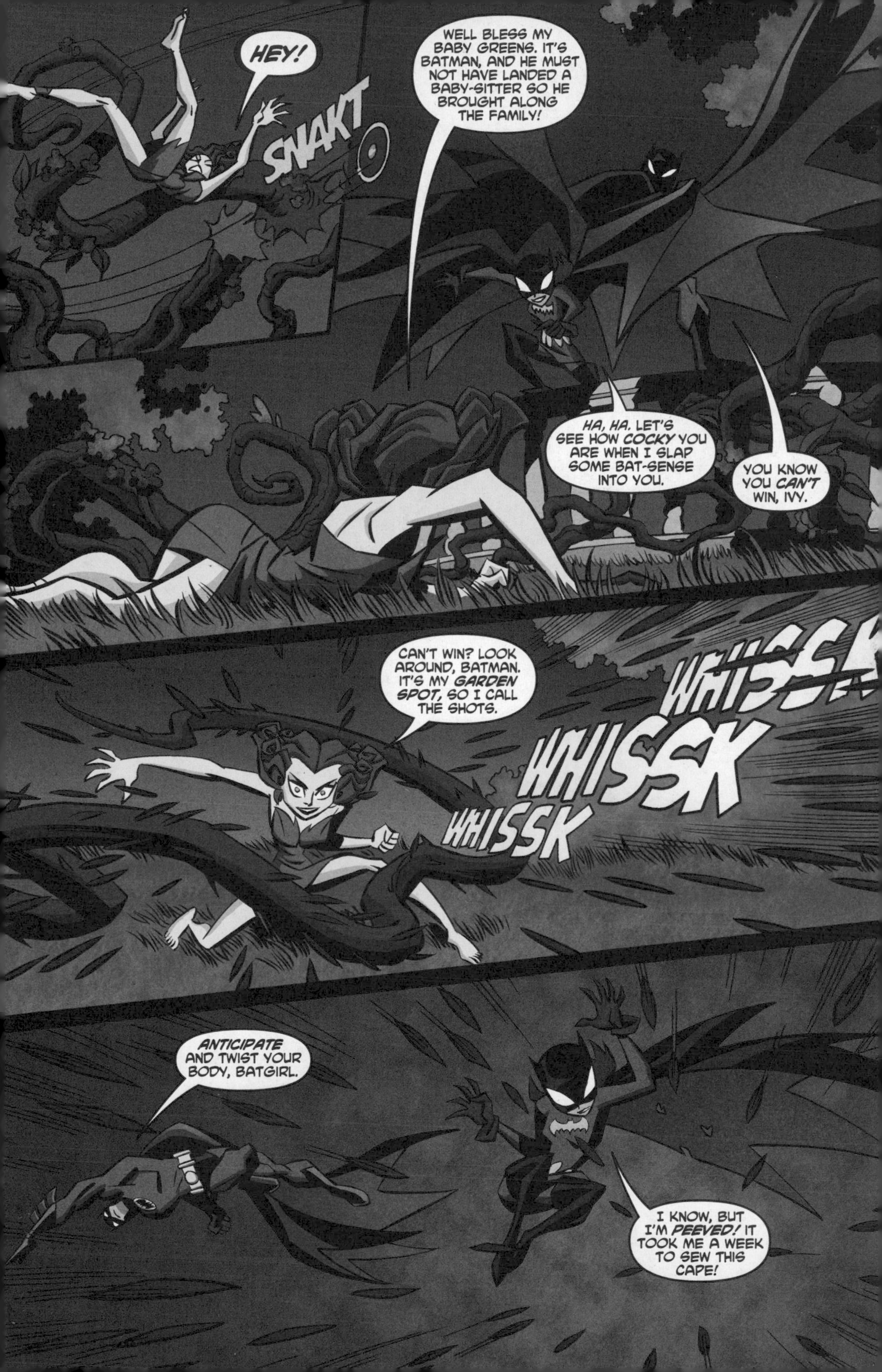
HEY!
SNAKT
WELL BLESS MY BABY GREENS. IT'S BATMAN, AND HE MUST NOT HAVE LANDED A BABY-SITTER SO HE BROUGHT ALONG THE FAMILY!
HA, HA. LET'S SEE HOW COCKY YOU ARE WHEN I SLAP SOME BAT-SENSE INTO YOU.
YOU KNOW YOU CAN'T WIN, IVY.
CAN'T WIN? LOOK AROUND, BATMAN. IT'S MY GARDEN SPOT, SO I CALL THE SHOTS.
WHISSK
WHISSK
ANTICIPATE AND TWIST YOUR BODY, BATGIRL.
I KNOW, BUT I'M PEEVED! IT TOOK ME A WEEK TO SEW THIS CAPE!

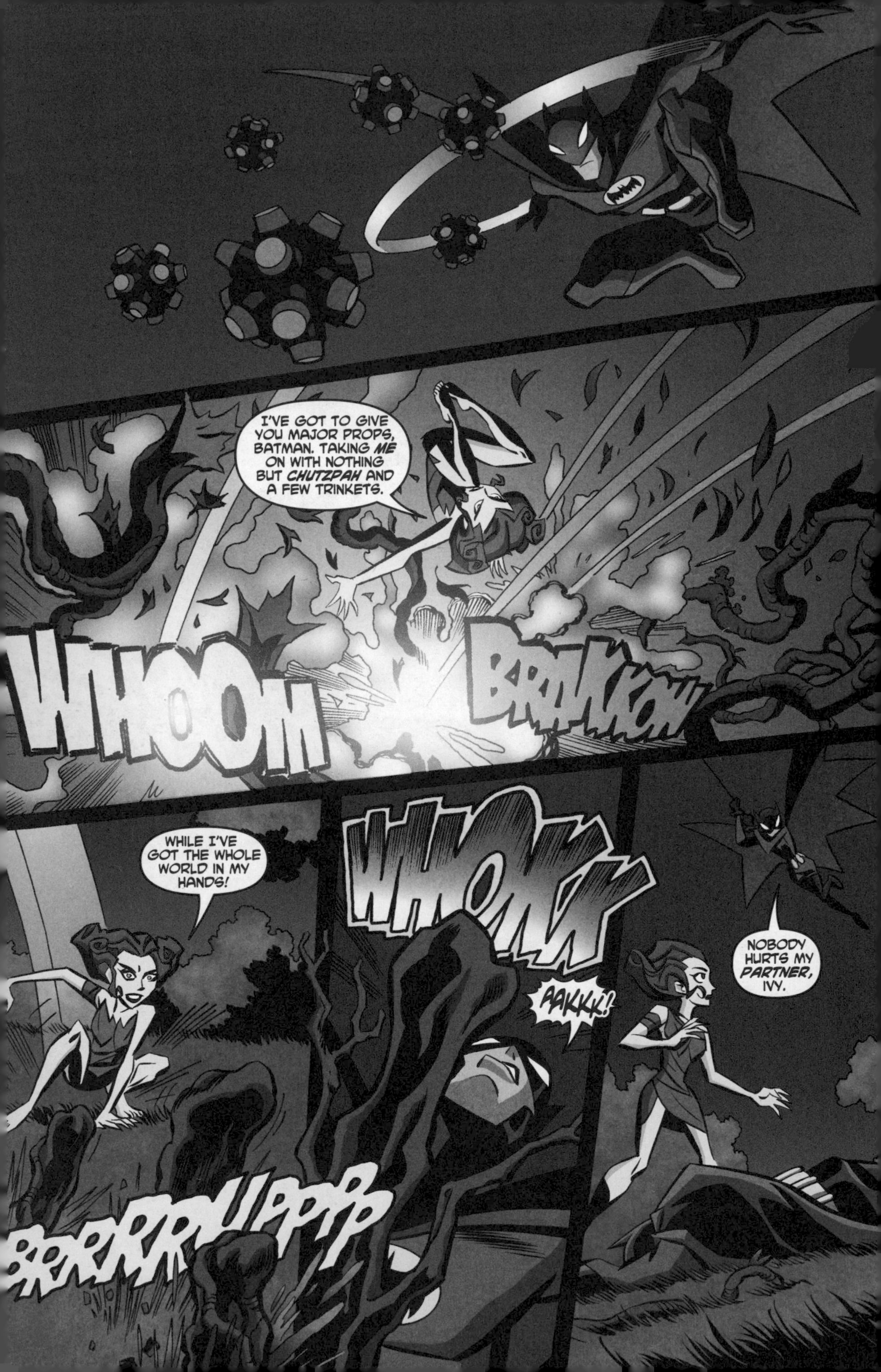
I'VE GOT TO GIVE YOU MAJOR PROPS, BATMAN. TAKING *ME* ON WITH NOTHING BUT *CHUTZPAH* AND A FEW TRINKETS.
WHOOM
BRAKKOW
WHILE I'VE GOT THE WHOLE WORLD IN MY HANDS!
BRRRRRUPPP
WHOKK
AAKKK!
NOBODY HURTS MY *PARTNER*, IVY.

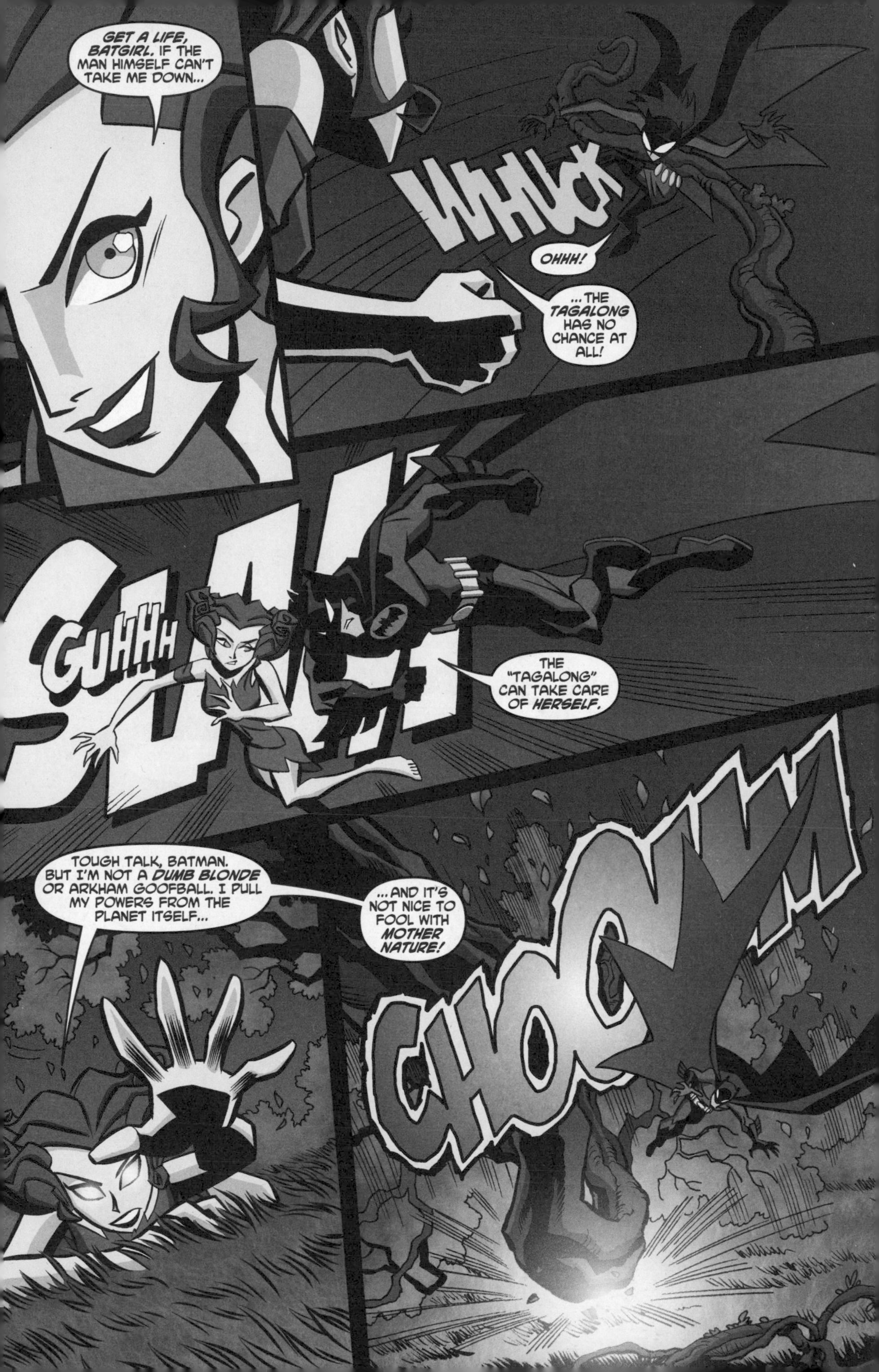
GET A LIFE, BATGIRL. IF THE MAN HIMSELF CAN'T TAKE ME DOWN...
WHUCK
OHHH!
...THE TAGALONG HAS NO CHANCE AT ALL!
GUHHH
THE "TAGALONG" CAN TAKE CARE OF HERSELF.
TOUGH TALK, BATMAN. BUT I'M NOT A DUMB BLONDE OR ARKHAM GOOFBALL. I PULL MY POWERS FROM THE PLANET ITSELF...
...AND IT'S NOT NICE TO FOOL WITH MOTHER NATURE!
CHOOM

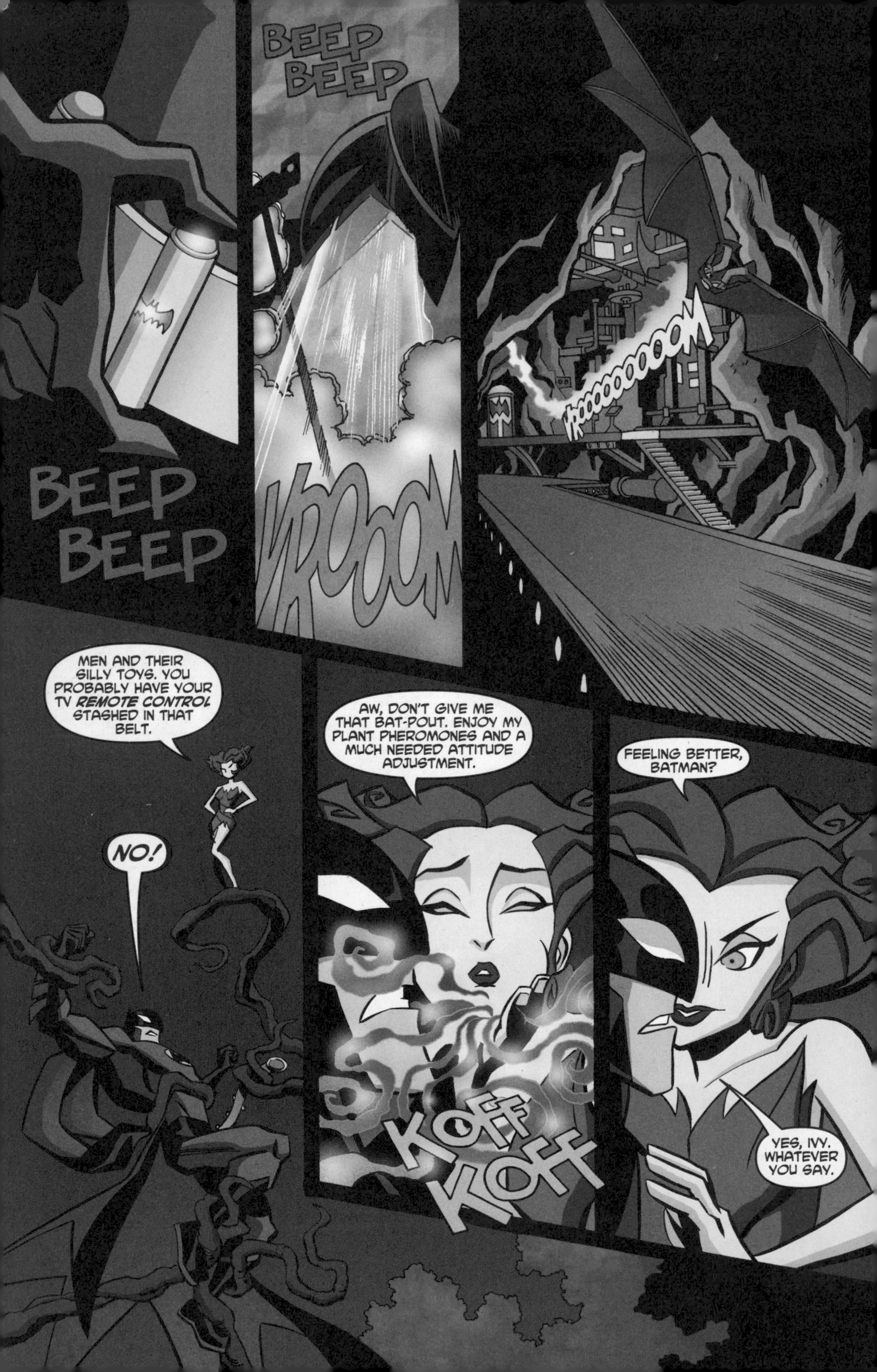
BEEP BEEP
BEEP BEEP
VROOOM
VROOOOOOOOOM
MEN AND THEIR SILLY TOYS. YOU PROBABLY HAVE YOUR TV REMOTE CONTROL STASHED IN THAT BELT.
NO!
AW, DON'T GIVE ME THAT BAT-POUT. ENJOY MY PLANT PHEROMONES AND A MUCH NEEDED ATTITUDE ADJUSTMENT.
KOFF KOFF
FEELING BETTER, BATMAN?
YES, IVY. WHATEVER YOU SAY.

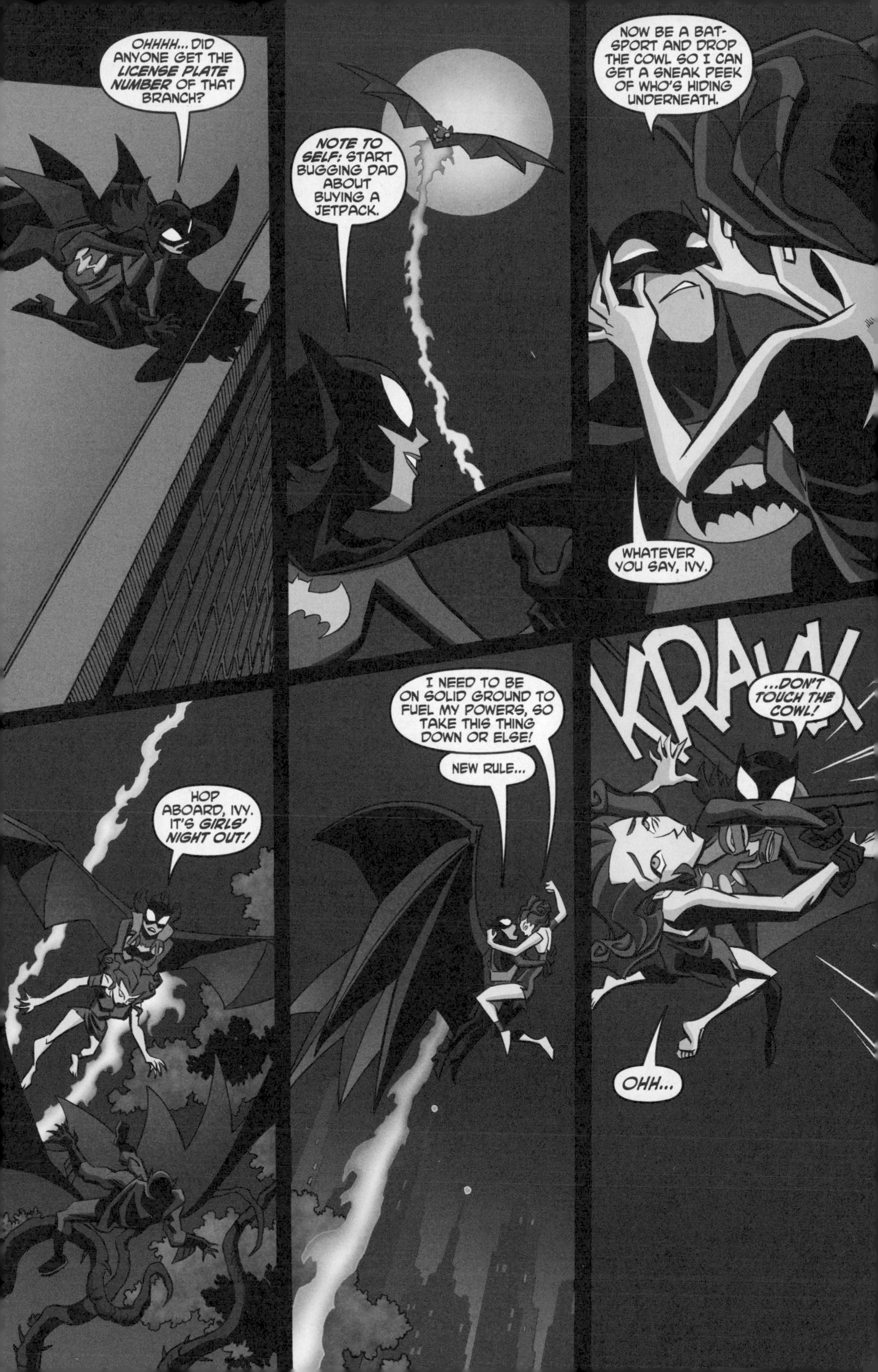
OHHHH... DID ANYONE GET THE LICENSE PLATE NUMBER OF THAT BRANCH?
NOTE TO SELF: START BUGGING DAD ABOUT BUYING A JETPACK.
NOW BE A BAT-SPORT AND DROP THE COWL SO I CAN GET A SNEAK PEEK OF WHO'S HIDING UNDERNEATH.
WHATEVER YOU SAY, IVY.
HOP ABOARD, IVY. IT'S GIRLS' NIGHT OUT!
I NEED TO BE ON SOLID GROUND TO FUEL MY POWERS, SO TAKE THIS THING DOWN OR ELSE!
NEW RULE...
KRAK!
...DON'T TOUCH THE COWL!
OHH...

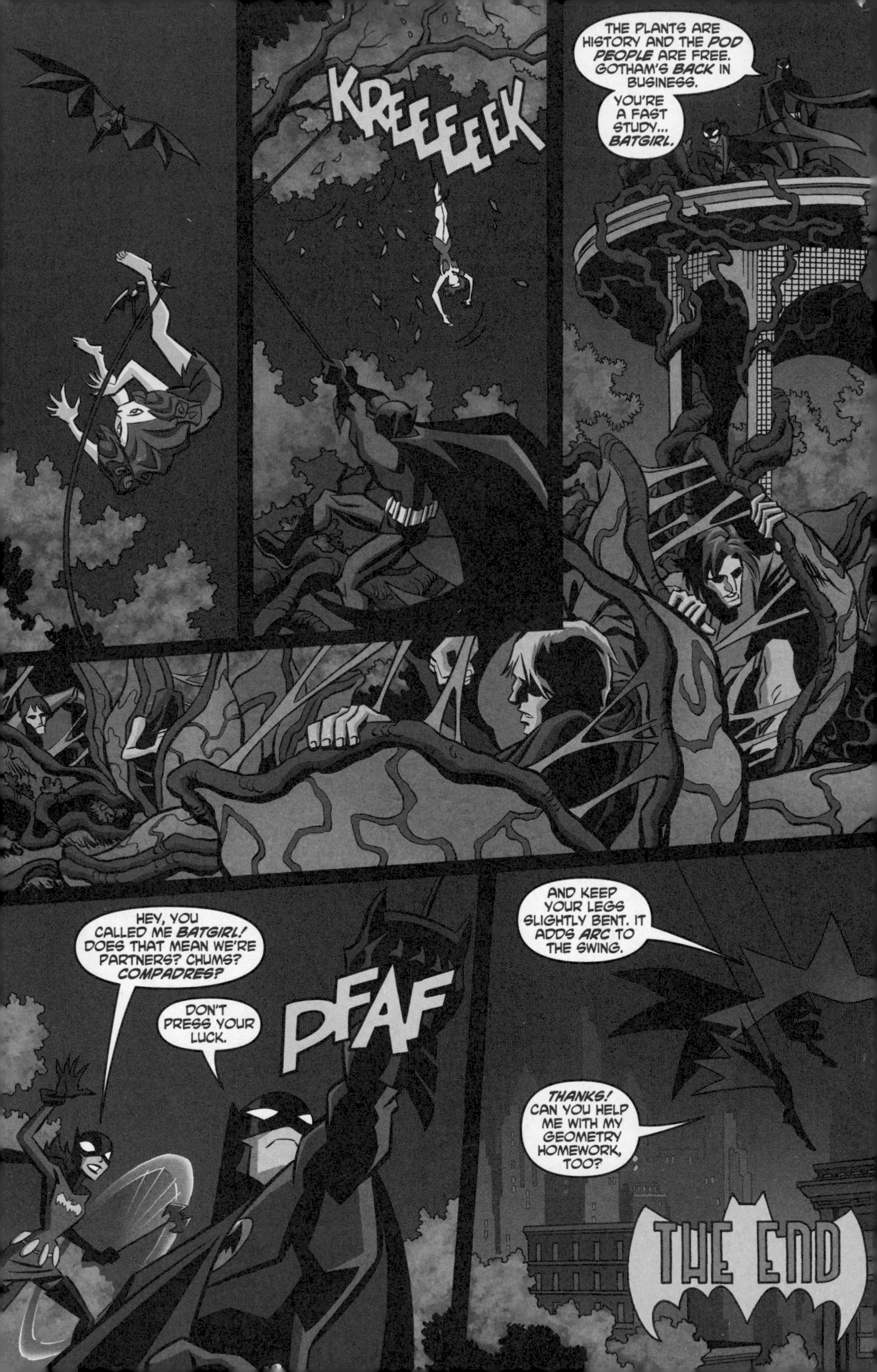
KREEEEEEK
THE PLANTS ARE HISTORY AND THE POD PEOPLE ARE FREE. GOTHAM'S BACK IN BUSINESS.
YOU'RE A FAST STUDY... BATGIRL.
HEY, YOU CALLED ME BATGIRL! DOES THAT MEAN WE'RE PARTNERS? CHUMS? COMPADRES?
DON'T PRESS YOUR LUCK.
PFAF
AND KEEP YOUR LEGS SLIGHTLY BENT. IT ADDS ARC TO THE SWING.
THANKS! CAN YOU HELP ME WITH MY GEOMETRY HOMEWORK, TOO?
THE END

COVER GALLERY

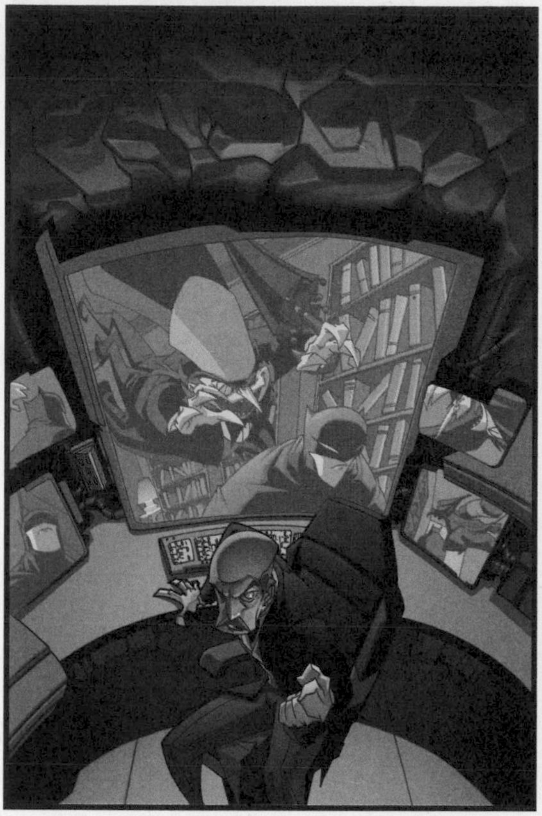

#11 ART BY **JEFF MATSUDA** COLOR BY **DAVE MCCAIG**

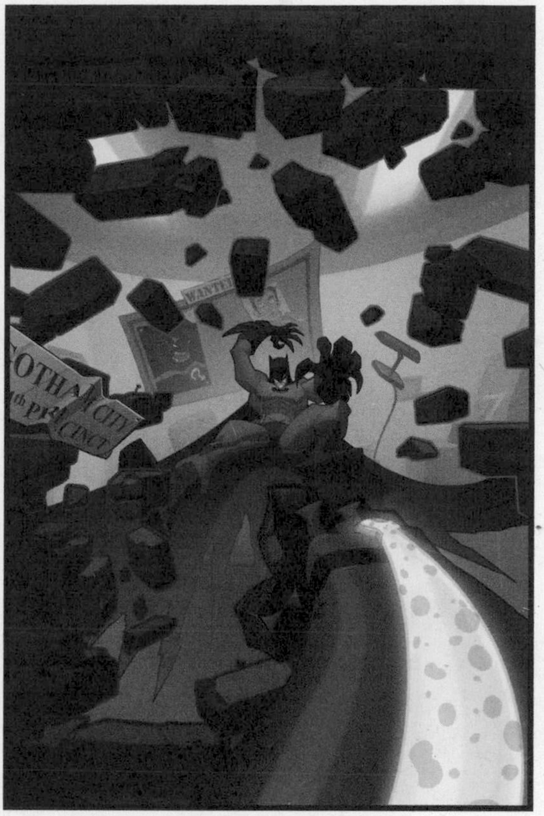

#12 ART BY AND COLOR BY **DAVE MCCAIG**

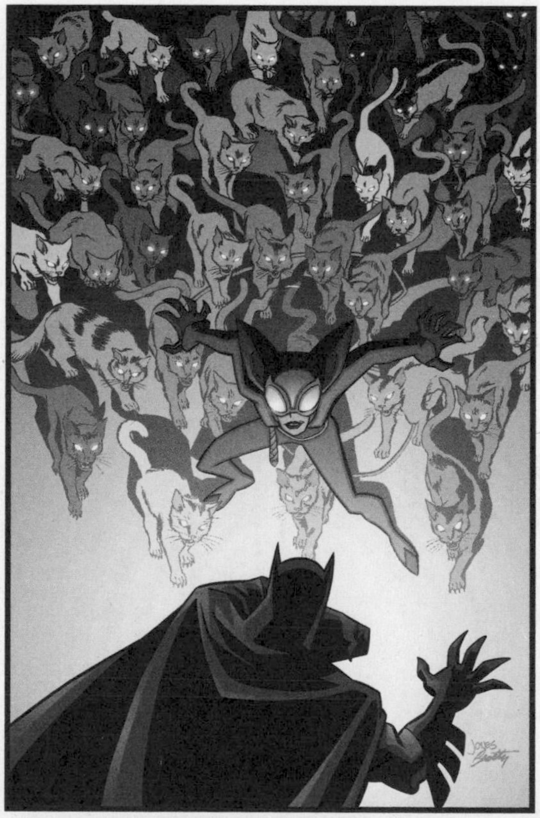

#13 PENCILS BY **CHRISTOPHER JONES** INKS BY **TERRY BEATTY**
COLOR BY **HEROIC AGE**

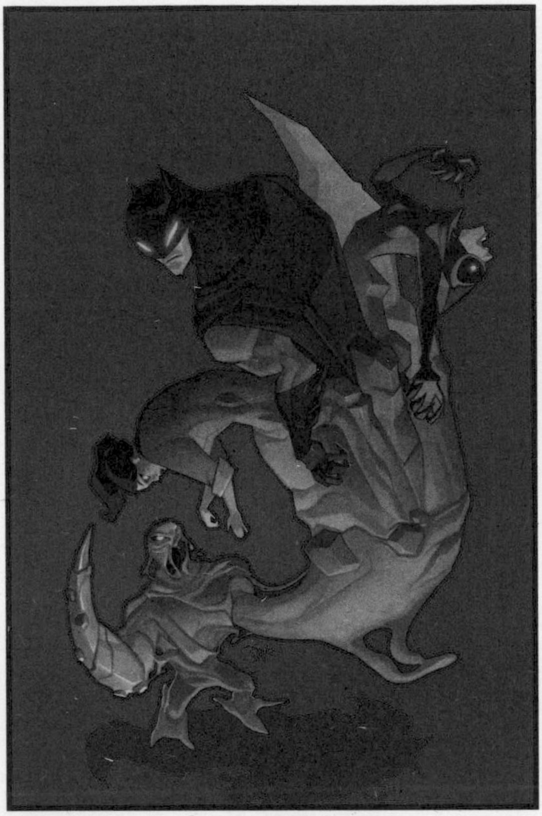

#14 ART AND COLOR BY **DAVE MCCAIG**

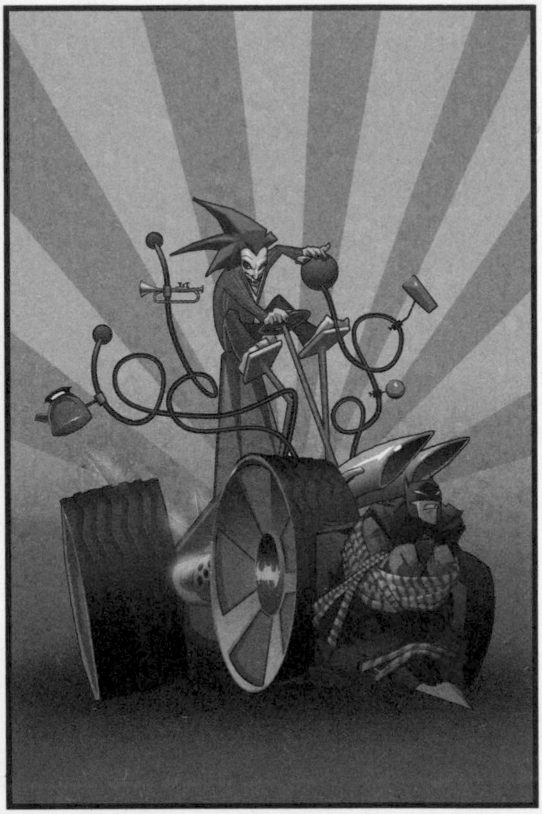

#16 ART AND COLOR BY **DAVE MCCAIG**

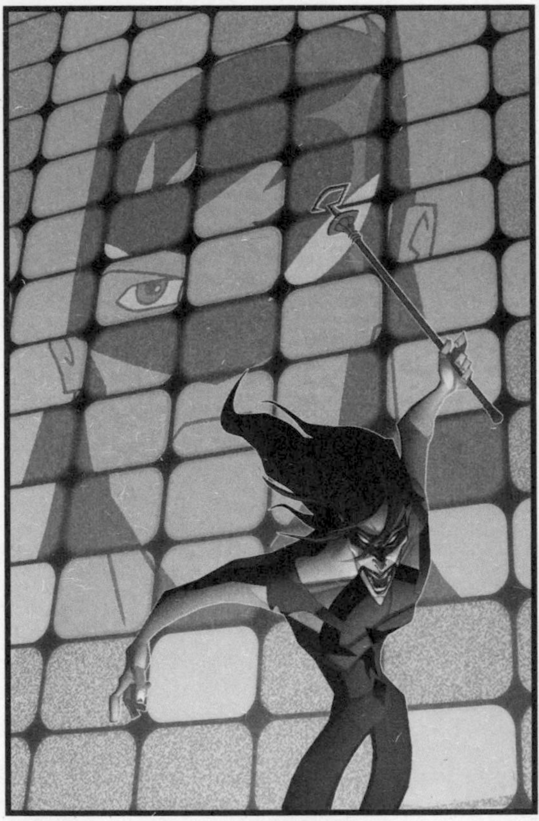

#17 ART AND COLOR BY **DAVE MCCAIG**

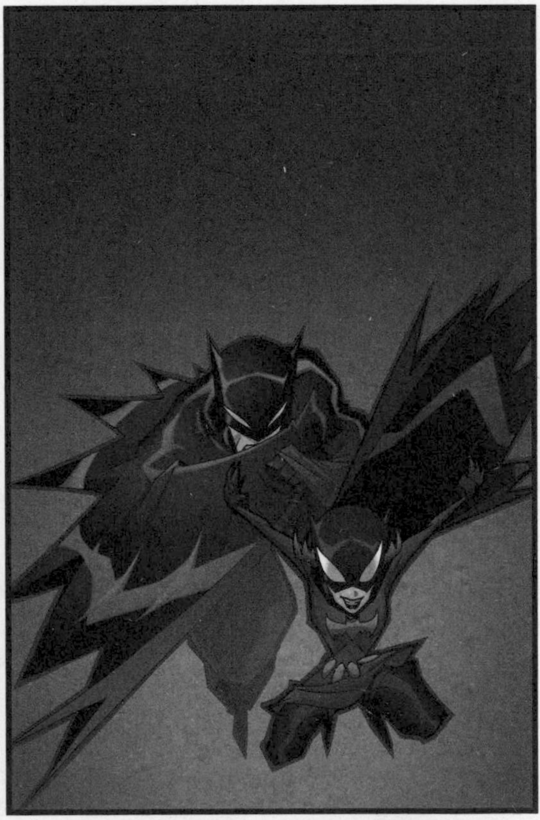

#18 ART BY **JEFF MATSUDA** COLOR BY **DAVE MCCAIG**